PENGUIN BOOKS

1191

SELECTED SHORT STORIES

Q

SELECTED
SHORT STORIES

Sir Arthur Quiller-Couch

PENGUIN BOOKS

Penguin Books Ltd, Harmondsworth, Middlesex
CANADA: Penguin Books (Canada) Ltd, 178 Norseman Street,
Toronto 18, Ontario
AUSTRALIA: Penguin Books Pty Ltd, 762 Whitehorse Road,
Mitcham, Victoria

—

This selection first published 1957

Made and printed in Great Britain
by C. Nicholls & Company Ltd

CONTENTS

BIBLIOGRAPHICAL NOTE   7

The Roll-call of the Reef   9
Visitors at the Gunnel Rock   26
Statement of Gabriel Foot, Highwayman   37
The Two Householders   49
A Cottage in Troy   61
   I. The Happy Voyage
   II. These-an'-That's Wife
The Affair of Bleakirk-on-Sands   71
Corporal Sam   83
The Mont-Bazillac   110
The Three Necklaces   119
Lieutenant Lapenotière   129
Frenchman's Creek   142
The Laird's Luck   170
Captain Knot   208
Mutual Exchange, Limited   224
Step o' One Side   239

BIBLIOGRAPHICAL NOTE

'The Roll-call of the Reef' and 'Visitors at the Gunnel Rock' were first published in *Wandering Heath* (1895, the Duchy edition 1928).

'The Two Householders' was first published in *I Saw Three Ships*, 'Statement of Gabriel Foot, Highwayman', 'A Cottage in Troy' (1 The Happy Voyage, 11 These-an'-That's Wife), and 'The Affair of Bleakirk-on-Sands' in *Noughts and Crosses* (1891); these five stories were included in the Duchy edition of *Noughts and Crosses* (1928).

'Corporal Sam' was first published in *Corporal Sam and Other Stories* (1911) and was included in the Duchy edition of *Two Sides of the Face* (1929).

'The Mont-Bazillac', 'The Three Necklaces', and 'Lieutenant Lapenotière' were first published in *News from the Duchy* (1913) and 'Frenchman's Creek' in *Shakespeare's Christmas* (1905); these four stories were included in the Duchy edition of *News from the Duchy* (1929).

'The Laird's Luck' was first published in *The Laird's Luck and Other Fireside Tales* (1901) and 'Captain Knot' in *Mortallone* (1917); they were both included in *Mystery Stories* (1937) with 'Mutual Exchange, Limited' and 'Step o' One Side', which were first published in that book.

Many of these stories had appeared in periodicals, such as *The Speaker*, *The Idler*, *The Strand Magazine*, and *The Times*, before being published in book form.

'YES, sir,' said my host the quarryman, reaching down the relics from their hook in the wall over the chimney-piece; 'they've hung there all my time, and most of my father's. The women won't touch 'em; they're afraid of the story. So here they'll dangle, and gather dust and smoke, till another tenant comes and tosses 'em out o' doors for rubbish. Whew! 'tis coarse weather.'

He went to the door, opened it, and stood studying the gale that beat upon his cottage-front, straight from the Manacle Reef. The rain drove past him into the kitchen, aslant like threads of gold silk in the shine of the wreckwood fire. Meanwhile by the same firelight I examined the relics on my knee. The metal of each was tarnished out of knowledge. But the trumpet was evidently an old cavalry trumpet, and the threads of its parti-coloured sling, though frayed and dusty, still hung together. Around the side-drum, beneath its cracked brown varnish, I could hardly trace a royal coat-of-arms, and a legend running – *Per Mare per Terram* – the motto of the Marines. Its parchment, though coloured and scented with wood-smoke, was limp and mildewed; and I began to tighten up the straps – under which the drumsticks had been loosely thrust – with the idle purpose of trying if some music might be got out of the old drum yet.

But as I turned it on my knee, I found the drum attached to the trumpet-sling by a curious barrel-shaped padlock, and paused to examine this. The body of the lock was composed of half a dozen brass rings, set accurately edge to edge; and, rubbing the brass with my thumb, I saw that each of the six had a series of letters engraved around it.

I knew the trick of it, I thought. Here was one of those word-padlocks, once so common; only to be opened by getting the rings to spell a certain word, which the dealer confides to you.

My host shut and barred the door, and came back to the hearth.

' 'Twas just such a wind – east by south – that brought in what you've got between your hands. Back in the year 'nine it was; my father has told me the tale a score o' times. You're twisting round the rings, I see. But you'll never guess the word. Parson Kendall, he made the word, and locked down a couple o' ghosts in their graves with it; and when his time came, he went to his own grave and took the word with him.'

'Whose ghosts, Matthew?'

'You want the story, I see, sir. My father could tell it better than I can. He was a young man in the year 'nine, unmarried at the time, and living in this very cottage just as I be. That's how he came to get mixed up with the tale.'

He took a chair, lit a short pipe, and unfolded the story in a low musing voice, with his eyes fixed on the dancing violet flames.

'Yes, he'd ha' been about thirty year old in January of the year 'nine. The storm got up in the night o' the twenty-first o' that month. My father was dressed and out long before daylight; he never was one to 'bide in bed, let be that the gale by this time was pretty near lifting the thatch over his head. Besides which, he'd fenced a small 'taty-patch that winter, down by Lowland Point, and he wanted to see if it stood the night's work. He took the path across Gunner's Meadow – where they buried most of the bodies afterwards. The wind was right in his teeth at the time, and once on the way (he's told me this often) a great strip of oreweed came flying through the darkness and fetched him a slap on the cheek like a cold hand. But he made shift pretty well till he got to Lowland, and then had to drop upon his hands and knees and crawl, digging his fingers every now and then into the shingle to hold on, for he declared to me that the stones, some of them as big as a man's head, kept rolling and driving past till it seemed the whole foreshore was moving westward under him. The fence was gone, of course; not a stick left to show where it stood; so that, when first he came to the place, he thought he must have missed his bearings. My father, sir, was a very religious man; and if he reckoned the end of the world was at hand – there in the great wind and night, among the moving stones – you may believe he was certain of it when he heard a gun fired, and, with the same, saw a flame shoot up out of the darkness to windward, making a sudden fierce light in all the place about. All he could find to think or say was, "The Second Coming – The Second Coming! The Bridegroom cometh, and the wicked He will toss like a ball into a large country!" and being already upon his knees, he just bowed his head and 'bided, saying this over and over.

'But by'm-by, between two squalls, he made bold to lift his head and look, and then by the light – a bluish colour 'twas – he saw all the coast clear away to Manacle Point, and off the Manacles, in the thick of the weather, a sloop-of-war with top-gallants housed, driving stern foremost towards the reef. It was she, of course, that was burning the flare. My father could see the white streak and the ports of her quite plain as she rose to it, a little outside the breakers, and he guessed easy enough that her captain had just managed to wear ship, and was trying to force her nose to the sea with the help of her small bower anchor and the scrap or two of canvas that hadn't yet been blown out of her. But while he looked, she fell off, giving her broadside to it foot by foot, and drifting back on the breakers around Carn dû and the Varses. The rocks lie so thick thereabouts, that 'twas a toss-up which she struck first; at any rate, my father couldn't tell at the time, for just then the flare died down and went out.

'Well, sir, he turned then in the dark and started back for Coverack to cry the dismal tidings – though well knowing ship and crew to be past any hope; and as he turned, the wind lifted him and tossed him forward "like a ball", as he'd been saying, and homeward along the foreshore. As you know, 'tis ugly work, even by daylight, picking your way among the stones there, and my father was prettily knocked about at first in the dark. But by this 'twas nearer seven than six o'clock, and the day spreading. By the time he reached North Corner, a man could see to read print; hows'ever, he looked neither out to sea nor towards Coverack, but headed straight for the first cottage – the same that stands above North Corner to-day. A man named Billy Ede lived there then, and when my father burst into the kitchen bawling, "Wreck! wreck!" he saw Billy Ede's wife, Ann, standing there in her clogs, with a shawl over her head, and her clothes wringing wet.

"'Save the chap!" says Billy Ede's wife, Ann. "What d' 'ee mean by crying stale fish at that rate?"

"'But 'tis a wreck, I tell 'ee. I've a-zeed 'n!'

"'Why, so 'tis," says she, "and I've a-zeed 'n too; and so has everyone with an eye in his head."

'And with that she pointed straight over my father's shoulder, and he turned; and there, close under Dolor Point, at the end of Coverack town, he saw *another* wreck washing, and the point black with people, like emmets, running to and fro in the morning light. While he stood staring at her, he heard a trumpet sounded on board, the notes coming in little jerks, like a bird rising against the wind; but faintly, of course, because of the distance and the gale blowing – though this had dropped a little.

"'She's a transport," said Billy Ede's wife, Ann, "and full of horse soldiers, fine long men. When she struck they must ha' pitched the hosses over first to lighten the ship, for a score of dead horses had washed in afore I left, half an hour back. An' three or four soldiers, too – fine long corpses in white breeches and jackets of blue and gold. I held the lantern to one. Such a straight young man!"

'My father asked her about the trumpeting.

"'That's the queerest bit of all. She was burnin' a light when me an' my man joined the crowd down there. All her masts had gone; whether they carried away, or were cut away to ease her, I don't rightly know. Anyway, there she lay 'pon the rocks with her decks bare. Her keelson was broke under her and her bottom sagged and stove, and she had just settled down like a sitting hen – just the leastest list to starboard; but a man could stand there easy. They had rigged up ropes across her, from bulwark to bulwark, an' beside these the men were mustered, holding on like grim death whenever the sea made a clean breach over them, an' standing up like heroes as soon as it passed. The captain an' the officers were clinging to the rail of the quarter-deck, all in their golden uniforms, waiting for the end as if 'twas King George they expected. There was no way to help, for she lay right beyond cast of line, though our folk tried it fifty times. And beside them clung a trumpeter, a whacking big man, an' between the heavy seas he would lift his trumpet with one hand, and blow a call; and every time he blew, the men gave a cheer. There" (she says) "–hark 'ee now – there he goes agen! But you won't hear no cheering any more, for few are left to cheer, and their voices weak. Bitter cold the wind is, and I reckon it numbs their grip o' the ropes, for they were dropping off fast with every sea when my man sent me home to get his breakfast. *Another* wreck, you say? Well, there's no hope for the tender dears, if 'tis the Manacles. You'd better run down and help yonder; though 'tis little help that any man can give. Not one came in alive while I was there. The tide's flowing, an' she won't hold together another hour, they say."

'Well, sure enough, the end was coming fast when my father got down to the point. Six men had been cast up alive, or just breathing – a seaman and five troopers. The seaman was the only one that had breath to speak; and while they were carrying him into the town, the word went round that the ship's name was the *Despatch*, transport, homeward bound from Corunna, with a detachment of the 7th Hussars, that had been fighting out there with Sir John Moore. The seas had rolled her farther over by this time, and given her decks a pretty sharp slope; but a dozen men still held on, seven by the ropes near the ship's waist, a couple near the break of the poop, and three on the quarter-deck. Of these three my father made out one to be the skipper; close by him clung an officer in full regimentals – his name, they heard after, was Captain Duncanfield; and last came the tall trumpeter; and if you'll believe me, the fellow was making shift there, at the very last, to blow *God Save the King*. What's more, he got to "Send us victorious" before an extra big sea came bursting across and washed them off the deck – every man but one of the pair beneath the poop – and *he* dropped his hold before the next wave; being stunned, I reckon. The others went out of sight at once, but the trumpeter – being, as I said, a powerful man as well as a tough swimmer – rose like a duck, rode out a couple of breakers, and came in on the crest of the third. The folks looked to see him broke like an egg at their feet; but when the smother cleared, there he was, lying face downward on a ledge below them; and one of the men that happened to have a rope round him – I forget the fellow's name, if I ever heard it – jumped down and grabbed him by the ankle as he began to slip back. Before the next big sea, the pair were hauled high enough to be out of harm, and another heave brought them up to grass. Quick work; but master trumpeter wasn't quite dead; nothing worse than a cracked head and three staved ribs. In twenty minutes or so they had him in bed, with the doctor to tend him.

'Now was the time – nothing being left alive upon the transport – for my father to tell of the sloop he'd seen driving upon the Manacles. And when he got a hearing, though the most were set upon salvage, and believed a wreck in the hand, so to say, to be worth half a dozen they couldn't see, a good few volunteered to start off with him and have a look. They crossed Lowland Point; no ship to be seen on the Manacles, nor anywhere upon the sea. One or two was for calling my father a liar. "Wait till we come to Dean Point," said he. Sure enough, on the far side of Dean Point, they found the sloop's mainmast washing about with half a dozen men lashed to it – men in red jackets – every mother's son drowned and staring; and a little farther on, just under the Dean, three or four bodies cast up on the shore, one of them a small drummer-boy, side-drum and all; and, near by, part of a ship's gig, with H.M.S. *Primrose* cut on the stern-board. From this point on, the shore was littered thick with wreckage and dead bodies – the most of them Marines in uniform; and in Godrevy Cove, in particular, a heap of furniture from the captain's cabin, and amongst it a water-tight box, not much damaged, and full of papers; by which, when it came to be examined next day, the wreck was easily made out to be the *Primrose*, of eighteen guns, outward bound from Portsmouth, with a fleet of transports for the

Spanish War – thirty sail, I've heard, but I've never heard what became of them. Being handled by merchant skippers, no doubt they rode out the gale and reached the Tagus safe and sound. Not but what the captain of the *Primrose* (Mein was his name) did quite right to try and club-haul his vessel when he found himself under the land: only he never ought to have got there if he took proper soundings. But it's easy talking.

'The *Primrose*, sir, was a handsome vessel – for her size, one of the handsomest in the King's service – and newly fitted out at Plymouth Dock. So the boys had brave pickings from her in the way of brass-work, ship's instruments, and the like, let alone some barrels of stores not much spoiled. They loaded themselves with as much as they could carry, and started for home, meaning to make a second journey before the preventive men got wind of their doings and came to spoil the fun. But as my father was passing back under the Dean, he happened to take a look over his shoulder at the bodies there. "Hullo," says he, and dropped his gear: "I do believe there's a leg moving!" And, running fore, he stooped over the small drummer-boy that I told you about. The poor little chap was lying there, with his face a mass of bruises and his eyes closed: but he had shifted one leg an inch or two, and was still breathing. So my father pulled out a knife and cut him free from his drum – that was lashed on to him with a double turn of Manila rope – and took him up and carried him along here, to this very room that we're sitting in. He lost a good deal by this, for when he went back to fetch his bundle the preventive men had got hold of it, and were thick as thieves along the foreshore; so that 'twas only by paying one or two to look the other way that he picked up anything worth carrying off: which you'll allow to be hard, seeing that he was the first man to give news of the wreck.

'Well, the inquiry was held, of course, and my father gave evidence; and for the rest they had to trust to the sloop's papers: for not a soul was saved besides the drummer-boy, and he was raving in a fever, brought on by the cold and the fright. And the seamen and the five troopers gave evidence about the loss of the *Despatch*. The tall trumpeter, too, whose ribs were healing, came forward and kissed the Book; but somehow his head had been hurt in coming ashore, and he talked foolish-like, and 'twas easy seen he would never be a proper man again. The others were taken up to Plymouth, and so went their ways; but the trumpeter stayed on in Cover-ack; and King George, finding he was fit for nothing, sent him down a trifle of a pension after a while – enough to keep him in board and lodging, with a bit of tobacco over.

'Now the first time that this man – William Tallifer, he called himself – met with the drummer-boy, was about a fort-night after the little chap had bettered enough to be allowed a short walk out of doors, which he took, if you please, in full regimentals. There was never a soldier so proud of his dress. His own suit had shrunk a brave bit with the salt water; but into ordinary frock an' corduroys he declared he would not get – not if he had to go naked the rest of his life; so my father, being a good-natured man and handy with the needle, turned to and repaired damages with a piece or two of scarlet cloth cut from the jacket of one of the drowned Marines. Well, the poor little chap chanced to be standing, in this rig-out, down by the gate of Gunner's Meadow, where they had buried two score and over of his comrades. The morning was a fine one, early in March month; and along came the cracked trumpeter, likewise taking a stroll.

'"Hullo!" says he; "good mornin'! And what might you be doin' here?"

'"I was a-wishin'," says the boy, "I had a pair o' drum-sticks. Our lads were buried yonder without so much as a drum tapped or a musket fired; and that's not Christian burial for British soldiers."

'"Phut!" says the trumpeter, and spat on the ground; "a parcel of Marines!"

'The boy eyed him a second or so, and answered up: "If I'd a tab of turf handy, I'd bung it at your mouth, you greasy cavalryman, and learn you to speak respectful of your betters. The Marines are the handiest body of men in the service."

'The trumpeter looked down on him from the height of six foot two, and asked: "Did they die well?"

"'They died very well. There was a lot of running to and fro at first, and some of the men began to cry, and a few to strip off their clothes. But when the ship fell off for the last time, Captain Mein turned and said something to Major Griffiths, the commanding officer on board, and the Major called out to me to beat to quarters. It might have been for a wedding, he sang it out so cheerful. We'd had word already that 'twas to be parade order, and the men fell in as trim and decent as if they were going to church. One or two even tried to shave at the last moment. The Major wore his medals. One of the seamen, seeing I had hard work to keep the drum steady – the sling being a bit loose for me and the wind what you remember – lashed it tight with a piece of rope; and that saved my life afterwards, a drum being as good as a cork until 'tis stove. I kept beating away until every man was on deck; and then the Major formed them up and told them to die like British soldiers, and the chaplain read a prayer or two – the boys standin' all the while like rocks, each man's courage keeping up the others'. The chaplain was in the middle of a prayer when she struck. In ten minutes she was gone. That was how they died, cavalryman."

"'And that was very well done, drummer of the Marines. What's your name?"

"'John Christian."

"'Mine is William George Tallifer, trumpeter, of the 7th Light Dragoons – the Queen's Own. I played *God Save the King* while our men were drowning. Captain Duncanfield told me to sound a call or two, to put them in heart; but that matter of *God Save the King* was a notion of my own. I won't say anything to hurt the feelings of a Marine, even if he's not much over five-foot tall; but the Queen's Own Hussars is a tearin' fine regiment. As between horse and foot, 'tis a question o' which gets the chance. All the way from Sahagun to Corunna 'twas we that took and gave the knocks – at Mayorga and Rueda, and Bennyventy." (The reason, sir, I can speak the names so pat is that my father learnt 'em by heart afterwards from the trumpeter, who was always talking about Mayorga and Rueda and Bennyventy.) "We made the rearguard, under General Paget, and drove the French every time; and all the infantry did was to sit about in wine-shops till we whipped 'em out, an' steal an' straggle an' play the tom-fool in general. And when it came to a stand-up fight at Corunna, 'twas the horse, or the best part of it, that had to stay sea-sick aboard the transports, an' watch the infantry in the thick o' the caper. Very well they behaved, too; 'specially the 4th Regiment, an' the 42nd Highlanders an' the Dirty Half-Hundred. Oh, ay; they're decent regiments, all three. But the Queen's Own Hussars is a tearin' fine regiment. So you played on your drum when the ship was goin' down? Drummer John Christian, I'll have to get you a new pair o' drum-sticks for that."

'Well, sir, it appears that the very next day the trumpeter marched into Helston, and got a carpenter there to turn him a pair of box-wood drum-sticks for the boy. And this was the beginning of one of the most curious friendships you ever heard tell of. Nothing delighted the pair more than to borrow a boat off my father and pull out to the rocks where the *Primrose* and the *Despatch* had struck and sunk; and on still days 'twas pretty to hear them out there off the Manacles, the drummer playing his tattoo – for they always took their music with them – and the trumpeter practising calls, and making his trumpet speak like an angel. But if the weather turned rough-ish, they'd be walking together and talking; leastwise, the youngster listened while the other discoursed about Sir John's campaign in Spain and Portugal, telling how each little skirmish befell; and of Sir John himself, and General Baird and General Paget, and Colonel Vivian, his own commanding officer, and what kind of men they were; and of the last bloody stand-up at Corunna, and so forth, as if neither could have enough.

'But all this had to come to an end in the late summer; for the boy, John Christian, being now well and strong again, must go up to Plymouth to report himself. 'Twas his own wish (for I believe King George had forgotten all about him), but his friend wouldn't hold him back. As for the trumpeter, my father had made an arrangement to take him on as a lodger as soon as the boy left; and on the morning fixed for the start, he was up at the door here by five o'clock, with his trumpet slung by his side, and all the rest of his kit in a small valise. A Monday morning it was, and after breakfast he had fixed to walk with the boy some way on the road towards Helston, where the coach started. My father left them at breakfast together, and went out to meat the pig, and do a few odd morning jobs of that sort. When he came back, the boy was still at table, and the trumpeter standing here by the chimney-place with the drum and trumpet in his hands, hitched together just as they be at this moment.

'"Look at this," he says to my father, showing him the lock; "I picked it up off a starving brass-worker in Lisbon, and it is not one of your common locks that one word of six letters will open at any time. There's *janius* in this lock; for you've only to make the rings spell any six-letter word you please, and snap down the lock upon that, and never a soul can open it – not the maker, even – until somebody comes along that knows the word you snapped it on. Now, Johnny here's goin', and he leaves his drum behind him; for, though he can make pretty music on it, the parchment sags in wet weather, by reason of the sea-water getting at it; an' if he carries it to Plymouth, they'll only condemn it and give him another. And, as for me, I shan't have the heart to put lip to the trumpet any more when Johnny's gone. So we've chosen a word together, and locked 'em together upon that; and, by your leave, I'll hang 'em here together on the hook over your fire-place. Maybe Johnny'll come back; maybe not. Maybe, if he comes, I'll be dead an' gone, an' he'll take 'em apart an' try their music for old sake's sake. But if he never comes, nobody can separate 'em; for nobody beside knows the word. And if you marry and have sons, you can tell 'em that here are tied together the souls of Johnny Christian, drummer of the Marines, and William George Tallifer, once trumpeter of the Queen's Own Hussars. Amen."

'With that he hung the two instruments 'pon the hook there; and the boy stood up and thanked my father and shook hands; and the pair went forth of the door, towards Helston.

'Somewhere on the road they took leave of one another; but nobody saw the parting, nor heard what was said between them. About three in the afternoon the trumpeter came walking back over the hill; and by the time my father came home from the fishing, the cottage was tidied up and the tea ready, and the whole place shining like a new pin. From that time for five years he lodged here with my father, looking after the house and tilling the garden; and all the while he was steadily failing, the hurt in his head spreading, in a manner, to his limbs. My father watched the feebleness growing on him, but said nothing. And from first to last neither spake a word about the drummer, John Christian; nor did any letter reach them, nor word of his doings.

'The rest of the tale you'm free to believe, sir, or not, as you please. It stands upon my father's words, and he always declared he was ready to kiss the Book upon it before judge and jury. He said, too, that he never had the wit to make up such a yarn; and he defied anyone to explain about the lock, in particular, by any other tale. But you shall judge for yourself.

'My father said that about three o'clock in the morning, April fourteenth of the year 'fourteen, he and William Tallifer were sitting here, just as you and I, sir, are sitting now. My father had put on his clothes a few minutes before, and was mending his spiller by the light of the horn lantern, meaning to set off before daylight to haul the trammel. The trumpeter hadn't been to bed at all. Towards the last he mostly spent his nights (and his days, too) dozing in the elbow-chair where you sit at this minute. He was dozing then (my father said), with his chin dropped forward on his chest, when a knock sounded upon the door, and the door opened, and in walked an upright young man in scarlet regimentals.

'He had grown a brave bit, and his face was the colour of wood-ashes; but it was the drummer, John Christian. Only his uniform was different from the one he used to wear, and the figures " 38 " shone in brass upon his collar.

'The drummer walked past my father as if he never saw him, and stood by the elbow-chair and said:

'"Trumpeter, trumpeter, are you one with me?"

'And the trumpeter just lifted the lids of his eyes, and answered, "How should I not be one with you, drummer Johnny – Johnny boy? The men are patient. 'Till you come, I count; while you march, I mark time; until the discharge comes."

'"The discharge has come to-night," said the drummer, "and the word is Corunna no longer"; and stepping to the chimney-place, he unhooked the drum and trumpet, and began to twist the brass rings of the lock, spelling the word aloud, so – C-O-R-U-N-A. When he had fixed the last letter, the padlock opened in his hand.

'"Did you know, trumpeter, that when I came to Plymouth they put me into a line regiment?"

'"The 38th is a good regiment," answered the old Hussar, still in his dull voice. "I went back with them from Sahagun to Corunna. At Corunna they stood in General Fraser's division, on the right. They behaved well."

'"But I'd fain see the Marines again," says the drummer, handing him the trumpet; "and you – you shall call once more for the Queen's Own. Matthew," he says, suddenly, turning on my father – and when he turned, my father saw for the first time that his scarlet jacket had a round hole by the breast-bone, and that the blood was welling there – "Matthew, we shall want your boat."

'Then my father rose on his legs like a man in a dream, while they two slung on, the one his drum, and t'other his trumpet. He took the lantern, and went quaking before them down to the shore, and they breathed heavily behind him; and they stepped into his boat, and my father pushed off.

'"Row you first for Dolor Point," says the drummer. So my father rowed them out past the white houses of Coverack to Dolor Point, and there, at a word, lay on his oars. And the trumpeter, William Tallifer, put his trumpet to his mouth and sounded the *reveille*. The music of it was like rivers running.

'"They will follow," said the drummer. "Matthew, pull you now for the Manacles."

'So my father pulled for the Manacles, and came to an easy close outside Carn dû. And the drummer took his sticks and beat a tattoo, there by the edge of the reef; and the music of it was like a rolling chariot.

'"That will do," says he, breaking off; "they will follow. Pull now for the shore under Gunner's Meadow."

'Then my father pulled for the shore, and ran his boat in under Gunner's Meadow. And they stepped out, all three, and walked up to the meadow. By the gate the drummer halted and began his tattoo again, looking out towards the darkness over the sea.

'And while the drum beat, and my father held his breath, there came up out of the sea and the darkness a troop of many men, horse and foot, and formed up among the graves; and others rose out of the graves and formed up – drowned Marines with bleached faces, and pale Hussars riding their horses, all lean and shadowy. There was no clatter of hoofs or accoutrements, my father said, but a soft sound all the while, like the beating of a bird's wing, and a black shadow lying like a pool about the feet of all. The drummer stood upon a little knoll just inside the gate, and beside him the tall trumpeter, with hand on hip, watching them gather; and behind them both my father, clinging to the gate. When no more came, the drummer stopped playing, and said, "Call the roll."

'Then the trumpeter stepped towards the end man of the rank and called, "Troop-Sergeant-Major Thomas Irons!" and the man in a thin voice answered "Here!"

'"Troop-Sergeant-Major Thomas Irons, how is it with you?"

'The man answered, "How should it be with me? When I was young, I betrayed a girl; and when I was grown, I betrayed a friend; and for these things I must pay. But I died as a man ought. God save the King!"

'The trumpeter called to the next man, "Trooper Henry Buckingham!" and the next man answered, "Here!"

'"Trooper Henry Buckingham, how is it with you?"

'"How should it be with me? I was a drunkard, and I stole, and in Lugo, in a wine-shop, I knifed a man. But I died as a man should. God save the King!"

'So the trumpeter went down the line; and when he had

finished, the drummer took it up, hailing the dead Marines in their order. Each man answered to his name, and each man ended with "God save the King!" When all were hailed, the drummer stepped back to his mound, and called:

'"It is well. You are content, and we are content to join you. Wait yet a little while."

'With this he turned and ordered my father to pick up the lantern, and lead the way back. As my father picked it up, he heard the ranks of dead men cheer and call, "God save the King!" all together, and saw them waver and fade back into the dark, like a breath fading off a pane.

'But when they came back here to the kitchen, and my father set the lantern down, it seemed they'd both forgot about him. For the drummer turned in the lantern-light – and my father could see the blood still welling out of the hole in his breast – and took the trumpet sling from around the other's neck, and locked drum and trumpet together again, choosing the letters on the lock very carefully. While he did this he said:

'"The word is no more Corunna, but Bayonne. As you left out an 'n' in Corunna, so must I leave out an 'n' in Bayonne." And before snapping the padlock, he spelt out the word slowly – "B-A-Y-O-N-E". After that, he used no more speech; but turned and hung the two instruments back on the hook; and then took the trumpeter by the arm; and the pair walked out into the darkness, glancing neither to right nor left.

'My father was on the point of following, when he heard a sort of sigh behind him; and there, sitting in the elbow-chair, was the very trumpeter he had just seen walk out by the door! If my father's heart jumped before, you may believe it jumped quicker now. But after a bit, he went up to the man asleep in the chair, and put a hand upon him. It was the trumpeter in flesh and blood that he touched; but though the flesh was warm, the trumpeter was dead.'

'Well, sir, they buried him three days after; and at first my father was minded to say nothing about his dream (as he thought it). But the day after the funeral, he met Parson Kendall coming from Helston market: and the parson called out: "Have 'ee heard the news the coach brought down this mornin'?" "What news?" says my father. "Why, that peace is agreed upon." "None too soon," says my father. "Not soon enough for our poor lads at Bayonne," the parson answered. "Bayonne!" cries my father, with a jump. "Why, yes"; and the parson told him all about a great sally the French had made on the night of April 13th. "Do you happen to know if the 38th Regiment was engaged?" my father asked. "Come, now," said Parson Kendall, "I didn't know you was so well up in the campaign. But, as it happens, I *do* know that the 38th was engaged, for 'twas they that held a cottage and stopped the French advance."

'Still my father held his tongue; and when, a week later, he walked into Helston and bought a *Mercury* off the Sherborne rider, and got the landlord of the "Angel" to spell out the list of killed and wounded, sure enough, there among the killed was Drummer John Christian, of the 38th Foot.

'After this, there was nothing for a religious man but to make a clean breast. So my father went up to Parson Kendall and told the whole story. The parson listened, and put a question or two, and then asked:

'"Have you tried to open the lock since that night?"

'"I hadn't dared to touch it," says my father.

'"Then come along and try." When the parson came to the cottage here, he took the things off the hook and tried the lock. "Did he say '*Bayonne*'? The word has seven letters."

'"Not if you spell it with one 'n' as *he* did," says my father.

'The parson spelt it out – B-A-Y-O-N-E. "Whew!" says he, for the lock had fallen open in his hand.

'He stood considering it a moment, and then he says, "I tell you what. I shouldn't blab this all round the parish, if I was you. You won't get no credit for truth-telling, and a miracle's wasted on a set of fools. But if you like, I'll shut down the lock again upon a holy word that no one but me shall know, and neither drummer nor trumpeter, dead or alive, shall frighten the secret out of me."

'"I wish to gracious you would, parson," said my father.

'The parson chose the holy word there and then, and shut

the lock back upon it, and hung the drum and trumpet back
in their place. He is gone long since, taking the word with
him. And till the lock is broken by force, nobody will ever
separate those twain.'

VISITORS AT THE GUNNEL ROCK

A Lightship Idyll

WHEN first the Trinity Brothers put a light out yonder by the Gunnel Rocks, it was just a trifling makeshift affair for the time – none of your proper lightships with a crew of twelve or fourteen hands; and my father and I used to tend it, taking turn and turn with two other fellows from the Islands. I'm talking of old days. The rule then – they have altered it since – was two months afloat and two ashore; and all the time we tossed out there on duty, not a soul would we see to speak to except when the Trinity boat put off with stores for us and news of what was doing in the world. This would be about once a fortnight in fair weather; but through the winter time it was oftener a month, and provisions ran low enough, now and then, to make us anxious. 'Was the life dreary?' Well, you couldn't call it gay; but, you see, it didn't kill me.

For the first week I thought the motion would drive me crazy – up and down, up and down, in that everlasting ground-swell – although I had been at the fishing all my life, and knew what it meant to lie-to in any ordinary sea. But after ten days or so I got not to mind it. And then there was the open air. It was different with the poor fellows on the lighthouse, eighteen miles to seaward of us, to the south-west. They drew better pay than ours, by a trifle; but they were landsmen, to start with; and cooped in that narrow tower at night, with the shutters closed and the whole building rocking like a tree, it's no wonder their nerves wore out. Four or five days of it have been known to finish a man; and in those times a lighthouse-keeper had three months of duty straight away, and only a fortnight on shore. Now he gets only a fortnight out there, and six weeks to recover in. With all that, they're mostly fit to start at their own shadow when the boat takes them off.

But on the lightship we fared tolerably. To begin with, we had the lantern to attend to. You'd be surprised how much

employment that gives a man – cleaning, polishing, and trimming. And my father, though particular to a scratch on the
reflector, or the smallest crust of salt on the glass, was a restful,
cheerful sort of a man to bide with. Not talkative, you understand – no light-keeper in the world was ever talkative – but
with a power of silence that was more comforting than speech.
And out there, too, we found all sorts of little friendly things
to watch and think over. Sometimes a school of porpoises; or
a line of little murrs flying; or a sail far to the south, making
for the Channel. And sometimes, towards evening, the
fishing-boats would come out and drop anchor a mile and a
half to south'ard, down sail, and hang out their riding lights;
and we knew that they took their mark from us, and that gave
a sociable feeling.

On clear afternoons, too, by swarming up the mast just
beneath the cage, I could see the Islands away in the east, with
the sun on their cliffs; and home wasn't so far off, after all.
The town itself, which lay low down on the shore, we could
never spy, but glimpsed the lights of it now and then, after
sunset. These always flickered a great deal, because of the
waves, like little hills of water, bobbing between them and us.
And always we had the lighthouse for company. In daytime,
through the glass, we could watch the keepers walking about
in the iron gallery round the top: and all night through, there
it was beckoning to us with its three white flashes every
minute. No, we weren't exactly gay out there, and sometimes
we made wild weather of it. Yet we did pretty well; except for
the fogs, when our arms ached with keeping the gong going.

But if we were comfortable then, you should have seen us
at the end of our two months, when the boat came off with the
relief, and took us on shore. John and Robert Pendlurian
were the names of the relief; brothers they were, oldsters of
about fifty-five and fifty; and John Pendlurian, the elder, a
widow-man same as my father, but with a daughter at home.
Living in the Islands, of course I'd known Bathsheba ever
since we'd sat in infant-school; and what more natural than to
ask after her health, along with the other news? But Old John
got to look sly and wink at my father when we came to this

question, out of the hundred others. And the other two would take it up and wink back solemn as mummers. I never lost my temper with the old idiots: 'twasn't worth while.

But the treat of all was to set foot on the quay steps, and the people crowding round and shaking your hand and chattering; and everything ashore going on just as you'd left it, and you not wishing it other, and everybody glad to see you all the same; and the smell of the gardens and the stinking fish at the quay corner – you might choose between them, but home was in both; and the nets drying; and to be out of oilskins and walking to meeting-house on the Sunday, and standing up there with the congregation, all singing in company, and the women taking stock of you till the newness wore off; and the tea-drinking, and Band of Hopes, and courants, and dances. We had all the luck of these; for the two Pendlurians, being up in years and easily satisfied so long as they were left quiet, were willing to take their holidays in the dull months, beginning with February and March. And so I had April and May, when a man can always be happy ashore; and August and September, which is the best of the fishing and all the harvest and harvest games; and again, December and January, with the courants and geesy-dancing, and carols and wassail-singing. Early one December, when he came to relieve us, Old John said to me in a haphazard way, 'It's all very well for me and Robert, my lad; for us two can take equal comfort in singin' *Star o' Bethl'em* ashore or afloat; but I reckon 'tis somebody's place to see that Bathsheba don't miss any of the season's joy an' dancin' on our account.'

Now, Bathsheba had an unmarried aunt – Aunt Hessy Pendlurian we called her – that used to take her to all the parties and courants when Old John was away at sea. So she wasn't likely to miss any of the fun, bein' able to foot it as clever as any girl in the Islands. She had the love of it, too – foot and waist and eyes all a-dancing, and body and blood all a-tingle as soon as ever the fiddle spoke. Maybe this same speech of Old John's set me thinking. Or, maybe I'd been thinking already – what with their May-game hints and the loneliness out there. Anyway, I dangled pretty close on

Bathsheba's heels all that Christmas. She was comely – you understand – very comely and tall, with dark blood, and eyes that put you in mind of a light shining steady upon dark water. And good as gold. She's dead and gone these twelve years – rest her soul! But (praise God for her!) I've never married another woman nor wanted to.

There, I've as good as told you already! When the time came and I asked her if she liked me, she said she liked no man half so well: and that being as it should be, the next thing was to put up the banns. There wasn't time that holiday: like a fool, I had been dilly-dallying too long, though I believe now I might have asked her a month before. So the wedding was held in the April following, my father going out to the Gunnel for a couple of days, so that Old John might be ashore to give his daughter away. The most I mind of the wedding was the wonder of beholding the old chap there in a long-tailed coat, having never seen him for years but in his oilskins.

Well, the rest of that year seemed pretty much like all the others, except that coming home was better than ever. But when Christmas went by, and February came and our turn to be out again on the Gunnel, I went with a dismal feeling I hadn't known before. For Bathsheba was drawing near her time, and the sorrow was that she must go through it without me. She had walked down to the quay with us, to see us off; and all the way she chatted and laughed with my father, as cheerful as cheerful – but never letting her eyes rest on me, I noticed, and I saw what that meant; and when it came to good-bye, there was more in the tightening of her arms about me than I'd ever read in it before.

The old man, I reckon, had a wisht time with me, the next two or three weeks; but, by the mercy of God, the weather behaved furious all the while, leaving a man no time to mope. 'Twas busy all, and busy enough, to keep a clear light inside the lantern, and warm souls inside our bodies. All through February it blew hard and cold from the north and north-west, and though we lay in the very mouth of the Gulf Stream, for ten days together there wasn't a halliard we could touch with the naked hand, nor a cloth nor handful of cotton-waste but had to be thawed at the stove before using. Then, with the beginning of March, the wind tacked round to south-west and stuck there, blowing big guns, and raising a swell that was something cruel. It was one of these gales that tore away the bell from the lighthouse, though hung just over a hundred feet above water-level. As for us, I wonder now how the little boat held by its two-ton anchors, even with three hundred fathom of chain cable to bear the strain and jerk of it; but with the spindrift whipping our faces, and the hail cutting them, we didn't seem to have time to think of *that*. Bathsheba thought of it, though, in her bed at home – as I've heard since – and lay awake more than one night thinking of it.

But the third week in March the weather moderated; and soon the sun came out and I began to think. On the second afternoon of the fair weather I climbed up under the cage and saw the Islands for the first time; and coming down, I said to my father:

'Suppose that Bathsheba is dead!'

We hadn't said more than a word or two to each other for a week; indeed, till yesterday we had to shout in each other's ear to be heard at all. My father filled a pipe and said, 'Don't be a fool.'

'I see your hand shaking,' said I.

Said he, 'That's with the cold. At my age the cold takes a while to leave a man's extremities.'

'But,' I went on in an obstinate way, 'suppose she is dead?'

My father answered, 'She is a well-built woman. The Lord is good.'

Not another word than this could I get from him. That evening – the wind now coming easy from the south, and the swell gone down in a wonderful way – as I was boiling water for the tea, we saw a dozen fishing-boats standing out from the Islands. They ran down to within two miles of us and then hove-to. The nets went out, and the sails came down, and by and by through the glass I could spy the smoke coming up from their cuddy-stoves.

'They might have brought news,' I cried out, 'even if 'tis sorrow!'

'Maybe there was no news to bring.'

''Twould have been neighbourly, then, to run down and say so.'

'And run into the current here, I suppose? With a chance of the wind falling light at any moment?'

I don't know if this satisfied my father: but I know that he meant it to satisfy me, which it was pretty far from doing. Before daylight the boats hoisted sail again, and were well under the Islands and out of sight by breakfast-time.

After this, for a whole long week I reckon I did little more than pace the ship to and fro; a fisherman's walk, as they say – three steps and overboard. I took the three steps and wished I was overboard. My father watched me queerly all the while; but we said no word to each other, not even at meals.

It was the eighth day after the fishing-boats left us, and about four in the afternoon, that we saw a brown sail standing towards us from the Islands, and my father set down the glass, resting it on the gunwale, and said:

'That's Old John's boat.'

I took the glass from him, and was putting it to my eye; but had to set it down and turn my back. I couldn't wait there with my eye on the boat; so I crossed to the other side of the ship and stood staring at the lighthouse away on the sky-line, and whispered: 'Come quickly!' But the wind had moved a couple of points to the east and then fallen very light, and the boat must creep towards us close-hauled. After a long while my father spoke again:

'That will be Old John steerin' her. I reckoned so: he've got her jib shakin' – that's it: sail her close till she strikes the tide-race, and that'll fetch her down, wind or no wind. Halloa! – Lad, lad! 'tis all right! See there, that bit o' red ensign run up to the gaff!'

'Why should that mean aught?' asked I.

'Would he trouble to hoist bunting if he had no news? Would it be there, close under the peak, if the news was bad? – and she his own daughter, his only flesh!'

It may have been twenty minutes later that Old John felt the Gunnel current, and, staying the cutter round, came down fast on us with the wind behind his beam. My father hailed to him once and twice, and the second time he must have heard. But, without answering, he ran forward and took in his foresail. And then I saw an arm and a little hand reached up to take hold of the tiller; and my heart gave a great jump.

It was she, my wife Bathsheba, laid there by the stern-sheets on a spare sail, with a bundle of oilskins to cushion her. With one hand she steered the boat up into the wind as Old John lowered sail and they fell alongside: and with the other she held a small bundle close against her breast.

'Such a whackin' boy I never see in my life!' – These were Old John's first words, and he shouted them. 'Born only yestiddy week, an' she ought to be abed: an' so I've been tellin' her ever since she dragged me out 'pon this wildy-go errand!'

But Bathsheba, as I lifted her over the lightship's side, said no more than 'Oh, Tom!' – and let me hold her, with her forehead pressed close against me. And the others kept very quiet, and everything was quiet about us, until she jumped back on a sudden and found all her speech in a flood.

'Tom,' she said, 'you're crushin' him, you great, awkward man!' And she turned back the shawl and snatched the handkerchief off the baby's face – a queer-looking face it was, too. 'Be all babies as queer as that?' thought I. Lucky I didn't say it, though. 'There, my blessed, my handsome! Look, my tender! Eh, Tom, but he kicks my side all to bruises; my merryun, my giant! Look up at your father, and you his very image!' That was pretty stiff. 'I declare,' she says, 'he's lookin' about an' takin' stock of everything' – and that was pretty stiff, too. 'So like a man; all for the sea and the boats! Tom, dear, father will tell you that all the way on the water he was as good as gold; and, on shore before that, kicking and fisting – all for the sea and the boats; the man of him! Hold him, dear, but be careful! A Sunday's child, too –

Sunday's child is full of grace . . .

and – the awkward you are! Here, give him back to me: but feel how far down in his clothes the feet of him reach.

Extraordinar'! Aun' Hessy mounted a chair and climbed 'pon the chest o' drawers with him, before takin' him downstairs; so that he'll go up in the world, an' not down.'

'If he wants to try both,' said I, 'he'd best follow his father and grandfathers, and live 'pon a lightship.'

'So this is how you live, Tom; and you, father; and you, father-in-law!' She moved about examining everything – the lantern, the fog-signals and life-buoys, the cooking-stove, bunks, and store-cupboards. 'To think that here you live, all the menkind belongin' to me, and I never to have seen it! All the menkind did I say, my rogue! And was I forgettin' you – you – you?' Kisses here, of course: and then she held the youngster up to look at his face in the light. 'Ah, heart of me, will you grow up too to live in a lightship and leave a poor woman at home to weary for you in her trouble? Rogue, rogue, what poor woman have I done this to, bringing you into the world to be her torture and her joy?'

'Dear,' says I, 'you're weak yet. Sit down by me and rest awhile before the time comes to go back.'

'But I'm not going back yet awhile. Your son, sir, and I are goin' to spend the night aboard.'

'Halloa!' I said, and looked towards Old John, who had made fast astern of us and run a line out to one of the anchor-buoys.

''Tisn't allowed, o' course,' he muttered, looking in turn and rather sheepishly towards my father. 'But once in a way – 'tis all Bathsheba's notion, and you mustn' ask *me*,' he wound up.

'"Once in a way!"' cried Bathsheba. 'And is it twice in a way that a woman comes to a man and lays his first child in his arms?'

My father had been studying the sunset and the sky to wind-ward; and now he answered Old John:

' 'Tis once in a way, sure enough, that a boat can lay along-side the Gunnel. But the wind's falling, and the night'll be warm. I reckon if you stay in the boat, Old John, she'll ride pretty comfortable; and I'll give the word to cast off at the leastest sign.'

'Once in a way' – ah, sirs, it isn't twice in a way there comes such a night as that was! We lit the light at sunset, and hoisted it, and made tea, talking like children all the while; and my father the biggest child of all. Old John had his share passed out to him, and ate it alone out there in the boat; and, there being a lack of cups, Bathsheba and I drank out of the same, and scalded our lips, and must kiss to make them well. Foolishness? Dear, dear, I suppose so. And the jokes we had, calling out to Old John as the darkness fell, and wishing him 'Good night!' 'Oh, aye; I hear 'ee,' was all he answered. After we'd eaten our tea and washed up, I showed Bathsheba how to crawl into her bunk, and passed in the baby and laid it in her arms, and so left her, telling her to rest and sleep. But by and by, as I was keeping watch, she came out, declaring the place stifled her. So I pulled out a mattress and blankets and strewed a bed for her out under the sky, and sat down beside her, watching while she suckled the child. She had him wrapped up so that the two dark eyes of him only could be seen, staring up from the breast to the great bright lantern above him. The moon was in her last quarter, and would not rise till close upon dawn; and the night pitchy dark around us, with a very few stars. In less than a minute Bathsheba gave a start and laid a hand on my arm.

'Oh, Tom, what was that?'

'Look up,' said I. ' 'Tis the birds flying about the light.'

For, of course, our light always drew the sea-birds, especially on dull nights, and 'twas long since we had grown used to the sound of their beating and flapping, and took no notice of it. A moment after I spoke one came dashing against the rigging, and we heard him tumble into the sea; and then one broke his neck against the cage overhead and tumbled dead at our feet. Bathsheba shivered as I tossed him overboard.

'Is it always like this?' she whispered. 'I thought 'twas only at the cost of a silly woman's fears that you saved men's lives out here.'

'Well,' said I, 'this is something more than usual, to be sure.'

For, looking up into the circle of light, we could see now at least a hundred birds flying round and round, and in half an hour's time there must have been many hundreds. Their white breasts were like a snowstorm; and soon they began to fall thick upon deck. They were not all sea-birds, either.

'Halloa!' said I, 'what's the day of the month?'

'The nineteenth of March.'

'Here's a wheatear, then,' I said. 'In a couple of weeks we shall have the swallows; and, a couple of weeks after, a cuckoo, maybe. So you see that even out here by the Gunnel we know when spring comes along.'

And I began to hum the old song that children sang in the Islands:

> The cuckoo is a pretty bird,
>   He sings as he flies:
> He brings us good tidings,
>   He tells us no lies:
> He sucks the sweet flow-ers
>   For to make his voice clear,
> And when he says 'Cuckoo!'
>   The summer is near.

Bathsheba's eyes were wet for the poor birds, but she took up the song, crooning it soft-like, and persuading the child to sleep.

> O, meeting is a pleasure,
>   But parting is grief,
> An inconstant lover
>   Is worse than a thief;
> For a thief at the worst
>   Will take all that I have;
> But an inconstant lover
>   Sends me to my grave.

Her hand stole into mine as the boy's eyes closed, and clasped my fingers, entreating me in silence to look and admire him. Our own eyes met over him, and I saw by the lantern-light the happy blush rise and spread over neck and chin and forehead. The flapping of the birds overhead had almost died away, and we lay still, watching the lighthouse flash, far down in the empty darkness.

By and by the clasp of her hand slackened. A star shot down the sky, and I turned. Her eyelids, too, had drooped, and her breath came and went as softly and regularly as the Atlantic swell around us. And my child slept in her arms.

Day was breaking before the first cry awoke her. My father had the breakfast ready, and Old John sang out to hurry. A fair wind went with them to the Islands – a light south-wester. As the boat dropped out of sight, I turned and drew a deep breath of it. It was full of the taste of flowers, and I knew that spring was already at hand, and coming up that way.

STATEMENT OF
GABRIEL FOOT, HIGHWAYMAN

THE jury re-entered the court after half an hour's consultation.

It all comes back to me as vividly as though I stood in the dock at this very moment. The dense fog that hung over the well of the court; the barristers' wigs that bobbed up through it, and were drowned again in that seething cauldron; the rays of the guttering candles (for the murder-trial had lasted far into the evening) that loomed through it and wore a sickly halo; the red robes and red face of my lord judge opposite, that stared through it and outshone the candles; the black crowd around, seen mistily; the voice of the usher calling 'Silence!'; the shuffling of the jurymen's feet; the pallor on their faces as I leant forward and tried to read the verdict on them; the very smell of the place, compounded of fog, jail-fever, the close air, and the dinners eaten earlier in the day by the crowd – all this strikes home upon me as sharply as it then did, after the numb apathy of waiting.

As the jury huddled into their places I stole a look at my counsel. He paused for a moment from his task of trimming a quill, shot a quick glance at the foreman's face, and then went on cutting as coolly as ever.

'Gentlemen of the jury' – it was the judge's voice – 'are you agreed upon your verdict?'

'We are.'

'Do you find the prisoner guilty or not guilty?'

'*Not guilty.*'

It must have been full a minute, as I leant back clutching the rail in front of me, before I saw anything but the bleared eyes of the candles, or heard anything but a hoarse murmur from the crowd. But as soon as the court ceased to heave, and I could stare about me, I looked towards my counsel again.

He was still shaping his pen. He made no motion to come

forward and shake hands over my acquittal, for which he had worked untiringly all day. He did not even offer to speak. He just looked up, nodded carelessly, and turned to his junior beside him; but in that glance I had read something which turned my heart cold, then sick, within me, and from that moment my hatred of the man was as deep as hell.

In the fog outside I got clear of the gaping crowd, but the chill of the night after that heated court pierced my very bones. I had on the clothes I had been taken in. It was June then, and now it was late in October. I remember that on the day when they caught me I wore my coat open for coolness. Four months and a half had gone out of my life. Well, I had money enough in my pocket to get a greatcoat; but I must put something warm inside me first, to get out the chill that cursed lawyer had laid on my heart.

I had purposely chosen the by-lanes of the town, but I remembered a certain tavern – the 'Lamb and Flag' – which lay down a side-alley. Presently the light from its windows struck across the street, ahead. I pushed open the door and entered.

The small bar was full of people newly come from the court, and discussing the trial in all its bearings. In the babel I heard a dozen different opinions given in as many seconds, and learnt enough, too, to make me content with the jury I had had. But the warmth of the place was pleasant, and I elbowed my way forward to the counter.

There was a woman standing by the door as I entered, who looked curiously at me for a moment, then turned to nudge a man at her side, and whisper. The whisper grew as I pressed forward, and before I could reach the counter a hand was laid on my shoulder from behind. I turned.

'Well?' said I.

It was a heavy-looking drover that had touched me.

'Are you the chap that was tried to-day for murder of Jewel-ler Todd?' he asked.

'Well?' said I again, but I could see the crowd falling back, as if I was a leper, at his question.

'Well? 'Tain't well then, as I reckon, to be making so free with respectable folk.'

There was a murmur of assent from the mouths turned towards me. The landlord came forward from behind the bar.

'I was acquitted,' I urged defiantly.

'Ac-quitted!' said he, with big scorn in the syllables. 'Hear 'im now – "ac-quitted"! Landlord, is this a respectable house?'

The landlord gave his verdict.

'Hout yer goes, and damn yer impudence!'

I looked round, but their faces were all dead against me.

'Hout yer goes!' repeated the landlord. 'And think yerself lucky it ain't worse,' added the drover.

With no further defence I slunk out into the night once more.

A small crowd of children (Heaven knows whence or how they gathered) followed me up the court and out into the street. Their numbers swelled as I went on, and some began to hoot and pelt me; but when I gained the top of the hill, and a lonelier district, I turned and struck among them with my stick. It did my heart good to hear their screams.

After that I was let alone, and tramped forward past the scattered houses, towards the open country and the moors. Up here there was scarcely any fog, but I could see it, by the rising moon, hanging like a shroud over the town below. The next town was near upon twelve miles off, but I do not remember that I thought of getting so far. I could not have thought at all, in fact, or I should hardly have taken the high road upon which the jeweller had been stopped and murdered.

There was a shrewd wind blowing, and I shivered all over; but the cold at my heart was worse, and my hate of the man who had set it there grew with every step. I thought of the four months and more which parted the two lives of Gabriel Foot, and what I should make of the new one. I had my chance again – a chance gained for me beyond hope by that counsel but for whom I should be sleeping to-night in the condemned cell; a chance, and a good chance, but for that same cursed lawyer. Ugh! how cold it was, and how I hated *him* for it!

There was a little whitewashed cottage on the edge of the

moorland just after the hedgerows ceased – the last house before the barren heath began, standing a full three hundred yards from any other dwelling. Its front faced the road, and at the back an outhouse and a wretched garden jutted out on the waste land. There was a light in each of its windows to-night, and as I passed down the road I heard the dismal music of a flute.

Perhaps it was this that jogged my thoughts and woke them up to my present pass. At any rate, I had not gone more than twenty yards before I turned and made for the door. The people might give me a night's lodging in the outhouse; at any rate, they would not refuse a crust to stay the fast which I had not broken since the morning. I tapped gently with my knuckles on the door, and listened.

I waited five minutes, and no one answered. The flute still continued its melancholy tune; it was evidently in the hands of a learner, for the air (a dispiriting one enough at the best) kept breaking off suddenly and repeating itself. But the performer had patience, and the sound never ceased for more than two seconds at a time. Besides this, nothing could be heard. The blinds were drawn in all the windows. The glow of the candles through them was cheerful enough, but nothing could be seen of the house inside. I knocked a second time, and a third, with the same result. Finally, tired of this, I pushed open the low gate which led into the garden behind, and stole round to the back of the cottage.

Here, too, the window on the ground floor was lit up behind its blinds, but that of the room above was shuttered. There was a hole in the shutter, however, where a knot of the wood had fallen out, and a thin shaft of light stretched across the blackness and buried itself in a ragged yew-tree at the end of the garden. From the loudness of the sounds I judged this to be the room where the flute-playing was going on. The crackling of my footsteps on the thin soil did not disturb the performer, so I gathered a handful of earth and pitched it up against the pane. The flute stopped for a minute or so, but just as I was expecting to see the shutter open, went on again: this time the air was 'Pretty Polly Oliver'.

I crept back again, and began to hammer more loudly at the door. 'Come,' said I, 'whoever this may be inside, I'll see for myself at any rate,' and with that I lifted the latch and gave the door a heavy kick. It flew open quite easily (it had not even been locked), and I found myself in a low kitchen. The room was empty, but the relics of supper lay on the deal table, and the remains of what must have been a noble fire were still smouldering on the hearthstone. A crazy, rusty blunderbuss hung over the fire-place. This, with a couple of rough chairs, a broken bacon-rack, and a small side-table, completed the furniture of the place. No; for as I sat down to make a meal off the remnants of supper, something lying on the lime-ash floor beneath this side-table caught my eye. I stepped forward and picked it up.

It was a barrister's wig.

'This is a queer business,' thought I; and I laid it on the table opposite me as I went on with my supper. It was a 'gossan' wig, as we call it in our parts; a wig grown yellow and rusty with age and wear. It looked so sly and wicked as it lay there, and brought back the events of the day so sharply, that a queer dread took me of being discovered with it. I pulled out my pistol, loaded it (they had given me back both the powder and pistol found on me when I was taken), and laid it beside my plate. This done, I went on with my supper – it was an excellent cold capon – and all the time the flute upstairs kept toot-tootling without stopping, except to change the tune. It gave me 'Hearts of Oak', 'Why, Soldiers, why?', 'Like Hermit Poor', and 'Come, Lasses and Lads', before I had fairly cleared the dish.

'And now,' thought I, 'I have had a good supper; but there are still three things to be done. In the first place I want drink, in the second I want a bed, and in the third I want to thank this kind person, whoever he is, for his hospitality. I'm not going to begin life No. 2 with housebreaking.'

I rose, slipped the pistol into my tail-pocket, and followed the sound up the ramshackle stairs. My footsteps made such a racket on their old timbers as fairly to frighten me, but it never disturbed the flute-player. He had harked back again to 'Like

Hermit Poor' by this time, and the dolefulness of it was fit to make the dead cry out, but he went whining on until I reached the head of the stairs and struck a rousing knock on the door.

The playing stopped. 'Come in,' said a cheery voice; but it gave me no cheerfulness. Instead of that, it sent all the comfort of my supper clean out of me, as I opened the door and saw *him* sitting there.

There he was, the man who had saved my neck that day, and whom most I hated in the world, sitting before a snug fire, with his flute on his knee, a glass of port wine at his elbow, and looking so comfortable, with that knowing light in his grey eyes, that I could have killed him where he sat.

'Oh, it's you, is it?' he said, just the very least bit surprised and no more. 'Come in.'

I stood in the doorway hesitating.

'Don't stay letting in that monstrous draught, man; but sit down. You'll find the bottle on the table and a glass on the shelf.'

I poured out a glassful and drank it off. The stuff was rare (I can remember its trick on the tongue to this day), but somehow it did not drive the cold out of my heart. I took another glass, and sat sipping it and staring from the fire to my companion.

He had taken up the flute again, and was blowing a few deep notes out of it, thoughtfully enough. He was a small, squarely built man, with a sharp ruddy face like a frozen pippin, heavy grey eyebrows, and a mouth like a trap when it was not pursed up for that everlasting flute. As he sat there with his wig off, the crown of his bald head was fringed with an obstinate-looking patch of hair, the colour of a badger's. My amazement at finding him here at this hour, and alone, was lost in my hatred of the man as I saw the depths of complacent knowledge in his face. I felt that I must kill him sooner or later, and the sooner the better.

Presently he laid down his flute again and spoke:

'I scarcely expected you.'

I grunted something in answer.

'But I might have known something was up, if I'd only

paid attention to my flute. It and I are not in harmony to-night. It doesn't like the secrets I've been blowing into it; it has heard a lot of queer things in its time, but it's an innocent-minded flute for all that, and I'm afraid that what I've told it to-night is a point beyond what it's prepared to go.'

'I take it, it knows a damned deal too much,' growled I.

He looked at me sharply for an instant, rose, whistled a bar or two of 'Like Hermit Poor', reached down a couple of clay pipes from the shelf, filled one for himself, and gravely handed the other with the tobacco to me.

– 'Beyond what it is prepared to go,' he echoed quietly, sinking back in his chair and puffing at the pipe. 'It's a nice point that we have been discussing together, my flute and I, and I won't say but that I've got the worst of it. By the way, what do you mean to do now that you have a fresh start?'

Now I had not tasted tobacco for over four months, and its effect upon my wits was surprising. It seemed to oil my thoughts till they worked without a hitch, and I saw my plan of action marked out quite plainly before me.

'Do you want to know the first step of all?' I asked.

'To be sure; the first step at any rate determines the direction.'

'Well then,' said I, very steadily, and staring into his face, 'the first step of all is that I am going to kill you.'

'H'm,' said he after a bit, and I declare that not so much as an eyelash of the man shook, 'I thought as much. I guessed *that* when you came into the room. And what next?'

'Time enough then to think of "what next",' I answered; for though I was set upon blowing his brains out, I longed for him to blaze out into a passion and warm up my blood for the job.

'Pardon me,' he said, as coolly as might be, 'that would be the very worst time to think of it. For, just consider: in the first place you will already be committed to your way of life, and secondly, if I know anything about you, you would be far too much flurried for any thought worth the name.'

There was a twinkle of frosty humour in his eye as he said this, and in the silence which followed I could hear him chuckling to himself, and tasting the words over again as though they were good wine. I sat fingering my pistol and waiting for him to speak again. When he did so, it was with another dry chuckle and a long puff of tobacco smoke.

'As you say, I know a deal too much. Shall I tell you how much?'

'Yes, you may if you'll be quick about it.'

'Very well, then, I will. Do you mind passing the bottle? Thank you. I probably know not only too much, but a deal more than you guess. First let us take the case for the Crown. The jeweller is travelling by coach at night over the moors. He has one postillion only, Roger Tallis by name, and by character shady. The jeweller has money (he was a niggardly fool to take only one postillion), and carries a diamond of great, or rather of an enormous and notable, value (he was a bigger fool to take this). In the dark morning two horses come galloping back frightened and streaming with sweat. A search party goes out, finds the coach upset by the Four Holed Cross, the jeweller lying beside it with a couple of pistol bullets in him, and the money, the diamond, and Roger Tallis – nowhere. So much for the murdered man. Two or three days after, you, Gabriel Foot, by character also shady, and known to be a friend of Roger Tallis, are whispered to have a suspicious amount of money about you, also blood-stains on your coat. It further leaks out that you were travelling on the moors afoot on the night in question, and that your pistols are soiled with powder. Case for the Crown closes. Have I stated it correctly?'

I nodded. He took a sip or two at his wine, laid down his pipe as if the tobacco spoiled the taste of it, took another sip, and continued:

'Case for the defence. That Roger Tallis has decamped, that no diamond has been found on you (or anywhere), and lastly that the bullets in the jeweller's body do not fit your pistols, but came from a larger pair. Not very much of a case, perhaps, but this last is a strong point.'

'Well?' I asked, as he paused.

'Now then for the facts of the case. Would you oblige me by casting a look over there in the corner?'

'I see nothing but a pickaxe and shovel.'

'Ha! very good; "nothing but a pickaxe and shovel." Well, to resume: facts of the case – Roger Tallis murders the jeweller, and you murder Roger Tallis. After that, as you say, "nothing but a pickaxe and shovel."'

And with this, as I am a living sinner, the rosy-faced old boy took up his flute and blew a stave or two of 'Come, Lasses and Lads'.

'Did you dig him up?' I muttered hoarsely; and although deathly cold I could feel a drop of sweat trickling down my forehead and into my eye.

'What, before the trial? My good sir, you have a fair, a very fair, aptitude for crime: but believe me, you have much to learn both of legal etiquette and of a lawyer's conscience.' And for the first time since I came in I saw something like indignation on his ruddy face.

'Now,' he continued, 'I either know too much or not enough. Obviously I know enough for you to wish, and perhaps wisely, to kill me. The question is, whether I know enough to make it worth your while to spare me. I think I do; but that is for you to decide. If I put you to-night, and in half an hour's time, in possession of property worth ten thousand pounds, will that content you?'

'Come, come,' I said, 'you need not try to fool me, nor think I am going to let you out of my sight.'

'You misunderstand. I desire neither; I only wish a bargain. I am ready to pledge you my word to make no attempt to escape before you are in possession of that property, and to offer no resistance to your shooting me in case you fail to obtain it, provided on the other hand you pledge your word to spare my life should you succeed within half an hour. And, my dear sir, considering the relative value of your word and mine, I think it must be confessed you have the better of the bargain.'

I thought for a moment. 'Very well then,' said I, 'so be it; but if you fail –'

'I know what happens,' replied he.

With that he blew a note or two on his flute, took it to

pieces, and carefully bestowed it in the tails of his coat. I put away my pistol in mine.

'Do you mind shouldering that spade and pickaxe, and following me?' he asked. I took them up in silence. He drained his glass and put on his hat.

'Now I think we are ready. Stop a moment.'

He reached across for the glass which I had emptied, took it up gingerly between thumb and forefinger, and tossed it with a crash on to the hearthstone. He then did the same to my pipe, after first snapping the stem into halves. This done, he blew out one candle, and with great gravity led the way down the staircase. I shouldered the tools and followed, while my heart hated him with a fiercer spite than ever.

We passed down the crazy stairs and through the kitchen. The candles were still burning there. As my companion glanced at the supper-table, 'H'm,' he said, 'not a bad beginning of a new leaf. My friend, I will allow you exactly twelve months in which to get hanged.'

I made no answer, and we stepped out into the night. The moon was now up, and the high road stretched like a white ribbon into the gloom. The cold wind bore up a few heavy clouds from the north-west, but for the most part we could see easily enough. We trudged side by side along the road in silence, except that I could hear my companion every now and then whistling softly to himself.

As we drew near to the Four Holed Cross and the scene of the murder I confess to an uneasy feeling and a desire to get past the place with all speed. But the lawyer stopped by the very spot where the coach was overturned, and held up a finger as if to call attention. It was a favourite trick of his with the jury.

'This was where the jeweller lay. Some fifteen yards off there was another pool of blood. Now the jeweller must have dropped instantly for he was shot through the heart. Yet no one doubted but that the other pool of blood was his. Fools!'

With this he turned off the road at right angles, and began to strike rapidly across the moor. At first I thought he was trying to escape me, but he allowed me to catch him up readily enough, and then I knew the point for which he was making. I followed doggedly. Clouds began to gather over the moon's face, and every now and then I stumbled heavily on the uneven ground; but he moved along nimbly enough, and even cried 'Shoo!' in a sprightly voice when a startled plover flew up before his feet. Presently, after we had gone about five hundred yards on the heath, the ground broke away into a little hollow, where a rough track led down to the lime kilns and the thinly wooded stream that washed the valley below. We followed this track for ten minutes or so, and presently the masonry of the disused kilns peered out, white in the moonlight, from between the trees.

There were three of these kilns standing close together beside the path; but my companion without hesitation pulled up almost beneath the very arch of the first, peered about, examined the ground narrowly, and then motioned to me.

'Dig here.'

'If we both know well enough what is underneath, what is the use of digging?'

'I very much doubt if we do,' said he. 'You had better dig.'

I can feel the chill creeping down my back as I write of it; but at that time, though I well knew what I was to discover, I dug away steadily enough. The man who had surprised my secret set himself down on a dark bank of ferns at about ten paces' distance, and began to whistle softly, though I could see his fingers fumbling with his coat-tails as though they itched to be at the flute again.

The moon's rays shone fitfully upon the white face of the kiln, and lit up my work. The little stream rushed noisily below. And so, with this hateful man watching, I laid bare the lime-burnt remains of the comrade whom, almost five months before, I had murdered and buried there. How I had then cursed my luck because forced to hide his corpse away before I could return and search for the diamond I had failed to find upon his body! But as I tossed the earth and lime aside, and discovered my handiwork, the moon's rays were suddenly caught and reflected from within the pit, and I fell forward with a short gasp of delight.

For there, kindled into quick shafts and points of colour – violet, green, yellow, and fieriest red – lay the missing diamond among Roger's bones. As I clutched the gem a black shadow fell between the moon and me. I looked up. My companion was standing over me, with the twinkle still in his eye and the flute in his hand.

'You were a fool not to guess that he had swallowed it. I hope you are satisfied with the bargain? As we are not, I trust, likely to meet again in this world, I will here bid you adieu, though possibly that is scarcely the word to use. But there is one thing I wish to tell you. I owe you a debt to-night for having prevented me from committing a crime. You saw that I had the spade and pickaxe ready in the cottage. Well, I confess I lusted for that gem. I was arguing out the case with my flute when you came in.'

'If,' said I, 'you wish a share –'

'Another word,' he interrupted very gravely, 'and I shall be forced to think that you insult me. As it is, I am grateful to you for supporting my flute's advice at an opportune moment. I will now leave you. Two hours ago I was in a fair way of becoming a criminal. I owe it to you, and to my flute, that I am still merely a lawyer. Farewell!'

With that he turned on his heel and was gone with a swinging stride up the path and across the moor. His figure stood out upon the skyline for a moment, and then vanished. But I could hear for some time the tootle-tootle of his flute in the distance, and it struck me that its note was unusually sprightly and clear.

THE TWO HOUSEHOLDERS

Extract from the Memories of Gabriel Foot,
Highwayman

I WILL say this – speaking as accurately as a man may, so long
afterwards – that when first I spied the house it put no desire
in me but just to give thanks.

For conceive my case. It was near midnight, and ever since
dusk I had been tramping the naked moors, in the teeth of as
vicious a nor'-wester as ever drenched a man to the skin, and
then blew the cold home to his marrow. My clothes were
sodden; my coat-tails flapped with a noise like pistol-shots; my
boots squeaked as I went. Overhead, the October moon was in
her last quarter, and might have been a slice of finger-nail for
all the light she afforded. Two-thirds of the time the wrack
blotted her out altogether; and I, with my stick clipped tight
under my armpit, eyes puckered up, and head bent aslant, had
to keep my wits alive to distinguish the road from the black
heath to right and left. For three hours I had met neither man
nor man's dwelling, and (for all I knew) was desperately lost.
Indeed, at the cross-roads, two miles back, there had been
nothing for me but to choose the way that kept the wind on
my face, and it gnawed me like a dog.

Mainly to allay the stinging of my eyes, I pulled up at last,
turned right-about-face, leant back against the blast with a
hand on my hat, and surveyed the blackness behind. It was at
this instant that, far away to the left, a point of light caught my
notice, faint but steady; and at once I felt sure it burnt in the
window of a house. 'The house,' thought I, 'is a good mile off,
beside the other road, and the light must have been an inch
over my hat-brim for the last half-hour.' This reflexion – that
on so wide a moor I had come near missing the information I
wanted (and perhaps a supper) by one inch – sent a strong
thrill down my back.

I cut straight across the heather towards the light, risking quags and pitfalls. Nay, so heartening was the chance to hear a fellow-creature's voice, that I broke into a run, skipping over the stunted gorse that cropped up here and there, and dreading every moment to see the light quenched. 'Suppose it burns in an upper window, and the family is going to bed, as would be likely at this hour —' The apprehension kept my eyes fixed on the bright spot, to the frequent scandal of my legs, that within five minutes were stuck full of gorse prickles.

But the light did not go out, and soon a flicker of moonlight gave me a glimpse of the house's outline. It proved to be a deal more imposing than I looked for — the outline, in fact, of a tall, square barrack, with a cluster of chimneys at either end, like ears, and a high wall, topped by the roofs of some outbuildings, concealing the lower windows. There was no gate in this wall, and presently I guessed the reason. I was approaching the place from behind, and the light came from a back window on the first floor.

The faintness of the light also was explained by this time. It shone behind a drab-coloured blind, and in shape resembled the stem of a wine-glass, broadening out at the foot; an effect produced by the half-drawn curtains within. I came to a halt, waiting for the next ray of moonlight. At the same moment a rush of wind swept over the chimney-stacks, and on the wind there seemed to ride a human sigh.

On this last point I may err. The gust had passed some seconds before I caught myself detecting this peculiar note, and trying to disengage it from the natural chords of the storm. From the next gust it was absent; and then, to my dismay, the light faded from the window.

I was half-minded to call out, when it appeared again, this time in two windows — those next on the right to that where it had shone before. Almost at once it increased in brilliance, as if the person who carried it from the smaller room to the larger were lighting more candles; and now the illumination was strong enough to make fine gold threads of the rain that fell within its radiance, and fling two shafts of warm yellow over the coping of the back wall. During the minute or more that I stood watching, no shadow fell on either blind.

Between me and the wall ran a ditch, into which the ground at my feet broke sharply away. Setting my back to the storm again, I followed the lip of this ditch around the wall's angle. Here it shallowed, and here, too, was shelter; but not wishing to mistake a bed of nettles or any such pitfall for solid earth, I kept pretty wide as I went on. The house was dark on this side, and the wall, as before, had no opening. Close beside the next angle there grew a mass of thick gorse bushes, and pushing through these I found myself suddenly on a sound high road, with the wind tearing at me as furiously as ever.

But here was the front; and I now perceived that the surrounding wall advanced some way before the house, so as to form a narrow courtlage. So much of it, too, as faced the road had been whitewashed, which made it an easy matter to find the gate. But as I laid hand on its latch I had a surprise.

A line of paving-stones led from the gate to a heavy porch; and along the wet surface of these there fell a streak of light from the front door, which stood ajar.

That a door should remain six inches open on such a night was astonishing enough, until I entered the court and found it as still as a room, owing to the high wall. But looking up and assuring myself that all the rest of the façade was black as ink, I wondered at the carelessness of the inmates.

It was here that my professional instinct received the first jog. Abating the sound of my feet on the paving-stones, I went up to the door and pushed it softly. It opened without noise.

I stepped into a fair-sized hall of modern build, paved with red tiles and lit by a small hanging lamp. To right and left were doors leading to the ground-floor rooms. Along the wall by my shoulder ran a line of pegs, on which hung half a dozen hats and greatcoats, every one of clerical shape; and full in front of me a broad staircase ran up, with a staring Brussels carpet, the colours and pattern of which I can recall as well as I can to-day's breakfast. Under this staircase was set a stand full of walking-sticks, and a table littered with gloves, brushes, a hand-bell, a riding-crop, one or two dog-whistles, and a bed-room candlestick with tinder-box beside it. This, with one notable exception, was all the furniture.

The exception – which turned me cold – was the form of a yellow mastiff dog, curled on a mat beneath the table. The arch of his back was towards me, and one forepaw lay over his nose in a natural posture of sleep. I leaned back on the wainscoting with my eyes tightly fixed on him, and my thoughts reverting, with something of regret, to the cruel storm I had come through.

But a man's habits are not easily denied. At the end of three minutes the dog had not moved, and I was down on the doormat unlacing my soaked boots. Slipping them off, and taking them in my left hand, I stood up, and tried a step towards the stairs, with eyes alert for any movement of the mastiff; but he never stirred. I was glad enough, however, on reaching the stairs, to find them newly built, and the carpet thick. Up I went, with a glance at every step for the table which now hid the brute's form from me, and never a creak did I wake out of that staircase till I was almost at the first landing, when my toe caught a loose stair-rod, and rattled it in a way that stopped my heart for a moment, and then set it going in double-quick time.

I stood still with a hand on the rail. My eyes were now on a level with the floor of the landing, out of which branched two passages – one turning sharply to my right, the other straight in front, so that I was gazing down the length of it. Almost at the end, a parallelogram of light fell across it from an open door.

A man who has once felt it knows there is only one kind of silence that can fitly be called 'dead'. This is only to be found in a great house at midnight. I declare that for a few seconds after I rattled the stair-rod you might have cut the silence with a knife. If the house held a clock, it ticked inaudibly.

Upon this silence, at the end of a minute, broke a light sound – the *tink-tink* of a decanter on the rim of a wine-glass. It came from the room where the light was.

Now perhaps it was that the very thought of liquor put warmth into my cold bones. It is certain that all of a sudden I straightened my back, took the remaining stairs at two strides, and walked down the passage as bold as brass, without caring a jot for the noise I made.

In the doorway I halted. The room was long, lined for the most part with books bound in what they call 'divinity calf', and littered with papers like a barrister's table on assize day. A leathern elbow-chair faced the fire-place, where a few coals burned sulkily, and beside it, on the corner of a writing-table, were set an unlit candle and a pile of manuscripts. At the opposite end of the room a curtained door led (as I guessed) to the chamber that I had first seen illuminated. All this I took in with the tail of my eye, while staring straight in front, where, in the middle of a great square of carpet, between me and the windows, stood a table with a red cloth upon it. On this cloth were a couple of wax candles lit, in silver stands, a tray, and a decanter three-parts full of liquor. And between me and the table stood a man.

He stood sideways, leaning a little back, as if to keep his shadow off the threshold, and looked at me over his left shoulder – a bald, grave man, slightly under the common height, with a long clerical coat of preposterous fit hanging loosely from his shoulders, a white cravat, black breeches, and black stockings. His feet were loosely thrust into carpet slippers. I judged his age at fifty, or thereabouts; but his face rested in the shadow, and I could only note a pair of eyes, very small and alert, twinkling above a large expanse of cheek.

He was lifting a wine-glass from the table at the moment when I appeared, and it trembled now in his right hand. I heard a spilt drop or two fall on the carpet. This was all the evidence he showed of discomposure.

Setting the glass back, he felt in his breast pocket for a handkerchief, failed to find one, and rubbed his hands together to get the liquor off his fingers.

'You startled me,' he said, in a matter-of-fact tone, turning his eyes upon me, as he lifted his glass again, and emptied it. 'How did you find your way in?'

'By the front door,' said I, wondering at his unconcern.

He nodded his head slowly.

'Ah! yes; I forgot to lock it. You came to steal, I suppose?'

'I came because I'd lost my way. I've been travelling this God-forsaken moor since dusk –'

'With your boots in your hand?' he put in quietly.

'I took them off out of respect to the yellow dog you keep.'

'He lies in a very natural attitude – eh?'

'You don't tell me he was *stuffed*?'

The old man's eyes beamed a contemptuous pity.

'You are indifferent sharp, my dear sir, for a housebreaker. Come in. Set down those convicting boots, and don't drip pools of water in the doorway. If I must entertain a burglar, I prefer him tidy.'

He walked to the fire, picked up a poker, and knocked the coals into a blaze. This done, he turned round on me with the poker still in his hand. The serenest gravity sat on his large, pale features.

'Why have I done this?' he asked.

'I suppose to get possession of the poker.'

'Quite right. May I inquire your next move?'

'Why?' said I, feeling in my tail-pocket, 'I carry a pistol.'

'Which I suppose to be damp?'

'By no means. I carry it, as you see, in an oil-cloth case.'

He stooped, and laid the poker carefully in the fender.

'That is a stronger card than I possess. I might urge that by pulling the trigger you would certainly alarm the house and the neighbourhood, and put a halter round your neck. But it strikes me as safer to assume you capable of using a pistol with effect at three paces. With what might happen subsequently I will not pretend to be concerned. The fate of your neck' – he waved a hand – 'Well, I have known you for just five minutes, and feel but a moderate interest in your neck. As for the inmates of this house, it will refresh you to hear that there are none. I have lived here two years with a butler and female cook, both of whom I dismissed yesterday at a minute's notice, for conduct which I will not shock your ears by explicitly naming. Suffice it to say, I carried them off yesterday to my parish church, two miles away, married them and dismissed them in the vestry without characters. I wish you had known that butler – but excuse me; with the information I have supplied, you ought to find no difficulty in fixing the price you will take to clear out of my house instanter.'

'Sir,' I answered, 'I have held a pistol at one or two heads in my time, but never at one stuffed with nobler indiscretion. Your chivalry does not, indeed, disarm me, but prompts me to desire more of your acquaintance. I have found a gentleman, and must sup with him before I make terms.'

This address seemed to please him. He shuffled across the room to a sideboard, and produced a plate of biscuits, another of dried figs, a glass, and two decanters.

'Sherry and Madeira,' he said. 'There is also a cold pie in the larder, if you care for it.'

'A biscuit will serve,' I replied. 'To tell the truth, I'm more for the bucket than the manger, as the grooms say: and the brandy you were tasting just now is more to my mind than wine.'

'There is no water handy.'

'I have soaked in enough to-night to last me with this bottle.'

I pulled over a chair, laid my pistol on the table, and held out the glass for him to fill. Having done so, he helped himself to a glass and a chair, and sat down facing me.

'I was speaking, just now, of my late butler,' he began, with a sip at his brandy. 'Does it strike you that, when confronted with moral delinquency, I am apt to let my indignation get the better of me?'

'Not at all,' I answered heartily, refilling my glass.

It appeared that another reply would have pleased him better.

'H'm. I was hoping that, perhaps, I had visited his offence too strongly. As a clergyman, you see, I was bound to be severe; but upon my word, sir, since Parkinson left I have felt like a man who has lost a limb.'

He drummed with his fingers on the cloth for a few moments, and went on:

'One has a natural disposition to forgive butlers – Pharaoh, for instance, felt it. There hovers around butlers an atmosphere in which common ethics lose their pertinence. But mine was a rare bird – a black swan among butlers! He was more than a butler: he was a quick and brightly gifted man. Of the accuracy of his taste, and the unusual scope of his endeavour, you will be able to form some opinion when I assure you he modelled himself upon *me*.'

I bowed, over my brandy.

'I am a scholar: yet I employed him to read aloud to me, and derived pleasure from his intonation. I talk with refinement: yet he learned to answer me in language as precise as my own. My cast-off garments fitted him not more irreproachably than did my amenities of manner. Divest him of his tray, and you would find his mode of entering a room hardly distinguishable from my own – the same urbanity, the same alertness of carriage, the same superfine deference towards the weaker sex. All – all my idiosyncrasies I saw reflected in him; and can you doubt that I was gratified? He was my *alter ego* – which, by the way, makes it harder for me to pardon his behaviour with the cook.'

'Look here,' I broke in; 'you want a new butler?'

'Oh, you really grasp that fact, do you?' he retorted.

'Why, then,' said I, 'let me cease to be your burglar and let me continue here as your butler.'

He leant back, spreading out the fingers of each hand on the table's edge.

'Believe me,' I went on, 'you might do worse. I have been in my time a demy of Magdalen College, Oxford, and retain some Greek and Latin. I'll undertake to read the Fathers with an accent that shall not offend you. My taste in wine is none the worse for having been formed in other men's cellars. Moreover, you shall engage the ugliest cook in Christendom, so long as I'm your butler. I've taken a liking to you – that's flat – and I apply for the post.'

'I give forty pounds a year,' said he.

'And I'm cheap at that price.'

He filled up his glass, looking up at me while he did so with the air of one digesting a problem. From first to last his face was grave as a judge's.

'We are too impulsive, I think,' was his answer, after a minute's silence; 'and your speech smacks of the amateur. You say, "Let me cease to be your burglar and let me be your butler." The aspiration is respectable; but a man might as well say, "Let me cease to write sermons, let me paint pictures." And truly, sir, you impress me as no expert even in your present trade.'

'On the other hand,' I argued, 'consider the moderation of my demands; that alone should convince you of my desire to turn over a new leaf. I ask for a month's trial; if at the end of that time I don't suit, you shall say so, and I'll march from your door with nothing in my pocket but my month's wages. Be hanged, sir! but when I reflect on the amount you'll have to pay to get me to face to-night's storm again, you seem to be getting off dirt cheap!' cried I, slapping my palm on the table.

'Ah, if you had only known Parkinson!' he exclaimed.

Now the third glass of clean spirit has always a deplorable effect on me. It turns me from bright to black, from levity to extreme sulkiness. I have done more wickedness over this third tumbler than in all the other states of comparative inebriety within my experience. So now I glowered at my companion and cursed.

'Look here, I don't want to hear any more of Parkinson, and I've a pretty clear notion of the game you're playing. You want to make me drunk, and you're ready to sit prattling there plying me till I drop under the table.'

'Do me the favour to remember that you came, and are staying, on your own motion. As for the brandy, I would remind you that I suggested a milder drink. Try some Madeira.'

He handed me the decanter, as he spoke, and I poured out a glass.

'Madeira!' said I, taking a gulp. 'Ugh! it's the commonest Marsala!'

I had no sooner said the words than he rose up, and stretched a hand gravely across to me.

'I hope you will shake it,' he said; 'though, as a man who after three glasses of neat spirit can distinguish between Madeira and Marsala, you have every right to refuse me. Two minutes ago you offered to become my butler, and I demurred. I now beg you to repeat that offer. Say the word, and I employ you gladly; you shall even have the second decanter (which contains genuine Madeira) to take to bed with you.'

We shook hands on our bargain, and catching up a candle-stick, he led the way from the room.

Picking up my boots, I followed him along the passage and down the silent staircase. In the hall he paused to stand on tiptoe, and turn up the lamp, which was burning low. As he did so, I found time to fling a glance at my old enemy, the mastiff. He lay as I had first seen him – a stuffed dog, if ever there was one. 'Decidedly,' thought I, 'my wits are to seek to-night'; and with the same, a sudden suspicion made me turn to my conductor, who had advanced to the left-hand door, and was waiting for me, with a hand on the knob.

'One moment!' I said: 'This is all very pretty, but how am I to know you're not sending me to bed while you fetch in all the country-side to lay me by the heels?'

'I'm afraid,' was his answer, 'you must be content with my word, as a gentleman, that never, to-night or hereafter, will I breathe a syllable about the circumstances of your visit. How-ever, if you choose, we will return upstairs.'

'No; I'll trust you,' said I; and he opened the door.

It led into a broad passage paved with slate, upon which three or four rooms opened. He paused by the second and ushered me into a sleeping-chamber, which, though narrow, was comfortable enough – a vast improvement, at any rate, on the mumpers' lodgings I had been used to for many months past.

'You can undress here,' he said. 'The sheets are aired, and if you'll wait a moment, I'll fetch a nightshirt – one of my own.'

'Sir, you heap coals of fire on me.'

'Believe me that for ninety-nine of your qualities I do not care a tinker's curse; but for your palate you are to be taken care of.'

He shuffled away, but came back in a couple of minutes with the nightshirt.

'Good night,' he called to me, flinging it in at the door; and without giving me time to return the wish, went his way upstairs.

Now it might be supposed I was only too glad to toss off my clothes and climb into the bed I had so unexpectedly acquired a right to. But, as a matter of fact, I did nothing of the kind. Instead, I drew on my boots and sat on the bed's edge, blinking at my candle till it died down in its socket, and afterwards at the purple square of window as it slowly changed to grey with the coming of dawn. I was cold to the heart, and my teeth chattered with an ague. Certainly I never suspected my host's word; but was even occupied in framing good resolutions and shaping out a reputable future, when I heard the front door gently pulled to, and a man's footsteps moving quietly to the gate.

The treachery knocked me in a heap for the moment. Then, leaping up and flinging my door wide, I stumbled through the uncertain light of the passage into the front hall.

There was a fan-shaped light over the door, and the place was very still and grey. A quick thought, or, rather, a sudden, prophetic guess at the truth, made me turn to the figure of the mastiff curled under the hall table.

I laid my hand on the scruff of his neck. He was quite limp, and my fingers sank into the flesh on either side of the vertebrae. Digging them deeper, I dragged him out into the middle of the hall and pulled the front door open to see the better.

His throat was gashed from ear to ear.

How many seconds passed after I dropped the senseless lump on the floor, and before I made another movement, it would puzzle me to say. Twice I stirred a foot as if to run out at the door. Then, changing my mind, I stepped over the mastiff, and ran up the staircase.

The passage at the top was now dark; but groping down it, I found the study door open, as before, and passed in. A sick light stole through the blinds – enough for me to distinguish the glasses and decanters on the table, and find my way to the curtain that hung before the inner room.

I pushed the curtain aside, paused for a moment, and listened to the violent beat of my heart; then felt for the door-handle and turned it.

All I could see at first was that the chamber was small; next, that the light patch in a line with the window was the white coverlet of a bed; and next that somebody, or something, lay on the bed.

I listened again. There was no sound in the room; no heart beating but my own. I reached out a hand to pull up the blind, and drew it back again. I dared not.

The daylight grew minute by minute on the dull oblong of the blind, and minute by minute that horrible thing on the bed took something of distinctness.

The strain beat me at last. I fetched a loud yell to give myself courage, and, reaching for the cord, pulled up the blind as fast as it would go.

The face on the pillow was that of an old man – a face waxen and peaceful, with quiet lines about the mouth and eyes, and long lines of grey hair falling back from the temples. The body was turned a little on one side, and one hand lay outside the bedclothes in a very natural manner. But there were two big dark stains on the pillow and coverlet.

Then I knew I was face to face with the real householder; and it flashed on me that I had been indiscreet in taking service as his butler, and that I knew the face his ex-butler wore.

And, being by this time awake to the responsibilities of the post, I quitted it three steps at a time, not once looking behind me. Outside the house the storm had died down, and white daylight was gleaming over the sodden moors. But my bones were cold, and I ran faster and faster.

A COTTAGE IN TROY

I

A HAPPY VOYAGE

THE cottage that I have inhabited these six years looks down on the one quiet creek in a harbour full of business. The vessels that enter beneath Battery Point move up past the grey walls and green quay-doors of the port to the jetties where their cargoes lie. All day long I can see them faring up and down past the mouth of my creek; and all the year round I listen to the sounds of them – the dropping or lifting of anchors, the *wh-h-ing!* of a siren-whistle cutting the air like a twanged bow, the concertina that plays at night, the rush of the clay cargo shot from the jetty into the lading ship. But all this is too far remote to vex me. Only one vessel lies beneath my terrace; and she has lain there for a dozen years. After many voyages she was purchased by the Board of Guardians in our district, dis-masted, and anchored up here to serve as a hospital-ship in case the cholera visited us. She has never had a sick man on board from that day to the present. But once upon a time three people spent a very happy night on her deck, as you shall hear. She is called *The Gleaner*.

I think I was never so much annoyed in my life as on the day when Annie, my only servant, gave me a month's 'warning'. That was four years ago; and she gave up cooking for me to marry a young watchmaker down at the town – a youth of no mark save for a curious distortion of the left eyebrow (due to much gazing through a circular glass into the bowels of watches), a frantic assortment of religious convictions, a habit of playing the fiddle in hours of ease, and an absurd name – Tubal Cain Bonaday. I noticed that Annie softened it to 'Tubey'.

Of course I tried to dissuade her: but my arguments were those of a wifeless man, and very weak. She listened to them with much patience, and went off to buy her wedding-frock. She was a plain girl, without a scintilla of humour; and had just that sense of an omelet that is vouchsafed to one woman in a generation.

So she and Tubal Cain were married at the end of the month, and disappeared on their honeymoon, no one quite knew whither. They went on the last day of April.

At halfpast eight in the evening of May 6th I had just finished my seventh miserable dinner. My windows were open to the evening, and the scent of the gorse-bushes below the terrace hung heavily underneath the veranda and stole into the room where I sat before the white cloth, in the lamp-light. I had taken a cigarette and was reaching for the matchbox when I chanced to look up, and paused to marvel at a singular beauty in the atmosphere outside.

It seemed a final atonement of sky and earth in one sheet of vivid blue. Of form I could see nothing; the heavens, the waters of the creek below, the woods on the opposite shore were simply indistinguishable – blotted out in this one colour. If you can recall certain advertisements of Mr. Reckitt, and can imagine one of these transparent, with a soft light glowing behind it, you will be as near as I can help you to guessing the exact colour. And, but for a solitary star and the red lamp of a steamer lying off the creek's mouth, this blue covered the whole firmament and face of the earth.

I lit my cigarette and stepped out upon the veranda. In a minute or so a sound made me return, fetch a cap from the hall, and descend the terrace softly.

My feet trod on bluebells and red-robins, and now and then crushed the fragrance out of a low-lying spike of gorse. I knew the flowers were there, though in this curious light I could only see them by peering closely. At the foot of the terrace I pulled up and leant over the oak fence that guarded the abrupt drop into the creek.

There was a light just underneath. It came from the deck of the hospital-ship, and showed me two figures standing there – a woman leaning against the bulwarks, and a man beside her.

The man had a fiddle under his chin, and was playing 'Annie Laurie', rather slowly and with a deal of sweetness.

When the melody ceased, I craned still farther over the oak fence and called down:

'Tubal Cain!'

The pair gave a start, and there was some whispering before the answer came up to me.

'Is that you, sir?'

'To be sure,' said I. 'What are you two about on board *The Gleaner*?'

Some more whispering followed, and then Tubal Cain spoke again –

'It doesn't matter now, sir. We've lived aboard here for a week, and to-night's the end of our honeymooning. If 'tis no liberty, sir, Annie's wishful that you should join us.'

Somehow, the invitation, coming through this mysterious atmosphere, seemed at once natural and happy. The fiddle began again as I stepped away from the fence and went down to get my boat out. In three minutes I was afloat, and a stroke or two brought me to the ship's ladder. Annie and Tubal Cain stood at the top to welcome me.

But if I had felt no incongruity in paying this respectful visit to my ex-cook and her lover, I own that her appearance made me stare. For, if you please, she was dressed out like a lady, in a gown of pale blue satin trimmed with swansdown – a low-necked gown, too, though she had flung a white shawl over her shoulders. Imagine this and the flood of blue light around us, and you will hardly wonder that, half-way up the ladder, I paused to take breath. Tubal Cain was dressed as usual, and tucking his fiddle under his arm, he led me up to shake hands with his bride as if she were a queen. I cannot say if she blushed. Certainly she received me with dignity: and then, inverting a bucket that lay on the deck, seated herself; while Tubal Cain and I sat down on the deck facing her, with our backs against the bulwarks.

'It's just this, sir,' explained the bridegroom, laying his fiddle across his lap, and speaking as if in answer to a question:

'it's just this: by trade you know me for a watchmaker, and for a Plymouth Brother by conviction. All the week I'm bending over a counter, and every Sabbath-day I speak in prayer-meeting what I hold, that life's a dull pilgrimage to a better world. If you ask me, sir, to-night, I ought to say the same. But a man may break out for once; and when so well as on his honeymoon? For a week I've been a free heathen: for a week I've been hiding here, living with the woman I love in the open air; and night after night for a week Annie here has clothed herself like a woman of fashion. Oh, my God! it has been a beautiful time – a happy beautiful time that ends to-night!'

He set down the fiddle, crooked up a knee and clasped his hands round it, looking at Annie.

'Annie, girl, what is it that we believe till to-morrow morning? You believe – eh? – that 'tis a rare world, full of delights, and with no ugliness in it?'

Annie nodded.

'And you love every soul – the painted woman in the streets no less than your own mother?'

Annie nodded again. 'I'd nurse 'em both if they were sick,' she said.

'One like the other?'

'No difference.'

'And there's nothing shames you?' Here he rose and took her hand. 'You wouldn't blush to kiss me before master here?'

'Why should I?' She gave him a sober kiss, and let her hand rest in his.

I looked at her. She was just as quiet as in the old days when she used to lay my table. It was like gazing at a play.

I should be ashamed to repeat the nonsense that Tubal Cain thereupon began to talk; for it was mere midsummer madness. But I smoked four pipes contentedly while the sound of his voice continued, and am convinced that he never performed so well at prayer-meeting. Down at the town I heard the church clock striking midnight, and then one o'clock; and was only aroused when the youth started up and grasped his fiddle.

'And now, sir, if you would consent to one thing, 'twould make us very happy. You can't play the violin, worse luck; but you might take a step or two round the deck with Annie, if I strike up a waltz tune for you to move to.'

It was ridiculous; but as he began to play I moved up to Annie, put my arm around her, and we began to glide round and round on the deck. Her face was turned away from mine, and looked over my shoulder; if our eyes had met, I am convinced I must have laughed or wept. It was half farce, half deadly earnest, and for me as near to hysterics as a sane man can go. Tubal Cain, that inspired young Plymouth Brother, was solemn as a judge. As for Annie, I would give a considerable amount, at this moment, to know what she thought of it. But she stepped very lightly and easily, and I am not sure I ever enjoyed a waltz so much. The blue light – that bewitching, intoxicating blue light – paled on us as we danced. The grey conquered it, and I felt that when we looked at each other the whole absurdity would strike us, and I should never be able to face these lovers again without a furious blush. As the day crept on, I stole a glance at Tubal Cain. He was scraping away desperately – *with his eyes shut*. For us the dance had become weariness, but we went on and on. We were afraid to halt.

Suddenly a string of the violin snapped. We stopped and I saw Tubal Cain's hand pointing eastward. A golden ripple came dancing down the creek, and, at the head of the combe beyond, the sun's edge was mounting.

'Morning!' said the bridegroom.

'It's all done,' said Annie, holding out a hand to me, without looking up. 'And thank you, sir.'

'We danced through the grey,' I answered; and that was all I could find to say, as I stepped towards the ladder.

Half an hour later as I looked out of the window before getting into bed I saw in the sunlight a boat moving down the creek towards the town. Tubal Cain was rowing, and Annie sat in the stern. She had changed her gown.

They have been just an ordinary couple ever since, and attend their chapel regularly. Sometimes Annie comes over to make me an omelet; and, as a matter of fact, she is now in the kitchen. But not a word has ever been spoken between us about her honeymoon.

2

THESE-AN'-THAT'S WIFE

IN the matter of These-an'-That himself, public opinion in Troy is divided. To the great majority he appears scandalously careless of his honour; while there are just six or seven who fight with a suspicion that there dwells something divine in the man.

To reach the town from my cottage I have to cross the Passage Ferry, either in the smaller boat which Eli pulls single-handed, or (if a market-cart or donkey, or drove of cattle be waiting on the slip) I must hang about till Eli summons his boy to help him with the horse-boat. Then the gangway is lowered, the beasts are driven on board, the passengers follow at a convenient distance, and the long sweeps take us slowly across the tide. It was on such a voyage, a few weeks after I settled in the neighbourhood, that I first met These-an'-That.

I was leaning back against the chain, with my cap tilted forward to keep off the dazzle of the June sunshine on the water, and lazily watching Eli as he pushed his sweep. Suddenly I grew aware that by frequent winks and jerks of the head he wished to direct my attention to a passenger on my right – a short, round man in black, with a basket of eggs on his arm.

There was quite a remarkable dearth of feature on this passenger's face, which was large, soft, and unhealthy in colour: but what surprised me was to see, as he blinked in the sunlight, a couple of big tears trickle down his cheeks and splash among the eggs in his basket.

'There's trouble agen, up at Kit's,' remarked Eli, finishing his stroke with a jerk, and speaking for the general benefit, though the words were particularly addressed to a drover opposite.

'Ho?' said the drover: 'that woman agen?'

The passengers, one and all, bent their eyes on the man in

black, who smeared his face with his cuff, and began weeping afresh, silently.

'Beat en blue las' night, an' turned en to doors – the dirty trollop.'

'Eli, don't 'ee –' put in the poor man, in a low, deprecating voice.

'Iss, an' no need to tell what for,' exclaimed a red-faced woman who stood by the drover, with two baskets of poultry at her feet. 'She's a low lot; a low trapesin' baggage. If These-an'-That, there, wasn' but a poor, ha'f-baked shammick, he'd ha' killed that wife o' his afore this.'

'Naybours, I'd as lief you didn't mention it,' appealed These-an'-That, huskily.

'I'm afeard you'm o' no account, These-an'-That: but sam-sodden, if I may say so,' the drover observed.

'Put in wi' the bread, an' took out wi' the cakes,' suggested Eli.

'Wife! – a pretty loitch, she an' the whole kit, up there!' went on the market-woman. 'If you durstn't lay finger 'pon your wedded wife, These-an'-That, but let her an' that long-legged gamekeeper turn 'ee to doors, you must be no better 'n a worm – that's all I say.'

I saw the man's face twitch as she spoke of the gamekeeper. But he only answered in the same dull way.

'I'd as lief you didn' mention it, friends – if 'tis all the same.'

His real name was Tom Warne, as I learnt from Eli after-wards; and he lived at St Kit's, a small fruit-growing hamlet two miles up the river, where his misery was the scandal of the place. The very children knew it, and would follow him in a crowd sometimes, pelting him with horrible taunts as he slouched along the road to the kitchen garden out of which he made his living. He never struck one; never even answered; but avoided the school-house as he would a plague; and if he saw the parson coming would turn a mile out of his road.

The parson had called at the cottage a score of times at least: for the business was quite intolerable. Two evenings out of the six, the long-legged gamekeeper, who was just a big, drunken bully, would swagger easily into These-an'-That's kitchen and sit himself down without so much as 'by your leave'. 'Good evenin', gamekeeper,' the husband would say in his dull, nerveless voice. Mostly he only got a jeer in reply. The fellow would sit drinking These-an'-That's cider and laughing with These-an'-That's wife, until the pair, very likely, took too much, and the woman without any cause broke into a passion, flew at the little man, and drove him out of doors, with broomstick or talons, while the gamekeeper hammered on the table and roared at the sport. His employer was an absentee who hated the parson: so the parson groaned in vain over the scandal.

Well, one Fair day I crossed in Eli's boat with the pair. The woman – a dark gipsy creature – was tricked out in violet and yellow, with a sham gold watch-chain and great aluminium ear-rings: and the gamekeeper had driven her down in his spring-cart. As Eli pushed off, I saw a small boat coming down the river across our course. It was These-an'-That, pulling down with vegetables for the Fair. I cannot say if the two saw him: but he glanced up for a moment at the sound of their laughter, then bent his head and rowed past us a trifle more quickly. The distance was too great to let me see his face.

I was the last to step ashore. As I waited for Eli to change my sixpence, he nodded after the couple, who by this time had reached the top of the landing-stage, arm in arm.

'A bad day's work for *her*, I reckon.'

It struck me at the moment as a moral reflexion of Eli's, and no more. Late in the afternoon, however, I was enlightened.

In the midst of the Fair, about four o'clock, a din of horns, beaten kettles and hideous yelling broke out in Troy. I met the crowd in the main street, and for a moment felt afraid of it. They had seized the woman in the tap-room of the 'Man-o'-War' – where the gamekeeper was lying in a drunken sleep – and were hauling her along in a Ramriding. There is nothing so cruel as a crowd, and I have seen nothing in my life like the face of These-an'-That's wife. It was bleeding; it was framed in tangles of black, dishevelled hair; it was livid; but, above all, it was possessed with an awful fear – a horror it turned a man white to look on. Now and then she bit and fought like a cat: but the men around held her tight, and mostly had to drag her, her feet trailing, and the horns and kettles dinning in her wake.

There lay a rusty old ducking-cage among the lumber up at the town-hall; and some fellows had fetched this down, with the poles and chain, and planted it on the edge of the Town Quay, between the American Shooting Gallery and the World-Renowned Swing Boats. To this they dragged her, and strapped her fast.

There is no need to describe what followed. Even the virtuous woman who stood and applauded would like to forget it, perhaps. At the third souse, the rusty pivot of the ducking-pole broke, and the cage, with the woman in it, plunged under water.

They dragged her ashore at the end of the pole in something less than a minute. They unstrapped and laid her gently down, and began to feel over her heart, to learn if it were still beating. And then the crowd parted, and These-an'-That came through it. His face wore no more expression than usual, but his lips were working in a queer way.

He went up to his wife, took off his hat, and producing an old red handkerchief from the crown, wiped away some froth and green weed that hung about her mouth. Then he lifted her limp hand, and patting the back of it gently, turned on the crowd. His lips were still working. It was evident he was trying to say something.

'Naybours,' the words came at last, in the old dull tone; 'I'd as lief you hadn' thought o' this.'

He paused for a moment, gulped down something in his throat, and went on –

'I wudn' say you didn' mean it for the best, an' thankin' you kindly. But you didn' know her. Roughness, if I may say, was never no good wi' her. It must ha' been very hard for her to die like this, axin your parden, for she wasn' one to bear pain.'

Another long pause.

'No, she cudn' bear pain. P'raps *he* might ha' stood it better

– though o' course you acted for the best, an' thankin' you kindly. I'd as lief take her home now, naybours, if 'tis all the same.'

He lifted the body in his arms, and carried it pretty steadily down the quay steps to his market-boat, that was moored below. Two minutes later he had pushed off and was rowing it quietly homewards.

There is no more to say, except that the woman recovered. She had fainted, I suppose, as they pulled her out. Anyhow, These-an'-That restored her to life – and she ran away the very next week with the gamekeeper.

THE AFFAIR OF
BLEAKIRK-ON-SANDS

The events, which took place on 23 November, 186–, are narrated by Reuben Cartwright, Esq., of Bleakirk Hall, Bleakirk-on-Sands, in the North Riding of Yorkshire.

A ROUGH, unfrequented bridle-road rising and dipping towards the coast, with here and there a glimpse of sea beyond the sad-coloured moors: straight overhead, a red and wintry sun just struggling to assert itself: to right and left, a stretch of barren down still coated white with hoar-frost.

I had flung the reins upon my horse's neck, and was ambling homewards. Between me and Bleakirk lay seven good miles, and we had come far enough already on the chance of the sun's breaking through; but as the morning wore on, so our prospect of hunting that day faded farther from us. It was now high noon, and I had left the hunt half an hour ago, turned my face towards the coast, and lit a cigar to beguile the way. When a man is twenty-seven he begins to miss the fun of shivering beside a frozen cover.

The road took a sudden plunge among the spurs of two converging hills. As I began to descend, the first gleam of sunshine burst from the dull heaven and played over the hoar-frost. I looked up and saw, on the slope of the hill to the right, a horseman also descending.

At first glance I took him for a brother sportsman who, too, had abandoned hope of a fox. But the second assured me of my mistake. The stranger wore a black suit of antique, clerical cut, a shovel hat, and gaiters; his nag was the sorriest of ponies, with a shaggy coat of flaring yellow, and so low in the legs that the broad flaps of its rider's coat all but trailed on the ground. A queerer turn-out I shall never see again, though I live to be a hundred.

He appeared not to notice me, but pricked leisurably down the slope, and I soon saw that, as our paths ran and at the pace we were going, we should meet at the foot of the descent: which we presently did.

'Ah, indeed!' said the stranger, reining in his pony as though now for the first time aware of me: 'I wish you a very good day, sir. We are well met.'

He pulled off his hat with a fantastic politeness. For me, my astonishment grew as I regarded him more closely. A mass of lanky, white hair drooped on either side of a face pale, pinched, and extraordinarily wrinkled; the clothes that wrapped his diminutive body were threadbare, greasy, and patched in all directions. Fifty years' wear could not have worsened them; and, indeed, from the whole aspect of the man, you might guess him a century old, were it not for the nimbleness of his gestures and his eyes, which were grey, alert, and keen as needles.

I acknowledged his salutation as he ranged up beside me.

'Will my company, sir, offend you? By your coat I suspect your trade: *venatorem sapit* – hey?'

His voice exactly fitted his eyes. Both were sharp and charged with expression; yet both carried also a hint that their owner had lived long in privacy. Somehow they lacked touch.

'I am riding homewards,' I answered.

'Hey? Where is that?'

The familiarity lay rather in the words than the manner; and I did not resent it.

'At Bleakirk.'

His eyes had wandered for a moment to the road ahead; but now he turned abruptly, and looked at me, as I thought, with some suspicion. He seemed about to speak, but restrained himself, fumbled in his waistcoat pocket, and producing a massive snuff-box, offered me a pinch. On my declining, he helped himself copiously; and then, letting the reins hang loose upon his arm, fell to tapping the box.

'To me this form of the herb *nicotiana* commends itself by its cheapness: the sense is tickled, the purse consenting – like the complaisant husband in *Juvenal*: you take me? I am well acquainted with Bleakirk-*super-sabulum*. By the way, how is Squire Cartwright of the Hall?'

'If,' said I, 'you mean my father, Angus Cartwright, he is dead these twelve years.'

'Hey?' cried the old gentleman, and added after a moment, 'Ah, to be sure, time flies – *quo dives Tullus et* – Angus, eh? And yet a hearty man, to all seeming. So you are his son?' He took another pinch. 'It is very sustaining,' he said.

'The snuff?'

'You have construed me, sir. Since I set out, just thirteen hours since, it has been my sole viaticum.' As he spoke he put his hand nervously to his forehead, and withdrew it.

'Then,' thought I, 'you must have started in the middle of the night,' for it was now little past noon. But looking at his face, I saw clearly that it was drawn and pinched with fasting. Whereupon I remembered my flask and sandwich-box, and pulling them out, assured him, with some apology for the offer, that they were at his service. His joy was childish. Again he whipped off his hat, and clapping it to his heart, swore my conduct did honour to my dead father; 'and with Angus Cartwright,' said he, 'kindness was intuitive. Being a habit, it outran reflexion; and his whisky, sir, was undeniable. Come, I have a fancy. Let us dismount, and, in heroic fashion, spread our feast upon the turf; or, if the hoar-frost deter you, see, here are boulders, and a running brook to dilute our cups; and, by my life, a foot-bridge, to the rail of which we may tether our steeds!'

Indeed, we had come to a hollow in the road, across which a tiny beck, now swollen with the rains, was chattering bravely. Falling in with my companion's humour, I dismounted, and, after his example, hitched my mare's rein over the rail. There was a raciness about the adventure that took my fancy. We chose two boulders from a heap of lesser stones close beside the beck, and divided the sandwiches; for though I protested I was not hungry, the old gentleman insisted on our sharing alike. And now, as the liquor warmed his heart and the sunshine smote upon his back, his eyes sparkled, and he launched on a flood of the gayest talk – yet always of a world that I felt was before my time. Indeed, as he rattled on, the feeling that this must be some Rip Van Winkle restored from a thirty years' sleep grew stronger and stronger upon me. He spoke of Bleakirk, and displayed a knowledge of it sufficiently thorough – intimate even – yet of the old friends for whom he inquired many names were unknown to me, many familiar only through their epitaphs in the windy cemetery above the cliff. Of the rest, the pretty girls he named were now grandmothers, the young men long since bent and rheumatic; the youngest well over fifty. This, however, seemed to depress him little. His eyes would sadden for a moment, then laugh again. 'Well, well,' he said, 'wrinkles, bald heads, and the deafness of the tomb – we have our day notwithstanding. Pluck the bloom of it – hey? A commonplace of the poets.'

'But, sir,' I put in as politely as I might, 'you have not yet told me with whom I have the pleasure of lunching.'

'Gently, young sir.' He waved his hand towards the encircling moors. 'We have feasted *more Homerico,* and in Homer, you remember, the host allowed his guest fourteen days before asking that question. Permit me to delay the answer only till I have poured libation on the turf here. Ah! I perceive the whisky is exhausted: but water shall suffice. May I trouble you – my joints are stiff – to fill your drinking-cup from the brook at your feet?'

I took the cup from his hands and stooped over the water. As I did so, he leapt on me like a cat from behind. I felt a hideous blow on the nape of the neck: a jagged flame leapt up: the sunshine turned to blood – then to darkness. With hands spread out, I stumbled blindly forward and fell at full length into the beck.

When my senses returned, I became aware, first that I was lying, bound hand and foot and securely gagged, upon the turf; secondly, that the horses were still tethered, and standing quietly at the foot-bridge; and, thirdly, that my companion had resumed his position on the boulder, and there sat watching my recovery.

Seeing my eyes open, he raised his hat and addressed me in tones of grave punctilio.

'Believe me, sir, I am earnest in my regret for this state of things. Nothing but the severest necessity could have persuaded me to knock the son of my late esteemed friend over the skull and gag his utterance with a stone – to pass over the fact that it fairly lays my sense of your hospitality under suspicion. Upon my word, sir, it places me in a cursedly equivocal position!'

He took a pinch of snuff, absorbed it slowly, and pursued.

'It was necessary, however. You will partly grasp the situation when I tell you that my name is Teague – the Reverend William Teague, Doctor of Divinity, and formerly incumbent of Bleakirk-on-Sands.'

His words explained much, though not everything. The circumstances which led to the Reverend William's departure from Bleakirk had happened some two years before my birth: but they were startling enough to supply talk in that dull fishing village for many a long day. In my nursery I had heard the tale that my companion's name recalled: and if till now I had felt humiliation, henceforth I felt absolute fear, for I knew that I had to deal with a madman.

'I perceive by your eyes, sir,' he went on, 'that with a part of my story you are already familiar: the rest I am about to tell you. It will be within your knowledge that late on a Sunday night, just twenty-nine years ago, my wife left the vicarage house, Bleakirk, and never returned; that subsequent inquiry yielded no trace of her flight, beyond the fact that she went provided with a small handbag containing a change of clothing; that, as we had lived together for twenty years in the entirest harmony, no reason could then, or afterwards, be given for her astonishing conduct. Moreover, you will be aware that its effect upon me was tragical; that my lively emotions underneath the shock deepened into a settled gloom; that my faculties (notoriously eminent) in a short time became clouded, nay, eclipsed – necessitating my removal (I will not refine) to a madhouse. Hey, is it not so?'

I nodded assent as well as I could. He paused, with a pinch between finger and thumb, to nod back to me. Though his eyes were now blazing with madness, his demeanour was formally, even affectedly, polite.

'My wife never came back: naturally, sir – for she was dead.'

He shifted a little on the boulders, slipped the snuff-box back into his waistcoat pocket, then crossing his legs and clasping his hands over one knee, bent forward and regarded me fixedly.

'I murdered her,' he said slowly, and nodded.

A pause followed that seemed to last an hour. The stone which he had strapped in my mouth with his bandanna was giving me acute pain; it obstructed, too, what little breathing my emotion left me; and I dare not take my eyes off his. The strain on my nerves grew so tense that I felt myself fainting when his voice recalled me.

'I wonder now,' he asked, as if it were a riddle – 'I wonder if you can guess why the body was never found?'

Again there was an intolerable silence before he went on.

'Lydia was a dear creature: in many respects she made me an admirable wife. Her affection for me was canine – positively. But she was fat, sir; her face a jelly, her shoulders mountainous. Moreover, her voice! it was my cruciation – monotonously, regularly, desperately voluble. If she talked of archangels, they became insignificant – and her themes, in ordinary, were of the pettiest. Her waist, sir, and my arm had once been commensurate: now not three of Homer's heroes could embrace her. Her voice could once touch my heart-strings into music; it frayed them now, between the millstones of the commonplace. Figure to yourself a man of my sensibility condemned to live on these terms!'

He paused, tightened his grasp on his knee, and pursued.

'You remember, sir, the story of the baker in Langius? He narrates that a certain woman conceived a violent desire to bite the naked shoulders of a baker who used to pass underneath her window with his wares. So imperative did this longing become, that at length the woman appealed to her husband, who (being a good-natured man, and unwilling to disoblige her) hired the baker, for a certain price, to come and be bitten. The man allowed her two bites, but denied a third, being unable to contain himself for pain. The author goes on to relate that, for want of this third bite, she bore one dead child, and two living. My own case,' continued the Reverend

William, 'was somewhat similar. Lydia's unrelieved babble reacted upon her bulk, and awoke in me an absorbing, fascinating desire to strike her. I longed to see her quiver. I fought against the feeling, stifled it, trod it down: it awoke again. It filled my thoughts, my dreams; it gnawed me like a vulture. A hundred times while she sat complacently turning her inane periods, I had to hug my fist to my breast, lest it should leap out and strike her senseless. Do I weary you? Let me proceed:

'That Sunday evening we sat, one on each side of the hearth, in the Vicarage drawing-room. She was talking – talking; and I sat tapping my foot and whispering to myself, 'You are too fat, Lydia! You are too fat!' Her talk ran on the two sermons I had preached that day, the dresses of the congregation, the expense of living, the parish ailments – inexhaustible, trivial, relentless. Suddenly she looked up and our eyes met. Her voice trailed off and dropped like a bird wounded in full flight. She stood up and took a step towards me. 'Is anything the matter, William?' she asked solicitously. 'You are too fat, my dear,' I answered, laughing, and struck her full in the face with my fist.

'She did not quiver much – not half enough – but dropped like a half-full sack on to the carpet. I caught up a candle and examined her. Her neck was dislocated. She was quite dead.'

The madman skipped up from his boulder, and looked at me with indescribable cunning.

'I am so glad, sir,' he said, 'that you did not bleed when I struck you; it was a great mercy. The sight of blood affects me – ah,' he broke off with a subtle quiver and drew a long breath. 'Do you know the sands by Woeful Ness – the Twin Brothers?' he asked.

I knew that dreary headland well. For half a mile beyond the grey Church and Vicarage of Bleakirk it extends, forming the northern arm of the small fishing-bay, and protecting it from the full set of the tides. Towards its end it breaks away sharply, and terminates in a dorsal ridge of slate-coloured rock that runs out for some two hundred feet between the sands we call the Twin Brothers. Of these, that to the south, and inside the bay, is motionless, and bears the name of the 'Dead-Boy'; but the 'Quick-Boy', to the north, shifts continually. It is a quick-sand, in short; and will swallow a man in three minutes.

'My mind,' resumed my companion, 'was soon made up. There is no murder, thought I, where there is no corpse. So I propped Lydia in the arm-chair, where she seemed as if nap-ping, and went quietly upstairs. I packed a small handbag carefully with such clothes as she would need for a journey, descended with it, opened the front door, went out to be sure the servants had blown out their lights, returned, and hoisting my wife on my shoulder, with the bag in my left hand, softly closed the door and stepped out into the night. In the shed beside the garden-gate the gardener had left his wheelbarrow. I fetched it out, set Lydia on the top of it, and wheeled her off towards Woeful Ness. There was just the rim of a waning moon to light me, but I knew every inch of the way.

'For the greater part of it I had turf underfoot; but where this ended and the rock began, I had to leave the barrow behind. It was ticklish work, climbing down; for footing had to be found, and Lydia was a monstrous weight. Pah! how fat she was and clumsy – lolling this way and that! Besides, the bag hampered me. But I reached the foot at last, and after a short rest clambered out along the ridge as fast as I could. I was sick and tired of the business.

'Well, the rest was easy. Arrived at the farthest spit of rock, I tossed the bag from me far into the northern sand. Then I turned to Lydia, whom I had set down for the moment. In the moonlight her lips were parted as though she were still chat-tering; so I kissed her once, because I had loved her, and dropped her body over into the Quick-Boy Sand. In three minutes or so I had seen the last of her.

'I trundled home the barrow, mixed myself a glass of whisky, sat beside it for half an hour, and then aroused the servants. I was cunning, sir; and no one could trace my foot-prints on the turf and rock of Woeful Ness. The missing hand-bag and the disarray I had been careful to make in the bed-room, provided them at once with a clue – but it did not lead them to the Quick-Boy. For two days they searched. At the expiration of that time it grew clear to them that grief was turning my brain. Your father, sir, was instant with his sympathy – at least ten times a day I had much ado to keep from laughing in his face. Finally two doctors visited me, and I was taken to a madhouse.

'I have remained within its walls twenty-nine years; but no – I have never been thoroughly at home there. Two days ago I discovered that the place was *boring* me. So I determined to escape; and this to a man of my resources presented few difficulties. I borrowed this pony from a stable not many yards from the madhouse wall; he belongs, I think, to a chimney-sweep, and I trust that, after serving my purpose, he may find a way back to his master.'

I suppose at this point he must have detected the question in my eyes, for he cried sharply.

'You wish to know my purpose? It is simple.' He passed a thin hand over his forehead. 'I have been shut up, as I say, for twenty-nine years, and I now discover that the madhouse bores me. If they retake me – and the hue and cry must be out long before this – I shall be dragged back. What, then, is my proposal? I ride to Bleakirk and out along the summit of Woeful Ness. There I dismount, turn my pony loose, and, descending along the ridge, step into the sand that swallowed Lydia. Simple, is it not? *Excessi, evasi, evanui.* I shall be there before sunset – which reminds me,' he added, pulling out his watch, 'that my time is nearly up. I regret to leave you in this plight, but you see how I am placed. I felt, when I saw you, a sudden desire to unbosom myself of a secret which, until the past half-hour, I have shared with no man. I see by your eyes again that if set at liberty you would interfere with my purpose. It is unfortunate that scarcely a soul ever rides this way – I know the road of old. But to-morrow is Sunday: I will scribble a line and fix it on the church-door at Bleakirk, so that the parish may at least know your predicament before twenty-four hours are out. I must now be going. The bandanna about your mouth I entreat you to accept as a memento. With renewed apologies, sir, I wish you good day; and count it extremely fortunate that you did not bleed.'

He nodded in the friendliest manner, turned on his heel, and walked quietly towards the bridge. As he untethered his pony, mounted, and ambled quietly off in the direction of the coast, I lay stupidly watching him. His black coat for some time lay, a diminishing blot, on the brown of the moors, stood for a brief moment on the sky-line, and vanished.

I must have lain above an hour in this absurd and painful position, wrestling with my bonds, and speculating on my chances of passing the night by the beck-side. My ankles were tied with my own handkerchief, my wrists with the thong of my own whip, and this especially cut me. It was knotted immovably; but by rolling over and rubbing my face into the turf, I contrived at length to slip the gag down below my chin. This done, I sat up and shouted lustily.

For a long time there was no reply but the whinnying of my mare, who seemed to guess something was wrong, and pulled at her tether until I thought she would break away. I think I called a score of times before I heard an answering 'Whoo-oop!' far back on the road, and a scarlet coat, then another, and finally a dozen or more appeared on the crest of the hill. It was the hunt returning.

They saw me at once, and galloped up, speechless from sheer amazement. I believe my hands were loosened before a word was spoken. The situation was painfully ridiculous; but my story was partly out before they had time to laugh, and the rest of it was gasped to the accompaniment of pounding hoofs and cracking whips.

Never did the Netherkirk Hunt ride after fox as it rode after the Reverend William Teague that afternoon. We streamed over the moor, a thin red wave, like a rank of charging cavalry, the whip even forgetting his tired hounds that straggled aimlessly in our wake. On the hill above Bleakirk we saw that the tide was out, and our company divided without drawing rein, some four horsemen descending to the beach, to ride along the sands out under Woeful Ness, and across the Dead-Boy, hoping to gain the ridge before the madman and cut him off. The rest, whom I led by a few yards, breasted the height above and thundered past the grey churchyard wall. Inside it I caught a flying glimpse of the yellow pony quietly cropping among the tombs. We had our prey, then, enclosed in that peninsula as in a trap; but there was one outlet.

I remember looking down towards the village as we tore along, and seeing the fisher-folk run out at their doors and stand staring at the two bodies of horsemen thus rushing to the sea. The riders on the beach had a slight lead of us at first; but this they quickly lost as their horses began to be distressed in the heavy sand. I looked back for an instant. The others were close at my heels; and, behind again, the bewildered hounds followed, yelping mournfully. But neither man nor hound could see him whom they hunted, for the cliff's edge hid the quicksand in front.

Presently the turf ceased. Dismounting, I ran to the edge and plunged down the rocky face. I had descended about twenty feet, when I came to the spot where, by craning forward, I could catch sight of the spit of rock, and the Quick-Boy sand to the right of it.

The sun – a blazing ball of red – was just now setting behind us, and its level rays fell full upon the man we were chasing. He stood on the very edge of the rocks, a black spot against the luminous yellow of sea and sand. He seemed to be meditating. His back was towards us, and he perceived neither his pursuers above nor the heads that at this moment appeared over the ridge behind him, and not fifteen yards away. The party on the beach had dismounted and was clambering up stealthily. Five seconds more and they could spring upon him.

But they under-estimated a madman's instinct. As if for no reason, he gave a quick start, turned, and at the same instant was aware of both attacking parties. A last gleam of sunlight fell on the snuff-box in his left hand; his right thumb and forefinger hung arrested, grasping the pinch. For fully half a minute nothing happened; hunters and hunted eyed each other and waited. Then carrying the snuff to his nose, and doffing his hat, with a satirical sweep of the hand and a low bow, he turned again and tripped off the ledge into the jaws of the Quick-Boy.

There was no help now. At his third step the sand had him by the ankles. For a moment he fought it, then, throwing up his arms, sank forward, slowly and as if bowing yet, upon his face. Second by second we stood and watched him disappear. Within five minutes the ripples of the Quick-Boy sand met once more above him.

In the course of the next afternoon the Vicar of Bleakirk called at the Hall with a paper which he had found pinned to the church door. It was evidently a scrap torn from an old letter, and bore, scribbled in pencil by a clerkly hand, these words: 'The young Squire Cartwright in straits by the foot-bridge, six miles towards Netherkirk. *Orate pro anima Gulielmi Teague.*'

CORPORAL SAM

I

SERGEANT DAVID WILKES, of the First (Royal) Regiment of Foot – third battalion, B Company – came trudging with a small fatigue party down the sandy slopes of Mount Olia, on the summit of which they had been toiling all day, helping the artillerymen to drag an extra 24-pounder into battery. They had brought it into position just half an hour ago, and already it had opened fire along with another 24-pounder and two howitzers mounted on the same rocky platform. The men as they descended heard the projectiles fly over their heads, and paused, distinguishing the scream of the shells from the dull hum of the round-shot, to watch the effect of the marksmanship, which was excellent.

Northwards, to their right, stretched the blue line of the Bay, where a single ship-of-war tacked lazily and kept a two-miles' offing. The smoke of the guns, drifting down on the land-breeze from the summit of Mount Olia, now hid her white sails, now lifted and revealed them in the late afternoon sunshine. But although blue held the upper heavens – cloudless blue of July – the sunshine that reached the ship was murky, almost copper-coloured; for it pierced through a cloud of denser smoke that rolled continuously along the western horizon from the burning houses of San Sebastian.

Sergeant Wilkes and his men, halting on the lower slope of the mountain where it fell away in sand dunes to the estuary of the Urumea, had the whole flank of the fortress in view. Just now, at half-tide, it rose straight out of the water on the farther bank – a low, narrow-necked isthmus that at its seaward end climbed to a cone-shaped rock four hundred feet high, crowned by a small castle. This was the citadel. The town, through which alone it could be taken by force, lay under it, across the neck of the isthmus; and this again was protected on the landward side by a high rampart or curtain, strengthened by a tall bastion in its centre and covered by a regular hornwork pushed out from its front. So much for the extremities, seaward and landward. That flank of the place which it presented to the sandhills across the Urumea was clearly more vulnerable, and yet not easily vulnerable. Deep water and natural rock protected Mount Orgullo, the citadel hill. The sea wall, for almost half its length, formed but a *fausse braye* for the hornwork towering formidably behind it. Only where it covered the town, in the space between citadel and hornwork, this wall became a simple rampart; stout indeed and solid and twenty-seven feet high, with two flanking towers for enfilading fire, besides a demi-bastion at the Mount Orgullo end; yet offering the weak spot in the defences.

The British batteries had found and were hammering at it; not the guns upon Mount Olia, which had been hauled thither to dominate those of the citadel, but a dozen 24-pounders disposed, with a line of mortars behind them, on the lower slope above the estuary, where an out-cropping ridge of rock gave firm ground among the sand-dunes. The undulating line of these dunes hid this, the true breaching battery, from view of Sergeant Wilkes and his men, though they had halted within a hundred yards of it, and for at least an hour the guns had been given a rest. Only, at long intervals one or other of the mortars threw a bomb to clear the breach – already close upon a hundred feet wide – driven between the two flanking towers. It was behind this breach that the town blazed. The smoke, carried down the estuary by the land-breeze, rolled heavily across the middle slopes of Mount Orgullo. But above it the small castle stood up clearly, silhouetted against the western light, and from time to time one of its guns answered the fire from Mount Olia. Save for this and the sound of falling timbers in the town, San Sebastian kept silence.

'Wonder what it feels like?'

Sergeant Wilkes, not catching the meaning of this, turned about slowly. The speaker was a tall young corporal, Sam Vicary by name, and by birth a Somerset lad – a curly-haired, broad-shouldered fellow with a simple engaging smile. He had come out with one of the later drafts, and nobody knew the cause of his enlisting, but it was supposed to be some poaching trouble at home. At all events, the recruiting sergeant had picked up a bargain in him; for, let alone his stature – and the Royals as a regiment prided themselves on their inches – he was easily the best marksman in B Company. Sergeant Wilkes, on whose recommendation he had been given his corporal's stripe, the day after Vittoria, looked on him as the hopefullest of his youngsters.

'Feels like?' echoed the sergeant, following the young man's gaze and observing that it rested on the great breach. 'Oh! 'tis the assault you mean? Well, it feels pretty much like any other part of the business, only your blood's up, and you don't have to keep yourself warm, waiting for the guns to tire. When we stormed the San Vincenty, now, at Badajoz –'

Someone interrupted, with a serio-comic groan.

'You've started him now, Sam Vicary! Johnnyraws of the Third Battalion, your kind attention, pray, for Daddy Wilkes and the good old days when pipeclay *was* pipeclay! Don't be afraid, for though he took the first-class fortress single-handed, you may sit upon his knee, and he'll tell you all about it.'

'It's children you are, anyway,' said the sergeant, with a tolerant smile. 'But I'll forgive ye, when the time comes, if ye'll do the Royals credit – and, what's more, I'll never cast up that 'twas but a third battalion against a third-class place. Nor will I need to,' he added, after a pause, 'if the general makes a throw for yon breach before clearing the hornwork.'

'I wasn't thinkin' of the assault,' explained the young corporal, simply, 'but of the women and children. It must be hell for them, this waitin'.'

The same voice that had mocked the sergeant put up a ribald guffaw.

'Didn't the general give warning,' it asked, 'when he summoned the garrison? "I've got Sam Vicary here along with me," he said, "and so I give you notice, for Sam's a terror when he starts to work."'

'If you fellows could quit foolin' a moment – ' began Corporal Sam, with an ingenuous blush. But here on a sudden the slope below them opened with a roar as the breaching battery – gun after gun – renewed its fire on the sea wall. Amid the din, and while the earth yet shook underfoot, the sergeant was the first to recover himself.

'Another breach!' he shouted between the explosions, putting up both hands like a pair of spectacles and peering through the smoke. 'See there – to the left; and that accounts for their quiet this last hour.' He watched the impact of the shot for a minute or so, and shook his head. 'They'd do better to clear the hornwork. At Badajoz, now –'

But here he checked himself in time, and fortunately no one had heard him. The men moved on and struck into the rutted track leading from the batteries to camp. He turned and followed them, in a brown study. Ever since Badajoz, siege operations had been Sergeant Wilkes's foible. His youngsters played upon it, drawing him into discussions over the camp fire, and winking one to another as he expounded and illustrated, using bits of stick to represent parallels, traverses, rampart and glaçis, scarp and counterscarp. But he had mastered something of the theory, after his lights, and our batteries' neglect of the hornwork struck him as unscientific.

As he pursued the path, a few dozen yards in rear of his comrades, at a turn where it doubled a sharp corner he saw their hands go up to the salute, and with this slight warning came upon two of his own officers – Major Frazer and Captain Archimbeau – perched on a knoll to the left, and attentively studying the artillery practice through their glasses. The captain (who, by the way, commanded B Company) signed to him to halt, and climbed down to him while the fatigue party trudged on. Major Frazer followed, closing his field telescope as he descended.

'What do you say to it?' asked Captain Archimbeau, with a jerk of his hand towards the great breach.

'It can be done, sir,' Sergeant Wilkes answered. 'Leastways, it ought to be done. But with submission, sir, 'twill be at wicked waste, unless they first clear the hornwork.'

'They can keep it pretty well swept while we assault. The

fact is,' said Major Frazer, a tall Scotsman, speaking in his slow Scots way, 'we assault it early to-morrow, and the general has asked me to find volunteers.'

'For the forlorn hope, sir?' The sergeant flushed a little, over the compliment paid to the Royals.

Major Frazer nodded. 'There's no need to make it common knowledge just yet. I am allowed to pick my men, but I have no wish to spend the night in choosing between volunteers. You understand?'

'Yes, sir. You will get a plenty without travelling outside the regiment.'

'Captain Archimbeau goes with us; and we thought, Wilkes, of asking you to join the party.'

'You are very good, sir.' There was hesitation, though, in the sergeant's manner, and Major Frazer perceived it.

'You understand,' he said coldly, 'that there is no obligation. I wouldn't press a man for this kind of service, even if I could.'

The sergeant flushed. 'I was thinkin' of the regiment, sir,' he answered, and turned to his captain. 'We shall have our men supportin'? – if I may make bold to ask.'

'The Royals are to show the way at the great breach, with the 9th in support. The 38th tackle the smaller breach. To make surer (as he says), the general has a mind to strengthen us up in the centre with a picked detachment of the whole division.'

Sergeant Wilkes shook his head. 'I am sorry for that, sir. 'Tisn't for me to teach the general; but I misdoubt all mixin' up of regiments. What the Royals can do they can do best by themselves.'

'Hurts your pride a bit, eh, Sergeant?' asked the major, with a short laugh. 'And yet, my friend, it was only yesterday I overheard you telling your company they weren't fit to carry the slops of the Fifth Division.'

'It does 'em good, sir. A man, if he wants to do good, must say a trifle more than he means, at times.'

'You *can* trust 'em, then?'

'And that again, sir – savin' your presence – would be sayin' more than I mean. For the lads, sir, are young lads, though willing enough; and young lads need to be nursed, however willing. As between you and me, sir' – here he appealed to Captain Archimbeau – 'B Company is the steadiest in the battalion. But if the major takes away its captain, and upon top of him its senior sergeant – well, beggin' your pardon, a compliment's a compliment, but it may be bought too dear.'

'Wilkes is right,' said the major, after a pause. 'To take the both of you would be risky; and unless I'm mistaken, Archimbeau, he thinks you will be the easier spared.'

'I haven't a doubt he does,' agreed Captain Archimbeau, laughing.

'But I do not, sir.' The sergeant seemed on the point to say more, but checked himself.

'Well?'

'It's not for me to give an opinion, sir, unless asked for it.'

'I ask for it then – your plain opinion, as a soldier.'

'An officer's an officer – that's my opinion. There's good and bad, to be sure; but an officer like the captain here, that the men can trust, is harder spared than any sergeant: let alone that you can easily spread officers too thick – even good ones, and even in a forlorn hope.'

'He wants my place,' said Captain Archimbeau; 'and he salves my feelings with a testimonial.'

'As for that, sir' – the sergeant conceded a grin – 'I reckon you won't be far behind us when the trouble begins. And if the major wants a good man from B Company, you'll agree with me, sir, that yonder he goes.' And Sergeant Wilkes jerked a thumb after the tall young corporal, a moment before the sandhills hid his retreating figure.

2

The assault had been a muddle from the start.

To begin with, after being ordered for one day (July 23rd) it had been deferred to the next; on reasonable grounds, indeed, for the town immediately behind the great breach was burning like a furnace; but it gave the troops an uneasy feeling that their leaders were distracted in counsel. Nor, divided by the river, did the artillery and the stormers work upon a mutual understanding. The heavy cannon, after a short experiment to the left of the great breach, had shifted their fire to the right of it, and had succeeded in knocking a practicable hole in it before dusk. But either this change of plan had not been reported to the trenches, or the officer directing the assault inexplicably failed to adapt his dispositions to it. The troops for the great breach were filed out ahead of the 38th, which had farther to go.

Worst of all, they were set in motion an hour before dawn, although Wellington had left orders that fair daylight should be waited for, and the artillerymen across the Urumea were still plying their guns on the sea wall, to dissuade the besieged from repairing it in the darkness. To be sure a signal for the assault – the firing of a mine against the hornwork – had been concerted, and was duly given; but in the din and the darkness it was either not heard or not understood.

Thus it happened that the forlorn hope and the supporting companies of the Royals had no sooner cleared the trenches than their ranks shook under a fire of grape, and from our own guns. There was no cure but to dash through it and take the chances, and Major Frazer, waving his sword, called on his men to follow him at the double. Ahead of them, along the foot of the sea wall, the receding tide had left a strip of strand foul with rock and rock pools and patches of seaweed, dark and slippery. Now and again a shell burst and illuminated these patches, or the still-dripping ooze twinkled under flashes of musketry from the wall above; for the defenders had hurried to the parapet and flanking towers, and their fire already crackled the whole length of the strand.

Sergeant Wilkes, running a pace or two behind the major, slipping and staggering at every second yard, was aware – though he could not see him – of young Corporal Sam close at his shoulder. The lad talked to himself as he ran: but his talk was no more than a babble of quiet unmeaning curses, and the sergeant, who understood how the lust of fighting works in different men, did not trouble to answer until, himself floundering up to his knees in a salt-water pool, he flung out a hand for support and felt it gripped.

'Damn them!' The corporal, dragging him to solid foothold, cast a look up as a shell burst high overhead, and his face showed white with passion in the glare of it. 'Can't anyone *tell* them there's no sense in it!'

'Take it easy, lad,' panted the sergeant, cheerfully. 'They're bound to understand in a minute, hearin' all this musketry. Accidents will happen – and anyway they can't help seein' us at the breach. Look at the light of it beyond the tower there!'

They floundered on together. The tower, not fifty yards away, jetted fire from every loophole; but its marksmen were aiming into the darkness, having been caught in a hurry and before they could throw down flares. As the sergeant rushed to get close under the wall of it, a bullet sent his shako whizzing; but still he ran on, and came bareheaded to the foot of the breach.

It ran down to the foreshore, a broadening scree of rubble, ruined masonry, broken beams of timber – some of them smouldering; and over the top of it shone the blaze of the town. But the actual gap appeared to be undefended, and, better still, the rubbish on the near side had so piled itself that for half the way up the stormers could climb under cover, protected from the enfilading fire. Already the major had dropped on hands and knees and was leading the way up, scrambling from heap to heap of rubbish. Close after him went an officer in the uniform of the Engineers, with Corporal Sam at his heels. The sergeant ducked his head and followed, dodging from block to block of masonry on the other side of which the bullets spattered

'Forward! Forward the Royals!'

The leaders were shouting it, and he passed on the shout. As yet, not a man had fallen on the slope of the breach. Two, more agile than he because younger by some years, overtook and passed him; but he was the sixth to reach the summit, and might reckon this very good work for a man of his weight. Then, as he turned to shout again, three more of the forlorn hope came blundering up, and the nine stood unscathed on the summit of the gap and apparently with none to oppose them.

But beyond it – between them and the town, and a sheer twenty feet below them, lay a pool of blazing tar, the flames of which roared up against their faces.

'Forward the Royals! Ladders – ladders! Oh, for your life, forward with the ladders!'

The major started the cry. Corporal Sam, taking it up, screamed it again and again. In the darkness, behind and below, the sergeant heard Captain Archimbeau calling to his men to hurry. One ladder-bearer came clattering up; but the ladders were in six-foot lengths, and a single length was useless. Nevertheless, in his rage of haste, Corporal Sam seized it from the man, and was bending to clamp it over the pit when from the parapet to the right a sudden cross-fire swept the head of the breach. A bullet struck him in the hand. He looked up, with the pain of it, in time to see Major Frazer spin about, topple past the sergeant's hand thrust out to steady him, and pitch headlong down the slope. The ladder-bearer and another tall Royal dropped at the same moment.

'Hi, Sergeant!' spoke up the young Engineer officer very sharply and clearly, at the same time stepping a couple of paces down from the ridge over which a frontal fire of bullets now flew whistling from the loopholed houses in the town. 'For God's sake, shout and hurry up your men, or our chance this night is gone!'

'I know it, sir – I know it,' groaned Wilkes.

'Then shout, man! Fifty men might do it yet, but every moment is odds against. See the swarm on the rampart there, to the right!'

They shouted together, but in vain. Four or five ladder-bearers mounted the slope, but only to be shot down almost at their feet. The Engineer officer, reaching forward to seize one of the ladder-lengths and drag it behind a pile of masonry under which he had taken cover, and thus for an instant exposing himself, dropped suddenly upon his face. And now but Sergeant Wilkes and Corporal Sam were left clinging, waiting for the help that still tarried.

What had happened was this. The supporting columns, disordered by the scramble along the foreshore, arrived at the foot of the breach in straggling twos and threes; and here, while their officers tried to form them up, the young soldiers behind, left for the moment without commanders and exasperated by the fire from the flanking tower, halted to exchange useless shots with its defenders and with the enemy on the rampart. Such fighting was worse than idle: it delayed them full in the path of the 38th, which now overtook them on its way to the lesser breach, and in five minutes the two columns were inextricably mixed, blocking the narrow space between wall and river, and exposed in all this dark confusion to a murderous fire.

At length, and though less than a third of his men followed him, Captain Archimbeau led the supporters up the breach; but by this time the enemy had packed the ramparts on either side. No soldiery could stand the hail of musketry, grape, and hand-grenades that rained upon the head of the column. It hesitated, pushed forward again, and broke some fifteen feet from the summit, like a spent wave. Then, as the Royals came pouring back, Lieutenant Campbell of the 9th, with all that could be collected of his picked detachment, forced his way up through the sheer weight of them, won clear, and made a fling for the crest. In vain! His first rush carried him abreast of the masonry under which Sergeant Wilkes and the corporal clung for cover. They rushed out to join him; but they had scarcely gained his side before the whole detachment began to give ground. It was not that the men fell back; rather, the apex of the column withered down as man after man dropped beside its leader. He himself had taken a wound. Yet he waved his sword and carried them forward on a second charge, only to reach where he had reached before, and be laid there by a second bullet.

Meanwhile the Royals, driven to the foot of the slope, were flung as a fresh obstacle in the path of the 38th still striving to press on for the lesser breach. From his perch half-way up the ruins, Sergeant Wilkes descried Captain Archimbeau endeavouring to rally them, and climbed down to help him. The corporal followed, nursing his wounded hand. As they reached him a bugle sounded the recall.

The assault had failed. At the foot of the breach a soldier of the 4th Regiment, mad with rage, foamed out a curse upon the Royals. Corporal Sam lifted his bleeding fist and struck him across the mouth. The sergeant dragged the two apart, slipped an arm under his comrade's, and led him away as one leads a child. A moment later the surge of the retreating crowd had almost carried them off their feet. But the sergeant kept a tight hold, and steered his friend back every yard of the way along the bullet-swept foreshore. They were less than half-way across when the dawn broke; and looking in his face he saw that the lad was crying silently – the powder-grime on his cheeks streaked and channelled with tears.

3

'I don't understand ye, lad,' said Sergeant Wilkes.

'Fast enough you'd understand, if you'd but look me in the face,' answered Corporal Sam, digging his heel into the sand.

The two men lay supine on a cushion of coarse grass; the sergeant smoking and staring up at the sky, the corporal with his sound hand clasping his wounded one behind his head, his gaze fixed gloomily between his knees and across the dunes, on the still unrepaired breach in San Sebastian.

A whole fortnight had dragged by since the assault; a fortnight of idleness for the troops, embittered almost intolerably by a sense that the Fifth Division had disgraced itself. One regiment blamed another, and all conspired to curse the artillery – whose practice, by the way, had been brilliant throughout the siege. Nor did the gunners fail to retort; but they were in luckier case, being kept busy all the while, first in shifting their batteries and removing their worst guns to the ships, next in hauling and placing the new train that had arrived piece-meal from England; and not only busy, but alert, on the watch against sorties. Also, and although the error of cannonading the columns of assault had never been cleared up, the brunt of Wellington's displeasure had fallen on the stormers. The Marquis ever laid stress on his infantry, whether to use them or blame them; and when he found occasion to blame, he had words – and methods – that scarified equally the general of division and the private soldier.

'Fast enough you understand,' repeated Corporal Sam, savagely.

'I do, then, and I don't,' admitted Sergeant Wilkes, after a pause. The lad puzzled him; gave him few confidences, asked for none at all, and certainly was no cheerful companion; and yet during these days of humiliation the two had become friends, almost inseparable. 'I've read it,' the sergeant pursued, 'in Scripture or somewhere, that a man what keeps a hold on himself does better than if he took a city. I don't say as I understand that altogether; but it *sounds* right.'

'Plucky lot of cities we take, in the Royals,' growled Corporal Sam. He nodded, as well as his posture allowed, towards San Sebastian. 'And you call that a third-class fortress!'

'Accidents will happen.' Sergeant Wilkes, puffing at his pipe, fell back philosophically on his old catchword. 'It takes you hard, because you're young; and it takes you harder because you had fed yourself up on dreams o' glory, and such like.'

'Well?'

'Well, and you have to get over it, that's all. A man can't properly call himself a soldier till he's learnt to get over it.'

'If that's all, the battalion is qualifyin' fast!' Corporal Sam retorted bitterly, and sat up, blinking in the strong sunlight. Then, as Sergeant Wilkes made no reply, or perhaps because he guessed something in Sergeant Wilkes's averted face, a sudden compunction seized him. 'You feel it too?'

'I got to, after all my trouble,' answered Sergeant Wilkes, brusquely.

'I'm sorry. Look here – I wish you'd turn your face about – it's worse for you and yet you get over it, as you say. How the devil do you manage?'

Still for a while Sergeant Wilkes leaned back without making reply. But of a sudden, he, too, sat upright, pulled down the peak of his shako to shade his eyes, and drawing his pipe from his mouth, jerked the stem of it to indicate a figure slowly crossing a rise of the sandhills between them and the estuary.

'You see that man?'

'To be sure I do. An officer, and in the R.A. – curse them! – though I can't call to mind the cut of his jib.'

'You wouldn't. His name's Ramsay, and he's just out of arrest.'

'What has he done?'

'A many things, first and last. At Fuentes d'Onoro the whole French cavalry cut him off – him and his battery – and he charged back clean through them; ay, lad, through 'em like a swathe, with his horses belly-down and the guns behind 'em bounding like skipjacks; not a gun taken, and scarce a gunner hurt. That's the sort of man.'

'Why has he been under arrest?'

'Because the Marquis gave him an order and forgot it. And because coming up later, expecting to find him where he wasn't and had no right to be, the Marquis lost his temper. And likewise because, when a great man loses his temper, right or wrong don't matter much. So there goes Captain Ramsay broken; a gentleman and a born fighter; and a captain he'll die. That's how the mills grind in this here all-conquering army. And the likes of us sit here and complain.'

'If a man did that wrong to me –' Corporal Sam jumped to his feet and stared after the slight figure moving alone across the sandhills.

Had his curiosity led him but a few paces farther, he had seen a strange sight indeed.

Captain Norman Ramsay, wandering alone and with a burning heart, halted suddenly on the edge of a sandpit. Below him four men stood, gathered in a knot – two of them artillery officers, the others officers of the line. His first impulse was to turn and escape, for he shunned all companionship just now. But a second glance told him what was happening; and, prompt on the understanding, he plunged straight down the sandy bank, walked up to a young artillery officer and took the pistol out of his hand. That was all, and it all happened in less than three minutes. The would-be-duellist – and challenges had been common since the late assault – knew the man and his story. For that matter, everyone in the army knew his story.

As a ghost he awed them. For a moment he stood looking from one to the other, and so, drawing the charge, tossed the pistol back at its owner's feet and resumed his way.

Corporal Sam, who had merely seen the slight figure pass beyond the edge of the dunes, went back and flung himself again on the warm bank.

'If a man did that wrong to me –' he repeated.

4

Certainly, just or unjust, the Marquis could make himself infernally unpleasant. Having ridden over from headquarters and settled the plans for the new assault, he returned to his main army and there demanded fifty volunteers from each of the fifteen regiments composing the First, Fourth, and Light Divisions – men (as he put it) *who could show other troops how to mount a breach*. It may be guessed with what stomach the Fifth Division digested this; and among them not a man was angrier than their old general, Leith, who now, after a luckless absence, resumed command. The Fifth Division, he swore, could hold their own with any soldiers in the Peninsula. He was furious with the seven hundred and fifty volunteers, and, evading the Marquis's order, which was implicit rather than direct, he added an oath that these interlopers should never lead his men to the breaches.

Rage begets rage. During the misty morning hours of August 31st, the day fixed for the assault, these volunteers, held back and chafing with the reserves, could scarcely be restrained from breaking out of the trenches. 'Why,' they demanded, 'had they been fetched here if not to show the way?' – a question for which their officers were in no mood to provide a soft answer.

Yet their turn came. Sergeant Wilkes, that amateur in siege operations, had rightly prophesied from the first that the waste of life at the breaches would be wicked and useless until the hornwork had been silenced and some lodgement made there. So, as the morning wore on, and the sea mists gave place to burning sunshine, and this again to heavy thunder clouds collected by the unceasing cannonade, still more and more of the reserves of the Fifth Division were pushed up, until none but the volunteers and a handful of the 9th Regiment remained in the trenches. Them, too, at length Leith was forced to unleash, and they swept forward on the breaches yelling like a pack of hounds; but on the crest-line they fared at first no better than the regiments they had taunted. Thrice and four times they reached it only to topple back. The general, watching the fight from the batteries across the Urumea, now directed the gunners to fire over the stormers' heads; and again a cry went up that our men were being slaughtered by their own artillery. Undismayed by this, with no recollections of the first assault to daunt them, a company of the Light Division took advantage of the fire to force their way over the rampart on the right of the great breach and seize a lodgement in some ruined houses actually within the town. There for an hour or so these brave men were cut off, for the assault in general made no headway.

It must have failed, even after five hours' fighting, but for an accident. A line of powder-barrels collected behind the traverses by the great breach took fire and blew up, driving back all the French grenadiers but the nearest, whom it scattered in mangled heaps. As explosion followed explosion, the bright flame spread and ran along the high curtain. The British leapt after it, breaking through the traverse and swarming up to the curtain's summit. Almost at the same moment the Thirteenth and Twenty-fourth Portuguese, who had crossed the river by a lower ford, hurled themselves over the lesser breach to the right; and as the swollen heavens burst in a storm of rain and thunder, from this point and that the besiegers, as over the lip of a dam, swept down into the streets.

'Treat men like dogs, and they'll behave like dogs,' grumbled Sergeant Wilkes, as he followed to prevent what mischief he might. But this, he well knew, would be little enough.

5

Corporal Sam Vicary, coming up to the edge of the campfire's light, stood there for a moment with a white face. The cause of it – though it would have been a sufficient one – was not the story to which the men around the fire had been listening; for the teller, at sight of the corporal, had broken off abruptly, knowing him to be a religious fellow after a fashion, with a capacity for disapproval and a pair of fists to back it up. So, while his comrades guffawed, he rather cleverly changed the subject.

'Oh, and by the way, talkin' of the convent' – he meant the Convent of Santa Teresa, a high building under the very slope of the citadel, protected by its guns and still held by the enemy, after three days' fighting –'do any of you know a small house to the left of it, with only a strip of garden between? Sort of a mud-nest, it is, like a swallow's, stuck under overhang o' the cliff. No? Well, that's a pity, for I hear tell the general has promised five pounds to the first man who breaks into that house.'

'But why, at all?' inquired a man close on his right.

'I know the place,' put in another; 'a mean kind of building, with one window lookin' down the street, and that on the second floor, as you might say. It don't look to me the sort of house to hold five pounds' worth, all told – let be that, to force it, a man must cross half the fire from the convent, and in full view. Five pounds be *damned*! Five pounds isn't so scarce in these times that a man need go there to fetch it for his widow.'

The corporal was turning away. For three days San Sebastian had been a hell, between the flames of which he had seen things that sickened his soul. They sickened it yet, only in remembrance. Yes, and the sickness had more than once come nigh to be physical. His throat worked at the talk of loot, now that he knew what men did for it.

'The general ain't after the furnitcher,' answered the first speaker. 'It consarns a child.'

'A child ain't no such rarity in San Sebastian that anybody need offer five pounds for one.'

'What's this talk about a child?' asked Sergeant Wilkes, coming in from his rounds, and dropping to a seat by the blaze. He caught sight of Corporal Sam standing a little way back, and nodded.

'Well, it seems that, barring this child, every soul in the house has been killed. The place is pretty certain death to approach, and the crittur, for all that's known, has been left without food for two days and more. 'Tis a boy, I'm told – a small thing, not above four at the most. Between whiles it runs to the window and looks out. The sentries have seen it more'n a dozen times; and one told me he'd a sight sooner look on a ghost.'

'Then why don't the Frenchies help?' someone demanded. 'There's a plenty of 'em close by, in the convent.'

'The convent don't count. There's a garden between it and the house, and on the convent side a blank wall – no windows at all, only loopholes. Besides which, there's a whole block of buildings in full blaze t'other side of the house, and the smoke of it drives across so that 'tis only between whiles you can see the child at all. The odds are, he'll be burnt alive or smothered before he starves outright; and, I reckon, put one against the other, 'twill be the mercifuller end.'

'Poor little beggar,' said the sergeant. 'But why don't the general send in a white flag, and take him off?'

'A lot the governor would believe – and after what you and me have seen these two days! A nice tenderhearted crew to tell him, "If you please, we've come for a poor little three-year-old." Why he'd as lief as not believe we meant to eat him.'

Sergeant Wilkes glanced up across the camp-fire to the spot where Corporal Sam had been standing. But Corporal Sam had disappeared.

6

Although the hour was close upon midnight, and no moon showed, Corporal Sam needed no lantern to light him through San Sebastian; for a great part of the upper town still burned fiercely, and from time to time a shell, soaring aloft from the mortar batteries across the river, burst over the citadel or against the rocks where the French yet clung, and each explosion flung a glare across the heavens.

He had passed into the town unchallenged. The fatigue

parties, hunting by twos and threes among the ruins of the river-front for corpses to burn or bury, doubtless supposed him to be about the same business. At any rate, they paid him no attention.

Just within the walls, where the conflagration had burnt itself out, there were patches of black shadow to be crossed carefully. The fighting had been obstinate here, and more than one blazing house had collapsed into the thick of it. The corporal picked his way gingerly, shivering a little at the thought of some things buried, or half-buried, among the loose stones. Indeed, at the head of the first street his foot entangled itself in something soft. It turned out to be nothing more than a man's cloak, or *poncho*, and he slipped it on, to hide his uniform and avoid explanations should he fall in with one of the patrols; but the feel of it gave him a scare for a moment.

The lad, in fact, was sick of fighting and slaughter – physically ill at the remembrance and thought of them. The rage of the assault had burnt its way through him like a fever and left him weak, giddy, queasy of stomach. He had always hated the sight of suffering, even the suffering of dumb animals: and as a sportsman, home in England, he had learnt to kill his game clean, were it beast or bird. In thought, he had always loathed the trade of a butcher, and had certainly never guessed that soldiering could be – as here in San Sebastian he had seen it – more bestial than the shambles.

For some reason, as he picked his road, his mind wandered away from the reek and stink of San Sebastian and back to England, back to Somerset, to the slopes of Mendip. His home there had overlooked an ancient battlefield, and as a boy, tending the sheep on the uplands, he had conned it often and curiously, having heard the old men tell tales of it. The battle had been fought on a wide plain intersected by many water-dykes. Twice or thrice he had taken a holiday to explore it, half expecting that a close view would tell him something of its history; but, having no books to help him, he had brought back very little beyond a sense of awe that so tremendous a thing had happened just there, and (unconsciously) a stored remembrance of the scents blown across the level from the flowers that lined the dykes – scents of mint and meadow-sweet at home there, as the hawthorn was at home on the hills above.

He smelt them now, across the reek of San Sebastian, and they wafted him back to England – to boyhood, dreaming of war but innocent of its crimes – to long thoughts, long summer days spent among the unheeding sheep, his dog Rover beside him – an almost thoroughbred collie, and a good dog, too, though his end had been tragic ... But why on earth should his thoughts be running on Rover just now?

Yet, and although, as he went, England was nearer to him and more real than the smoking heaps between which he picked his way, he steered all the while towards the upper town, through the square, and up the hill overlooked by the convent and the rocky base of the citadel. He knew the exact position of the house, and he chose a narrow street – uninhabited now, and devastated by fire – that led directly to it.

The house was untouched by fire as yet, though another to the left of it blazed furiously. It clung, as if it were a swallow's nest, to the face of the cliff. A garden wall ran under the front; and, parallel with the wall, a road pretty constantly swept by musketry fire from the convent. At the head of the street Corporal Sam stumbled against a rifleman who, sheltered from bullets at the angle of the crossing, stood calmly watching the conflagration.

'Hallo!' said the rifleman, cheerfully; 'I wanted some more audience, and you're just in time.'

'There's a child in the house, eh?' panted Corporal Sam, who had come up the street at a run.

The rifleman nodded. 'Poor little devil! He'll soon be out of his pain, though.'

'Why, there's heaps of time! The fire won't take hold for another half-hour. What's the best way in? ... You an' me can go shares, if that's what you're hangin' back for,' added Corporal Sam, seeing that the man eyed him without stirring.

'Hi! Bill!' the rifleman whistled to a comrade, who came slouching out of a doorway close by, with a clock in one hand, and in the other a lantern by the help of which he had been

examining the inside of this piece of plunder. 'Here's a boiled
lobster in an old woman's cloak, wants to teach us the way
into the house yonder.'

'Tell him to go home,' said Bill, still peering into the works
of the clock. 'Tell him we've *been* there' He chuckled a moment, looked up, and addressed himself to Corporal Sam.
'What regiment?'

'The Royals.'

The two burst out laughing, scornfully. 'Don't wonder you
cover it up,' said the first rifleman.

Corporal Sam pulled off his *poncho*. 'I'd offer to fight the
both of you,' he said: 'but 'tis time wasted with a couple of
white-livers that don't dare fetch a poor child across a roadway. Let me go by; *you*'ll keep, anyway.'

'Now look here, sonny –' The first rifleman blocked his
road. 'I don't bear no malice for a word spoken in anger: so
stand quiet and take my advice. That house isn't goin' to take
fire. 'Cos why? 'Cos, as Bill says, we've *been* there – there and
in the next house, now burnin' – and we know. 'Cos before
leavin' –' the night before last it was – some of our boys set
two barrels o' powder somewheres in the next house, on the
ground floor, *with* a slow match. That's why *we* left; though, as
it happened, the match missed fire. But the powder's there, and if
you'll wait a few minutes now you'll not be disapp'inted.'

'You left the child behind!'

'Well, we left in a hurry, as I tell you, and somehow in the
hurry nobody brought him along. I'm sorry for the poor little
devil, too.' The fellow swung about. 'See him there at the
window, now! If you want him put out of his pain –'

He lifted his rifle. Corporal Sam made a clutch at his arm to
drag it down, and in the scuffle both men swayed out upon the
roadway. And with that, or a moment later, he felt the rifleman
slip down between his arms, and saw the blood gush from his
mouth as he collapsed on the cobbles.

Corporal Sam heard the man Bill shout a furious oath, cast
one puzzled look up the roadway towards the convent, saw
the flashes jetting from its high wall, and raced across unscathed. A bullet sang past his ear as he found the gate and

hurled himself into the garden. It was almost dark here, but dark only for a moment . . . For as he caught sight of a flight of steps leading to a narrow doorway, and ran for them – and even as he set foot on the lowest – of a sudden the earth heaved under him, seemed to catch him up in a sheet of flame, and flung him backwards – backwards and flat on his back, into a clump of laurels.

Slowly he picked himself up. The sky was dark now; but, marvellous to say, the house stood. The mass of it yet loomed over the laurels. Yes, and a light showed under the door at the head of the steps. He groped his way up and pushed the door open.

The light came through a rent in the opposite wall; and on the edge of this jagged hole some thin laths were just bursting into a blaze. He rushed across the room to beat out the flame, and this was easily done; but, as he did it, he caught sight of a woman's body, stretched along the floor by the fire-place and of a child cowering in the corner, watching him.

'Come and help, little one!' said Corporal Sam, still beating at the laths.

The child understood no English, and moreover was too small to help. But it seemed that the corporal's voice emboldened him, for he drew near and stood watching.

'Who did *this*, little one?' asked Corporal Sam, nodding towards the corpse, as he rubbed the charred dust from his hands.

For a while the child stared at him, not comprehending, but by and by pointed beneath the table and then back at its mother.

The corporal walked to the table, stooped, and drew from under it a rifle and a pouch half filled with cartridges.

'Tell him we've *been* there.' He seemed to hear the rifleman Bill's voice repeating the words close at hand. He recognized the badge on the pouch.

He was shaking where he stood; and this, perhaps, was why the child stared at him so oddly. But, looking into the wondering young eyes, he read only the question, 'What are you going to do?'

He hated these riflemen. Nay, looking around the room, how he hated all the foul forces that had made this room what it was! ... And yet, on the edge of resolve, he knew that he must die for what he meant to do ... that the thing was unpardonable, that in the end he must be shot down, and rightly, as a dog.

He remembered his dog Rover, how the poor brute had been tempted to sheep-killing, at night, on the sly; and the look in his eyes when, detected at length, he had crawled forward to his master to be shot. No other sentence was possible, and Rover had known it.

Had he no better excuse? Perhaps not ... He only knew that he could not help it; that this thing had been done, and by the consent of many ... and that as a man he must kill for it, though as a soldier he deserved only to be killed.

With the child's eyes still resting on him in wonder, he set the rifle on its butt and rammed down a cartridge, and so, dropping on hands and knees, crept to the window.

7

Early next morning Sergeant Wilkes picked his way across the ruins of the great breach and into the town, keeping well to windward of the fatigue parties already kindling fires and collecting the dead bodies that remained unburied.

Within and along the sea wall San Sebastian was a heap of burnt-out ruins. Amid the stones and rubble encumbering the streets, lay broken muskets, wrenched doors, shattered sticks of furniture – mirrors, hangings, women's apparel, children's clothes – loot dropped by the pillagers as valueless, wreckage of the flood. He passed a very few inhabitants, and these said nothing to him; indeed, did not appear to see him, but sat by the ruins of their houses with faces set in a stupid horror. Even the crash of a falling house near by would scarcely persuade them to stir, and hundreds during the last three days had been overwhelmed thus and buried.

The sergeant had grown callous to these sights. He walked on, heeding scarcely more than he was heeded, came to the great square, and climbed a street leading northwards, a little to the left of the great convent. The street was a narrow one, for half its length lined on both sides with fire-gutted houses; but the upper half, though deserted, appeared to be almost intact. At the very head, and close under the citadel walls, it took a sharp twist to the right, and another twist, almost equally sharp, to the left before it ended in a broader thoroughfare, crossing it at right angles and running parallel with the ramparts.

At the second twist the sergeant came to a halt; for at his feet, stretched across the causeway, lay a dead body.

He drew back with a start, and looked about him. Corporal Sam had been missing since nine o'clock last night, and he felt sure that Corporal Sam must be here or hereabouts. But no living soul was in sight.

The body at his feet was that of a rifleman; one of the volunteers whose presence had been so unwelcome to General Leith and the whole Fifth Division. The dead fist clutched its rifle; and the sergeant stooping to disengage this, felt that the body was warm.

'Come back, you silly fool!'

He turned quickly. Another rifleman had thrust his head out of a doorway close by. The sergeant, snatching up the weapon, sprang and joined him in the passage where he sheltered.

'I – I was looking for a friend, hereabouts.'

'Fat lot of friend you'll find at the head of *this* street!' snarled the rifleman, and jerked his thumb towards the corpse. 'That makes the third already this morning. These Johnnies ain't no sense of honour left – firing on outposts as you may call it.'

'Where are they firing from?'

'No "they" about it. You saw that cottage – or didn't you? – right above there, under the wall; the place with one window in it? There's a devil behind it somewheres; he fires from the back of the room, and what's more, he never misses his man. You have Nick's own luck – the pretty target you made, too; that is unless, like some that call themselves Englishmen and ought to know better, he's a special spite on the Rifles.'

The sergeant paid no heed to the sneer. He was beginning to think.

'How long has this been going on?' he asked.

'Only since daylight. There was a child, up yonder, last night; but it stands to reason a child can't be doing this. He never misses, I tell you. Oh, you had luck, just now!'

'I wonder,' said Sergeant Wilkes, musing. 'I'll try it again, anyway.' And while the rifleman gasped he stepped out boldly into the road.

He knew that his guess might, likely enough, be wrong: that, even were it right, the next two seconds might see him a dead man. Yet he was bound to satisfy himself. With his eyes on the sinister window – it stood half open and faced straight down the narrow street – he knelt by the corpse, found its ammunition pouch, unbuckled the strap and drew out a handful of cartridges. Then he straightened himself steadily – but his heart was beating hard – and as steadily walked back and rejoined the rifleman in the passage.

'You have a nerve,' said the rifleman, his voice shaking a little. 'Looks like he don't fire on redcoats; but you have a nerve all the same.'

'Or else he may be gone,' suggested the sergeant, and on the instant corrected himself; 'but I warn you not to reckon upon that. Is there a window facing on him anywhere, round the bend of the street?'

'I dunno.'

The rifleman peered forth, turning his head sideways for a cautious reconnoitre. 'Maybe he *has* gone, after all – '

It was but his head he exposed beyond the angle of the doorway; and yet, on the instant, a report cracked out sharply, and he pitched forward into the causeway. His own rifle clattered on the stones beside him, and where he fell he lay, like a stone.

Sergeant Wilkes turned with a set jaw and mounted the stairs of the deserted house behind him. They led him up to the roof, and there he dropped on his belly and crawled. Across three roofs he crawled, and lay down behind a balustrade overlooking the transverse roadway. Between the pillars of the balustrade he looked right across the roadway and into the half-open window of the cottage. The room within was dark, save for the glimmer of a mirror on the back wall.

'Kill him I must,' growled the sergeant through his teeth, 'though I wait the day for it.'

And he waited there, crouching, for an hour – for two hours.

He was shifting his cramped attitude a little – a very little – for about the twentieth time, when a smur of colour showed on the mirror, and the next instant passed into a dark shadow. It may be that the marksman within the cottage had spied yet another rifleman in the street. But the sergeant had noted the reflection in the glass, that it was red. Two shots rang out together. But the sergeant, after peering through the parapet, stood upright, walked back across the roofs, and regained the stairway.

The street was empty. From one of the doorways a voice called to him to come back. But he walked on, up the street and across the roadway to a green-painted wicket. It opened upon a garden, and across the garden he came to a flight of steps with an open door above. Through this, too, he passed and stared into a small room. On the far side of it, in an arm-chair, sat Corporal Sam, leaning back, with a hand to his breast; and facing him, with a face full of innocent wonder, stood a child – a small, grave, curly-headed child.

8

'I'm glad you done it quick,' said Corporal Sam.

His voice was weak, yet he managed to get out the words firmly, leaning back in the wooden armchair, with one hand on his left breast, spread and covering the lower ribs.

The sergeant did not answer at once. Between the spread fingers he saw a thin stream welling, darker than the scarlet tunic which it discoloured. For perhaps three seconds he watched it. To him the time seemed as many minutes, and all the while he was aware of the rifle-barrel warm in his grasp.

'Because,' Corporal Sam pursued with a smile that wavered a little, halfwistfully seeking his eyes, 'you'd'a had to do it, anyway

– wouldn't you? And any other way it – might – 'a been hard.'

'Lad, what *made* you?'

It was all Sergeant Wilkes could say, and he said it, wondering at the sound of his own voice. The child, who, seeing that the two were friends and not, after all, disposed to murder one another, had wandered to the head of the stairs to look down into the sunlit garden shining below, seemed to guess that something was amiss, and, wandering back, stood at a little distance, finger to lip.

'I don't know,' the corporal answered, like a man with difficulty trying to collect his thoughts. 'Leastways, not to explain to you. It must 'a been comin' on for some time.'

'But *what*, lad – *what*?'

'Ah – "what?" says you. That's the trouble, and I can't never make you *see* – yes, make you *see* – the hell of it. It began with thinkin' – just with thinkin' – *that first night you led me home from the breach*. And the things I saw and heard; and then, when I came here, only meanin' to save *him* –'

He broke off and nodded at the child, who catching his eye, nodded back smiling.

He and the corporal had evidently made great friends.

But the corporal's gaze, wavering past him, had fixed itself on a trestle bed in the corner.

'There was a woman,' he said. 'She was stone cold; but the child told me – until I stopped his mouth and made a guess at the rest. I took her down and buried her in the garden. And with that it came over me that the whole of it – the whole business – was wrong and that to put myself right I must kill, and keep on killing. Of course I knew what the end would be. But I never looked for such luck as *your* coming ... I was ashamed, first along, catching sight 'o' you ... no, not ashamed, only I didn't want you to see. But when you took cover an' waited – though I wouldn't a' hurt you for worlds – why then I knew how the end would be.'

'Lad,' said the sergeant, watching him as he panted, 'I don't understand you, except that you're desperate wrong. But I saw you – saw you by the lookin' glass, behind there; and 'tis right you should know.'

'O' course you saw me . . . I'm not blamin', am I? You had to do it, and I had to take it. That was the easiest way. I couldn' do no other, an' you couldn' do no other, that bein' your duty. An' the child, there – '

Sergeant Wilkes turned for a moment to the child, who met his gaze, round-eyed; then to his friend again.

But the corporal's head had dropped forward on his chest.

The sergeant touched his shoulder, to make sure; then, with one look behind him, but ignoring the child, reeled out of the room and down the stairs, as in a dream. In the sunny garden the fresh air revived him and he paused to stare at a rose-bush, rampant, covered with white blossoms against which the bees were humming. Their hum ran in his head so that he failed to notice that the sound of musketry had died down. An hour before it had been death to walk, as he did, under the convent wall and out into the street leading to the lesser breach. The convent had, in fact, surrendered, and its defenders were even now withdrawing up the hill to the citadel. He found the lesser breach and climbed down it to the shore of the Urumea, beside the deserted ford across which the Portuguese had waded on the morning of the second assault. Beyond it shone the sand-hills, hiding our batteries.

He sat down on the bank and pulled off boots and socks, preparing to wade; but turned at a slight sound.

The child had followed him and stood half-way down the ruins of the breach, wistful, uncertain.

In a rage, as one threatens off an importunate dog, Sergeant Wilkes waved an arm. The child turned and slunk away, back into San Sebastian.

THE MONT-BAZILLAC

I HAVE a sincere respect and liking for the Vicar of Gantick – 'th' old Parson Kendall', as we call him – but have somewhat avoided his hospitality since Mrs Kendall took up with the teetotal craze. I say nothing against a lady's renouncing, an she choose, the light dinner claret, the cider, the port (pale with long maturing in the wood) which her table afforded of yore: nor do I believe that the Vicar, excellent man, repines deeply – though I once caught the faint sound of a sigh as we stood together and conned his cider-apple trees, ungarnered, shedding their fruit at random in the long grasses. For his glebe contains a lordly orchard, and it used to be a treat to watch him, his greenish third-best coat stuck all over with apple-pips and shreds of pomace, as he helped to work the press at the great annual cider-making. But I agree with their son, Master Dick, that 'it's rough on the guests'.

Master Dick is now in his second year at Oxford; and it was probably for his sake, to remove temptation from the growing lad, that Mrs Kendall first discovered the wickedness of all alcoholic drink. Were he not an ordinary, good-natured boy – had he, as they say, an ounce of vice in him – I doubt the good lady's method might go some way towards defeating her purpose. As things are, it will probably take no worse revenge upon her solicitude than by weaning him insensibly away from home, to use his vacation times in learning to be a man.

Last Long Vacation, in company with a friend he calls Jinks, Master Dick took a Canadian canoe out to Bordeaux by steamer, and spent six adventurous weeks in descending the Dordogne and exploring the Garonne with its tributaries. On his return he walked over, to find me smoking in my garden after dinner, and gave me a gleeful account of his itinerary.

' . . . and the next place we came to was Bergerac,' said he, after ten minutes of it.

'Ah!' I murmured. 'Bergerac!'

'You know it?'

'Passably well,' said I. 'It lies toward the edge of the claret country; but it grows astonishing claret. When I was about your age it grew a wine yet more astonishing.'

'Hallo!' Master Dick paused in the act of lighting his pipe and dropped the match hurriedly as the flame scorched his fingers.

'It was grown on a hill just outside the town – the Mont-Bazillac. I once drank a bottle of it.'

'Lord! You too? . . . *Do* tell me what happened!'

'Never,' I responded firmly. 'The Mont-Bazillac is extinct, swept out of existence by the phylloxera when you were a babe in arms. *Infandum jubes renovare* – no one any longer can tell you what that wine was. They made it of the ripe grape. It had the raisin flavour with something – no more than a hint – of Madeira in it: the leathery tang – how to describe it?'

'You need not try, when I have two bottles of it at home, at this moment!'

'When I tell you – ' I began.

'Oh, but wait till you've heard the story!' he interrupted. 'As I was saying, we came to Bergerac and put up for the night at the *Couronne d'Or* – first-class cooking. Besides ourselves there were three French bagmen at the *table d'hôte.* The usual sort. Jinks, who talks worse French than I do (if that's possible), and doesn't mind, got on terms with them at once. . . . For my part I can always hit it off with a commercial – it's the sort of mind that appeals to me – and these French bagmen *do* know something about eating and drinking. That's how it happened. One of them started chaffing us about the *ordinaire* we were drinking – quite a respectable tap, by the way. He had heard that Englishmen drank only the strongest wine, and drank it in any quantities. Then another said: "Ah, messieurs, if you would drink for the honour of England, *justement* you should match yourselves here in this town against the famous Mont-Bazillac." "What is this Mont-Bazillac?" we asked: and they told us – well, pretty much what you told me just now – adding, however, that the landlord kept a few precious bottles of it. They were quite fair in their warnings.'

'Which, of course, you disregarded.'

'For the honour of England. We rang for the landlord – a decent fellow, Sébillot by name – and at first, I may tell you, he wasn't at all keen on producing the stuff; kept protesting that he had but a small half-dozen left, that his daughter was to be married in the autumn, and he had meant to keep it for the wedding banquet. However, the bagmen helping, we persuaded him to bring up two bottles. A frantic price it was, too – frantic for *us*. Seven francs a bottle.'

'It was four francs fifty even in my time.'

'The two bottles were opened. Jinks took his, and I took mine. We had each *arrosé* the dinner with about a pint of Bordeaux; nothing to count. We looked at each other straight. I said, "Be a man, Jinks! *À votre santé, messieurs!*" and we started . . . As you said just now, it's a most innocent-tasting wine.'

'As a matter of fact, I didn't say so. Still, you are right.'

'The fourth and fifth glasses, too, seemed to have no more kick in them than the first . . . Nothing much seemed to be happening, except that Sébillot had brought in an extra lamp – at any rate, the room was brighter, and I could see the bagmen's faces more distinctly as they smiled and congratulated us. I drank off the last glass "to the honour of England", and suggested to Jinks – who had kept pace with me, glass for glass – that we should take a stroll and view the town. There was a fair (as I had heard) across the bridge . . . We stood up together. I had been feeling nervous about Jinks, and it came as a relief to find that he was every bit as steady on his legs as I was. We said good evening to the bagmen and walked out into the street. "Up the hill or down?" asked Jinks, and I explained to him very clearly that, since rivers followed the bottoms of their valleys, we should be safe in going downhill if we wanted to find the bridge. And I'd scarcely said the words before it flashed across me that I was drunk as Chloe.

'Here's another thing – I'd never been drunk before, and I haven't been drunk since: but all the same I knew that this wasn't the least like ordinary drunkenness: it was too – what shall I say? – too brilliant. The whole town of Bergerac belonged to me: and, what was better, it was lit so that I could steer my way perfectly, although the street seemed to be quite amazingly full of people, jostling and chattering. I turned to call Jinks's attention to this, and was saying something about a French crowd – how much cheerfuller it was than your average English one – when all of a sudden Jinks wasn't there! No, nor the crowd! I was alone on Bergerac bridge, and I leaned with both elbows on the parapet and gazed at the Dordogne flowing beneath the moon.

'It was not an ordinary river, for it ran straight up into the sky: and the moon, unlike ordinary moons, kept whizzing on an axis like a Catherine-wheel, and swelled every now and then and burst into showers of the most dazzling fireworks. I leaned there and stared at the performance, feeling just like a king – proud, you understand, but with a sort of noble melancholy. I knew all the time that I was drunk; but that didn't seem to matter. The bagmen had told me – '

I nodded again.

'That's one of the extraordinary things about the Mont-Bazillac,' I corroborated. 'It's all over in about an hour, and there's not (as the saying goes) a headache in a hogshead.'

'I wouldn't quite say that,' said Dick reflectively. 'But you're partly right. All of a sudden the moon stopped whizzing, the river lay down in its bed, and my head became clear as a bell. "The trouble will be," I told myself, "to find the hotel again." But I had no trouble at all. My brain picked up bearing after bearing. I worked back up the street like a prize Baden-Powell scout, found the portico, remembered the stairway to the left, leading to the lounge, went up it, and recognizing the familiar furniture, dropped into an armchair with a happy sigh. My only worry, as I picked up a copy of the *Gil Blas* and began to study it, was about Jinks. But, you see, there wasn't much call to go searching after him when my own experience told me it would be all right.

'There were, maybe, half a dozen men in the lounge, scattered about in the armchairs and smoking. By and by, glancing up from my newspaper, I noticed that two or three had their eyes fixed on me pretty curiously. One of them – an old boy with a grizzled moustache – set down his paper, and came slowly across the room. "Pardon, monsieur," he said in the politest way, "but have we the honour of numbering you amongst our members?" "Good Lord!" cried I, sitting up, "isn't this the *Couronne d'Or*?" "Pray let monsieur not discommode himself," said he, with a quick no-offence sort of smile, "but he has made a little mistake. This is the *Cercle Militaire*."

'I must say those French officers were jolly decent about it: especially when I explained about the Mont-Bazillac. They saw me back to the hotel in a body; and as we turned in at the porchway, who should come down the street but Jinks, striding elbows to side, like a man in a London-to-Brighton walking competition! ... He told me, as we found our bedrooms, that "*of course*, he had gone up the hill, and that the view had been magnificent." I did not argue about it, luckily: for – here comes in another queer fact – *there was no moon at all that night.* Next morning I wheedled two more bottles of the stuff out of old Sébillot – which leaves him two for the wedding. I thought that you and I might have some fun with them ... Now tell me *your* experience.'

'That,' said I, 'must wait until you unlock my tongue; if indeed you have brought home the genuine Mont-Bazillac.'

As it happened, Master Dick was called up to Oxford unexpectedly, a week before the beginning of term, to start practice in his college 'four'. Our experiment had to be postponed; with what result you shall hear.

About a fortnight later I read in our local paper that the Bishop had been holding a Confirmation service in Gantick Parish Church. The paragraph went on to say that 'a large and reverent congregation witnessed the ceremony, but general regret was expressed at the absence of our respected Vicar through a temporary indisposition. We are glad to assure our readers that the reverend gentleman is well on the way to recovery, and indeed has already resumed his ministration in the parish, where his genial presence and quick sympathies,' etc.

This laid an obligation upon me to walk over to Gantick and inquire about my old friend's health: which I did that same afternoon. Mrs Kendall received me with the information that her husband was quite well again, and out and about; that in fact he had started, immediately after luncheon, to pay a round of visits on the outskirts of the parish. On the nature of his late indisposition she showed herself reticent, not to say 'short' in her answers; nor, though the hour was four o'clock, did she invite me to stay and drink tea with her.

On my way back, and just within the entrance-gate of the vicarage drive, I happened on old Trewoon, who works at odd jobs under the gardener, and was just now busy with a besom, sweeping up the first fall of autumn leaves. Old Trewoon, I should tell you, is a Wesleyan, and a Radical of the sardonic sort; and, as a jobbing man, holds himself free to criticize his employers.

'Good afternoon!' said I. 'This is excellent news that I hear about the Vicar. I was afraid, when I first heard of his illness, that it might be something serious – at his age – '

'Serious?' Old Trewoon rested his hands on the besom-handle and eyed me, with a twist of his features, 'Missus didn' tell you the natur' of the complaint, I reckon?'

'As a matter of fact she did not.'

'I bet she didn'. Mind you, I don't know, nuther.' He upended his besom and plucked a leaf or two from between the twigs before adding, 'And what, makin' so bold, did she tell about the Churchwardens?'

'The Churchwardens?' I echoed.

'Aye, the Churchwardens: Matthey Hancock an' th' old Farmer Truslove. They was took ill right about the same time. Aw, my dear' – Mr Trewoon addresses all mankind impartially as 'my dear' – 'th' hull parish knaws about *they*. Though there warn't no concealment, for that matter.'

'What about the Churchwardens?' I asked innocently, and of a sudden became aware that he was rocking to and fro in short spasms of inward laughter.

' – It started wi' the Bishop's motor breakin' down; whereby he and his man spent the better part of two hours in a God-forsaken lane somewhere t'other side of Hen's Beacon, tryin' to make her go. He'd timed hisself to reach here punctual for the lunchin' the Missus always has ready on Confirmation Day: nobody to meet his Lordship but their-selves and the two Churchwardens; an' you may guess that Hancock and Truslove had turned up early in their best broadcloth, lookin' to have the time o' their lives.

'They were pretty keen-set, too, by one o'clock, bein' used to eat their dinners at noon sharp. One o'clock comes – no Bishop: two o'clock and still no Bishop. "There's been a nac-cydent," says the Missus: "but thank the Lord the vittles is cold!" "Maybe he've forgot the day," says the Vicar; "but any way, we'll give en another ha'f-hour's grace an' then set-to," says he, takin' pity on the noises old Truslove was makin' inside his weskit ... So said, so done. At two-thirty – service bein' fixed for ha'f-after-three – they all fell to work.

'You d'know, I dare say, what a craze the Missus have a-took o' late against the drinkin' habit. Sally, the parlourmaid, told me as how, first along, th' old lady set out by hintin' that the Bishop, bein' a respecter o' conscience, wouldn' look for anything stronger on the table than home-brewed lemonade. But there the Vicar struck; and findin' no way to shake him, she made terms by outin' with two bottles o' wine that, to her scandal, she'd rummaged out from a cupboard o' young Master Dick's since he went back to Oxford College. She decanted 'em (chuckle), an' th' old Vicar allowed, havin' tasted the stuff, that – though he had lost the run o' wine lately, an' didn' reckernize whether 'twas port or what-not – seemin' to him 'twas a sound wine and fit for any gentleman's table. "Well, at any rate," says the Missus, "my boy shall be spared the temptation: an' I hope 'tis no sign he's betaken his-self to secret drinkin'!"'

'Well, then, it was decanted: an' Hancock and Truslove, nothin' doubtful, begun to lap it up like so much milk – the Vicar helpin', and the Missus rather encouragin' than not, to the extent o' the first decanter; thinkin' that 'twas good rid-dance to the stuff and that if the Bishop turned up, he wouldn't look, as a holy man, for more than ha'f a bottle. I'm tellin' it you as Sally told it to me. She says that everything went on as easy as eggs in a nest until she started to hand round the sweets, and all of a sudden she didn' know what was happenin' at table, nor whether she was on her head or her heels. ... All I can tell you, sir, is that me and Battershall' – Battershall is the vicarage gardener, stableman, and factotum – 'was waitin' in the stables, wonderin' when in the deuce the Bishop would turn up, when we heard the whistle blown from the kitchen: which was the signal. Out we ran; an' there to be sure was the Bishop comin' down the drive in a hired trap. But between him and the house – slap-bang, as you might say, in the middle of the lawn – was our two Churchwardens, stripped mother-naked to the waist, and sparring: and from the window just over the porch the old Missus screaming out to us to separate 'em. No, nor that wasn't the worst: for, as his Lordship's trap drove up, the two tom-fools stopped their boxin' to stand 'pon their toes and blow kisses at him!

'I must say that Battershall showed great presence o' mind. He shouted to me to tackle Truslove, while he ran up to Matthey Hancock an' butted him in the stomach; an' together we'd heaved the two tom-fools into the shrubbery almost afore his Lordship could believe his eyes. I won't say what had happened to the Vicar, for I don't rightways know. All I can get out o' Sally – she's a modest wench – is that – that – *he wanted to be a Statoo*! ...'

'Quite so,' I interrupted, edging towards the gate and signifying with a gesture of the hand that I had heard enough.

Old Trewoon's voice followed me.

'I reckon, sir, we best agree, for the sake o' the dear old fella, that such a sight as them two Churchwardens was enough to make any gentleman take to his bed. But' – as the gate rang on its hasp and rang again – 'I've been thinkin' powerful *what might ha' happened if his Lordship had turned up in due time to partake.*'

Master Dick is a good boy; and when we met in the Christmas vacation no allusion was made to the Mont-Bazillac. On my part, I am absolved from my promised confession, and my lips shall remain locked. That great, that exhilarating, that redoubtable wine, has – with the nuptials of M. Sébillot's daughter – perished finally from earth. I wonder what happened in Bergerac on that occasion, and if it had a comparable apotheosis!

THE THREE NECKLACES

'A GREAT nation!' said the little curé. 'But yes, indeed, the English are a very great nation. And now I have seen them at home! But it passes expression, monsieur, what a traveller I find myself!'

We stood together on the deck of the steamer, watching – after an eight hours' passage from Plymouth – the Breton coast as it loomed out of the afternoon haze. Our crossing had been smooth, yet sea-sickness had prostrated all his compatriots on board – five or six priests, as many *religieuses*, and maybe a dozen peasants, whom I supposed to be attached in some way to the service of the religious orders the priests represented. (Of late years, since the French Government expelled them, quite a number of these orders have found a home in our West Country.) On my way to the docks that morning I had overtaken and passed them straggling by twos and threes to the steamer, the men in broad-brimmed hats with velvet ribbons, the women coifed and bodiced after the fashion of their country, each group shepherded by a priest; and I had noted how strange and almost forlorn a figure they cut in the grey English streets. If some of the strangeness had worn off, they certainly appeared no less forlorn as they sat huddled in physical anguish, dumb, immobile, staring at the sea.

The little curé, however, was vivacious enough for ten. It was impossible to avoid making friends with him. He had nothing to do, he told me, with his companions, but was just a plain parish priest returning from an errand of business.

He announced this with a fine roll of the voice.

'Of business,' he repeated. 'The English are a great nation for business. But how warm of heart, notwithstanding!'

'That is not always reckoned to us,' said I.

'But *I* reckon it ... *Tenez,* that will be Île Vierge – there, with the lighthouse standing white – as it were, beneath the cliffs; but the cliffs belong in fact to the mainland ... And now

in a few minutes we come abreast of *my* parish – the Île Lezan
… See, see!' He caught my arm as the tide raced us down
through the Passage du Four. 'My church – how her spire
stands up!' He turned to me, his voice shaking with emotion.
'You English are accustomed to travel. Probably you do not
guess, monsieur, with what feelings I see again Île Lezan – I,
who have never crossed the Channel before nor indeed have
visited any foreign land. But I am glad: it spreads the mind.'
Here he put his hands together and drew them apart as though
extending a concertina. 'I have seen you English at home. If
monsieur, who is on tour, could only spare the time to visit
me on Île Lezan!'

Well, the end of it was that before we parted on the quay at
Brest I found myself under half a promise, and a week later,
having (as I put it to myself) nothing better to do, I took the
train to a little wind-swept terminus, whence a ramshackle
cart jolted me to Port Lezan, on the coast, whence again by
sail and oar a ferry-boat conveyed me over to the Island.

My friend the curé greeted me with something not far short
of ecstasy.

'But this is like you English – you keep your word … You
will hardly believe,' he confided, as I shared his admirable
déjeuner – soup, *langouste*, an incomparable omelet, stuffed
veal, and I forget what beside – 'you will hardly believe with
what difficulty I bring myself back to this horizon.' He waved
a hand to the blue sea-line beyond his window. 'When one has
tasted progress – ' He broke off. 'But, thanks be to God, we
too, on Île Lezan, are going to progress. You will visit my
church and see how much we have need.'

He took me to it: a bleak, decayed building, half ruinated,
the slated pavement uneven as the waves of the sea, the
plastered walls dripping with saline ooze. From the roof
depended three or four rudely carved ships, hung there *ex voto*
by parishioners preserved from various perils of the deep. He
narrated their histories at length.

'The roof leaks,' he said, 'but we are to remedy that. At
length the blessed Mary of Lezan will be housed, if not as
befits her, at least not shamefully.' He indicated a niched

statue of the Virgin, with daubed red cheeks and a robe of crude blue overspread with blotches of sea-salt. 'Thanks to your England,' he added.

'Why "thanks to England"?'

He chuckled – or perhaps I had better say chirruped.

'Did I not say I had been visiting your country on business? Eh? You shall hear the story – only I tell no names.'

He took snuff.

'We will call them,' he said, 'only by their Christian names, which are Lucien and Jeanne ... I am to marry them next month, when Lucien gets his relief from the lighthouse on Île Ouessant.

'They are an excellent couple. As between them, the wits are with Lucien, who will doubtless rise in his profession. He has been through temptation, as you shall hear. For Jeanne, she is *un coeur simple*, as again you will discover; not clever at all – oh, by no means! – yet one of the best of my children. It is really to Jeanne that we owe it all ... I have said so to Lucien, and just at the moment Lucien was trying to say it to me.

'They were betrothed, you understand. Lucien was nineteen, and Jeanne maybe a year younger. From the beginning, it had been an understood thing: to this extent understood, that Lucien, instead of sailing to the fishery (whither go most of the young men of Île Lezan and the coast hereabouts) was destined from the first to enter the lighthouse service under Government. The letters I have written to Government on his behalf! ... I am not one of those who quarrel with the Republic. Still – a priest, and in this out-of-the-way spot – what is he?

'However, Lucien got his appointment. The pay? Enough to marry on, for a free couple. But the families were poor on both sides – long families, too. Folk live long on Île Lezan – women-folk especially; accidents at the fishery keep down the men. Still, and allowing for that, the average is high. Lucien had even a great-grandmother alive – a most worthy soul – and on Jeanne's side the grandparents survived on both sides. Where there are grandparents they must be maintained.

'No one builds on Île Lezan. Lucien and Jeanne – on either

side their families crowded to the very windows. If only the smallest hovel might fall vacant! ... For a week or two it seemed that a cottage might drop in their way; but it happened to be what you call picturesque, and a rich man snapped it up. He was a stranger from Paris, and called himself an artist; but in truth he painted little, and that poorly – as even *I* could see. He was fonder of planning what he would have, and what not, to indulge his mood when it should be in the key for painting. Happening here just when the cottage fell empty, he offered a price for it far beyond anything Lucien could afford, and bought it. For a month or two he played with this new toy, adding a studio and a veranda, and getting over many large crates of furniture from the mainland. Then by and by a restlessness overtook him – that restlessness which is the disease of the rich – and he left us, yet professing that it delighted him always to keep his little *pied-à-terre* in Île Lezan. He has never been at pains to visit us since.

'But meanwhile Lucien and Jeanne had no room to marry and set up house. It was a heavy time for them. They had some talk together of crossing over and finding a house on the mainland; but it came to nothing. The parents on both sides would not hear of it, and in truth Jeanne would have found it lonely on the mainland, away from her friends and kin; for Lucien, you see, must in any case spend half his time on the lighthouse on Île Ouessant. So many weeks on duty, so many weeks ashore – thus it works, and even so the loneliness wears them; though our Bretons, being silent men by nature, endure it better than the rest.

'Lucien and Jeanne must wait – wait for somebody to die. In plain words it came to that. Ah, monsieur! I have heard well-to-do folk talk of our poor as unfeeling. That is an untruth. But suppose it were true. Where would the blame lie in such a story as this? Like will to like, and young blood is hot ... Lucien and Jeanne, however, were always well conducted ... Yes, yes, my story? Six months passed, and then came word that our rich artist desired to sell his little *pied-à-terre*; but he demanded the price he had given for it, and, moreover, what he called compensation for the buildings he had added.

Also he would only sell or let it with the furniture; he wished, in short, to disencumber himself of his purchase, and without loss. This meant that Lucien less than ever could afford to buy; and there are no money-lenders on Île Lezan. The letter came as he was on the point of departing for another six weeks on Île Ouessant: and that evening the lovers' feet took them to the nest they had so often dreamed of furnishing. There is no prettier cottage on the island – I will show it to you on our way back. Very disconsolately they looked at it, but there was no cure. Lucien left early next morning.

'That was last autumn, a little before the wreck of your great English steamship the *Rougemont Castle*. Days after, the tides carried some of the bodies even here, to Île Lezan; but not many – four or five at the most – and we, cut off from shore around this corner of the coast, were long in hearing the terrible news. Even the lighthouse-keepers on Île Ouessant knew nothing of it until morning, for she struck in the night, you remember, attempting to run through the Inner Passage and save her time.

'I believe – but on this point will not be certain – that the alarm first came to Lucien, and in the way I shall tell you. At any rate he was walking alone in the early morning, and some-where along the shore to the south of the lighthouse, when he came on a body lying on the seaweed in a gully of the rocks.

'It was the body of a woman, clad only in a nightdress. As he stooped over her, Lucien saw that she was exceeding beautiful; yet not a girl, but a well-developed woman of thirty or thereabouts, with heavy coils of dark hair, well-rounded shoulders, and (as he described it to me later on) a magnificent throat.

'He had reason enough to remark her throat, for as he turned the body over – it lay on its right side – to place a hand over the heart, if perchance some life lingered, the nightdress, open at the throat, disclosed one, two, three superb necklaces of diamonds. There were rings of diamonds on her fingers, too, and afterwards many fine gems were found sewn within a short vest or camisole of silk she wore under her nightdress. But Lucien's eyes were fastened on the three necklaces.

'Doubtless the poor lady, aroused in her berth as the ship struck, had clasped these hurriedly about her throat before rushing on deck. So, might her life be spared, she would save with it many thousands of pounds. They tell me since that in moments of panic women always think first of their jewels.

'But here she lay drowned, and the jewels – as I said, Lucien could not unglue his eyes from them. At first he stared at them stupidly. Not for some minutes did his mind grasp that they represented great wealth; and even when the temptation grew, it whispered no more than that here was money – maybe even a hundred pounds – but enough, at all events, added to his savings, to purchase the cottage at home, and make him and Jeanne happy for the rest of their lives.

'His fingers felt around to the clasps. One by one he detached the necklaces and slipped them into his trousers' pocket.

'He also managed to pull off one of the rings; but found this a more difficult matter, because the fingers were swollen somewhat with the salt water. So he contented himself with one, and ran back to the lighthouse to give the alarm to his comrades.

'When his comrades saw the body there was great outcry upon the jewels on its fingers; but none attempted to disturb them, and Lucien kept his own counsel. They carried the poor thing to a store-chamber at the base of the lighthouse, and there before nightfall they had collected close upon thirty bodies. There was much talk in the newspapers afterwards concerning the honesty of our poor Bretons, who pillaged none of the dead, but gave up whatever they found. The relatives and the great shipping company subscribed a fund, of which a certain small portion came even to Île Lezan to be administered by me.

'The poor lady with the necklaces? If you read the accounts in the newspapers, as no doubt you did, you will already have guessed her name. Yes, in truth, she was your great soprano, whom they called Madame Chiara, or La Chiara: so modest are you English, at least in all that concerns the arts, that when an incomparable singer is born to you she must go to Italy to borrow a name. She was returning from South Africa, where the finest of the three necklaces had been presented to her by subscription amongst her admirers. They say her voice so ravished the audiences at Johannesburg and Pretoria that she might almost, had she willed, have carried home the great diamond they are sending to your King. But that, no doubt, was an invention of the newspapers.

'For certain, at any rate, the necklace was a superb one; nor do I speak without knowledge, as you shall hear. Twenty-seven large stones – between each a lesser stone – and all of the purest water! The other two were scarcely less magnificent. It was a brother who came over and certified the body; for her husband she had divorced in America, and her father was an English clergyman, old and infirm, seldom travelling beyond the parish where he lives in a *château* and reigns as a king. It seems that these things happen in England. At first he was only a younger son, and dwelt in the rectory as a plain parish priest, and there he married and brought up his family; but his elder brother dying, he became *seigneur* of the parish too, and moved into a great house, yet with little money to support it until his only daughter came back from studying at Milan and conquered London. The old gentleman speaks very modestly about it. Oh, yes, I have seen and talked with him. And what a garden! The azaleas! the rhododendrons! But he is old, and his senses somewhat blunted. He lives in the past – not his own, but his family's rather. He spoke to me of his daughter without emotion, and said that her voice was undoubtedly derived from three generations back, when an ancestor – a baronet – had married with an opera singer.

'But we were talking of the necklaces and of the ring which Lucien had taken . . . He told his secret to nobody, but kept them ever in his trousers' pocket. Only, when he could escape away from his comrades to some corner of the shore, he would draw the gems forth and feast his eyes on them. I believe it weighed on him very little that he had committed a crime or a sin. Longshore folk have great ease of conscience respecting all property cast up to them by the sea. They regard all such as their rightful harvest: the feeling is in their blood, and I have many times argued in vain against it. Once while I argued, here in Île Lezan, an old man asked me, "But, Father, if it were not for such chances, why should any man choose to dwell by the sea?" If, monsieur, you lived among them and knew their hardships, you would see some rude sense in that question.

'To Lucien, feasting his eyes by stealth on the diamonds and counting the days to his relief, the stones meant that Jeanne and happiness were now close within his grasp. There would be difficulty, to be sure, in disposing of them; but with Jeanne's advice – she had a practical mind – and perhaps with Jeanne's help, the way would not be hard to find. He was inclined to plume himself on the ease with which, so far, it had been managed. His leaving the rings, and the gems sewn within the camisole – though to be sure these were not discovered for many hours – had been a masterstroke. He and his comrades had been complimented together upon their honesty.

'The relief came duly; and in this frame of mind – a little sly, but more than three parts triumphant – he returned to Île Lezan and was made welcome as something of a hero. (To do him credit, he had worked hard in recovering the bodies from the wreck.) At all times it is good to arrive home after a spell on the lighthouse. The smell of nets drying and of flowers in the gardens, the faces on the quay, and the handshakes, and the first church-going – they all count. But to Lucien these things were for once as little compared with the secret he carried. His marriage now was assured, and that first evening – the Eve of Noël – he walked with Jeanne up the road to the cottage, and facing it, told her his secret. They could be married now. He promised it, and indicated the house with a wave of the hand almost proprietary.

'But Jeanne looked at him as one scared, and said: "Shall I marry a thief?"

'Then, very quietly, she asked for a look at the jewels, and he handed them to her. She had never set eyes on diamonds before, but all women have an instinct for jewels, and these made her gasp. "Yes," she owned, "I could not have believed that the world contained such beautiful things. I am sorry thou hast done this wickedness, but I understand how they tempted thee."

'"What is this you are chanting?" demanded Lucien. "The stones were nothing to me. I thought only that by selling them we two could set up house as man and wife."

'"My dear one," said Jeanne, "what happiness could we have known with this between us?" What with the diamonds in her hand and the little cottage there facing her, so long desired, she was forced to shut her eyes for a moment; but when she opened them again her voice was quite firm. "We must restore them where they belong. It may be that Père Thomas can help us; but I must think of a way. Give them to me, and let me keep them while I think of a way."

'"You do not love me as I love you," said Lucien in his anger and disappointment; but he knew, all the same, that he spoke an untruth.

' Jeanne took the diamonds home with her, to her bedroom, and sat for some time on the edge of her bed, thinking out a way. In the midst of her thinking she stood up, walked over to the glass, and clasped the finest of the necklaces about her throat . . . I suppose no woman of this country ever wore the like of it – no, not in the days when there were kings and queens of Léon . . . Jeanne was not beautiful, but she gazed at herself with eyes like those of a patient in a fever . . . Then of a sudden she felt the stones burning her as though they had been red-hot coals. She plucked them off, and cast herself on her knees beside the bed.

' You will remember that this was the Eve of Noël, when the children of the parish help me to deck the *crèche* for the infant Christ. We take down the images – see, there is St Joseph, and there yonder Our Lady, in the side chapel, the two oxen and a sheep are put away in the vestry, in a cupboard full of camphor. We have the Three Kings too . . . in short, we put our hearts into the dressing-up. By nightfall all is completed, and I turn the children out, reserving some few last touches which I invent to surprise them when they come again on Christmas morning. Afterwards I celebrate the Mass for the Vigil, and then always I follow what has been a custom in this parish, I believe, ever since the church was built. I blow out all the candles but two, and remain here, seated, until the day breaks, and the folk assemble to celebrate the first Mass of Noël. Eh? It is discipline, but I bring rugs, and I will not say that all the time my eyes are wide open.

'Certainly I closed them on this night of which I am telling. For I woke up with a start, and almost, you might say, in trepidation, for it seemed to me that someone was moving in the church. My first thought was that some mischievous child had crept in, and was playing pranks with my *crèche*, and to that first I made my way. Beyond the window above it rode the flying moon, and in the rays of it what did I see?

'The figures stood as I had left them. But above the manger, over the shoulders of the Virgin, blazed a rope of light – of diamonds such as I have never seen nor shall see again – all flashing green and blue and fieriest scarlet and piercing white. Of the Three Kings also each bore a gift, two of them a necklace apiece, and the third a ring. I stood before the miracle, and my tongue clave to the roof of my mouth, and then a figure crept out of the shadows and knelt in the pool of moonlight at my feet. It was Jeanne. She caught at the skirt of my *soutane*, and broke into sobbing.

'"My father, let the Blessed One wear them ever, or else help me to give them back!"

'You will now guess, monsieur, on what business I have been visiting England. It is a great country. The old clergyman sat among his azaleas and rhododendrons and listened to all my story. Then he took the box that held his daughter's jewels, and, emptying it upon the table, chose out one necklace and set it aside. "This one," said he, "shall be sold, my friend, and with the money you shall, after giving this girl a marriage portion, re-adorn your church on Île Lezan to the greater glory of God!"'

On our way back to his lodging the little curé halted me before the cottage. Gay curtains hung in the windows, and the veranda had been freshly painted.

'At the end of the month Lucien gets his relief, and then they are to be married,' said the little curé.

LIEUTENANT LAPENOTIÈRE

THE night porter at the Admiralty had been sleeping in his chair. He was red-eyed and wore his livery coat buttoned at random. He grumbled to himself as he opened the great door.

He carried a glass-screened candle, and held it somewhat above the level of his forehead – which was protuberant and heavily pock-marked. Under the light he peered out at the visitor, who stood tall and stiff, with uniform overcoat buttoned to the chin, between the Ionic pillars of the portico.

'Who's there?'

'Lieutenant Lapenotière, of the *Pickle* schooner – with dispatches.'

'Dispatches?' echoed the night porter. Out beyond the screen of masonry that shut off the Board of Admiralty's forecourt from Whitehall, one of the tired post-horses started blowing through its nostrils on this foggy night.

'From Admiral Collingwood – Mediterranean Fleet off Cadiz – sixteen days,' answered the visitor curtly. 'Is everyone abed?'

'Admiral Collingwood? Why Admiral Collingwood?' The night porter fell back a pace, opening the door a trifle wider. 'Good God, sir! You don't say as how –'

'You can fetch down a secretary or someone, I hope?' said Lieutenant Lapenotière, quickly stepping past him into the long dim hall. 'My dispatches are of the first importance. I have posted up from Falmouth without halt but for relays.'

As the man closed the door, he heard his post-boy of the last relay slap one of the horses encouragingly before heading home to stable. The chaise wheels began to move on the cobbles.

'His lordship himself will see you, sir. Of that I make no doubt,' twittered the night porter, fumbling with the bolt. 'There was a terrible disturbance, back in July, when Captain Bettesworth arrived – not so late as this, to be sure, but towards midnight – and they waited till morning, to carry up the dispatches with his lordship's chocolate. Thankful was I next day not to have been on duty at the time . . . If you will follow me, sir – '

Lieutenant Lapenotière had turned instinctively towards a door on the right. It admitted to the waiting room, and there were few officers in the service who did not know – and only too well – that Chamber of Hope Deferred.

'No, sir . . . this way, if you please,' the night porter corrected him, and opened a door on the left. 'The Captains' Room,' he announced, passing in and steering for the chimney-shelf, on which stood a pair of silver sconces each carrying three wax candles. These he took down, lit, and replaced. 'Ah, sir! Many's the time I've showed Lord Nelson himself into this room, in the days before Sir Horatio, and even after. And you were sayin' – '

'I said nothing.'

The man moved to the door; but halted there and came back, as though in his own despite.

'I can't help it, sir . . . Half a guinea he used to give me, regular. But the last time – and hard to believe 'twas little more than a month ago – he halts on his way out, and says he, searchin' awkward-like in his breeches' pocket with his left hand, "Ned," says he, "my old friend" – aye, sir, his old friend he called me – "Ned," says he, pullin' out a fistful o' gold, "my old friend," says he, "I'll compound with you for two guineas, this bein' the last time you may hold the door open for me, in or out. But you must pick 'em out," says he, spreadin' his blessed fingers with the gold in 'em: "for a man can't count money who's lost his right flapper." Those were his words, sir. "Old friend," he called me, in that way of his.'

Lieutenant Lapenotière pointed to his left arm. Around the sleeve a black scarf was knotted.

'*Dead*, sir,' the night porter hushed his voice.

'Dead,' echoed Lieutenant Lapenotière, staring at the Turkey carpet, of which the six candles, gaining strength, barely illumined the pattern. 'Dead, at the top of victory; a great victory. Go: fetch somebody down.'

The night porter shuffled off. Lieutenant Lapenotière, erect and sombre, cast a look around the apartment, into which he had never before been admitted. The candles lit up a large painting – a queer bird's-eye view of Venice. Other pictures, dark and bituminous, decorated the panelled walls – portraits of dead admirals, a sea piece or two, some charts ... This was all he discerned out in the dim light; and in fact he scanned the walls, the furniture of the room, inattentively. His stomach was fasting, his head light with rapid travel; above all, he had a sense of wonder that all this should be happening to *him*. For, albeit a distinguished officer, he was a modest man, and by habit considered himself of no great importance; albeit a brave man, too, he shrank at the thought of the message he carried – a message to explode and shake millions of men in a confusion of wild joy or grief.

For about the tenth time in those sixteen days it seemed to burst and escape in an actual detonation, splitting his head – there, as he waited in the strange room where never a curtain stirred ... It was a trick his brain played him, repeating, echoing the awful explosion of the French seventy-four *Achille*, which had blown up towards the close of the battle. When the ship was ablaze and sinking, his own crew had put off in boats to rescue the Frenchmen, at close risk of their own lives, for her loaded guns, as they grew red-hot, went off at random among rescuers and rescued ...

As had happened before when he felt this queer shock, his mind travelled back and he seemed to hear the series of discharges running up at short intervals to the great catastrophe ... To divert his thoughts, he turned to study the view of Venice above the chimney-piece ... and on a sudden faced about again.

He had a sensation that someone was in the room – someone standing close behind him.

But no ... For the briefest instant his eyes rested on an indistinct shadow – his own perhaps, cast by the candle-light? Yet why should it lie lengthwise there, shaped like a coffin, on the dark polished table that occupied the middle of the room?

The answer was that it did not. Before he could rub his eyes it had gone. Moreover, he had turned to recognize a living being ... and no living person was in the room, unless by chance (absurd supposition) one were hidden behind the dark red window curtains.

'Recognize' may seem a strange word to use; but here had lain the strangeness of the sensation – that the someone standing there was a friend, waiting to be greeted. It was with eagerness and a curious warmth of the heart that Lieutenant Lapenotière had faced about – upon nothing.

He continued to stare in a puzzled way at the window curtains, when a voice by the door said:

'Good evening! – or perhaps, to be correct, good morning! You are Mr – '

'Lapenotière,' answered the lieutenant, who had turned sharply. The voice – a gentleman's and pleasantly modulated – was not one he knew; nor did he recognize the speaker – a youngish, shrewd-looking man, dressed in civilian black, with knee-breeches. 'Lapenotière – of the *Pickle* schooner.'

'Yes, yes – the porter bungled your name badly, but I guessed. Lord Barham will see you personally. He is, in fact, dressing with all haste at this moment ... I am his private secretary,' explained the shrewd-looking gentleman in his quiet, business-like voice. 'Will you come with me upstairs?'

Lieutenant Lapenotière followed him. At the foot of the great staircase the secretary turned.

'I may take it, sir, that we are not lightly disturbing his lordship – who is an old man.'

'The news is of great moment, sir. Greater could scarcely be.'

The secretary bent his head. As they went up the staircase Lieutenant Lapenotière looked back and caught sight of the night porter in the middle of the hall, planted there and gazing up, following their ascent.

On the first-floor landing they were met by a truly ridiculous spectacle. There emerged from a doorway on the left of the wide corridor an old gentleman clad in night-cap, nightshirt and bedroom slippers, buttoning his breeches and cursing vigorously; while close upon him followed a valet with dressing-gown on one arm, waistcoat and wig on the other, vainly striving to keep pace with his master's impatience.

'The braces, my lord – your lordship has them forepart behind, if I may suggest – '

'Damn the braces!' swore the old gentleman. 'Where is he? Hi, Tylney!' as he caught sight of the secretary. 'Where are we to go? My room, I suppose?'

'The fire is out there, my lord ... 'Tis past three in the morning. But after sending word to awake you, I hunted round and by good luck found a plenty of promising embers in the board room grate. On top of these I've piled what remained of my own fire, and Dobson has set a lamp there – '

'You've been devilish quick, Tylney. Dressed like a buck you are, too!'

'Your lordship's wig,' suggested the valet.

'Damn the wig!' Lord Barham snatched it and attempted to stick it on top of his night-cap, damned the night-cap, and, plucking it off, flung it to the man.

'I happened to be sitting up late, my lord, over the *Æolus* papers,' said Mr Secretary Tylney.

'Ha?' Then, to the valet, 'The dressing-gown there! Don't fumble! ... So this is Captain – '

'Lieutenant, sir: Lapenotière, commanding the *Pickle* schooner.'

The lieutenant saluted.

'From the Fleet, my lord – off Cadiz; or rather, off Cape Trafalgaro.'

He drew the sealed dispatch from an inner breast pocket and handed it to the First Lord.

'Here, step into the board room ... Where the devil are my spectacles?' he demanded of the valet, who had sprung forward to hold open the door.

Evidently the board room had been but a few hours ago the scene of a large dinner-party. Glasses, dessert-plates, dishes of fruit, decanters empty and half empty, cumbered the great mahogany tables, as dead and wounded, guns and tumbrils, might a battlefield. Chairs stood askew; crumpled napkins lay as they had been dropped or tossed, some on the floor, others across the table between the dishes.

'Looks cosy, eh?' commented the First Lord. 'Maggs, set a screen around the fire, and look about for a decanter and some clean glasses.'

He drew a chair close to the reviving fire, and glanced at the cover of the dispatch before breaking its seal.

'Nelson's handwriting?' he asked. It was plain that his old eyes, unaided by spectacles, saw the superscription only as a blur.

'No, my lord: Admiral Collingwood's,' said Lieutenant Lapenotière, inclining his head.

Old Lord Barham looked up sharply. His wig set awry, he made a ridiculous figure in his hastily donned garments. Yet he did not lack dignity.

'Why Collingwood?' he asked, his fingers breaking the seal. 'God! you don't tell me – '

'Lord Nelson is dead, sir.'

'Dead – dead? ... Here, Tylney – you read what it says. Dead? ... No, damme, let the captain tell his tale. Briefly, sir.'

'Briefly, sir – Lord Nelson had word of Admiral Villeneuve coming out of the Straits, and engaged the combined fleets off Cape Trafalgaro. They were in single line, roughly; and he bore down in two columns, and cut off their van under Dumanoir. This was at dawn or thereabouts, and by five o'clock the enemy was destroyed.'

'How many prizes?'

'I cannot say precisely, my lord. The word went, when I was signalled aboard the Vice-Admiral's flagship, that either fifteen or sixteen had struck. My own men were engaged, at the time, in rescuing the crew of a French seventy-four that had blown up; and I was too busy to count, had counting been possible. One or two of my officers maintain to me that our gains were higher. But the dispatch will tell, doubtless.'

'Aye, to be sure ... Read, Tylney. Don't sit there clearing your throat, but read, man alive!' And yet it appeared that while the secretary was willing enough to read, the First Lord had no capacity, as yet, to listen. Into the very first sentence he broke with –

'No, wait a minute. "Dead", d'ye say? ... My God! ...

Lieutenant, pour yourself a glass of wine and tell us first how it happened.'

Lieutenant Lapenotière could not tell very clearly. He had twice been summoned to board the *Royal Sovereign* – the first time to receive the command to hold himself ready. It was then that, coming alongside the great ship, he had read in all the officers' faces an anxiety hard to reconcile with the evident tokens of victory around them. At once it had occurred to him that the Admiral had fallen, and he put the question to one of the lieutenants – to be told that Lord Nelson had indeed been mortally wounded and could not live long; but that he must be alive yet, and conscious, since the *Victory* was still signalling orders to the Fleet.

'I think, my lord,' said he, 'that Admiral Collingwood must have been doubtful, just then, what responsibility had fallen upon him, or how soon it might fall. He had sent for me to "stand by", so to speak. He was good enough to tell me the news as it had reached him – '

Here Lieutenant Lapenotière, obeying the order to fill his glass, let spill some of the wine on the table. The sight of the dark trickle on the mahogany touched some nerve of the brain: he saw it widen into a pool of blood, from which, as they picked up a shattered seaman and bore him below, a lazy stream crept across the deck of the flag-ship towards the scuppers. He moved his feet, as he had moved them then, to be out of the way of it: but recovered himself in another moment and went on –

'He told me, my lord, that the *Victory* after passing under the *Bucentaure's* stern, and so raking her that she was put out of action, or almost, fell alongside the *Redoutable*. There was a long swell running, with next to no wind, and the two ships could hardly have cleared had they tried. At any rate, they hooked, and it was then a question which could hammer the harder. The Frenchman had filled his tops with sharp-shooters, and from one of these – the mizen-top, I believe – a musket-ball struck down the Admiral. He was walking at the time to and fro on a sort of gangway he had caused to be planked over his cabin skylight, between the wheel and the ladder-way . . .

Admiral Collingwood believed it had happened about half-past one ...'

'Sit down, man, and drink your wine,' commanded the First Lord as the dispatch-bearer swayed with a sudden faintness.

'It is nothing, my lord – '

But it must have been a real swoon, or something very like it: for he recovered to find himself lying in an arm-chair. He heard the secretary's voice reading steadily on and on ... Also they must have given him wine, for he awoke to feel the warmth of it in his veins and coursing about his heart. But he was weak yet, and for the moment well content to lie still and listen.

Resting there and listening, he was aware of two sensations that alternated within him, chasing each other in and out of his consciousness. He felt all the while that he, John Richards Lapenotière, a junior officer in His Majesty's service, was assisting in one of the most momentous events in his country's history; and alone in the room with these two men, he felt it as he had never begun to feel it amid the smoke and roar of the actual battle. He had seen the dead hero but half a dozen times in his life: he had never been honoured by a word from him: but like every other naval officer, he had come to look up to Nelson as to the splendid particular star among commanders. *There* was greatness: *there* was that which lifted men to such deeds as write man's name across the firmament! And, strange to say, Lieutenant Lapenotière recognized something of it in this queer old man, in dressing-gown and ill-fitting wig, who took snuff and interrupted now with a curse and anon with a 'bravo!' as the secretary read. He was absurd: but he was no common man, this Lord Barham. He had something of the ineffable aura of greatness.

But in the lieutenant's brain, across this serious, even awful sense of the moment and of its meaning, there played a curious secondary sense that the moment was not – that what was happening before his eyes had either happened before or was happening in some vacuum in which past, present, future, and the ordinary divisions of time had lost their bearings. The great twenty-four-hour clock at the end of the board room, ticking on and on while the secretary read, wore an unfamiliar face ... Yes, time had gone wrong, somehow: and the events of the passage home to Falmouth, of the journey up to the doors of the Admiralty, though they ran on a chain, had no intervals to be measured by a clock, but followed one another like pictures on a wall. He saw the long, indigo-coloured swell thrusting the broken ships shoreward. He felt the wind freshening as it southered and he left the Fleet behind: he watched their many lanterns as they sank out of sight, then the glow of flares by the light of which dead-tired men were repairing damages, cutting away wreckage. His ship was wallowing heavily now, with the gale after her – and now dawn was breaking clean and glorious on the swell off Lizard Point. A Mount's Bay lugger had spied them, and lying in wait, had sheered up close alongside, her crew bawling for news. He had not forbidden his men to call it back, and he could see the fellows' faces now, as it reached them from the speaking-trumpet: 'Great victory – twenty taken or sunk – Admiral Nelson killed!' They had guessed something, noting the *Pickle's* ensign at half-mast: yet as they took in the purport of the last three words, these honest fishermen had turned and stared at one another; and without one answering word, the lugger had been headed straight back to the mainland.

So it had been at Falmouth. A ship entering port has a thousand eyes upon her, and the *Pickle's* errand could not be hidden. The news seemed in some mysterious way to have spread even before he stepped ashore there on the Market Strand. A small crowd had collected, and, as he passed through it, many doffed their hats. There was no cheering at all – no, not for this the most glorious victory of the war – outshining even the Nile or Howe's First of June.

He had set his face as he walked to the inn. But the news had flown before him, and fresh crowds gathered to watch him off. The post-boys knew ... and *they* told the post-boys at the next stage, and the next – Bodmin and Plymouth – not to mention the boatmen at Torpoint Ferry. But the country-side did not know: nor the labourers gathering in cider apples heaped under Devon apple-trees, nor, next day, the sportsmen banging off guns at the partridges around Salisbury. The slow, jolly life of England on either side of the high road turned leisurely as a wagon-wheel on its axle, while between hedge-rows, past farm hamlets, church towers, and through the cobbled streets of market towns, he had sped and rattled with Collingwood's dispatch in his sealed case. The news had reached London with him. His last post-boys had carried it to their stables, and from stable to tavern. To-morrow – to-day, rather – in an hour or two – all the bells of London would be ringing – or tolling! ...

'He's as tired as a dog,' said the voice of the secretary. 'Seems almost a shame to waken him.'

The lieutenant opened his eyes and jumped to his feet with an apology. Lord Barham had gone, and the secretary hard by was speaking to the night porter, who bent over the fire, raking it with a poker. The hands of the Queen Anne clock indicated a quarter to six.

'The First Lord would like to talk with you ... later in the day,' said Mr Tylney gravely, smiling a little these last words. He himself was white and haggard. 'He suggested the early afternoon, say half-past two. That will give you time for a round sleep ... You might leave me the name of your hotel, in case he should wish to send for you before that hour.'

' "The Swan with Two Necks," Lad Lane, Cheapside,' said Lieutenant Lapenotière.

He knew little of London, and gave the name of the hostelry at which, many years ago, he had alighted from a West Country coach with his box and midshipman's kit ... A moment later he found himself wondering if it still existed as a house of entertainment. Well, he must go and seek it.

The secretary shook hands with him, smiling wanly.

'Few men, sir, have been privileged to carry such news as you have brought us to-night.'

'And I went to sleep after delivering it,' said Lieutenant Lapenotière, smiling back.

The night porter escorted him to the hall, and opened the great door for him. In the portico he bade the honest man good night, and stood for a moment, mapping out in his mind his way to 'The Swan with Two Necks'. He shivered slightly, after his nap, in the chill of the approaching dawn.

As the door closed behind him he was aware of a light shining out beyond the screen of the fore-court, and again a horse blew through its nostrils on the raw air.

'Lord!' thought the Lieutenant. 'That fool of a post-boy cannot have mistaken me and waited all this time!'

He hurried out into Whitehall. Sure enough a chaise was drawn up there, and a post-boy stood by the near lamp, conning a scrap of paper by the light of it. No, it was a different chaise, and a different post-boy. He wore the buff and black, whereas the other had worn the blue and white. Yet he stepped forward confidently, and with something of a smile.

'Lieutenant Lapenotière?' he asked, reaching back and holding up his paper to the lamp to make sure of the syllables.

'That is my name,' said the amazed Lieutenant.

'I was ordered here – five-forty-five – to drive you down to Merton.'

'To Merton?' echoed Lieutenant Lapenotière, his hand going to his pocket. The post-boy's smile, or so much as could be seen of it by the edge of the lamp, grew more knowing.

'I ask no questions, sir.'

'But – but who ordered you?'

The post-boy did not observe, or disregarded, his bewilderment.

'A Briton's a Briton, sir, I hope? I ask no questions, knowing my place . . . But if so be as you were to tell me there's been a great victory –' He paused on this.

'Well, my man, you're right so far, and no harm in telling you.'

'Aye,' chirruped the post-boy. 'When the maid called me up with the order, and said as how *he* and no other had called with it –'

'He?'

The fellow nodded.

'She knew him at once, from his portraits. Who wouldn't? With his right sleeve pinned across so . . . And, said I,

"'Then there's been a real victory. Never would you see him back, unless." And I was right, sir!' he concluded triumphantly.

'Let me see that piece of paper.'

'You'll let me have it back, sir? – for a memento,' the post-boy pleaded. Lieutenant Lapenotière took it from him – a plain half-sheet of note-paper roughly folded. On it was scribbled in pencil, back-handwise, 'Lt. Lapenotière. Admiralty, White-hall. At 6.30 a.m., not later. For Merton, Surrey.'

He folded the paper very slowly, and handed it back to the post-boy.

'Very well, then. For Merton.'

*

The house lay but a very little distance beyond Wimbledon. Its blinds were drawn as Lieutenant Lapenotière alighted from the chaise and went up to the modest porch.

His hand was on the bell-push. But some pressure checked him as he was on the point of ringing. He determined to wait for a while and turned away towards the garden.

The dawn had just broken; two or three birds were singing. It did not surprise – at any rate, it did not frighten – Lieutenant Lapenotière at all, when, turning into a short pleached alley, he looked along it and saw *him* advancing.

– Yes, *him,* with the pinned sleeve, the noble, seamed, eager face. They met as friends ... In later years the lieutenant could never remember a word that passed, if any passed at all. He was inclined to think that they met and walked together in complete silence, for many minutes. Yet he ever maintained that they walked as two friends whose thoughts hold converse without need of words. He was not terrified at all. He ever insisted, on the contrary, that there, in the cold of the breaking day, his heart was light and warm as though flooded with first love – not troubled by it, as youth in first love is wont to be – but bathed in it; he, the ardent young officer, bathed in a glow of affection, ennobling, exalting him, making him free of a brotherhood he had never guessed.

He used also, in telling the story, to scandalize the clergyman of his parish by quoting the evangelists, and especially St John's narrative of Mary Magdalen at the sepulchre.

For the door of the house opened at length; and a beautiful woman, scarred by knowledge of the world, came down the alley, slowly, unaware of him. Then (said he), as she approached, his hand went up to his pocket for the private letter he carried, and the shade at his side left him to face her in the daylight.

FRENCHMAN'S CREEK

A Reported Tale

FRENCHMAN'S CREEK runs up between overhanging woods from the western shore of Helford River, which flows down through an earthly paradise and meets the sea midway between Falmouth and the dreadful Manacles – a river of gradual golden sunsets such as Wilson painted; broadbosomed, holding here and there a village as in an arm maternally crook'd, but with a brooding face of solitude. Off the main flood lie creeks where the oaks dip their branches in the high tides, where the stars are glassed all night long without a ripple, and where you may spend whole days with no company but herons and sandpipers:

> *Helford River, Helford River,*
> *Blessed may you be!*
> *We sailed up Helford River*
> *By Durgan from the sea . . .*

And about three-quarters of a mile above the ferry-crossing (where is the best anchorage) you will find the entrance of the creek they call Frenchman's, with a cob-built ruin beside it, and perhaps, if you come upon it in the morning sunlight, ten or a dozen herons aligned like statues on the dismantled walls.

Now, why they call it Frenchman's Creek no one is supposed to know, but this story will explain. And the story I heard on the spot from an old verderer, who had it from his grandfather, who bore no unimportant part in it – as will be seen. Maybe you will find it out of keeping with its scenery. In my own words you certainly would: and so I propose to relate it just as the verderer told it to me.

I

First of all you'll let me say that a bad temper is an affliction, whoever owns it, and shortening to life. I don't know what

your opinion may be: but my grandfather was parish constable in these parts for forty-seven years, and you'll find it on
his headstone in Manaccan churchyard that he never had a
cross word for man, woman, or child. He took no credit for it:
it ran in the family, and to this day we're all terribly mild to
handle.

Well, if ever a man was born bad in his temper, 'twas Captain Bligh, that came from St Tudy parish, and got himself
known to all the world over that dismal business aboard the
Bounty. Yes, sir, that's the man – 'Breadfruit Bligh', as they
called him. They made an Admiral of him in the end, but they
never cured his cussedness: and my grandfather, that followed
his history (and good reason for why) from the day he first set
foot in this parish, used to rub his hands over every fresh item
of news. 'Darn it!' he'd say, 'here's that old Turk broke loose
again. Lord, if he ain't a warrior!' Seemed as if he took a delight in the man, and kept a sort of tenderness for him till the
day of his death.

Bless you, though folks have forgotten it, that little affair of
the *Bounty* was only the beginning of Bligh. He was a left'nant
when it happened, and the King promoted him post-captain
straight away. Later on, no doubt because of his experiences in
mutinies, he was sent down to handle the big one at the Nore.
'Now, then, you dogs!' – that's how he began with the men's
delegates – 'His Majesty will be graciously pleased to hear
your grievances: and afterwards I'll be graciously pleased to
hang the lot of you and rope-end every fifth man in the Fleet.
That's plain sailing, I hope!' says he. The delegates made a
rush at him, triced him up hand and foot, and in two two's
would have heaved him to the fishes with an eighteen-pound
shot for ballast if his boat's crew hadn't swarmed on by the
chains and carried him off. After this he commanded a ship at
Camperdown, and another at Copenhagen, and being a good
fighter as well as a man of science, was chosen for Governor of
New South Wales. He hadn't been forty-eight hours in the
colony, I'm told, before the music began, and it ended with
his being clapped into irons by the military and stuck in prison
for two years to cool his heels. At last they took him out, put

him on board a ship of war and played farewell to him on a brass band: and, by George, sir, if he didn't fight with the captain of the ship all the way home, making claim that as senior in the service he ought to command her! By this time, as you may guess, there was nothing to be done with the fellow but make him an Admiral; and so they did; and as Admiral of the Blue he died in the year seventeen, only a couple of weeks ahead of my poor grandfather, that would have set it down to the finger of Providence if he'd only lived to hear the news.

Well, now, the time that Bligh came down to Helford was a few months before he sailed for Australia, and that will be a hundred years ago next summer: and I guess the reason of his coming was that the folks at the Admiralty couldn't stand him in London, the weather just then being sultry. So they pulled out a map and said, 'This Helford looks a nice cool far-away place; let the man go down and take soundings and chart the place'; for Bligh, you must know, had been a pupil of Captain Cook's, and at work of this kind there was no man cleverer in the Navy.

To do him justice, Bligh never complained of work. So off he packed and started from London by coach in the early days of June; and with him there travelled down a friend of his, a retired naval officer by the name of Sharl, that was bound for Falmouth to take passage in the Lisbon packet; but whether on business or a pleasure trip is more than I can tell you.

So far as I know, nothing went wrong with them until they came to Torpoint Ferry: and there, on the Cornish side of the water, stood the Highflyer coach, the inside of it crammed full of parcels belonging to our Vicar's wife, Mrs Polwhele, that always visited Plymouth once a year for a week's shopping. Having all these parcels to bring home, Mrs Polwhele had crossed over by a waterman's boat two hours before, packed the coach as full as it would hold, and stepped into the Ferry Inn for a dish of tea. 'And glad I am to be across the river in good time,' she told the landlady; 'for by the look of the sky there's a thunderstorm coming.'

Sure enough there was, and it broke over the Hamoaze with a bang just as Captain Bligh and his friend put across in the ferry-boat. The lightning whizzed, and the rain came down like the floods of Deva, and in five minutes' time the streets and gutters of Torpoint were pouring on to the Quay like so many shutes, and turning all the inshore water to the colour of pea-soup. Another twenty minutes and 'twas over; blue sky above and the birds singing, and the roof and trees all a-twinkle in the sun; and out steps Mrs Polwhele very gingerly in the landlady's pattens, to find the Highflyer ready to start, the guard unlashing the tarpaulin that he'd drawn over the out-side luggage, the horses steaming and anxious to be off, and on the box-seat a couple of gentlemen wet to the skin, and one of them looking as ugly as a chained dog in a street fight. This was Bligh, of course. His friend, Mr Sharl, sat alongside, talk-ing low and trying to coax him back to a good temper: but Mrs Polwhele missed taking notice of this. She hadn't seen the gentlemen arrive, by reason that, being timid of thunder, at the very first peal she'd run upstair, and crawled under one of the bed-ties: and there she bided until the chambermaid brought word that the sky was clear and the coach waiting.

If ever you've had to do with timmersome folks I dare say you've noted how talkative they get as soon as danger's over. Mrs Polwhele took a glance at the inside of the coach to make sure that her belongings were safe, and then, turning to the ladder that the Boots was holding for her to mount, up she trips to her outside place behind the box-seat, all in a fluff and commotion, and chattering so fast that the words hitched in each other like beer in a narrow-necked bottle.

'Give you good morning, gentlemen!' said Mrs Polwhele, 'and I do hope and trust I haven't kept you waiting; but thun-der makes me *that* nervous! 'Twas always the same with me from a girl; and la! what a storm while it lasted! I declare the first drops looked to me a'most so big as crown-pieces. Most unfortunate it should come on when you were crossing – most unfortunate, I vow! There's nothing so unpleasant as sitting in damp clothes, especially if you're not accustomed to it. My husband, now – if he puts on a shirt that hasn't been double-aired I always know what's going to happen: it'll be lumbago next day to a certainty. But maybe, as travellers, you're not so susceptible. I find hotel-keepers so careless with their damp sheets! May I ask, gentlemen, if you've come from far? You'll be bound for Falmouth, as I guess: and so am I. You'll find much on the way to admire. But perhaps this is not your first visit to Cornwall?'

In this fashion she was rattling away, good soul – settling her wraps about her and scarcely drawing breath – when Bligh slewed himself around in his seat, and for answer treated her to a long stare.

Now, Bligh wasn't a beauty at the best of times, and he carried a scar on his cheek that didn't improve matters by turning white when his face was red, and red when his face was white. They say the King stepped up to him at Court once and asked him how he came by it and in what action. Bligh had to tell the truth – that he'd got it in the orchard at home: he and his father were trying to catch a horse there: the old man flung a hatchet to turn the horse and hit his boy in the face, marking him for life. Hastiness, you see, in the family.

Well, the sight of his face, glowering back on her over his shoulder, was enough to dry up the speech in Mrs Polwhele or any woman. But Bligh, it seems, couldn't be content with this. After withering the poor soul for ten seconds or so, he takes his eyes off her, turns to his friend again in a lazy, insolent way, and begins to talk loud to him in French.

'Twas a terrible unmannerly thing to do for a fellow supposed to be a gentleman. I've naught to say against modern languages: but when I see it in the newspaper nowadays that naval officers ought to give what's called 'increased attention' to French and German, I hope that they'll use it better than Bligh, that's all! Why, sir, my eldest daughter threw up a situation as parlour-maid in London because her master and mistress pitched to parleyvooing whenever they wanted to talk secrets at table. 'If you please, ma'am,' she told the lady, 'you're mistaking me for the governess and I never could abide compliments.' She gave a month's warning then and there, and I commend the girl's spirit.

But the awkward thing for Bligh, as it turned out, was that Mrs Polwhele didn't understand his insolence. Being a woman that wouldn't hurt a fly if she could help it, and coming from a parish where every man, her husband included, took pleasure in treating her respectfully, she never dreamed that an affront was meant. From the moment she heard Bligh's lingo, she firmly believed that here were two Frenchies on the coach; and first she went white to the lips and shivered all over, and then caught at the seat to steady herself, and then she flung back a look at Jim the guard, to make sure he had his blunderbuss handy. She couldn't speak to Sammy Hosking, the coachman, or touch him by the arm without reaching across Bligh: and by this time the horses were at the top of the hill and settling into a gallop. She thought of the many times she'd sat up in bed at home in a fright that the Frenchmen had landed and were marching up to burn Manaccan Vicarage: and how often she had warned her husband against abusing Boney from the pulpit – 'twas dangerous, she always maintained, for a man living so nigh the seashore. The very shawl beside her was scarlet, same as the women-folk wore about the fields in those days in hopes that the invaders, if any came, would mistake them for red-coats. And here she was, perched up behind two of her country's enemies – one of them as ugly as Old Nick or Boney himself – and bowling down towards her peaceful home at anything from sixteen to eighteen miles an hour.

I dare say, too, the thunderstorm had given her nerves a shaking; at any rate, Jim the guard came crawling over the coach-roof after a while, and, said he, 'Why, Mrs Polwhele, whatever is the matter? I han't heard you speak six words since we started.'

And with that, just as he settled himself down for a comfortable chat with her, after his custom, the poor lady points to the two strangers, flings up both hands, and tumbles upon him in a fit of hysterics.

'Stop the hosses!' yells Jim; but already Sammy Hosking was pulling up for dear life at the sound of her screams.

'What in thunder's wrong with the female?' asks Bligh.

'Female yourself!' answers up Sammy in a pretty passion. 'Mrs Polwhele's a lady, and I reckon your cussed rudeness upset her. I say nothing of your face, for that you can't help.'

Bligh started up in a fury, but Mr Sharl pulled him down on the seat, and then Jim the guard took a turn.

'Pitch a lady's luggage into the road, would you?' for this, you must know, was the reason of Bligh's sulkiness at starting. He had come up soaking from Torpoint Ferry, walked straight to the coach, and pulled the door open to jump inside, when down on his head came rolling a couple of Dutch cheeses that Mrs Polwhele had crammed on the top of her belongings. This raised his temper, and he began to drag parcel after parcel out and fling them in the mud, shouting that no passenger had a right to fill up the inside of a coach in that fashion. Thereupon Jim sent an ostler running to the landlady that owned the Highflyer, and she told Bligh that he hadn't booked his seat yet: that the inside was reserved for Mrs Polwhele: and that he could either take an outside place and behave himself, or be left behind to learn manners. For a while he showed fight: but Mr Sharl managed to talk sense into him, and the parcels were stowed again and the door shut but a minute before Mrs Polwhele came downstairs and took her seat as innocent as a lamb.

'Pitch a lady's luggage into the road, would you?' struck in Jim the guard, making himself heard above the pillaloo. 'Carry on as if the coach belonged to ye, hey? Come down and take your coat off, like a man, and don't sit there making fool faces at me!'

'My friend is not making faces,' began Mr Sharl, very gentle-like, trying to keep the peace.

'Call yourself his friend!' Jim snapped him up. 'Get off, the pair of you. Friend indeed! Go and buy him a veil.'

But 'twas easily seen that Mrs Polwhele couldn't be carried farther. So Sammy Hosking pulled up at a farmhouse a mile beyond St Germans: and there she was unloaded, with her traps, and put straight to bed: and a farm-boy sent back to Torpoint to fetch a chaise for her as soon as she recovered. And the Highflyer – that had been delayed three-quarters of an hour – rattled off at a gallop, with all on board in the worst of tempers.

When they reached Falmouth – which was not till after ten o'clock at night – and drew up at the 'Crown and Anchor', the first man to hail them was old Parson Polwhele, standing there under the lamp in the entry and taking snuff to keep himself awake.

'Well, my love,' says he, stepping forward to help his wife down and give her a kiss. 'And how have you enjoyed the journey?'

But instead of his wife 'twas a bull-necked-looking man that swung himself off the coach-roof, knocking the parson aside, and bounced into the inn without so much as a 'beg your pardon'.

Parson Polwhele was taken aback for the moment by reason that he'd pretty nigh kissed the fellow by accident; and before he could recover, Jim the guard leans out over the darkness, and, says he, speaking down: 'Very sorry, Parson, but your missus wasn't taken very well t'other side of St Germans, and we've been forced to leave her 'pon the road.'

Now, the parson doted on his wife, as well he might. He was a very learned man, you must know, and wrote a thundering great history of Cornwall: but outside of book-learning his head rambled terribly, and Mrs Polwhele managed him in all the little business of life. ' 'Tis like looking after a museum,' she used to declare. 'I don't understand the contents, I'm thankful to say; but, please God, I can keep 'em dusted.' A better-suited couple you couldn't find, nor a more affectionate; and whenever Mrs Polwhele tripped it to Plymouth, the parson would be at Falmouth to welcome her back, and they'd sleep the night at the 'Crown and Anchor' and drive home to Manaccan next morning.

'Not taken well?' cried the parson. 'Oh, my poor Mary – my poor, dear Mary!'

' 'Tisn' so bad as all that,' says Jim, as soothing as he could; but he thought it best to tell nothing about the rumpus.

'If 'tis on the wings of an eagle, I must fly to her!' cries the parson, and he hurried indoors and called out for a chaise and pair.

He had some trouble in persuading a post-boy to turn out at such an hour, but before midnight the poor man was launched and rattling away eastward, chafing at the hills and singing out that he'd pay for speed, whatever it cost. And at Grampound in the grey of the morning he almost ran slap into a chaise and pair proceeding westward, and likewise as if its postilion wanted to break his neck.

Parson Polwhele stood up in his vehicle and looked out ahead. The two chaises had narrowly missed doubling each other into a cocked hat; in fact, the boys had pulled up within a dozen yards of smash, and there stood the horses face to face and steaming.

'Why, 'tis my Mary!' cries the parson, and takes a leap out of the chaise.

'Oh, Richard! Richard!' sobs Mrs Polwhele. 'But you can't possibly come in here, my love,' she went on, drying her eyes.

'Why not, my angel?'

'Because of the parcels, dearest. And Heaven only knows what's underneath me at this moment, but it feels like a flat-iron. Besides,' says she, like the prudent woman she was, 'we've paid for two chaises. But 'twas good of you to come in search of me, and I'll say what I've said a thousand times, that I've the best husband in the world.'

The parson grumbled a bit; but, indeed, the woman was piled about with packages up to the neck. So, very sad-like, he went back to his own chaise – that was now slewed about for Falmouth – and off the procession started at an easy trot, the good man bouncing up in his seat from time to time to blow back a kiss.

But after a while he shouted to the post-boy to pull up again.

'What's the matter, love?' sings out Mrs Polwhele, over-taking him and coming to a stand likewise.

'Why, it occurs to me, my angel, that *you* might get into *my* chaise, if you're not too tightly wedged.'

'There's no saying what will happen when I once begin to move,' said Mrs Polwhele: 'but I'll risk it. For I don't mind telling you that one of my legs went to sleep somewhere near St Austell, and 'tis dreadfully uncomfortable.'

So out she was fetched and climbed in beside her husband.

'But what was it that upset you?' he asked, as they started again.

Mrs Polwhele laid her cheek to his shoulder and sobbed aloud; and so by degrees let out her story.

'But, my love, the thing's impossible!' cried Parson Polwhele. 'There's no Frenchman in Cornwall at this moment, unless maybe 'tis the Guernsey merchant* or some poor wretch of a prisoner escaped from the hulks in the Hamoaze.'

'Then, that's what these men were, you may be sure,' said Mrs Polwhele.

'Tut-tut-tut! You've just told me that they came across the ferry, like any ordinary passengers.'

'Did I? Then I told more than I know; for I never saw them cross.'

'A couple of escaped prisoners wouldn't travel by coach in broad daylight, and talk French in everyone's hearing.'

'We live in the midst of mysteries,' said Mrs Polwhele. 'There's my parcels, now – I packed 'em in the Highflyer most careful, and I'm sure Jim the guard would be equally careful in handing them out – you know the sort of man he is: and yet I find a good dozen of them plastered in mud, and my new Moldavia cap, that I gave twenty-three shillings for only last Tuesday, pounded to a jelly, quite as if someone had flung it on the road and danced on it!'

The poor soul burst out into fresh tears, and there against her husband's shoulder cried herself fairly asleep, being tired out with travelling all night. By and by the parson, that wanted a nap just as badly, dozed off beside her: and in this fashion they were brought back through Falmouth streets and into the yard of the 'Crown and Anchor', where Mrs Polwhele woke up with a scream, crying out: 'Prisoners or no prisoners, those men were up to no good: and I'll say it if I live to be a hundred!'

That same afternoon they transhipped the parcels into a cart, and drove ahead themselves in a light gig, and so came down, a little before sunset, to the 'Passage Inn' yonder. There, of course, they had to unload again and wait for the ferry to bring them across to their own parish. It surprised the parson a bit to find the ferry-boat lying ready by the shore and

*Euphemistic for 'smuggler's agent'.

my grandfather standing there head to head with old Arch'laus Spry, that was constable of Mawnan parish.

'Hallo, Calvin!' the parson sings out. 'This looks bad – Mawnan and Manaccan putting their heads together. I hope there's nothing gone wrong since I've been away?'

'Aw, Parson dear,' says my grandfather, 'I'm glad you've come – yea, glad sure 'nuff. We've a-been enjoying a terrible time!'

'Then something *has* gone wrong?' says the parson.

'As for that,' my grandfather answers, 'I only wish I could say yes or no: for 'twould be a relief even to know the worst.' He beckoned very mysterious-like and led the parson a couple of hundred yards up the foreshore, with Arch'laus Spry following. And there they came to a halt, all three, before a rock that someone had been daubing with whitewash. On the top of the cliff, right above, was planted a stick with a little white flag.

'Now, sir, as a Justice of the Peace, what d'ee think of it?'

Parson Polwhele stared from the rock to the stick and couldn't say. So he turns to Arch'laus Spry and asks: 'Any person taken ill in your parish?'

'No, sir.'

'You're sure Billy Johns hasn't been drinking again?' Billy Johns was the landlord of the 'Passage Inn', a very ordinary man by rule, but given to breaking loose among his own liquors. 'He seemed all right yesterday when I hired the trap off him; but he does the most unaccountable things when he's taken bad.'

'He never did anything so far out of nature as this here; and I can mind him in six outbreaks,' answered my grandfather. 'Besides, 'tis not Billy Johns nor anyone like him.'

'Then you know who did it?'

'I do and I don't, sir. But take a look round, if you please.'

The parson looked up and down and across the river; and, sure enough, whichever way he turned, his eyes fell on splashes of whitewash and little flags fluttering. They seemed to stretch right away from Porthnavas down to the river's mouth; and though he couldn't see it from where he stood, even Mawnan churchtower had been given a lick of the brush.

'But,' said the parson, fairly puzzled, 'all this can only have happened in broad daylight, and you must have caught the fellow at it, whoever he is.'

'I wouldn't go so far as to say I caught him,' answered my grandfather, modest-like; 'but I came upon him a little above Bosahan in the act of setting up one of his flags, and I asked him, in the King's name, what he meant by it.'

'And what did he answer?'

My grandfather looked over his shoulder. 'I couldn't, sir, not for a pocketful of crowns, and your good lady, so to speak, within hearing.'

'Nonsense, man! She's not within a hundred yards.'

'Well, then, sir, he up and hoped the devil would fly away with me, and from that he went on to say — ' But here my grandfather came to a dead halt. 'No, sir, I can't; and as a Minister of the Gospel, you'll never insist on it. He made such horrible statements that I had to go straight home and read over my old mother's marriage lines. It fairly dazed me to hear him talk so confident, and she in her grave, poor soul!'

'You ought to have demanded his name.'

'I did, sir; naturally I did. And he told me to go to the naughty place for it.'

'Well, but what like is he?'

'Oh, as to that, sir, a man of ordinary shape, like yourself, in a plain blue coat and a wig shorter than ordinary; nothing about him to prepare you for the language he lets fly.'

'And,' put in Arch'laus Spry, 'he's taken lodgings down to Durgan with the Widow Polkinghorne, and eaten his dinner — a fowl and a jug of cider with it. After dinner he hired Robin's boat and went for a row. I thought it my duty, as he was pushing off, to sidle up in a friendly way. I said to him "The weather, sir, looks nice and settled": that is what I said, neither more nor less, but using those very words. What d'ee think he answered? He said, "That's capital, my man: now go along and annoy somebody else." Wasn't that a disconnected way of talking? If you ask my opinion, putting two and two together, I say he'd most likely some poor wandering loonatic.'

The evening was dusking down by this time, and Parson

Polwhele, though a good bit puzzled, called to mind that his wife would be getting anxious to cross the ferry and reach home before dark: so he determined that nothing could be done before morning, when he promised Arch'laus Spry to look into the matter. My grandfather he took across in the boat with him, to look after the parcels and help them up to the Vicarage: and on the way they talked about a grave that my grandfather had been digging – he being sexton and parish clerk, as well as constable and the parson's right-hand man, as you might call it, in all public matters.

While they discoursed, Mrs Polwhele was taking a look about her to make sure the country hadn't altered while she was away at Plymouth. And by and by she cries out:

'Why, my love, whatever are these dabs o' white stuck up and down the foreshore?'

The parson takes a look at my grandfather before answering: 'My angel, to tell you the truth, that's more than we know.'

'Richard, you're concealing something from me,' said Mrs Polwhele. 'If the French have landed and I'm going home to be burnt in my bed, it shall be with my eyes open.'

'My dear Mary,' the parson argued, 'you've a-got the French on your brain. If the French landed they wouldn't begin by sticking dabs of whitewash all over the parish; now, would they?'

'How in the world should I know what a lot of Papists would do or not do?' she answered. ''Tis no more foolish to my mind than eating frogs or kissing a man's toe.'

Well, say what the parson would, the notion had fixed itself in the poor lady's head. Three times that night she woke in the bed with her curl-papers crackling for very fright; and the fourth time 'twas at the sound of a real dido below stairs. Some person was down by the back door knocking and rattling upon it with all his might.

The sun had been up for maybe an hour – the time of year, as I told you, being near about mid-summer – and the parson, that never wanted for pluck, jumped out and into his breeches in a twinkling, while his wife pulled the counterpane over her head. Down along the passage he skipped to a little window opening over the back porch.

'Who's there!' he called, and out from the porch stepped my grandfather, that had risen early and gone to the churchyard to finish digging the grave before breakfast. 'Why, what on the earth is wrong with ye? I made sure the French had landed, at the least.'

'Couldn't be much worse if they had,' said my grandfather. 'Some person 've a-stole my shovel, pick, and biddicks.'

'Nonsense!' said the parson.

'The corpse won't find it nonsense, sir, if I don't get 'em back in time. I left 'em lying, all three, at the bottom of the grave overnight.'

'And now they're missing?'

'Not a trace of 'em to be seen.'

'Someone has been playing you a practical joke, Calvin. Here, stop a moment – ' The parson ran back to his room, fetched a key, and flung it out into the yard. 'That'll unlock the tool-shed in the garden. Get what you want, and we'll talk about the theft after breakfast. How soon will the grave be ready?'

'I can't say sooner than ten o'clock after what has happened.'

'Say ten o'clock, then. This is Saturday, and I've my sermon to prepare after breakfast. At ten o'clock I'll join you in the churchyard.'

2

My grandfather went off to unlock the tool-shed, and the parson back to comfort Mrs Polwhele – which was no easy matter. 'There's something wrong with the parish since I've been away, and that you can't deny,' she declared. 'It don't feel like home any longer, and my poor flesh is shivering like a jelly, and my hand almost too hot to make the butter.' She kept up this lidden all through breakfast, and the meal was no sooner cleared away than she slipped on a shawl and stepped across to the churchyard to discuss the robbery.

The parson drew a chair to the window, lit his pipe, and

pulled out his pocket Bible to choose a text for his next day's sermon. But he couldn't fix his thoughts. Try how he would, they kept harking back to his travels in the post-chaise, and his wife's story, and those unaccountable flags and splashes of whitewash. His pipe went out, and he was getting up to find a light for it, when just at that moment the garden gate rattled, and, looking down the path towards the sound, his eyes fell on a square-cut, fierce-looking man in blue, standing there with a dirty bag in one hand and a sheaf of tools over his right shoulder.

The man caught sight of the parson at the window, and set down his tools inside the gate – shovel and pick and biddicks.

'Good-mornin'! I may come inside, I suppose?' says he, in a gruff tone of voice. He came up the path and the parson unlatched the window, which was one of the long sort reaching down to the ground.

'My name's Bligh,' said the visitor, gruff as before. 'You're the parson, eh? Bit of an antiquarian, I'm given to understand? These things ought to be in your line, then, and I hope they are not broken: I carried them as careful as I could.' He opened the bag and emptied it out upon the table – an old earthenware pot, a rusted iron ring, four or five burnt bones, and a handful or so of ashes. 'Human, you see,' said he, picking up one of the bones and holding it under the parson's nose. 'One of your ancient Romans, no doubt.'

'Ancient Romans? Ancient Romans?' stammered Parson Polwhele. 'Pray, sir, where did you get these – these articles?'

'By digging for them, sir; in a mound just outside that old Roman camp of yours.'

'Roman camp? There's no Roman camp within thirty miles of us as the crow flies: and I doubt if there's one within fifty!'

'Shows how much you know about it. That's what I complain about in you parsons: never glimpse a thing that's under your noses. Now, I come along, making no pretence to be an antiquarian, and the first thing I see out on your headland yonder, is a Roman camp, with a great mound beside it – '

'No such thing, sir!' the parson couldn't help interrupting.

Bligh stared at him for a moment, like a man hurt in his

feelings but keeping hold on his Christian compassion. 'Look here,' he said; 'you mayn't know it, but I'm a bad man to contradict. This here Roman camp, as I was sayin' – '

'If you mean Little Dinnis Camp, sir, 'tis as round as my hat.'

'Damme, if you interrupt again – '

'But I will. Here, in my own parlour, I tell you that Little Dinnis is as round as my hat!'

'All right; don't lose your temper, shouting out what I never denied. Round or square, it don't matter a ha'porth to me. This here round Roman camp – '

'But I tell you, once more, there's no such thing!' cried the parson, stamping his foot. 'The Romans never made a round camp in their lives. Little Dinnis is British; the encampment's British; the mound, as you call it, is a British barrow; and as for you – '

'As for me,' thunders Bligh, 'I'm British too, and don't you forget it. Confound you, sir! What the devil do I care for your pettifogging bones? I'm a British sailor, sir; I come to your God-forsaken parish on a Government job, and I happen on a whole shopful of ancient remains. In pure kindness – pure kindness, mark you – I interrupt my work to dig 'em up; and this is all the thanks I get!'

'Thanks!' fairly yelled the parson. 'You ought to be horse-whipped, rather, for disturbing an ancient tomb that's been the apple of my eye ever since I was inducted to this parish!' Then, as Bligh drew back, staring: 'My poor barrow!' he went on; 'my poor, ransacked barrow! But there may be something to save yet – ' and he fairly ran for the door, leaving Bligh at a standstill.

For a while the man stood there like a fellow in a trance, opening and shutting his mouth, with his eyes set on the doorway where the parson had disappeared. Then, his temper overmastering him, with a sweep of his arm, he sent the whole bag of tricks flying on to the floor, kicked them to right and left through the garden, slammed the gate, pitched across the road, and flung through the churchyard towards the river like a whirlwind.

Now, while this was happening, Mrs Polwhele had picked her way across the churchyard, and after chatting a bit with my grandfather over the theft of his tools, had stepped into the church to see that the place, and especially the table and communion-rails and the parsonage pew, was neat and dusted, this being her regular custom after a trip to Plymouth. And no sooner was she within the porch than who should come dandering along the road but Arch'laus Spry. The road, as you know, goes downhill after passing the parsonage gate, and holds on round the churchyard wall like a sunk way, the soil inside being piled up to the wall's coping. But, my grandfather being still behindhand with his job, his head and shoulders showed over the grave's edge. So Arch'laus Spry caught sight of him.

'Why, you're the very man I was looking for,' says Arch-'laus, stopping.

'Death halts for no man,' answers my grandfather, shovelling away.

'That furrin' fellow is somewhere in this neighbourhood at this very moment,' says Arch'laus, wagging his head. 'I saw his boat moored down by the Passage as I landed. And I've a-got something to report. He was up and off by three o'clock this morning, and knocked up the Widow Polkinghorne, trying to borrow a pick and shovel.'

'Pick and shovel!' My grandfather stopped working and slapped his thigh. 'Then he's the man that 've walked off with mine: and a biddicks too.'

'He said nothing of a biddicks, but he's quite capable of it.'

'Surely in the midst of life we are in death,' said my grandfather. 'I was al'ays inclined to believe that text, and now I'm sure of it. Let's go and see the parson.'

He tossed his shovel on to the loose earth above the grave and was just about to scramble out after it when the churchyard gate shook on its hinges, and across the path and by the church porch went Bligh, as I've said, like a whirlwind. Arch'laus Spry, that had pulled his chin up level with the coping, ducked at the sight of him, and even my grandfather ducked down a little in the grave as he passed.

'The very man!' said Spry, under his breath.

'The wicked flee, whom no man pursueth,' said my grand-father, looking after the man; but Bligh turned his head neither to the right hand nor to the left.

'Oh – oh – oh!' squealed a voice inside the church.

'Whatever was *that*,' cries Arch'laus Spry, giving a jump. They both stared at the porch.

'Oh – oh – oh!' squealed the voice again.

'It certainly comes from inside,' said Arch'laus Spry.

'It's Mrs Polwhele!' said my grandfather; 'and by the noise of it she's having hysterics.'

And with that he scrambled up and ran; and Spry heaved himself over the wall and followed. And there, in the south aisle, they found Mrs Polwhele lying back in a pew and kicking like a stallion in a loose-box.

My grandfather took her by the shoulders, while Spry ran for the jug of holy water that stood by the font. As it happened 'twas empty: but the sight of it fetched her to, and she raised herself up with a shiver.

'The Frenchman!' she cries out, pointing. 'The Frenchman – on the coach! O Lord, deliver us!'

For a moment, as you'll guess, my grandfather was puzzled: but he stared where the poor lady pointed, and after a bit he began to understand. I dare say you've seen our church, sir, and if so, you must have taken note of a monstrous fine fig-tree growing out of the south wall – 'the marvel of Manaccan', we used to call it. When they restored the church the other day nobody had the heart to destroy the tree, for all the damage it did to the building – having come there the Lord knows how, and grown there since the Lord knows when. So they took and patched up the wall around it, and there it thrives. But in the times I'm telling of, it had split the wall so that from inside you could look straight through the crack into the church-yard; and 'twas to this crack that Mrs Polwhele's finger pointed.

'Eh?' said my grandfather. 'The furriner* that went by just now, was it he that frightened ye, ma'am?'

Mrs Polwhele nodded.

* In Cornwall a 'foreigner' is anyone from east of the Tamar.

'But what put it into your head that he's a Frenchman?'

'Because French is his language. With these very ears I heard him talk it! He joined the coach at Torpoint, and when I spoke him fair in honest English not a word could he answer me. Oh, Calvin, Calvin! what have I done – a poor weak woman – to be mixed up in these plots and invasions?'

But my grandfather couldn't stop to answer that question, for a terrible light was breaking in upon him. 'A Frenchman?' he called out. 'And for these twenty-four hours he's been marking out the river and taking soundings!' He glared at Arch'laus Spry, and Arch'laus dropped the brazen ewer upon the pavement and smote his forehead. 'The Devil,' says he, 'is among us, having great wrath!'

'And for aught we know,' says my grandfather, speaking in a slow and fearsome whisper, 'the French ships may be hanging off the coast while we'm talking here!'

'You don't mean to tell us,' cried Mrs Polwhele, sitting up stiff in the pew, 'that this man has been mapping out the river under your very noses!'

'He has, ma'am. Oh, I see it all! What likelier place could they choose on the whole coast? And from here to Falmouth what is it but a step?'

'Let them that be in Judæa flee to the mountains,' said Arch'laus Spry solemn-like.

'And me just home from Plymouth with a fine new roasting-jack!' chimed in Mrs Polwhele. 'As though the day of wrath weren't bad enough without *that* waste o' money! Run, Calvin – run and tell the vicar this instant – no, no, don't leave me behind! Take me home, that's a good man: else I shall faint at my own shadow!'

Well, they hurried off to the Vicarage: but, of course, there was no parson to be found, for by this time he was half-way towards Little Dinnis, and running like a madman under the hot sun to see what damage had befallen his dearly-loved camp. The servants hadn't seen him leave the house; ne'er a word could they tell of him except that Martha, the cook, when she cleared away the breakfast things, had left him seated in his chair and smoking.

'But what's the meaning of this?' cried out Mrs Polwhele pointing to the tablecloth that Bligh had pulled all awry in his temper. 'And the window open too!'

'And – hallo!' says my grandfather, staring across the patch of turf outside. 'Surely here's signs of a violent struggle. Human, by the look of it,' says he, picking up a thigh-bone and holding it out towards Mrs Polwhele.

She began to shake like a leaf. 'Oh, Calvin!' she gasps out. 'Oh, Calvin, not in this short time – it couldn't be!'

'Charred, too,' says my grandfather, inspecting it: and with that they turned at a cry from Martha the cook, that was down on hands and knees upon the carpet.

'Ashes! See here, mistress – ashes all over your best carpet!'

The two women stared at the fireplace: but, of course, that told them nothing, being empty, as usual at the time of year, with only a few shavings stuck about it by way of ornament. Martha, the first to pick up her wits, dashed out into the front hall.

'Gone without his hat, too!' she fairly screamed, running her eye along the row of pegs.

Mrs Polwhele clasped her hands. 'In the midst of life we are in death,' said Arch'laus Spry: 'that's my opinion if you ask it.'

'Gone! Gone without his hat, like the snuff of a candle!' Mrs Polwhele dropped into a chair and rocked herself and moaned.

My grandfather banged his fist on the table. He never could abide the sight of a woman in trouble.

'Missus,' says he, 'if the parson's anywhere alive, we'll find 'en: and if that Frenchman be Old Nick himself, he shall rue the day he ever set foot in Manaccan parish! Come'st along, Arch'laus — '

He took Spry by the arm and marched him out and down the garden path. There, by the gate, what should his eyes light upon but his own stolen tools! But by this time all power of astonishment was dried up within him. He just raised his eyes aloft, as much as to say, 'Let the sky open and rain miracles!' and then and there he saw, coming down the road, the funeral that both he and the parson had clean forgotten.

The corpse was an old man called 'Pollas Hockaday; and Sam Trewhella, a fish-curer that had married Hockaday's eldest daughter, walked next behind the coffin as chief mourner. My grandfather waited by the gate for the procession to come by, and with Trewhella caught sight of him, and says he, taking down the handkerchief from his nose:

'Well, you're a pretty fellow, I must say! What in thunder d'ee mean by not tolling the minute-bell?'

'Take 'en back,' answers my grandfather, pointing to the coffin. 'Take 'en back, 'co!'

'Eh?' says Trewhella. 'Answer my question, I tell 'ee. You've hurt my feelings and the feelings of everyone connected with the deceased: and if this weren't not azackly the place for it, I'd up and give you a dashed good hiding,' says he.

'Aw, take 'en back,' my grandfather goes on. 'Take 'en back, my dears, and put 'en somewhere, cool and temporary! The grave's not digged, and the parson's kidnapped, and the French be upon us, and down by the river ther's a furrin spy taking soundings at this moment! In the name of King George,' said he, remembering that he was constable, 'I command you all except the females to come along and collar 'en!'

While this was going on, sir, Bligh had found his boat – which he'd left by the shore – and was pulling up the river to work off his rage. Ne'er a thought had he, as he flounced through the churchyard, of the train of powder he dribbled behind him: but all the way he blew off steam, cursing Parson Polwhele and the whole cloth from Land's End to Johnny Groats, and glowering at the very gates by the road as though he wanted to kick 'em to relieve his feelings. But when he reached his boat and began rowing, by little and little the exercise tamed him. With his flags and whitewash he'd marked out most of the lines he wanted for soundings: but there were two creeks he hadn't yet found time to explore – Porthnavas, on the opposite side, and the very creek by which we're sitting. So, as he came abreast of this one, he determined to have a look at it; and after rowing a hundred yards or so, lay on his oars, lit his pipe, and let his boat drift up with the tide.

The creek was just the same lonesome place that it is to-day, the only difference being that the pallace* at the entrance had a roof on it then, and was rented by Sam Trewhella – the same that followed old Hockaday's coffin, as I've told you. But above the pallace the woods grew close to the water's edge, and lined both shores with never a clearing till you reached the end, where the cottage stands now and the stream comes down beside it: in those days there wasn't any cottage, only a piece of swampy ground. I don't know that Bligh saw much in the scenery, but it may have helped to soothe his mind: for by and by he settled himself on the bottom-boards, lit another pipe, pulled his hat over his nose, and lay there blinking at the sky, while the boat drifted up, hitching sometimes in a bough and sometimes floating broadside-on to the current, until she reached this bit of marsh and took the mud very gently.

After a while, finding she didn't move, Bligh lifted his head for a look about him and found that he'd come to the end of the creek. He put out a hand and felt the water, that was almost luke-warm with running over the mud. The trees shut him in; not a living soul was in sight; and by the quietness he might have been a hundred miles from anywhere. So what does my gentleman do but strip himself for a comfortable bathe.

He folded his clothes very neatly in the stern-sheets, waded out across the shallows as naked as a babe, and took to the water with so much delight that after a minute or so he must needs lie on his back and kick. He splashed away, one leg after the other, with his face turned towards the shore, and was just on the point of rolling over for another swim, when, as he lifted a leg for one last kick, his eyes fell on the boat. And there on the top of his clothes, in the stern of her, sat my grandfather sucking a pipe.

Bligh let down his legs and stood up, touching bottom, but neck-deep in water.

'Hi, you there!' he sings out.

'Wee, wee, parleyvou!' my grandfather answers, making use of pretty well all the French he knew.

'Confound you, sir, for an impident dirty dog! What in the

* Fish-store.

name of jiminy' – I can't give you, sir, the exact words, for my grandfather could never be got to repeat 'em – 'What in the name of jiminy d'ee mean by sitting on my clothes?'

'Wee, wee,' my grandfather took him up, calm as you please. 'You shocked me dreadful yesterday with your blasphemious talk: but now, seeing 'tis French, I don't mind so much. Take your time: but when you come out you go to prison. Wee, wee – preeson,' says my grandfather.

'Are you drunk?' yells Bligh. 'Get off my clothes this instant, you hobnailed son of a something-or-other!' And he began striding for shore.

'In the name of His Majesty King George the Third I charge you to come along quiet,' says my grandfather, picking up a stretcher.

Bligh, being naked and unarmed, casts a look round for some way to help himself. He was a plucky fellow enough in a fight, as I've said: but I leave you to guess what he felt like when to right and left of him the bushes parted, and forth stepped half a dozen men in black suits with black silk weepers a foot and a half wide tied in great bunches round their hats. These were Sam Trewhella, of course, and the rest of the funeral-party, that had left the coffin in a nice shady spot inside the Vicarage garden gate, and come along to assist the law. They had brought along pretty nearly all the menkind of the parish beside: but these, being in their work-a-day clothes, didn't appear, and for a reason you'll learn by and by. All that Bligh saw was this dismal company of mourners backed by a rabble of school-children, the little ones lining the shore and staring at him fearsomely with their fingers in their mouths.

For the moment Bligh must have thought himself dreaming. But there they stood, the men in black and the crowd of children, and my grandfather with the stretcher ready, and the green woods so quiet all round. And there he stood up to the ribs in water, and the tide and his temper rising.

'Look here, you something-or-other yokels,' he called out, 'if this is one of your village jokes, I promise you shall smart for it. Leave the spot this moment, fetch that idiot out of the boat, and take away the children. I want to dress, and it isn't decent!'

'Mounseer,' answers my grandfather, 'I dare say you've a-done it for your country; but we've a-caught you, and now you must go to prison – wee, wee, to preeson,' he says, lisping it in a Frenchified way so as to make himself understood.

Bligh began to foam. 'The longer you keep up this farce, my fine fellows, the worse you'll smart for it! There's a magistrate in this parish, as I happen to know.'

'There *was*,' said my grandfather; 'but we've strong reasons to believe he's been made away with.'

'The only thing we could find of 'en,' put in Arch'laus Spry, 'was a shin-bone and a pint of ashes. I don't know if the others noticed it, but to my notion there was a sniff of brimstone about the premises; and I've always been remarkable for my sense of smell.'

'You won't deny,' my grandfather went on, 'that you've been making a map of this here river; for here it is in your tailcoat pocket.'

'You insolent ruffian, put that down at once! I tell you that I'm a British officer and a gentleman!'

'*And* a Papist,' went on my grandfather, holding up a ribbon with a bullet threaded to it. ('Twas the bullet Bligh used to weigh out allowances with on his voyage in the open boat after the mutineers had turned him adrift from the *Bounty*, and he wore it ever after.) 'See here, friends: did you ever know an honest Protestant to wear such a thing about him inside his clothes?'

'Whether you're a joker or a numskull is more than I can fathom,' says Bligh; 'but for the last time I warn you I'm a British officer, and you'll go to jail for this as sure as eggs.'

'The question is, will you surrender and come along quiet?'

'No, I won't,' says Bligh, sulky as a bear; 'not if I stay here all night!'

With that my grandfather gave a wink to Sam Trewhella, and Sam Trewhella gave a whistle, and round the point came Trewhella's sean-boat that the village lads had fetched out and launched from his store at the mouth of the creek. Four men pulled her with all their might; in the stern stood Trewhella's foreman, Jim Bunt, with his two-hundred-fathom net: and along the shore came running the rest of the lads to see the fun.

'Heva, heva!' yelled Sam Trewhella, waving his hat with the black streamers.

The sean-boat swooped up to Bligh with a rush, and then, just as he faced upon it with his fists up, to die fighting, it swerved off on a curve round him, and Jim Bunt began shooting the sean hand over hand like lightning. Then the poor man understood, and having no mind to be rolled up and afterwards tucked in a sean-net, he let out an oath, ducked his head, and broke for the shore like a bull. But 'twas no manner of use. As soon as he touched land a dozen jumped for him and pulled him down. They handled him as gentle as they could, for he fought with fists, legs, and teeth, and his language was awful: but my grandfather in his foresight had brought along a couple of wainropes, and within ten minutes they had my gentleman trussed, heaved him into the boat, covered him over, and were rowing him off and down the creek to land him at Helford Quay.

By this 'twas past noon; and at one o'clock, or a little before, Parson Polwhele come striding along home from Little Dinnis. He had tied a handkerchief about his head to keep off the sun; his hands and knees were coated with earth; and he sweated like a furze-bush in a mist, for the footpath led through cornfields and the heat was something terrible. Moreover, he had just called the funeral to mind; and this and the damage he'd left at Little Dinnis fairly hurried him into a fever.

But worse was in store. As he drew near the Parsonage, he spied a man running towards him: and behind the man the most dreadful noises were sounding from the house. The parson came to a halt and swayed where he stood.

'Oh, Calvin! Calvin!' he cried – for the man running was my grandfather – 'don't try to break it gently, but let me know the worst!'

'Oh, blessed day! Oh, fearful and yet blessed day!' cries my grandfather, almost catching him in both arms. 'So you're not dead! So you're not dead, the Lord be praised, but only hurt!'

'Hurt?' says the parson. 'Not a bit of it – or only in my feelings. Oh, 'tis the handkerchief you're looking at? I put that up against sunstroke. But whatever do these dreadful sounds mean? Tell me the worst, Calvin, I implore you!'

'Oh, as for that,' says my grandfather cheerfully, 'the Frenchman's the worst by a long way – not but what your good lady made noise enough when she thought you'd been made away with: and afterwards, when she went upstairs and, taking a glance out of window, spied a long black coffin laid out under the lilac bushes, I'm told you could hear her a mile away. But she've been weakening this half-hour: her nature couldn't keep it up: whereas the longer we keep that Frenchman, the louder he seems to bellow.'

'Heaven defend us, Calvin!' – the parson's eyes fairly rolled in his head – 'are you gone clean crazed? Frenchman! What Frenchman?'

'The same that frightened Mrs Polwhele, sir, upon the coach. We caught him drawing maps of the river, and very nigh tucked him in Sam Trewhella's sean: and now he's in your tool-shed right and tight, and here's the key, sir, making so bold, that you gave me this morning. But I didn't like to take him into the house, with your good lady tumbling out of one fit into another. Hark to 'en, now! Would you ever believe one man could make such a noise?'

'Fits! My poor, dear, tender Mary having fits!' The parson broke away for the house and dashed upstairs three steps at a time: and when she caught sight of him, Mrs Polwhele let out a louder squeal than ever. But the next moment she was hanging round his neck, and laughing and sobbing by turns. And how long they'd have clung to one another there's no knowing, if it hadn't been for the language pouring from the tool-shed.

'My dear,' said the parson, holding himself up and listening, 'I don't think that can possibly be a Frenchman. He's too fluent.'

Mrs Polwhele listened too, but after a while she was forced to cover her face with both hands. 'Oh, Richard, I've often heard 'en described as gay, but – but they can't surely be so gay as all that!'

The parson eased her into an armchair and went downstairs to the courtyard, and there, as you may suppose, he found the parish gathered.

'Stand back all of you,' he ordered. 'I've a notion that some mistake has been committed: but you had best hold yourselves ready in case the prisoner tries to escape.'

'But Parson dear, you're never going to unlock that door!' cried my grandfather.

'If you'll stand by me, Calvin,' says the parson, plucky as ginger, and up he steps to the very door, all the parish holding its breath.

He tapped once – no answer: twice – and no more answer than before. There was a small trap open in the roof and through this the language kept pouring with never a stop, only now and then a roar like a bull's. But at the third knock it died down to a sort of rumbling, and presently came a shout, 'Who's there?'

'A clergyman and justice of the peace,' answers the parson.

'I'll have your skin for this!'

'But you'll excuse me – '

'I'll have your skin for this, and your blood in a bottle! I'm a British officer and a gentleman, and I'll have you stuffed and put in a glass case, as sure as my name's Bligh!'

'Bligh?' says the parson, opening the door. 'Any relation to the Blighs of St Tudy? Oh, no it can't be!' he stammered, taken all aback to see the man stark naked on the threshold. 'Why – why, you're the gentleman that called this morning!' he went on, the light breaking in upon him: 'excuse me, I recognize you by – by the slight scar on your face.'

Well, sir, there was nothing for Bligh to do – the whole parish staring at him – but to slip back into the shed and put on the clothes my grandfather handed in at the door: and while he was dressing the whole truth came out. I won't say that he took the parson's explanations in a nice spirit: for he vowed to have the law on everyone concerned. But that night he walked back to Falmouth and took the London coach. As for Helford River, 'twasn't charted that year nor for a score of years after. And now you know how this creek came by its name; and I'll say again, as I began, that a bad temper is an affliction, whoever owns it.

THE LAIRD'S LUCK

[In a General Order issued from the Horse-Guards on New Year's Day, 1836, His Majesty King William IV was pleased to direct, through the Commander-in-Chief, Lord Hill, that 'with the view of doing the fullest justice to Regiments, as well as to Individuals who had distinguished themselves in action against the enemy', an account of the services of every Regiment in the British Army should be published, under the supervision of the Adjutant-General.

With fair promptitude this scheme was put in hand, under the editorship of Mr Richard Cannon, Principal Clerk of the Adjutant-General's Office. The duty of examining, sifting, and preparing the records of that distinguished Regiment which I shall here call the Moray Highlanders (concealing its real name for reasons which the narrative will make apparent) fell to a certain Major Reginald Sparkes; who in the course of his researches came upon a number of pages in manuscript sealed under one cover and docketed 'Memoranda concerning Ensign D. M. J. Mackenzie. J. R., 3rd Jan., 1816' – the initials being those of Lieut.-Colonel Sir James Ross, who had commanded the 2nd Battalion of the Morays through the campaign of Waterloo. The cover also bore, in the same handwriting, the word 'Private', twice underlined.

Of the occurrences related in the enclosed papers – of the private ones, that is – it so happened that of the four eye-witnesses none survived at the date of Major Sparkes' discovery. They had, moreover, so carefully taken their secret with them that the Regiment preserved not a rumour of it. Major Sparkes' own commission was considerably more recent than the Waterloo year, and he at least had heard no whisper of the story. It lay outside the purpose of his inquiry, and he judiciously omitted it from his report. But the time is past when its publication might conceivably have been injurious; and with some alterations in the names – to carry out the disguise of the Regiment – it is here given. The reader will understand that I use the *ipsissima verba* of Colonel Ross. – Q.]

I

I HAD the honour of commanding my Regiment, the Moray Highlanders, on the 16th of June 1815, when the late Ensign

David Marie Joseph Mackenzie met his end in the bloody struggle of Quatre Bras (his first engagement). He fell beside the colours, and I gladly bear witness that he had not only borne himself with extreme gallantry, but maintained, under circumstances of severest trial, a coolness which might well have rewarded me for my help in procuring the lad's commission. And yet at the moment I could scarcely regret his death, for he went into action under a suspicion so dishonouring that, had it been proved, no amount of gallantry could have restored him to the respect of his fellows. So at least I believed, with three of his brother officers who shared the secret. These were Major William Ross (my half-brother), Captain Malcolm Murray, and Mr Ronald Braintree Urquhart, then our senior ensign. Of these, Mr Urquhart fell two days later, at Waterloo, while steadying his men to face that heroic shock in which Pack's skeleton regiments were enveloped yet not overwhelmed by four brigades of the French infantry. From the others I received at the time a promise that the accusation against young Mackenzie should be wiped off the slate by his death, and the affair kept secret between us. Since then, however, there has come to me an explanation which – though hard indeed to credit – may, if true, exculpate the lad. I laid it before the others, and they agreed that if, in spite of precautions, the affair should ever come to light, the explanation ought also in justice to be forthcoming; and hence I am writing this memorandum.

It was in the late September of 1814 that I first made acquaintance with David Mackenzie. A wound received in the battle of Salamanca – a shattered ankle – had sent me home invalided, and on my partial recovery I was appointed to command the 2nd Battalion of my Regiment, then being formed at Inverness. To this duty I was equal; but my ankle still gave trouble (the splinters from time to time working through the flesh), and in the late summer of 1814 I obtained leave of absence with my step-brother, and spent some pleasant weeks in cruising and fishing about the Moray Firth. Finding that my leg bettered by this idleness, we hired a smaller boat and embarked on a longer excursion, which took us almost to the south-western end of Loch Ness.

Here, on 18th September, and pretty late in the afternoon, we were overtaken by a sudden squall, which carried away our mast (we found afterwards that it had rotted in the step), and put us for some minutes in no little danger; for my brother and I, being inexpert seamen, did not cut the tangle away, as we should have done, but made a bungling attempt to get the mast on board, with the rigging and drenched sail; and thereby managed to knock a hole in the side of the boat, which at once began to take in water. This compelled us to desist and fall to baling with might and main, leaving the raffle and jagged end of the mast to bump against us at the will of the waves. In short, we were in a highly unpleasant predicament, when a coble or row-boat, carrying one small lug-sail, hove out of the dusk to our assistance. It was manned by a crew of three, of whom the master (though we had scarce light enough to distinguish features) hailed us in a voice which was patently a gentleman's. He rounded up, lowered sail, and ran his boat alongside; and while his two hands were cutting us free of our tangle, inquired very civilly if we were strangers. We answered that we were, and desired him to tell us of the nearest place alongshore where we might land and find a lodging for the night, as well as a carpenter to repair our damage.

'In any ordinary case,' said he, 'I should ask you to come aboard and home with me. But my house lies five miles up the lake; your boat is sinking, and the first thing is to beach her. It happens that you are but half a mile from Ardlaugh and a decent carpenter who can answer all requirements. I think, if I stand by you, the thing can be done; and afterwards we will talk of supper.'

By diligent baling we were able, under his direction, to bring our boat to a shingly beach, over which a light shone warm in a cottage window. Our hail was quickly answered by a second light. A lantern issued from the building, and we heard the sound of footsteps.

'Is that you, Donald?' cried our rescuer (as I may be permitted to call him).

Before an answer could be returned, we saw that two men were approaching; of whom the one bearing the lantern was a grizzled old carlin with bent knees and a stoop of the shoulders. His companion carried himself with a lighter step. It was he who advanced to salute us, the old man holding the light obediently; and the rays revealed to us a slight, up-standing youth, poorly dressed, but handsome, and with a touch of pride in his bearing.

'Good evening, gentlemen.' He lifted his bonnet politely, and turned to our rescuer. 'Good evening, Mr Gillespie,' he said – I thought more coldly. 'Can I be of any service to your friends?'

Mr Gillespie's manner had changed suddenly at sight of the young man, whose salutation he acknowledged more coldly and even more curtly than it had been given. 'I can scarcely claim them as my friends,' he answered. 'They are two gentlemen, strangers in these parts, who have met with an accident to their boat: one so serious that I brought them to the nearest landing, which happened to be Donald's.' He shortly explained our mishap, while the young man took the lantern in hand and inspected the damage with Donald.

'There is nothing,' he announced, 'which cannot be set right in a couple of hours; but we must wait till morning. Meanwhile if, as I gather, you have no claim on these gentlemen, I shall beg them to be my guests for the night.'

We glanced at Mr Gillespie, whose manners seemed to have deserted him. He shrugged his shoulders. 'Your house is the nearer,' said he, 'and the sooner they reach a warm fire the better for them after their drenching.' And with that he lifted his cap to us, turned abruptly, and pushed off his own boat, scarcely regarding our thanks.

A somewhat awkward pause followed as we stood on the beach, listening to the creak of the thole-pins in the departing boat. After a minute our new acquaintance turned to us with a slightly constrained laugh.

'Mr Gillespie omitted some of the formalities,' said he. 'My name is Mackenzie – David Mackenzie; and I live at Ardlaugh Castle, scarcely half a mile up the glen behind us. I warn you that its hospitality is rude, but to what it affords you are heartily welcome.'

He spoke with a high, precise courtliness which contrasted oddly with his boyish face (I guessed his age at nineteen or twenty), and still more oddly with his clothes, which were threadbare and patched in many places, yet with a deftness which told of a woman's care. We introduced ourselves by name, and thanked him, with some expressions of regret at inconveniencing (as I put it, at hazard) the family at the Castle.

'Oh!' he interrupted, 'I am sole master there. I have no parents living, no family, and,' he added, with a slight sullenness which I afterwards recognized as habitual, 'I may almost say, no friends: though to be sure, you are lucky enough to have one fellow-guest to-night – the minister of the parish, a Mr Saul, and a very worthy man.'

He broke off to give Donald some instructions about the boat, watched us while we found our plaids and soaked valises, and then took the lantern from the old man's hand. 'I ought to have explained,' said he, 'that we have neither cart here nor carriage: indeed, there is no carriage-road. But Donald has a pony.'

He led the way a few steps up the beach, and then halted, perceiving my lameness for the first time. 'Donald, fetch out the sheltie. Can you ride bareback?' he asked: 'I fear there's no saddle but an old piece of sacking.' In spite of my protestations the pony was led forth; a starved little beast, on whose oversharp ridge I must have cut a sufficiently ludicrous figure when hoisted into place with the valises slung behind me.

The procession set out, and I soon began to feel thankful for my seat, though I took no ease in it. For the road climbed steeply from the cottage, and at once began to twist up the bottom of a ravine so narrow that we lost all help of the young moon. The path, indeed, resembled the bed of a torrent, shrunk now to a trickle of water, the voice of which ran in my ears while our host led the way, springing from boulder to boulder, avoiding pools, and pausing now and then to hold his lantern over some slippery place. The pony followed with admirable caution, and my brother trudged in the rear and took his cue from us. After five minutes of this the ground grew easier and at the same time steeper, and I guessed that we were slanting up the hillside and away from the torrent at an acute angle. The many twists and angles, and the utter darkness (for we were now moving between trees) had completely baffled my reckoning when – at the end of twenty minutes, perhaps – Mr Mackenzie halted and allowed me to come up with him.

I was about to ask the reason of this halt when a ray of his lantern fell on a wall of masonry; and with a start almost laughable I knew we had arrived. To come to an entirely strange house at night is an experience which holds some taste of mystery even for the oldest campaigner; but I have never in my life received such a shock as this building gave me – naked, unlit, presented to me out of a darkness in which I had imagined a steep mountain scaur dotted with dwarfed trees – a sudden abomination of desolation standing, like the prophet's, where it ought not. No light showed on the side where we stood – the side over the ravine; only one pointed turret stood out against the faint moonlight glow in the upper sky: but feeling our way around the gaunt side of the building, we came to a back court-yard and two windows lit. Our host whistled, and helped me to dismount.

In an angle of the court a creaking door opened. A woman's voice cried: 'That will be you, Ardlaugh, and none too early! The minister – '

She broke off, catching sight of us. Our host stepped hastily to the door and began a whispered conversation. We could hear that she was protesting, and began to feel awkward enough. But whatever her objections were, her master cut them short.

'Come in, sirs,' he invited us: 'I warned you that the fare would be hard, but I repeat that you are welcome.'

To our surprise and, I must own, our amusement, the woman caught up his words with new protestations, uttered this time at the top of her voice.

The fare hard? Well, it might not please folks accustomed to city feasts; but Ardlaugh was not yet without a joint of venison in the larder and a bottle of wine, maybe two, maybe three, for any guest its master chose to make welcome. It was 'an ill bird that 'filed his own nest' – with more to this effect, which our host tried in vain to interrupt.

'Then I will lead you to your rooms,' he said, turning to us as soon as she paused to draw breath.

'Indeed, Ardlaugh, you will do nothing of the kind.' She ran into the kitchen, and returned holding high a lighted torch – a grey-haired woman, with traces of past comeliness, overlaid now by an air of worry, almost of fear. But her manner showed only a defiant pride as she led us up the uncarpeted stairs, past old portraits sagging and rotting in their frames, through bleak corridors, where the windows were patched and the plastered walls discoloured by fungus. Once only she halted. 'It will be a long way to your ap-partments. A grand house!' She had faced round on us, and her eyes seemed to ask a question of ours. 'I have known it filled,' she added – 'filled with guests, and the drink and fiddles never stopping for a week. You will see it better to-morrow. A grand house!'

I will confess that, as I limped after this barbaric woman and her torch, I felt some reasonable apprehensions of the bed-chamber towards which they were escorting me. But here came another surprise. The room was of moderate size, poorly furnished indeed, but comfortable and something more. It bore traces of many petty attentions, even– in its white dimity curtains and valances – of an attempt at daintiness. The sight of it brought quite a pleasant shock after the dirt and disarray of the corridor. Nor was the room assigned to my brother one whit less habitable. But if surprised by all this, I was fairly astounded to find in each room a pair of candles lit – and quite recently lit – beside the looking-glass, and an ewer of hot water standing, with a clean towel upon it, in each washhand basin. No sooner had the woman departed than I visited my brother and begged him (while he unstrapped his valise) to explain this apparent miracle. He could only guess with me that the woman had been warned of our arrival by the noise of footsteps in the courtyard, and had dispatched a servant by some back stairs to make ready for us.

Our valises were, fortunately, waterproof. We quickly

exchanged our damp clothes for dry ones, and groped our way together along the corridors, helped by the moon which shone through their uncurtained windows, to the main staircase. Here we came on a scent of roasting meat – appetizing to us after our day in the open air – and at the foot found our host waiting for us. He had donned his Highland dress of ceremony – velvet jacket, filibeg and kilt, with the tartan of his clan – and looked (I must own) extremely well in it, though the garments had long since lost their original gloss. An apology for our rough touring suits led to some few questions and replies about the regimental tartan of the Morays, in the history of which he was passably well informed.

Thus chatting, we entered the great hall of Ardlaugh Castle – a tall but narrow and ill-proportioned apartment, having an open timber roof, a stone-paved floor, and walls sparsely decorated with antlers and round targes – where a very small man stood warming his back at an immense fireplace. This was the Reverend Samuel Saul, whose acquaintance we had scarce time to make before a cracked gong summoned us to dinner in the adjoining room.

The young Laird of Ardlaugh took his seat in a roughly carved chair of state at the head of the table; but before doing so treated me to another surprise by muttering a Latin grace and crossing himself. Up to now I had taken it for granted he was a member of the Scottish Kirk. I glanced at the minister in some mystification; but he, good man, appeared to have fallen into a brown study, with his eyes fastened upon a dish of apples which adorned the centre of our promiscuously furnished board.

Of the furniture of our meal I can only say that poverty and decent appearance kept up a brave fight throughout. The table-cloth was ragged, but spotlessly clean; the silver-ware scanty and worn with high polishing. The plates and glasses displayed a noble range of patterns, but were for the most part chipped or cracked. Each knife had been worn to a point, and a few of them joggled in their handles. In a lull of the talk I caught myself idly counting the darns in my table-napkin. They were – if I remember – fourteen, and all exquisitely stitched. The dinner, on the other hand, would have tempted men far less hungry than we – grilled steaks of salmon, a roast haunch of venison, grouse, a milk-pudding, and, for dessert, the dish of apples already mentioned; the meats washed down with one wine only, but that wine was claret, and beautifully sound. I should mention that we were served by a grey-haired retainer, almost stone deaf, and as hopelessly cracked as the gong with which he had beaten us to dinner. In the long waits between the courses we heard him quarrelling outside with the woman who had admitted us; and gradually – I know not how – the conviction grew on me that they were man and wife, and the only servants of our host's establishment. To cover the noise of one of their altercations I began to congratulate the Laird on the quality of his venison, and put some idle question about his care for his deer.

'I have no deer-forest,' he answered. 'Elspeth is my only housekeeper.'

I had some reply on my lips, when my attention was distracted by a sudden movement by the Rev. Samuel Saul. This honest man had, as we shook hands in the great hall, broken into a flood of small talk. On our way to the dining-room he took me, so to speak, by the button-hole, and within the minute so drenched me with gossip about Ardlaugh, its climate, its scenery, its crops, and the dimensions of the parish, that I feared a whole evening of boredom lay before us. But from the moment we seated ourselves at table he dropped to an absolute silence. There are men, living much alone, who by habit talk little during their meals; and the minister might be reserving himself. But I had almost forgotten his presence when I heard a sharp exclamation, and, looking across, saw him take from his lips a wineglass of claret and set it down with a shaking hand. The Laird, too, had heard, and bent a darkly questioning glance on him. At once the little man – whose face had turned to a sickly white – began to stammer and excuse himself.

It was nothing – a spasm. He would be better of it in a moment. No, he would take no wine: a glass of water would set him right – he was more used to drinking water, he explained, with a small, nervous laugh.

Perceiving that our solicitude embarrassed him, we resumed our talk, which now turned upon the last Peninsular campaign and certain engagements in which the Morays had borne part; upon the stability of the French Monarchy, and the career (as we believed, at an end) of Napoleon. On all these topics the Laird showed himself well informed, and while preferring the part of listener (as became his youth), from time to time put in a question which convinced me of his intelligence, especially in military affairs.

The minister, though silent as before, had regained his colour; and we were somewhat astonished when, the cloth being drawn and the company left to its wine and one dish of dessert, he rose and announced that he must be going. He was decidedly better, but (so he excused himself) would feel easier at home in his own manse; and so, declining our host's offer of a bed, he shook hands and bade us good night. The Laird accompanied him to the door, and in his absence I fell to peeling an apple, while my brother drummed with his fingers on the table and eyed the faded hangings. I suppose that ten minutes elapsed before we heard the young man's footsteps returning through the flagged hall and a woman's voice uplifted.

But had the minister any complaint, whatever – to ride off without a word? She could answer for the collops –

'Whist, woman! Have done with your clashin', ye doited old fool!' He slammed the door upon her, stepped to the table, and with a sullen frown poured himself a glass of wine. His brow cleared as he drank it. 'I beg your pardon, gentlemen; but this indisposition of Mr Saul has annoyed me. He lives at the far end of the parish – a good seven miles away – and I had invited him expressly to talk of parish affairs.'

'I believe,' said I, 'you and he are not of the same religion?'

'Eh?' He seemed to be wondering how I had guessed. 'No, I was bred a Catholic. In our branch we have always held to the Old Profession. But that doesn't prevent my wishing to stand well with my neighbours and do my duty towards them. What disheartens me is, they won't see it.' He pushed the wine aside, and for a while, leaning his elbows on the table and resting his chin on his knuckles, stared gloomily before him. Then, with sudden boyish indignation, he burst out: 'It's an infernal shame; that's it – an infernal shame! I haven't been home here a twelve-month, and the people avoid me like the plague. What have I done? My father wasn't popular – in fact, they hated him. But so did I. And he hated me, God knows: misused my mother, and wouldn't endure me in his presence. All my miserable youth I've been mewed up in a school in England – a private seminary. Ugh, what a den it was, too! My mother died calling for me – I was not allowed to come: I hadn't seen her for three years. And now, when the old tyrant is dead, and I come home meaning – so help me! – to straighten things out and make friends – come home, to the poverty you pretend not to notice, though it stares you in the face from every wall – come home, only asking to make the best of it, live on good terms with my fellows, and be happy for the first time in my life – damn them, they won't fling me a kind look! What have I *done*? – that's what I want to know. The queer thing is they behaved more decently at first. There's that Gillespie, who brought you ashore: he came over the first week, offered me shooting, was altogether as pleasant as could be. I quite took to the fellow. Now, when we meet, he looks the other way! If he has anything against me, he might at least explain: it's all I ask. What have I done?'

Throughout this outburst I sat slicing my apple and taking now and then a glance at the speaker. It was all so hotly and honestly boyish! He only wanted justice. I know something of youngsters, and recognized the cry. Justice! It's the one thing every boy claims confidently as his right, and probably the last thing on earth he will ever get. And this boy looked so handsome, too, sitting in his father's chair, petulant, restive under a weight too heavy (as any one could see) for his age. I couldn't help liking him.

My brother told me afterwards that I pounced like any recruiting-sergeant. This I do not believe. But what, after a long pause, I said was this: 'If you are innocent or unconscious of offending, you can only wait for your neighbours to explain themselves. Meanwhile, why not leave them? Why not travel, for instance?'

'Travel!' he echoed, as much as to say, 'You ought to know, without my telling, that I cannot afford it.'

'Travel,' I repeated; 'see the world, rub against men of your age. You might by the way do some fighting.'

He opened his eyes wide. I saw the sudden idea take hold of him, and again I liked what I saw.

'If I thought – ' He broke off. 'You don't mean – ' he began, and broke off again.

'I mean the Morays,' I said. 'There may be difficulties; but at this moment I cannot see any real ones.'

By this time he was gripping the arms of his chair. 'If I thought – ' he harked back, and for the third time broke off. 'What a fool I am! It's the last thing they ever put in a boy's head at that infernal school. If you will believe it, they wanted to make a priest of me!'

He sprang up, pushing back his chair. We carried our wine into the great hall, and sat there talking the question over before the fire. Before we parted for the night I had engaged to use all my interest to get him a commission in the Morays; and I left him pacing the hall, his mind in a whirl, but his heart (as was plain to see) exulting in his new prospects.

And certainly, when I came to inspect the castle by the next morning's light, I could understand his longing to leave it. A gloomier, more pretentious, or worse-devised structure I never set eyes on. The Mackenzie who erected it may well have been (as the saying is) his own architect, and had either come to the end of his purse or left his heirs to decide against planting gardens, laying out approaches, or even maintaining the pile in decent repair. In place of a drive a grassy cart-track, scored deep with old ruts, led through a gateless entrance into a courtyard where the slates had dropped from the roof and lay strewn like autumn leaves. On this road I encountered the young Laird returning from an early tramp with his gun; and he stood still and pointed to the castle with a grimace.

'A white elephant,' said I.

'Call it rather the corpse of one,' he answered. 'Cannot you imagine some *genie* of the Oriental Tales dragging the beast across Europe and dumping it down here in a sudden fit of disgust? As a matter of fact my grandfather built it, and cursed us with poverty thereby. It soured my father's life. I believe the only soul honestly proud of it is Elspeth.'

'And I suppose,' said I, 'you will leave her in charge of it when you join the Morays?'

'Ah!' he broke in, with a voice which betrayed his relief: 'you are in earnest about that? Yes, Elspeth will look after the castle, as she does already. I am just a child in her hands. When a man has only one servant it's well to have her devoted.' Seeing my look of surprise, he added, 'I don't count old Duncan, her husband; for he's half-witted, and only serves to break the plates. Does it surprise you to learn that, barring him, Elspeth is my only retainer.'

'H'm,' said I, considerably puzzled – I must explain why.

I am by training an extraordinarily light sleeper; yet nothing had disturbed me during the night until at dawn my brother knocked at the door and entered, ready dressed.

'Hallo!' he exclaimed, 'are you responsible for this?' and he pointed to a chair at the foot of the bed where lay, folded in a neat pile, not only the clothes I had tossed down carelessly overnight, but the suit in which I had arrived. He picked up this latter, felt it, and handed it to me. It was dry, and had been carefully brushed.

'Our friend keeps a good valet,' said I; 'but the queer thing is that, in a strange room, I didn't wake. I see he has brought hot water too.'

'Look here,' my brother asked: 'did you lock your door?'

'Why, of course not – the more by token that it hasn't a key.'

'Well,' said he, 'mine has, and I'll swear I used it; but the same thing has happened to me!'

This, I tried to persuade him, was impossible; and for the while he seemed convinced. 'It *must* be,' he owned; 'but if I didn't lock that door I'll never swear to a thing again in all my life.'

The young Laird's remark set me thinking of this, and I

answered after a pause: 'In one of the pair, then, you possess a remarkably clever valet.'

It so happened that, while I said it, my eyes rested, without the least intention, on the sleeve of his shooting-coat; and the words were scarcely out before he flushed hotly and made a motion as if to hide a neatly mended rent in its cuff. In another moment he would have retorted, and was indeed drawing himself up in anger, when I prevented him by adding:

'I mean that I am indebted to him or to her this morning for a neatly brushed suit; and I suppose to your freeness in plying me with wine last night that it arrived in my room without waking me. But for that I could almost set it down to the supernatural.'

I said this in all simplicity, and was quite unprepared for its effect upon him, or for his extraordinary reply. He turned as white in the face as, a moment before, he had been red. 'Good God!' he said eagerly, 'you haven't missed anything, have you?'

'Certainly not,' I assured him. 'My dear sir – '

'I know, I know. But you see,' he stammered, 'I am new to these servants. I know them to be faithful, and that's all. Forgive me; I feared from your tone one of them – Duncan perhaps . . .'

He did not finish his sentence, but broke into a hurried walk and led me towards the house. A minute later, as we approached it, he began to discourse half-humorously on its more glaring features, and had apparently forgotten his perturbation.

I too attached small importance to it, and recall it now merely through unwillingness to omit any circumstance which may throw light on a story sufficiently dark to me. After breakfast our host walked down with us to the loch-side, where we found old Donald putting the last touches on his job. With thanks for our entertainment we shook hands and pushed off: and my last word at parting was a promise to remember his ambition and write any news of my success.

2

I anticipated no difficulty, and encountered none. The *Gazette* of January, 1815, announced that David Marie Joseph Mackenzie, gentleman, had been appointed to an ensigncy in the —th Regiment of Infantry (Moray Highlanders); and I timed my letter of congratulation to reach him with the news. Within a week he had joined us at Inverness, and was made welcome.

I may say at once that during his brief period of service I could find no possible fault with his bearing as a soldier. From the first he took seriously to the calling of arms, and not only showed himself punctual on parade and in all the small duties of barracks, but displayed, in his reserved way, a zealous resolve to master whatever by book or conversation could be learned of the higher business of war. My junior officers – though when the test came, as it soon did, they acquitted themselves most creditably – showed, as a whole, just then no great promise. For the most part they were young lairds, like Mr Mackenzie, or cadets of good Highland families; but, unlike him, they had been allowed to run wild, and chafed under harness. One or two of them had the true Highland addiction to card-playing; and though I set a pretty stern face against this curse – as I dare to call it – its effects were to be traced in late hours, more than one case of shirking 'rounds', and a general slovenliness at morning parade.

In such company Mr Mackenzie showed to advantage, and I soon began to value him as a likely officer. Nor, in my dissatisfaction with them, did it give me any uneasiness – as it gave me no suprise – to find that his brother-officers took less kindly to him. He kept a certain reticence of manner, which either came of a natural shyness or had been ingrained in him at the Roman Catholic seminary. He was poor, too; but poverty did not prevent his joining in all the regimental amusements, figuring modestly but sufficiently on the subscription lists, and even taking a hand at cards for moderate stakes. Yet he made no headway, and his popularity diminished instead of growing. All this I noted, but without discovering any definite reason. Of his professional promise, on the other hand, there could be no question; and the men liked and respected him.

Our senior ensign at this date was a Mr Urquhart, the eldest son of a West Highland laird, and heir to a considerable estate. He had been in barracks when Mr Mackenzie joined; but a week later his father's sudden illness called for his presence at home, and I granted him a leave of absence, which was afterwards extended. I regretted this, not only for the sad occasion, but because it deprived the battalion for a time of one of its steadiest officers, and Mr Mackenzie in particular of the chance to form a very useful friendship. For the two young men had (I thought) several qualities which might well attract them each to the other, and a common gravity of mind in contrast with their companions' prevalent and somewhat tiresome frivolity. Of the two I judged Mr Urquhart (the elder by a year) to have the more stable character. He was a good-looking, dark-complexioned young Highlander, with a serious expression which, without being gloomy, did not escape a touch of melancholy. I should judge this melancholy of Mr Urquhart's constitutional and the boyish sullenness which lingered on Mr Mackenzie's equally handsome face to have been imposed rather by circumstances.

Mr Urquhart rejoined us on the 24th of February. Two days later, as all the world knows, Napoleon made his escape from Elba; and the next week or two made it certain not only that the Allies must fight, but that the British contingent must be drawn largely, if not in the main, from the second battalions then drilling up and down the country. The 29th of March brought us our marching orders; and I will own that, while feeling no uneasiness about the great issue, I mistrusted the share my raw youngsters were to take in it.

On the 12th of April we were landed at Ostend, and at once marched up to Brussels, where we remained until the middle of June, having been assigned to the 5th (Picton's) Division of the Reserve. For some reason the Highland regiments had been massed into the Reserve, and were billeted about the capital, our own quarters lying between the 92nd (Gordons) and General Kruse's Nassauers, whose lodgings stretched out along the Louvain road; and although I could have wished some harder and more responsible service to get the Morays into training, I felt what advantage they derived from rubbing shoulders with the fine fellows of the 42nd, 79th, and 92nd, all First Battalions toughened by Peninsular work. The gaieties of life in Brussels during these two months have been described often enough; but among the military they were chiefly confined to those officers whose means allowed them to keep the pace set by rich civilians, and the Morays played the part of amused spectators. Yet the work and the few gaieties which fell to our share, while adding to our experiences, broke up to some degree the old domestic habits of the battalion. Excepting on duty I saw less of Mr Mackenzie and thought less about him; he might be left now to be shaped by active service. But I was glad to find him often in company with Mr Urquhart.

I come now to the memorable night of June 15th, concerning which and the end it brought upon the festivities of Brussels so much has been written. All the world has heard of the Duchess of Richmond's ball, and seems to conspire in decking it out with pretty romantic fables. To contradict the most of these were waste of time; but I may point out (1) that the ball was over and, I believe, all the company dispersed, before the actual alarm awoke the capital; and (2) that all responsible officers gathered there shared the knowledge that such an alarm was impending, might arrive at any moment, and would almost certainly arrive within a few hours. News of the French advance across the frontier and attack on General Zieten's outposts had reached Wellington at three o'clock that afternoon. It should have been brought five hours earlier; but he gave his orders at once, and quietly, and already our troops were massing for defence upon Nivelles. We of the Reserve had secret orders to hold ourselves prepared. Obedient to a hint from their Commander-in-Chief, the generals of division and brigade who attended the Duchess's ball withdrew themselves early on various pleas. Her Grace had honoured me with an invitation, probably because I represented a Highland regiment; and Highlanders (especially the Gordons, her brother's regiment) were much to the fore that night with reels, flings, and strathspeys. The many withdrawals warned me that something was in the wind, and after remaining just so long as seemed respectful I took leave of my hostess and walked homewards across the city as the clocks were striking eleven.

We of the Morays had our headquarters in a fairly large building – the Hôtel de Liège – in time of peace a resort of *commis-voyageurs* of the better class. It boasted a roomy hall, out of which opened two coffee-rooms, converted by us into guard- and mess-room. A large drawing-room on the first floor overlooking the street served me for sleeping as well as working quarters, and to reach it I must pass the *entresol,* where a small apartment had been set aside for occasional uses. We made it, for instance, our ante-room, and assembled there before mess; a few would retire there for smoking or card-playing; during the day it served as a waiting-room for messengers or any one whose business could not be for the moment attended to.

I had paused at the entrance to put some small question to the sentry, when I heard the crash of a chair in this room, and two voices broke out in fierce altercation. An instant after, the mess-room door opened, and Captain Murray, without observing me, ran past me and up the stairs. As he reached the *entresol,* a voice – my brother's – called down from an upper landing, and demanded: 'What's wrong there?'

'I don't know, Major,' Captain Murray answered, and at the same moment flung the door open. I was quick on his heels, and he wheeled round in some surprise at my voice, and to see me interposed between him and my brother, who had come running downstairs, and now stood behind my shoulder in the entrance.

'Shut the door,' I commanded quickly. 'Shut the door, and send away anyone you may hear outside. Now, gentlemen, explain yourselves, please.'

Mr Urquhart and Mr Mackenzie faced each other across a small table, from which the cloth had been dragged and lay on the floor with a scattered pack of cards. The elder lad held a couple of cards in his hand; he was white in the face.

'He cheated!' He swung round upon me in a kind of indignant fury, and tapped the cards with his forefinger.

I looked from him to the accused. Mackenzie's face was dark, almost purple, rather with rage (as it struck me) than with shame.

'It's a lie.' He let out the words slowly, as if holding rein on his passion. 'Twice he's said so, and twice I've called him a liar.' He drew back for an instant, and then lost control of himself. 'If that's not enough – ' He leapt forward, and almost before Captain Murray could interpose had hurled himself upon Urquhart. The table between them went down with a crash, and Urquhart went staggering back from a blow which just missed his face and took him on the collarbone, before Murray threw both arms around the assailant.

'Mr Mackenzie,' said I, 'you will consider yourself under arrest. Mr Urquhart, you will hold yourself ready to give me a full explanation. Whichever of you may be in the right, this is a disgraceful business, and dishonouring to your regiment and the cloth you wear: so disgraceful, that I hesitate to call up the guard and expose it to more eyes than ours. If Mr Mackenzie' – I turned to him again – 'can behave himself like a gentleman, and accept the fact of his arrest without further trouble, the scandal can at least be postponed until I discover how much it is necessary to face. For the moment, sir, you are in the charge of Captain Murray. Do you understand?'

He bent his head sullenly. 'He shall fight me, whatever happens,' he muttered.

I found it wise to pay no heed to this. 'It will be best,' I said to Murray, 'to remain here with Mr Mackenzie until I am ready for him. Mr Urquhart may retire to his quarters, if he will – I advise it, indeed – but I shall require his attendance in a few minutes. You understand,' I added significantly, 'that for the present this affair remains strictly between ourselves.' I knew well enough that, for all the King's regulations, a meeting would inevitably follow sooner or later, and will own I looked upon it as the proper outcome, between gentlemen, of such a quarrel. But it was not for me, their Colonel, to betray this knowledge or my feelings, and by imposing secrecy

I put off for the time all the business of a formal challenge with seconds. So I left them, and requesting my brother to follow me, mounted to my own room. The door was no sooner shut than I turned on him.

'Surely,' I said, 'this is a bad mistake of Urquhart's? It's an incredible charge. From all I've seen of him, the lad would never be guilty ...' I paused, expecting his assent. To my surprise he did not give it, but stood fingering his chin and looking serious.

'I don't know,' he answered unwillingly. 'There are stories against him.'

'What stories?'

'Nothing definite.' My brother hesitated. 'It doesn't seem fair to him to repeat mere whispers. But the others don't like him.'

'Hence the whispers, perhaps. They have not reached me.'

'They would not. He is known to be a favourite of yours. But they don't care to play with him.' My brother stopped, met my look, and answered it with a shrug of the shoulders, adding: 'He wins pretty constantly.'

'Any definite charge before to-night's?'

'No: at least, I think not. But Urquhart may have been put up to watch.'

'Fetch him up, please,' said I promptly; and seating myself at the writing-table I lit candles (for the lamp was dim), made ready the writing materials and prepared to take notes of the evidence.

Mr Urquhart presently entered, and I wheeled round in my chair to confront him. He was still exceedingly pale – paler, I thought, than I had left him. He seemed decidedly ill at ease, though not on his own account. His answer to my first question made me fairly leap in my chair.

'I wish,' he said, 'to qualify my accusation of Mr Mackenzie. That he cheated I have the evidence of my own eyes; but I am not sure how far he knew he was cheating.'

'Good heavens, sir!' I cried. 'Do you know you have accused that young man of a villainy which must damn him for life? And now you tell me – ' I broke off in sheer indignation.

'I know,' he answered quietly. 'The noise fetched you in upon us on the instant, and the mischief was done.'

'Indeed, sir,' I could not avoid sneering, 'to most of us it would seem that the mischief was done when you accused a brother-officer of fraud to his face.'

He seemed to reflect. 'Yes, sir,' he assented slowly; 'it is done. I saw him cheat: that I must persist in; but I cannot say how far he was conscious of it. And since I cannot, I must take the consequences.'

'Will you kindly inform us how it is possible for a player to cheat and not know that he is cheating?'

He bent his eyes on the carpet as if seeking an answer. It was long in coming. 'No,' he said at last, in a slow, dragging tone, 'I cannot.'

'Then you will at least tell us exactly what Mr Mackenzie did.'

Again there was a long pause. He looked at me straight, but with hopelessness in his eyes. 'I fear you would not believe me. It would not be worth while. If you can grant it, sir, I would ask time to decide.'

'Mr Urquhart,' said I sternly, 'are you aware you have brought against Mr Mackenzie a charge under which no man of honour can live easily for a moment? You ask me without a word of evidence in substantiation to keep *him* in torture while I give *you* time. It is monstrous, and I beg to remind you that, unless your charge is proved, you can – and will – be broken for making it.'

'I know it, sir,' he answered firmly enough; 'and because I knew it, I asked – perhaps selfishly – for time. If you refuse, I will at least ask permission to see a priest before telling a story which I can scarcely expect you to believe.' Mr Urquhart too was a Roman Catholic.

But my temper for the moment was gone. 'I see little chance,' said I, 'of keeping this scandal secret, and regret it the less if the consequences are to fall on a rash accuser. But just now I will have no meddling priest share the secret. For the present, one word more. Had you heard before this evening of any hints against Mr Mackenzie's play?'

He answered reluctantly: 'Yes.'

'And you set yourself to lay a trap for him?'

'No, sir; I did not. Unconsciously I may have been set on the watch: no, that is wrong – I *did* watch. But I swear it was in every hope and expectation of clearing him. He was my friend. Even when I *saw*, I had at first no intention to expose him until – '

''That is enough, sir,' I broke in, and turned to my brother. 'I have no option but to put Mr Urquhart too under arrest. Kindly convey him back to his room, and send Captain Murray to me. He may leave Mr Mackenzie in the *entresol*.'

My brother led Urquhart out, and in a minute Captain Murray tapped at my door. He was an honest Scot, not too sharp-witted, but straight as a die. I am to show him this description, and he will cheerfully agree with it.

'This is a hideous business, Murray,' said I as he entered. 'There's something wrong with Urquhart's story. Indeed, between ourselves it has the fatal weakness that he won't tell it.'

Murray took half a minute to digest this: then he answered: 'I don't know anything about Urquhart's story, sir. But there's something wrong about Urquhart.' Here he hesitated.

'Speak out, man,' said I: 'in confidence. That's understood.'

'Well, sir,' said he, 'Urquhart won't fight.'

'Ah! so that question came up, did it?' I asked, looking at him sharply.

He was abashed, but answered, with a twinkle in his eye: 'I believe, sir, you gave me no orders to stop their talking, and in a case like this – between youngsters – some question of a meeting would naturally come up. You see, I know both the lads. Urquhart I really like; but he didn't show up well, I must own – to be fair to the other, who is in the worse fix.'

'I am not so sure of that,' I commented; 'but go on.'

He seemed surprised. 'Indeed, Colonel? Well,' he resumed, 'I being the sort of fellow they could talk before, a meeting *was* discussed. The question was how to arrange it without seconds – that is, without breaking your orders and dragging in outsiders. For Mackenzie wanted blood at once, and for a

while Urquhart seemed just as eager. All of a sudden, when
. . .' here he broke off suddenly, not wishing to commit himself.

'Tell me only what you think necessary,' said I.

He thanked me. 'That is what I wanted,' he said. 'Well, all
of a sudden, when we had found out a way and Urquhart was
discussing it, he pulled himself up in the middle of a sentence,
and with his eyes fixed on the other – a most curious look it
was – he waited while you could count ten, and, "No," says
he, "I'll not fight you at once" – for we had been arranging
something of the sort – "not to-night, anyway, nor to-morrow,"
he says. "I'll fight you; but I won't have your blood on my
head *in that way*." Those were his words. I have no notion what
he meant; but he kept repeating them, and would not explain,
though Mackenzie tried him hard and was for shooting across
the table. He was repeating them when the Major interrupted
us and called him up.'

'He has behaved ill from the first,' said I. 'To me the whole
affair begins to look like an abominable plot against Mackenzie. Certainly I cannot entertain a suspicion of his guilt upon a
bare assertion which Urquhart declines to back with a tittle of
evidence.'

'The devil he does!' mused Captain Murray. 'That looks
bad for him. And yet, sir, I'd sooner trust Urquhart than
Mackenzie, and if the case lies against Urquhart –'

'It will assuredly break him,' I put in, 'unless he can prove
the charge, or that he was honestly mistaken.'

'Then, sir,' said the Captain, 'I'll have to show you this.
It's ugly, but it's only justice.'

He pulled a sovereign from his pocket and pushed it on the
writing-table under my nose.

'What does this mean?'

'It is a marked one,' said he.

'So I perceive.' I had picked up the coin and was examining
it.

'I found it just now,' he continued, 'in the room below. The
upsetting of the table had scattered Mackenzie's stakes about
the floor.'

'You seem to have a pretty notion of evidence!' I observed sharply. 'I don't know what accusation this coin may carry; but why need it be Mackenzie's? He might have won it from Urquhart.'

'I thought of that,' was the answer. 'But no money had changed hands. I inquired. The quarrel arose over the second deal, and as a matter of fact Urquhart had laid no money on the table, but made a pencil-note of the few shillings he lost by the first hand. You may remember, sir, how the table stood when you entered.'

I reflected. 'Yes, my recollection bears you out. Do I gather that you have confronted Mackenzie with this?'

'No. I found it and slipped it quietly into my pocket. I thought we had trouble enough on hand for the moment.'

'Who marked this coin?'

'Young Fraser, sir, in my presence. He has been losing small sums, he declares, by pilfering. We suspected one of the orderlies.'

'In this connexion you had no suspicion of Mr Mackenzie?'

'None, sir.' He considered for a moment, and added: 'There was a curious thing happened three weeks ago over my watch. It found its way one night to Mr Mackenzie's quarters. He brought it to me in the morning; said it was lying, when he awoke, on the table beside his bed. He seemed utterly puzzled. He had been to one or two already to discover the owner. We joked him about it, the more by token that his own watch had broken down the day before and was away at the mender's. The whole thing was queer, and has not been explained. Of course in that instance he was innocent: everything proves it. It just occurred to me as worth mentioning, because in both instances the lad may have been the victim of a trick.'

'I am glad you did so,' I said; 'though just now it does not throw any light that I can see.' I rose and paced the room. 'Mr Mackenzie had better be confronted with this, too, and hear your evidence. It's best he should know the worst against him; and if he be guilty it may move him to confession.'

'Certainly, sir,' Captain Murray assented. 'Shall I fetch him?'

'No, remain where you are,' I said; 'I will go for him myself.'

I understood that Mr Urquhart had retired to his own quarters or to my brother's, and that Mr Mackenzie had been left in the *entresol* alone. But as I descended the stairs quietly I heard within that room a voice which at first persuaded me he had company, and next that, left to himself, he had broken down and given way to the most childish wailing. The voice was so unlike his, or any grown man's, that it arrested me on the lowermost stair against my will. It resembled rather the sobbing of an infant mingled with short strangled cries of contrition and despair.

'What shall I do? What shall I do? I didn't mean it – I meant to do good! What shall I do?'

So much I heard (as I say) against my will, before my astonishment gave room to a sense of shame at playing, even for a moment, the eavesdropper upon the lad I was to judge. I stepped quickly to the door, and with a warning rattle (to give him time to recover himself) turned the handle and entered.

He was alone, lying back in an easy chair – not writhing there in anguish of mind, as I had fully expected, but sunk rather in a state of dull and hopeless apathy. To reconcile his attitude with the sounds I had just heard was merely impossible; and it bewildered me worse than any in the long chain of bewildering incidents. For five seconds or so he appeared not to see me but when he grew aware his look changed suddenly to one of utter terror, and his eyes, shifting from me, shot a glance about the room as if he expected some new accusation to dart at him from the corners. His indignation and passionate defiance were gone: his eyes seemed to ask me: 'How much do you know?' before he dropped them and stood before me, sullenly submissive.

'I want you upstairs,' said I: 'not to hear your defence on this charge, for Mr Urquhart has not yet specified it. But there is another matter.'

'Another?' he echoed dully, and, I observed, without surprise.

I led the way back to the room where Captain Murray waited. 'Can you tell me anything about this?' I asked, pointing to the sovereign on the writing-table.

He shook his head, clearly puzzled, but anticipating mischief.

'The coin is marked, you see. I have reason to know that it was marked by its owner in order to detect a thief. Captain Murray found it just now among your stakes.'

Somehow – for I liked the lad – I had not the heart to watch his face as I delivered this. I kept my eyes upon the coin, and waited, expecting an explosion – a furious denial, or at least a cry that he was the victim of a conspiracy. None came. I heard him breathing hard. After a long and very dreadful pause some words broke from him, so lowly uttered that my ears only just caught them.

'This too? O my God!'

I seated myself, the lad before me, and Captain Murray erect and rigid at the end of the table. 'Listen, my lad,' said I. 'This wears an ugly look, but that a stolen coin has been found in your possession does not prove that you've stolen it.'

'I did not. Sir, I swear to you on my honour, and before Heaven, that I did not.'

'Very well,' said I. 'Captain Murray asserts that he found this among the moneys you had been staking at cards. Do you question that assertion?'

He answered almost without pondering. 'No, sir. Captain Murray is a gentleman, and incapable of falsehood. If he says so, it was so.'

'Very well again. Now, can you explain how this coin came into your possession?'

At this he seemed to hesitate; but answered at length: 'No, I cannot explain.'

'Have you any idea? Or can you form any guess?'

Again there was a long pause before the answer came in low and strained tones: 'I can guess.'

'What is your guess?'

He lifted a hand and dropped it hopelessly. 'You would not believe,' he said.

I will own a suspicion flashed across my mind on hearing these words – the very excuse given a while ago by Mr Urquhart – that the whole affair was a hoax and the two young men were in conspiracy to befool me. I dismissed it at once: the sight of Mr Mackenzie's face was convincing. But my temper was gone.

'Believe you?' I exclaimed. 'You seem to think the one thing I can swallow as credible, even probable, is that an officer in the Morays has been pilfering and cheating at cards. Oddly enough, it's the last thing I'm going to believe without proof, and the last charge I shall pass without clearing it up to my satisfaction. Captain Murray, will you go and bring me Mr Urquhart and the Major?'

As Captain Murray closed the door I rose, and with my hands behind me took a turn across the room to the fireplace, then back to the writing-table.

'Mr Mackenzie,' I said, 'before we go any further I wish you to believe that I am your friend as well as your Colonel. I did something to start you upon your career, and I take a warm interest in it. To believe you guilty of these charges will give me the keenest grief. However unlikely your defence may sound – and you seem to fear it – I will give it the best consideration I can. If you are innocent, you shall not find me prejudiced because many are against you and you are alone. Now, this coin – ' I turned to the table.

The coin was gone.

I stared at the place where it had lain; then at the young man. He had not moved. My back had been turned for less than two seconds, and I could have sworn he had not budged from the square of carpet on which he had first taken his stand, and on which his feet were still planted. On the other hand, I was equally positive the incriminating coin had lain on the table at the moment I turned my back.

'It is gone!' cried I.

'Gone?' he echoed, staring at the spot to which my finger pointed. In the silence our glances were still crossing when my brother tapped at the door and brought in Mr Urquhart, Captain Murray following.

Dismissing for a moment this latest mystery, I addressed Mr Urquhart. 'I have sent for you, sir, to request in the first place that here in Mr Mackenzie's presence and in colder blood you will either withdraw or repeat and at least attempt to substantiate the charge you brought against him.'

'I adhere to it, sir, that there was cheating. To withdraw would be to utter a lie. Does he deny it?'

I glanced at Mr Mackenzie. 'I deny that I cheated,' said he sullenly.

'Further,' pursued Mr Urquhart, 'I repeat what I told you, sir. He *may*, while profiting by it, have been unaware of the cheat. At the moment I thought it impossible; but I am willing to believe – '

'*You* are willing!' I broke in. 'And pray, sir, what about me, his Colonel, and the rest of his brother-officers? Have you the coolness to suggest – '

But the full question was never put, and in this world it will never be answered. A bugle call, distant but clear, cut my sentence in half. It came from the direction of the Place d'Armes. A second bugle echoed it from the height of the Montagne du Parc, and within a minute its note was taken up and answered across the darkness from quarter after quarter of the city.

We looked at one another in silence. 'Business,' said my brother at length, curtly and quietly.

Already the rooms above us were astir. I heard windows thrown open, voices calling questions, feet running.

'Yes,' said I, 'it is business at length, and for the while this inquiry must end. Captain Murray, look to your company. You, Major, see that the lads tumble out quickly to the alarm-post. One moment!' – and Captain Murray halted with his hand on the door – 'It is understood that for the present no word of to-night's affair passes our lips.' I turned to Mr Mackenzie and answered the question I read in the lad's eyes. 'Yes, sir; for the present I take off your arrest. Get your sword. It shall be your good fortune to answer the enemy before answering me.'

To my amazement Mr Urquhart interposed. He was, if

possible, paler and more deeply agitated than before. 'Sir, I entreat you not to allow Mr Mackenzie to go. I have reasons – I was mistaken just now – '

'Mistaken, sir?'

'Not in what I saw. I refused to fight him – under a mistake. I thought – '

But I cut his stammering short. 'As for you,' I said, 'the most charitable construction I can put on your behaviour is to believe you mad. For the present you, too, are free to go and do your duty. Now leave me. Business presses, and I am sick and angry at the sight of you.'

It was just two in the morning when I reached the alarm-post. Brussels by this time was full of the rolling of drums and screaming of pipes; and the regiment formed up in darkness rendered tenfold more confusing by a mob of citizens, some wildly excited, others paralysed by terror, and all intractable. We had, moreover, no small trouble to disengage from our ranks the wives and families who had most unwisely followed many officers abroad, and now clung to their dear ones bidding them farewell. To end this most distressing scene I had in some instances to use a roughness which it still afflicts me to remember. Yet in actual time it was soon over, and dawn scarcely breaking when the Morays with the other regiments of Pack's brigade filed out of the park and fell into stride on the road which leads southward to Charleroi.

In this record it would be immaterial to describe either our march or the since-famous engagement which terminated it. Very early we began to hear the sound of heavy guns far ahead and to make guesses at their distance; but it was close upon two in the afternoon before we reached the high ground above Quatre Bras, and saw the battle spread below us like a picture. The Prince of Orange had been fighting his ground stubbornly since seven in the morning. Ney's superior artillery and far superior cavalry had forced him back, it is true; but he still covered the cross-roads which were the key of his defence, and his position remained sound, though it was fast becoming critical. Just as we arrived, the French, who had already mastered the farm of Piermont on the left of the Charleroi road, began to push their skirmishers into a thicket below it and commanding the road running east to Namur. Indeed, for a short space they had this road at their mercy, and the chance within grasp of doubling up our left by means of it.

This happened, I say, just as we arrived; and Wellington, who had reached Quatre Bras a short while ahead of us (having fetched a circuit from Brussels through Ligny, where he paused to inspect Field-Marshal Blücher's dispositions for battle), at once saw the danger, and detached one of our regiments, the 95th Rifles, to drive back the *tirailleurs* from the thicket; which, albeit scarcely breathed after their march, they did with a will, and so regained the Allies' hold upon the Namur road. The rest of us meanwhile defiled down this same road, formed line in front of it, and under a brisk cannonade from the French heights waited for the next move.

It was not long in coming. Ney, finding that our artillery made poor play against his, prepared to launch a column against us. Warned by a cloud of skirmishers, our light companies leapt forward, chose their shelter, and began a very pretty exchange of musketry. But this was preliminary work only, and soon the head of a large French column appeared on the slope to our right, driving the Brunswickers slowly before it. It descended a little way, and suddenly broke into three or four columns of attack The mischief no sooner threatened than Picton came galloping along our line and roaring that our division would advance and engage with all speed. For a raw regiment like the Morays this was no light test; but, supported by a veteran regiment on either hand, they bore it admirably. Dropping the Gordons to protect the road in case of mishap, the two brigades swung forward in the prettiest style, their skirmishers running in and forming on their flank as they advanced. Then for a while the work was hot; but, as will always happen when column is boldly met by line, the French quickly had enough of our enveloping fire, and wavered. A short charge with the bayonet finished it, and drove them in confusion up the slope: nor had I an easy task to resume a hold on my youngsters and restrain them from pursuing too far. The brush had been sharp, but I had the satisfaction of knowing that the Morays had behaved well. They also knew it, and fell to jesting in high good humour as General Pack withdrew the brigade from the ground of its exploit and posted us in line with the 42nd and 44th Regiments on the left of the main road to Charleroi.

To the right of the Charleroi road, and some way in advance of our position, the Brunswickers were holding ground as best they could under a hot and accurate artillery fire. Except for this, the battle had come to a lull, when a second mass of the enemy began to move down the slopes: a battalion in line heading two columns of infantry direct upon the Brunswickers, while squadron after squadron of lancers crowded down along the road into which by weight of numbers they must be driven. The Duke of Brunswick, perceiving his peril, headed a charge of his lancers upon the advancing infantry, but without the least effect. His horsemen broke. He rode back and called on his infantry to retire in good order. They also broke, and in the attempt to rally them he fell mortally wounded.

The line taken by these flying Brunswickers would have brought them diagonally across the Charleroi road into our arms, had not the French lancers seized this moment to charge straight down it in a body. They encountered, and the indiscriminate mass was hurled on to us, choking and overflowing the causeway. In a minute we were swamped – the two Highland regiments and the 44th bending against a sheer weight of French horsemen. So suddenly came the shock that the 42nd had not time to form square, until two companies were cut off and well-nigh destroyed; *then* that noble regiment formed around the horsemen who could boast of having broken it, and left not one to bear back the tale. The 44th behaved more cleverly, but not more intrepidly: it did not attempt to form square, but faced its rear rank round and gave the Frenchmen a volley; before they could check their impetus the front rank poured in a second; and the light company, which had held its fire, delivered a third, breaking the crowd in two, and driving the hinder-part back in disorder and up the Charleroi road. But already the fore-part had fallen upon the Morays, fortunately the last of the three regiments to receive the shock. Though most fortunate, they had least experience, and were consequently slow in answering my shout. A wedge of lancers broke through us as we formed around the two standards, and I saw Mr Urquhart with the King's colours hurled back in the rush. The pole fell with him, after swaying within a yard of a French lancer, who thrust out an arm to grasp it. And with that I saw Mackenzie divide the rush and stand – it may have been for five seconds – erect, with his foot upon the standard. Then three lances pierced him, and he fell. But the lateral pressure of their own troopers broke off the head of the wedge which the French had pushed into us. Their leading squadrons were pressed down the road and afterwards accounted for by the Gordons. Of the seven-and-twenty assailants around whom the Morays now closed, not one survived.

Towards nightfall, as Ney weakened and the Allies were reinforced, our troops pushed forward and recaptured every important position taken by the French that morning. The Morays, with the rest of Picton's division, bivouacked for the night in and around the farmsteads of Gemiancourt.

So obstinately had the field been contested that darkness fell before the wounded could be collected with any thoroughness; and the comfort of the men around many a camp-fire was disturbed by groans (often quite near at hand) of some poor comrade or enemy lying helpless and undiscovered, or exerting his shattered limbs to crawl towards the blaze. And these interruptions at length became so distressing to the Morays, that two or three officers sought me and demanded leave to form a fatigue party of volunteers and explore the hedges and thickets with lanterns. Among them was Mr Urquhart; and having readily given leave and accompanied them some little way on their search, I was bidding them good night and good speed when I found him standing at my elbow.

'May I have a word with you, Colonel?' he asked.

His voice was low and serious. Of course I knew what subject filled his thoughts. 'Is it worth while, sir?' I answered. 'I have lost to-day a brave lad for whom I had a great affection. For him the account is closed; but not for those who liked him

and are still concerned in his good name. If you have anything
further against him, or if you have any confession to make,
I warn you that this is a bad moment to choose.'

'I have only to ask,' said he, 'that you will grant me the
first convenient hour for explaining; and to remind you that
when I besought you not to send him into action to-day, I had
no time to give you reasons.'

'This is extraordinary talk, sir. I am not used to command
the Morays under advice from my subalterns. And in this
instance I had reasons for not even listening to you.' He was
silent. 'Moreover,' I continued, 'you may as well know,
though I am under no obligation to tell you, that I do most
certainly not regret having given that permission to one who
justified it by a signal service to his king and country.'

'But would you have sent him *knowing* that he must die?
Colonel,' he went on rapidly, before I could interrupt, 'I
beseech you to listen. I *knew* he had only a few hours to live.
I saw his wraith last night. It stood behind his shoulder in the
room when in Captain Murray's presence he challenged me to
fight him. You are a Highlander, sir: you may be sceptical
about the second sight; but at least you must have heard many
claim it. I swear positively that I saw Mr Mackenzie's wraith
last night, and for that reason, and no other, tried to defer the
meeting. To fight him, knowing he must die, seemed to me as
bad as murder. Afterwards, when the alarm sounded and you
took off his arrest, I knew that his fate must overtake him –
that my refusal had done no good. I tried to interfere again,
and you would not hear. Naturally you would not hear; and
very likely, if you had, his fate would have found him in some
other way. That is what I try to believe. I hope it is not selfish,
sir; but the doubt tortures me.'

'Mr Urquhart,' I asked, 'is this the only occasion on which
you have possessed the second sight, or had reason to think
so?'

'No, sir.'

'Was it the first or only time last night you believed you
were granted it?'

'It was the *second* time last night,' he said steadily.

We had been walking back to my bivouac fire, and in the light of it I turned and said: 'I will hear your story at the first opportunity. I will not promise to believe, but I will hear and weigh it. Go now and join the others in their search.'

He saluted, and strode away into the darkness. The opportunity I promised him never came. At eleven o'clock next morning we began our withdrawal, and within twenty-four hours the battle of Waterloo had begun. In one of the most heroic feats of that day – the famous resistance of Pack's brigade – Mr Urquhart was among the first to fall.

3

Thus it happened that an affair which so nearly touched the honour of the Morays, and which had been agitating me at the very moment when the bugle sounded in the Place d'Armes, became a secret shared by three only. The regiment joined in the occupation of Paris, and did not return to Scotland until the middle of December.

I had ceased to mourn for Mr Mackenzie, but neither to regret him nor to speculate on the mystery which closed his career, and which, now that death had sealed Mr Urquhart's lips, I could no longer hope to penetrate, when, on the day of my return to Inverness, I was reminded of him by finding, among the letters and papers awaiting me, a visiting-card neatly indited with the name of the Reverend Samuel Saul. On inquiry I learnt that the minister had paid at least three visits to Inverness during the past fortnight, and had, on each occasion, shown much anxiety to learn when the battalion might be expected. He had also left word that he wished to see me on a matter of much importance.

Sure enough, at ten o'clock next morning the little man presented himself. He was clearly bursting to disclose his business, and our salutations were scarce over when he ran to the door and called to someone in the passage outside.

'Elspeth! Step inside, woman. The housekeeper, sir, to the late Mr Mackenzie of Ardlaugh,' he explained, as he held the door to admit her.

She was dressed in ragged mourning, and wore a grotesque and fearful bonnet. As she saluted me respectfully I saw that her eyes indeed were dry and even hard, but her features set in an expression of quiet and hopeless misery. She did not speak, but left explanation to the minister.

'You will guess, sir,' began Mr Saul, 'that we have called to learn more of the poor lad.' And he paused.

'He died most gallantly,' said I: 'died in the act of saving the colours. No soldier could have wished for a better end.'

'To be sure, to be sure. So it was reported to us. He died, as one might say, without a stain on his character?' said Mr Saul, with a sort of question in his tone.

'He died,' I answered, 'in a way which could only do credit to his name.'

A somewhat constrained silence followed. The woman broke it. 'You are not telling us all,' she said, in a slow harsh voice.

It took me aback. 'I am telling all that needs to be known,' I assured her.

'No doubt, sir, no doubt,' Mr Saul interjected. 'Hold your tongue, woman. I am going to tell Colonel Ross a tale which may or may not bear upon anything he knows. If not, he will interrupt me before I go far; but if he says nothing I shall take it I have his leave to continue. Now, sir, on the 16th day of June last, and at six in the morning – that would be the day of Quatre Bras – '

He paused for me to nod assent, and continued. 'At six in the morning or a little earlier, this woman, Elspeth Mackenzie, came to me at the Manse in great perturbation. She had walked all the way from Ardlaugh. It had come to her (she said) that the young Laird abroad was in great trouble since the previous evening. I asked: What trouble? Was it danger of life, for instance? – asking it not seriously, but rather to compose her; for at first I set down her fears to an old woman's whimsies. Not that I would call Elspeth *old* precisely – '

Here he broke off and glanced at her; but, perceiving she paid little attention, went on again at a gallop. 'She answered that it was worse – that the young Laird stood very near disgrace, and (the worst of all was) at a distance she could not help him. Now, sir, for reasons I shall hereafter tell you, Mr Mackenzie's being in disgrace would have little surprised me; but that she should know of it, he being in Belgium, was incredible. So I pressed her, and she being distraught and (I verily believe) in something like anguish, came out with a most extraordinary story: to wit, that the Laird of Ardlaugh had in his service, unbeknown to him (but, as she protested, well known to her), a familiar spirit – or, as we should say commonly, a 'brownie' – which in general served him most faithfully but at times erratically, having no conscience nor any Christian principle to direct him. I cautioned her, but she persisted, in a kind of wild terror, and added that at times the spirit would, in all good faith, do things which no Christian allowed to be permissible, and further, that she had profited by such actions. I asked her: Was thieving one of them? She answered that it was, and indeed the chief.

'Now, this was an admission which gave me some eagerness to hear more. For to my knowledge there were charges lying against young Mr Mackenzie – though not pronounced – which pointed to a thief in his employment and presumably in his confidence. You will remember, sir, that when I had the honour of meeting you at Mr Mackenzie's table, I took my leave with much abruptness. You remarked upon it, no doubt. But you will no longer think it strange when I tell you that there – under my nose – were a dozen apples of a sort which grows nowhere within twenty miles of Ardlaugh but in my own Manse garden. The tree was a new one, obtained from Herefordshire, and planted three seasons before as an experiment. I had watched it, therefore, particularly; and on that very morning had counted the fruit, and been dismayed to find twelve apples missing. Further, I am a pretty good judge of wine (though I taste it rarely), and could there and then have taken my oath that the claret our host set before us was the very wine I had tasted at the table of his neighbour Mr Gillespie. As for the venison – I had already heard whispers that deer and all game were not safe within a mile or two of Ardlaugh. These were injurious tales, sir, which I had no mind to believe; for, bating his religion, I saw everything in Mr Mackenzie which disposed me to like him. But I knew (as neighbours must) of the shortness of his purse; and the multiplied evidence (particularly my own Goodrich pippins staring me in the face) overwhelmed me for a moment.

'So then, I listened to this woman's tale with more patience – or, let me say, more curiosity – than you, sir, might have given it. She persisted, I say, that her master was in trouble; and that the trouble had something to do with a game of cards, but that Mr Mackenzie had been innocent of deceit, and the real culprit was this spirit I tell of – '

Here the woman herself broke in upon Mr Saul. 'He had nae conscience – he had nae conscience. He was just a poor luck-child, born by mischance and put away without baptism. He had nae conscience. How should he?'

I looked from her to Mr Saul in perplexity.

'Whist!' said he; 'we'll talk of that anon.'

'We will not,' said she. 'We will talk of it now. He was my own child, sir, by the young Laird's own father. That was before he was married upon the wife he took later – '

Here Mr Saul nudged me, and whispered: 'The old Laird had her married to that daunderin' old half-wit Duncan, to cover things up. This part of the tale is true enough, to my knowledge.'

'My bairn was overlaid, sir,' the woman went on; 'not by purpose, I will swear before you and God. They buried his poor body without baptism; but not his poor soul. Only when the young Laird came, and my own bairn clave to him as Mackenzie to Mackenzie, and wrought and hunted and mended for him – it was not to be thought that the poor innocent, without knowledge of God's ways – '

She ran on incoherently, while my thoughts harked back to the voice I had heard wailing behind the door of the *entresol* at Brussels; to the young Laird's face, his furious indignation, followed by hopeless apathy, as of one who in the interval had learnt what he could never explain; to the marked coin so mysteriously spirited from sight; to Mr Urquhart's words before he left me on the night of Quatre Bras.

'But he was sorry,' the woman ran on; 'he was sorry – sorry. He came wailing to me that night; yes, and sobbing. He meant no wrong; it was just that he loved his own father's son, and knew no better. There was no priest living within thirty miles; so I dressed, and ran to the minister here. *He* gave me no rest until I started.'

I addressed Mr Saul. 'Is there reason to suppose that, besides this woman and (let us say) her accomplice, any one shared the secret of these pilferings?'

'Ardlaugh never knew,' put in the woman quickly. 'He may have guessed we were helping him; but the lad knew nothing, and may the saints in heaven love him as they ought! He trusted me with his purse, and slight it was to maintain him. But until too late he never knew – no, never, sir!'

I thought again of that voice behind the door of the *entresol*.

'Elspeth Mackenzie,' I said, 'I and two other living men alone know of what your master was accused. It cannot affect him; but these two shall hear your exculpation of him. And I will write the whole story down, so that the world, if it ever hears the charge, may also hear your testimony, which of the two (though both are strange) I believe to be not the less credible.'

CAPTAIN KNOT

AARON KNOT, master of the Virginia barque *Jehoiada*, though a member of the Society of Friends and a religious man by nature, had a tolerant and catholic mind, a quiet but insatiable curiosity in the ways of his fellow-men (seafarers and sinners especially), with a temperate zest for talking with strangers and listening to them. He liked his company to be honest, yet could stretch a point or two in charity. He knew, and liked to think, that it takes all sorts to make a world. At sea – and he had passed forty-five of his sixty years at sea – he would spend long hours, night after night, in his cabin, peaceably thinking about God, and God's wonders, and the purpose of it all. Ashore, his heart warmed to the red light behind the blinds of a decent tavern. He was old enough, and wise enough, to know that for him the adventure would be sober. He knew at first taste good ale and good company from bad, and no stranger to whom he offered a pipeful could deny the quality of his tobacco, the best grown on the Rappahannock. He wore the strict Quaker dress, from broad hat down to square toes with buckles. His features had a large Roman gravity. His hair, of an iron-grey, still strong in growth and combed over temples noticeably massive, was tied at the back with a wisp of black ribbon. His stature was six feet or a little over, and his build proportionate. In a man of sixty years one looks less to the waistband than to the depth of chest.

This Captain Knot, having brought the *Jehoiada* up Avon on a full spring tide, moored her off Wyatt's Wharf, settled with his crew, declared his cargo (mainly tobacco), and done all necessary business with his consignee, bent his steps towards the Welcome Home Tavern at the head of Quay Street. The date was Saturday, 11th August, 1742: the time about seven o'clock in the evening.

Of all the taverns in all the ports known to him the Welcome Home was Captain Knot's favourite house of call, and to-night it looked as cosy and well-to-do as ever; the sign newly painted and varnished, the doorstep white with holystone, the brick floor clean as a pin, fresh sawdust in the spittoons; the brass candlesticks on the chimney-piece, the brass chains of the clock-weights, the copper warming-pan on the wall, the ware on the dresser all a-twinkle in so much of evening light as drifted in by the open doorway or over the red window-blinds.

Yes, the place still prospered. 'But why, then, is it so empty?' wondered Captain Knot – 'and on a Saturday night?'

There were, in fact, but two customers in the room, two seafaring men seated and talking together on the settle beyond the fire-place; or rather, the one talking low and earnestly, the other listening. The listener – who was clearly the elder – held a long pipe and had a mug of beer beside him. The other had neither pipe nor mug. He leaned forward with his wrists on his knees and his hands clasped, nor did he shift his position when answering Captain Knot's 'Good evening' with a 'Good evening, sir.' Lowering his voice, he went on with his argument, the murmur of which could not hide a Scottish accent.

Captain Knot threw the pair a look before rapping on the table. 'House!' he called, threw the younger man a second, slightly longer look as if searching his face in the dusk, and walking to the window, stared out upon the street.

The landlady entered, and he whipped about.

'Mrs Walters?'

'At your service, sir . . . Why, if it isn't Captain Knot! For a moment – and you standing there with your back to the light –'

'Husband well?'

'Quite well, sir, the Lord be praised! – and what's more, sir, he warned me the *Jehoiada* had come in . . . but with so much housework on one's mind! And I hope it's been a good passage, Captain? Haler I never saw you looking.'

'Pretty fair, ma'am: nothing to grumble at,' the Captain answered, but absent-mindedly. His brows had drawn to-gether in a slight frown as one of the men on the settle made a sudden shuffling movement with his feet. 'Much, on the contrary, to be thankful for,' he went on briskly, pulling himself together. 'And pretty hale yet, as you say, for a man of sixty. But where's thy husband, that he neglects his old customers? Thou gave me a start, ma'am – a scare, till I took notice thy cap was no widow-woman's.'

'Walters?' said the wife. 'Oh, Walters is like every other fool in Bristol, crazy after the new preacher. You wouldn't think it in a man of his solid habits. He started at four o'clock to walk all the way to Kingswood – on a Saturday, too!'

'But who is this new preacher, ma'am?'

'Why, haven't you heard? Oh, but I forgot – you have only arrived to-day, and all the way from – from – '

'From the Potomac, ma'am.'

'But even in America, sir, you must have heard tell of him – the great John Wesley, that is setting half England by the ears.'

'Well, as a fact, ma'am,' said Captain Knot coolly, 'I *have* heard tell of him once or twice, and the first time was over in Georgia, where I'm sorry to say they did not think much of him.'

'Not think much of him!' The younger of the two seamen rose abruptly from the settle and thrust himself into the conversation. 'Show me the man as dares to say he doesn't think much of John Wesley, and I'll say to his face: "John Wesley was sent straight from Heaven, as sure as John the Baptist."' The man's hands and muscles of his still youthful face twitched with excitement.

'You mustn't mind Peter Williamson, sir,' interposed Mrs Walters. 'He's young yet, and was converted almost a week ago – '

'Glory!' put in Williamson. 'Hallelujah – and I don't care who knows it.'

'Though I wonder, Pete,' Mrs Walters went on, 'that with all your fervour you're not out at Kingswood, too, this fine evening, but sitting here and all the time ordering nothing. One way or the other you're losing your privileges, and that you can't gainsay.'

'I'm here, ma'am, on my Father's business,' stammered Williamson. 'If I've forgot the due of your house in this zeal o' mine – '

'Fetch Master Williamson a mug of your strong home-brewed, and another for me,' ordered Captain Knot briskly. He ignored the younger seaman, who had twice made as if to rise and go, and twice faltered and sat down again.

'My young friend,' said Captain Knot to Williamson, when the landlady had gone out, 'so thou art on thy Father's business? And what might that be?'

'The saving of souls, sir,' answered Williamson promptly. 'This man's, for instance.' He jerked a thumb at his companion.

'Ah? What's his name?'

'Haynes, sir – Jim Haynes. I know his need, and it's a bitter hard one.'

'Haynes?' Captain Knot pondered. 'No, I don't recall the name. Well, friend, I'll take thy word about knowing his need. As to knowing his soul, and dealing with it, on a seven-days'-old conversion, I am not so sure. Souls are kittle, friend, as they say up in thy country of North Britain. Take mine, for example – and I dare say a passable example, as souls go. It has its need, God knows; yet I have a notion that the cure of 'em would give thee much trouble and yield me much amusement.'

'I take ye for a releegious man, sir; though it beats me how you guessed I was out of Scotland. At first sight I said: "Yon elderly gentleman has had convictions of sin at least, or I'm mistaken."'

'Plenty.' Captain Knot walked over to the empty fire-place, turned his back to it, and parted his broad coat-tails so that one hung over each arm. 'Plenty, my friend, at one time and another. But I never crowd sail on my conscience, nor will I allow another man to do it. I'm master of that ship; and so it is, or should be to my notion, with every man. "The Kingdom of God is within you." Ah, here comes Mrs Walters with the beer! Thy good health, my friend. As I was saying, or about to say, every man has a soul of his own, and is responsible for it. That's a tidy number, and all different. On top of that, there's animals, as some hold. Why there's Indians, over on my side of the world, make gods of the very vermin on their bodies. And what shall we say about ships now?'

'You're talking too deep for me, sir,' said Williamson, rubbing his jaw. 'A ship with a soul, you say?'

'Why not? I put it to thee as a seaman. Well, I won't press the word "soul": but there's a something belonging to her, and to her only, whats'ever ship she may be.'

'I'm not denying as a ship may have a character,' owned Williamson, who was young enough, and enough of a Scotsman, to rub shoulders fondly against anything hard and metaphysical.

'Character?' echoed Captain Knot with a faint accent of scorn, and still nursing his coat-tails. 'Thou art old enough, by thy looks, to have seen a ship – ay, and felt her – running down the trades, with t' gallant sails set and stuns'ls out like the wings on a butterfly, floating and striving after heaven. Hast never had that feeling?'

'I know what you mean, sir,' confessed Williamson.

'Then,' advised Captain Knot, sharply, 'don't pretend to me she was sailing to heaven on her character, like a servant maid after a situation. I don't know at what point in building or rigging the Lord puts the spirit in; but a spirit there is, and a soul, even in my old *Jehoiada*. For all that, she'll nag and sulk like a man's old wife. Ships? There be ships afloat comely as Mary Magdalen, and, like her, torn with devils; beautiful, born to be damned. I've known and pitied 'em, as I'd pity a girl with her pretty face set t'ards hell. Why, I could tell of the –'

Here Captain Knot with a start disengaged both hands from under his coat-tails, smote the palm of his left with the knuckles of his right, and cried: 'I have it! I never forget a face! That man' – he pointed a finger at the older seaman, who shrank back sideways on the settle before it – 'I never heard his name till five minutes ago, but the *Rover* was his ship. I remember his face on the deck of her as we parted. Ay, the *Rover*, Captain Kennedy – Mrs Walters!'

The older seaman staggered up from the settle. He would have made for the door; but Captain Knot had stepped to the exit and stood barring it.

'You can't harm me,' stammered the seaman. 'I got the King's pardon for it these four years.'

'Who wants to harm thee?' asked Captain Knot gently. 'I only want to see thy face. Mrs Walters, ma'am, the nights are closing in, and I'll ask the favour of a candle.'

Mrs Walters brought a candle and handed it to Captain Knot. 'We will have a third mug of ale, ma'am, if thou please, and this one mulled hot, with a clove or two.'

He took the candle, placed it on the high chimney-piece, and under it studied the seaman's features, keeping silence until the landlady had left the room. The wick burned dimly in the tallow, and at first the light showed him but a pair of eyes staring out from a frame or fringe of black hair. They were at once defiant in the surface and timid in their depths, eyes of a man at bay, hunted, and even haunted. Captain Knot took up the candle again, and held it close. The lower part of the face was weak, but neither sensual nor unrefined.

'When you've quite finished,' growled the man.

'So Jim Haynes is his name?' Captain Knot set back the candle, and addressed the younger seaman, 'Jim Haynes, formerly of Kennedy's gang in the *Rover*. If either of ye wants to convert this man I would advise thee and thy Master Wesley against starting him to confess his sins in public.'

'I got the King's pardon,' repeated Haynes. 'Can't you let a man alone as has turned a new leaf?'

'I never saw the *Rover*, sir,' put in Williamson. 'But, as it happens, I came across a good part of her crew one time, and this Jim Haynes amongst 'em. What's more, I know how most of 'em ended.'

'On the gallows, I make no doubt,' said Captain Knot. 'Let me hear thy tale presently. But 'tis the *Rover* – the ship herself – that I'm concerned about; the ship and the soul of her. A beautiful ship, hey?' He swung round on Haynes.

'Pretty enough,' Haynes admitted in a hoarse voice.

' "Beautiful" was my word. Dutch built, as I've heard, and Dutch manned when that blackguard Howell Davies took her. But the man who designed her must have despised to call his craft by the name of any nation, for he had been up to heaven and fetched away the Lord's own pattern of a ship. The sheer of her! and the entry! It isn't enough to say that the wave off her cut-water never had time to catch so much as her heel, the dainty! For she cut no water, or none that showed. She touched it, and it made room. The first time I crossed her 'twas in a gale of wind, and she'd come up for a look at us. It couldn't have been but for that, and for wantonness, the seas being too steep and the weather too heavy for so much as hailing us, let alone boarding. I was young in those days – young and proud as a cock, it being my first command. My ship? Oh, the same old *Jehoiada*. I've commanded her and never another these thirty-five years. By rights I should have laid her to, hours and hours before. Nowadays I should lay-to as a matter of course. But I was proud, as I say, and venturesome, and anxious to cut a dash with my owners. So I held her on under close-reefed main-tops'l and a napkin of a fores'l, which answered well enough until the gale moderated, and the seas growing as it lessened began to knock the wind out of our sails, so that she fell slow to her helm in the troughs, why then I began to see my vainglory in a new light. And just then, out of the dirt astern, this *Rover* came overhauling us, leaping almost atop of us. She had sighted us, no doubt, and made sure we were running in fear of her. So, just to give us a shake, she passed us to windward and close. At one moment she was high up over our heads – high as our mainyard almost; the next I'd be holding hard by the rigging and looking over as she went down and down, craning my neck over her deck and half wondering if she'd spike our very hull as she lifted again. There were two men at her wheel, and a third man just aft of them; and right aft, on her very taffrail, a monkey, cracking nuts and grinning.'

'Roberts's ape,' blurted Jim Haynes.

'I reckoned the third man would be Roberts. He was grinning almost as comfortable as his ape, and once he looked up and shook his fist for a joke. A light-featured man, with a wig, as I remember; but his ship! Dancing past like a fairy on cork heels, the very deck of her dry, and three times the *Jehoiada* had taken it green. She passed us, downed helm, put breast to wave, went over it like a lark over a wall, right across our bows, and left us.

'That was the first time. The second, 'twas about thirty leagues off Barbados, and the *Jehoiada* standing for home with a hold full of negroes from the Guinea Coast. This time she came up on us out of a summer sea, every stitch set, to her butterflies.' Captain Knot turned on Haynes. 'She carried a genius of a sailmaker?'

Haynes nodded. 'Corson – Zeph Corson. He went with the rest.'

'Ay! I can guess how. Well, then, they hanged an artist. The old Greeks or the Romans – I forget which – used to figure the soul in the shape of a butterfly. Master Haynes, what like was the soul of that ship? The beautiful! – I tell thee "beautiful" was my word – and the hands she had passed through! Howell first, then Roberts, and now with that hulking Kennedy for master.

'Kennedy had given Roberts the slip – left him (as I've heard) to rot in a waterless boat – and now was in his shoes, full sail for Execution Dock. There's a silly proverb tells ye to speak of a man as you find him. I found Kennedy well enough. Partly in fun, belike, and it happening to be his humour, he let me off easy. But I sensed him for one of the worst rogues I had ever run across. A hollow man, filled up with dirt – that's what I made of Kennedy.'

'I can tell you his end, sir,' put in Williamson. 'He got back to London and kept a bad house on Deptford Road. One of his women, in a tiff, laid information against him for robbery. While he was in Bridewell on this charge she sought out the ex-mate of a ship that he'd plundered. Grant was his name. Grant pays a visit to Bridewell, spots Kennedy as his man, swears to a warrant for piracy, and gets him shipped to Marshalsea. The rogue, to save his neck, offered King's Evidence against eight or ten old comrades then in hiding.'

'I was one,' said Jim Haynes. 'He was a dirty rogue, was Walter Kennedy – as you say, sir. But the judge wouldn't listen. So they took him from the Marshalsea and turned him off at Execution Dock. That would be in the summer of twenty-one, as I make out.'

'There or thereabouts,' agreed Captain Knot. 'That would

be about the length of rope I gave him. I haven't exactly what they call second sight, and yet I saw the hemp about his neck as plain as plain ... notwithstanding that he used me very civilly.

'I have told you that I was proud in those days. On one point I've continued proud as I was then. I belong to the Society of Friends. Not a gun have I ever carried on the *Jehoiada*; not a pistol nor sword nor cutlass would I ever permit to be brought aboard of her, much less to be worn. My owners called me a fool, and, what was more, they proved it. To which I made no answer but that they must take me or leave me. They took me.

'I had a sprinkling of friends among my crew; but the rest, who would have fought the ship if we'd carried arms, treated me to some pretty black looks when the *Rover* bore down upon us. I kept my face as stiff as I could, making believe not to notice; and indeed I saw very little to fear. These gentry would have little use for my ship, which is, and ever was, a good plain sailer in sea-room, but no consort for theirs – not within six points of the wind. "Why," said I to my mate, Mr Greenaway, that stood grumbling, "the *Jehoida's* as good-looking as any man's wife has a right to be; but this here dancing beauty, angel or devil, is not coming to enlist the likes of the *Jehoiada*. And as for her cargo, Friend Greenaway," I said, "didst thou ever hear of a pirate that was hungry for a cargo of blacks? However much treasure he may carry, or however little, he takes only what stows close for its worth, and nine times out of ten he's in trouble to feed his own mouths. He'll take victual from us, and victual we have in plenty" – for I always feed my slaves fat as pigs; it's Christian, and it brings its earthly reward in the market. "But for the rest," said I, "thou mark my words, he'll leave us alone."

'Well, so it turned out and to my astonishment even a little better. For what should prove to be this Kennedy's real reason for bringing us to? Victual he took from us, indeed, and enough to last him for three weeks. But his main purpose, he explained to me, coming aboard to my cabin. It seemed that he and his men, having taken much wealth, were weighted by it, and not only oppressed but frightened. "Of what use is wealth, Master Quaker," he asked, "if it don't bring a man peace and comfort?" "Of none at all, friend," said I, "and I am glad that repentance sits so heavy on thee." "Devil a bit it does," said he. "But I want to enjoy my earnings, and it's the same with my men. Now wealth made at sea will only bring enjoyment ashore, and the enjoyment we seek is not to be found in the islands, or, to my mind, anywhere on this Main. The most of us are dying to drop this trade, get back to England, bury the past, and live respectable, more or less. But that's the curse of it," said he. "You took note of my ship, maybe, as she came up on you?" "As one seaman to another, Captain Kennedy," I said, "she's the loveliest thing I ever saw on the face of the waters." "She's a devil," says he. "And I'm chained to her. Worse than a devil she is, being damned herself. Face of the waters – ay, there's her prison. Homeless, houseless, fleet as a bird, with all the law and the gospels in chase and giving her no rest. For all my pride in her she might sink under my shoes to-night, so I could win home to a tidy little parlour in Deptford." "It's there, friend," said I, "that I cannot help thee, being bound for the Capes." "No," said he; "but you can take off eight, or maybe nine, men of my company that have a mind to settle in Virginia. They will bring their share of the money, and I don't doubt they'll pay you well. I'm overmanned," said he, "for anything but fighting; and I'm sick of fighting and plundering; I only ask to get away home and live clean."

'The upshot was that I took over eight pirates with their chests and a light cutter boat, in which four of them had a mind to make, as soon as we neared the coast, for Maryland. Eight they were, and, as I remember, Jim Haynes, thou watched 'em pull from ship to ship, yourself in two minds to make the ninth. I had my glass on thee, and I never forget a face.'

'What became of them?' asked Haynes.

Captain Knot made a purring noise in his throat.

'I carried them safe,' said he, 'and delivered them. They made me a present of ten chests of sugar, ten rolls of Brazil tobacco, thirty moidores and some gold dust, in all to the value of two hundred and fifty pounds. They also made presents to the sailors. But they gave me a great deal of trouble with their jovial ways, and it was difficult for me to keep any discipline because they wore arms day and night. So I was glad enough when we reached coast water, and half the party left us in the boat to make across the bay for Maryland. For the other four, I may tell thee that, coming to Hampton and anchoring, I made haste ashore to Mr Spottswood, the Governor, who sent off a guard, had them all bound, and hanged them out of hand. Nay, he did more, being a man of great energy. He sent patrols up the coast after the four that were making for Maryland, but (as it happened) had been forced by weather to land where they could, and were having good entertainment with the planters in those parts. These also he hanged. So all the eight were accounted for.'

'And a d—n dirty trick!' swore Haynes, 'when they had paid their passage.'

'Ah, to be sure,' said Captain Knot. 'I forgot to tell that I handed the Governor all their property taken on board, and all the presents they had made me, and forced my men to do the like. I've no taste – never had – for pirates or pirates' money.'

'Well, I'm glad I made up my mind as I did – that's all,' Haynes growled.

Captain Knot fairly beamed on him. 'I thought I had made it clear, friend,' said he, ' 'twas the ship, and only the ship, that moved my bowels of pity. The beauty she was! ' He sighed. 'I never saw her again, nor heard what became of her.'

Peter Williamson took up the story.

'I canna tell you, sir, what became of the ship. But I ken very well how the crew came to land, and it was not in this same *Rover*.

'Jamie Haynes, here, did once tell me a part of your tale, sir – how that they fell in with a Virginiaman, the master of which was a Quaker (saving your presence), and would carry no arms. He named me the eight men that went along with you, but the names, you'll understand, don't stick in my head.'

'Nor in mine,' Captain Knot assured him heartily.

'I dare say Jamie could put names to them now.' William-son glanced at Haynes, who had thrust his shoulders back into the settle-corner and was brooding inattentive, with his chin sunk on his chest. 'But there! they're hanged long syne and don't signify. He said he'd often wished he had gone along with them.'

'Ha?' was Captain Knot's comment, short and grim.

'But he said, sir, that some days after parting company with you, cruising off Jamaica, they took a sloop thitherbound from Boston, loaded with bread and flour. Aboard of this sloop went all hands that was in compact for breaking the gang and living honest – or all but Kennedy himself. They mistrusted Kennedy for his dirty ways, forbye that he had no skill in navigation, nor even in the reading and writing, but was only useful in a fight. He pleaded so bitterly, however, when they were about to throw him overboard – he having got ahead of them and sneaked into the sloop – that in the end they took him along, having first made him swear to be faithful, putting his hand upon the Bible, and taking the most dread-fullest oaths.

'So the *Rover* was left on the high seas, with the few that had a mind to hold on in her; and the sloop, with Kennedy's party (as we'll call them) and their shares of plunder aboard, shaped right away for Ireland, where they had agreed to land and scatter. By bad navigation, however, they ran away to the north-west of Scotland, and into one gale upon another; whereby, with all bearings lost, they came near to perishing.

'Upon this coast, sir, in those days, my father kept what you might call a shebeen, a mile from Clashnessie, to the south of Eddruchillis Bay. Alec Williamson his name was, a widower, and myself a lad of sixteen, very industrious to learn penman-ship and the casting of accounts – my father doing some business off and on in the Free Trade, and, as he maintained, losing half his just profits by reason of his ignorance in these branches.

'Late one night, then – and the wind still blowing hard – there came a knocking at the door, and I opened it upon this

very James Haynes as you see on this settle. He was we
through, and scared; and his first word was: "Shut the door
for God's sake, and for God's sake close that chink of ligh
between your shutters!" "Is it a run?" asked my father, awak
and coming downstairs at the noise of the latch. "If, so," say
my father, "no warning has been put on me; and, what's more
my man, I never saw your face in my life." "By the smell o
this house," says Haynes, "the *usquebah* is not very far away
Fetch me a drink, and in the morning, if ye're early risers, I'l
make ye rich for life." I went with the jug, and, that side o
the house being dead to leeward, I heard a roaring of tipsy
voices away beyond the cross-roads. When I brought it to
him the man took the liquor down like milk. "I gave 'em the
slip at the turning," says he, and laughs. "They're for Edin-
burgh, poor devils." He would answer no questions. Afte
another drink and a bite he laid himself down in his sodder
clothes before what was left of the fire, and was asleep as soor
as his head touched the hearthstone.

'But before day he was up and led us – a little unsurely,
having come in the dark – down to a cove we called the Sow's
Shelter; a hole well-kenned as serviceable by the free-traders,
running in narrow and steep-to, with a shelf of sand for the
landing. What should we see there in the light of morning,
but a good-sized sloop almost filling the hole, stem-on to the
beach, and there grounded, hard and fast! . . . "Take your run
through her," says this Haynes, pointing, "and take your
pickings before the whole country's on top of 'ee – as it will be
within these two hours. For the fools who ran her here," says
he, "are rolling south down the road and passing themselves
for shipwrecked men; and the money is in their pockets and
the drink in their heads. So help yourselves, honest men, while
you may," says he. "There's silks aboard, and chinaware, and
plenty good tobacco; but to look for the dollars and the
precious stones and the gold dust will only waste your time."

"'Tis hard we three must work then before his lordship's
factor comes and claims wreckage," said my father. "Begging
your pardon," says Haynes, "but it will not be healthy for me
to be taken here. You two must do without me, and that not

until your lad here has taken me to safe hiding." There was reason in this, and I led the man around a point of the fore-shore to a snug cave. His clothing was stuffed with money so that he clinked as he climbed across the rocks. Well, in this cave by day, and by night in our cottage, we kept him hid for more than a month, it being sure capture for him within that time to try south after the rest of the crew. For I must tell you, sir–'

'I am curious to hear about this man,' put in Captain Knot, with a pretty grim look at Haynes, 'seeing that I missed the pleasure to hang him. He's alive, as I see, so we will say no more about it. As for the rest, it will content me to hear that they came to the gallows – never mind how.'

'Very well, sir,' said Williamson; 'then I'll be as short as you please. Kennedy cut loose from them at Cromarty, and by some means got himself shipped across to Ireland; which delayed *his* sail into Execution Dock for a season. Six or seven others had sense after a while to break away singly or in couples, and reached London without being disturbed or sus-picioned. But the main gang flamed it down through Scotland, drinking and roaring at such a rate that in places folk shut themselves within doors. In others they treated the whole township to drink; which procured two of their stragglers to be knocked on the head, their bodies being found murdered on the road and their money taken from them. The residue, to the number of seventeen, won almost to the gates of Edin-burgh. But, a post having ridden ahead, they were arrested and put into jail on suspicion of they kent not what. The magistrates were not long at a loss over warrants; for two of the pact, offering themselves for evidence, were accepted; which put the others on trial: whereby nine were convicted and executed. To get back to Jamie Haynes here – '

'I tell thee,' Captain Knot interrupted, 'I am fair sick hear-ing of Haynes.'

Haynes stood up, wiping his mouth weakly with the back of his hand. His knees shook as he straightened himself. He seemed like a man in a twitter after long drinking.

'Is it the *Rover*? . . . I can tell you, sir, about the *Rover*. She was a fine ship, sir. There was no mistaking her – '

'Look here, my man,' put in Captain Knot. 'There's no need to stand up and tell what I have been telling thee these twenty minutes.'

'There was no mistaking her,' Haynes went on, as though not hearing. His eyes were as if they withdrew their look deep in his head, and anon they stared out past the captain as though they saw a picture out in the twilight beyond the window-pane. He paused and gulped.

–'No mistaking her,' he went on. 'In the end I got away, first to Wick, then to Leith. There I shipped honest on the *Anna* brig for Jamaica. We called at St Vincent in the Wind'-ard Islands. Two days out from St Vincent – and me forward, it being my watch – at daybreak there stood the *Rover* right ahead, and not two miles from us. There was no mistaking her, *as* you say, sir. She came on me out of the night like, as if she had been searching, with all her sins aboard – her sins and mine, sir. Instead of calling out I ran aft to the master, and threw myself down, there by the wheel, at his feet, crying out her name, and how that was once a lost ship.'

Haynes passed a hand over his eyes.

'There she was, sir – heeling to it – the main t'gallant sail blown away, and all the rest of her canvas crowded. The master put up his glass. 'They must be mad aboard then,' says he; 'or else blazing drunk – the way she's behaving' – For she fetched up in the wind, staggered dead, and after a bit the breeze fetched her a clap that laid her rail under. She righted, paid off again, and again she fetched up shivering. 'We'll hail her,' says the old man. 'I'm not afraid of any seaman that handles his ship so.' He hailed, and none answered.

'The master, then, manning up close, saw that her decks were empty. There was no one at the wheel, which wasn't even lashed. He ordered me and five others to board her along with him.'

Haynes covered his eyes again, and henceforth to the end kept them covered.

'There was no crew aboard, sir: no trace of a crew. The hold was empty, but for nine niggers – live niggers, starved to the bone – sitting there with the whites of their eyes shining. Oh, ny God! Nine niggers, and not a word to be got from them!

'What is it you say, sir? There was no trace, I swear! Not a spot of blood on her decks or anywhere. Cleaned down from 'o'c'sle to cabin. Food enough on board, too. No, the men were not chained. But there they sat, the flesh shrunk on their bones and the whites of their eyes shining . . .'

Haynes dropped back on the settle, and covered his face with both hands.

'Well?' asked Captain Knot. 'What did your skipper do with her?'

'Put half a dozen hands aboard of her, sir: with orders to keep company and bear up with us for Kingston.'

'And – '

'And that night she skipped ahead . . . We never saw her again. She never came to port.'

'Amen,' said Captain Knot after a pause. 'She never was for port.'

MUTUAL EXCHANGE, LIMITED

I

MILLIONAIRE though he was, Mr Markham (*né* Markheim) never let a small opportunity slip. To be sure the enforced idleness of the Atlantic crossing bored him and kept him restless; it affected him with malaise to think that for these five days, while the solitude of ocean swallowed him, men on either shore, with cables at their command, were using them to get rich on their own account – it might even be at his expense. The first day out from New York he had spent in his cabin, immersed in correspondence. Having dealt with this and exhausted it, on the second, third, and fourth days he found nothing to do. He never played cards; he eschewed all acquaintance with his fellow-men except in the way of business; he had no vanity, and to be stared at on the promenade deck because of the fame of his wealth merely annoyed him. On the other hand, he had not the smallest excuse to lock himself up in his stuffy state-room. He enjoyed fresh air, and had never been sea-sick in his life.

It was just habit – the habit of never letting a chance go, or the detail of a chance – that on the fourth morning carried him the length of the liner, to engage in talk with the fresh-coloured young third officer busy on the high deck forward.

'A young man, exposed as you are, ought to insure himself,' said Mr Markham.

The third officer – by name Dick Rendal – knew something of the inquisitiveness and idle ways of passengers. This was his fifth trip on the *Carnatic*. He took no truck in passengers beyond showing them the patient politeness enjoined by the Company's rules. He knew nothing of Mr Markham, who dispensed with the services of a valet and dressed with a shabbiness only pardonable in the extremely rich. Mr Markham, 'The Insurance King', had arrayed himself this morning in grey flannel, with a reach-me-down overcoat, cloth cap, and carpet slippers that betrayed his flat, oriental instep. Dick Rendal sized him up for an insurance tout; but behaved precisely as he would have behaved on better information. He refrained from ordering the intruder aft; but eyed him less than amiably – being young, keen on his ship, and just now keen on his job.

'I saw you yesterday,' said Mr Markham. (It had blown more than half a gale, and late in the afternoon three heavy seas had come aboard. The third officer at that moment was employed with half a dozen seamen in repairing damages.) 'I was watching. As I judged, it was the nicest miss you weren't overboard. Over and above employers' liability you should insure. The Hands Across Mutual Exchange – that's your office.'

Mr Markham leaned back, and put a hand up to his inner breast-pocket – it is uncertain whether for his cigar-case, or for some leaflet relating to the Hands Across.

'Take care, sir!' said the third officer sharply. 'That stanchion – '

He called too late. The hand as it touched the breast-pocket, shot up and clawed at the air. With a voice that was less a cry than a startled grunt, Mr Markham pitched backwards off the fore-deck into the sea.

The third officer stared for just a fraction of a second; ran, seized a life-belt as the liner's length went shooting past; and hurled it – with pretty good aim, too – almost before a man of his working party had time to raise the cry of 'Man Overboard!' Before the alarm reached the bridge, he had kicked off his shoes; and the last sound in his ears as he dived was the ping of the bell ringing down to the engine-room – a thin note, infinitely distant, speaking out of an immense silence.

2

It was a beautifully clean dive; but in the flurry of the plunge the third officer forgot for an instant the right upward slant of the palms, and went a great way deeper than he had intended. By the time he rose to the surface the liner had slid by, and for a moment or two he saw nothing; for instinctively he came up facing aft, towards the spot where Mr Markham had fallen, and the long sea running after yesterday's gale threw up a ridge that seemed to take minutes – though in fact it took but a few seconds – to sink and heave up the trough beyond. By and by a life-belt swam up into sight: then another – at least a dozen had been flung; and beyond these at length, on the climbing crest of the swell two hundred yards away, the head and shoulders of Mr Markham. By great luck the first life-belt had fallen within a few feet of him, and Mr Markham had somehow managed to get within reach and clutch it – a highly creditable feat when it is considered that he was at best a poor swimmer, that the fall had knocked more than half the breath out of his body, that he had swallowed close on a pint of salt water, and that a heavy overcoat impeded his movements. But after this fair first effort Mr Markham, as his clothes weighed him down, began – as the phrase is – to make very bad weather of it. He made worse and worse weather of it as Dick Rendal covered the distance between them with a superlatively fine side-stroke, once or twice singing out to him to hold on, and keep a good heart. Mr Markham, whether he heard or no, held on with great courage, and even coolness – up to a point. Then of a sudden his nerve deserted him. He loosed his hold of the life-belt, and struck out for his rescuer. Worse, as he sank in the effort and Dick gripped him, he closed and struggled. For half a minute Dick, shaking free of the embrace – and this only by striking him on the jaw and half stunning him as they rose on the crest of a swell – was able to grip him by the collar and drag him within reach of the life-belt. But here the demented man managed to wreath his legs and arms in another and more terrible hold. The pair of them were now cursing horribly, cursing whenever a wave desisted from choking them and allowed them to cough and splutter for breath. They fought as two men whose lives had pent up an unmitigable hate for this moment. They fought, neither losing his hold, as their strength ebbed, and the weight of their clothes dragged them lower. Dick Rendal's hand still clutched the cord of the life-belt, but both bodies were under water, fast locked, when the liner's boat at length reached the spot. They were hauled on board, as on a long-line you haul a fish with a crab fastened upon him; and were laid in the stern-sheets, where their grip was with some difficulty loosened.

It may have happened in the struggle. Or again it may have happened when they were hoisted aboard and lay, for a minute or so, side by side on the deck. Both men were insensible; so far gone indeed that the doctor looked serious as he and his helpers set to work inducing artificial respiration.

The young third officer came round after five or ten minutes of this; but, strangely enough, in the end he was found to be suffering from a severer shock than Mr Markham, on whom the doctor had operated for a full thirty-five minutes before a flutter of the eyelids rewarded him. They were carried away – the third officer, in a state of collapse, to his modest berth; Mr Markham to his white-and-gold deck-cabin. On his way thither Mr Markham protested cheerily that he saw no reason for all this fuss; he was as right now, or nearly as right, as the Bank.

3

'How's Rendal getting on?'

Captain Holditch, skipper of the *Carnatic,* put this question next morning to the doctor, and was somewhat surprised by the answer.

'Oh, Rendal's all right. That is to say, he will be all right. Just now he's suffering from shock. My advice – supposing, of course, you can spare him – is to pack him straightaway off to his people on a month's leave. In less than a month he'll be fit as a fiddle.' The doctor paused and added: 'Wish I could feel as easy about the millionaire.'

'Why, what's the matter with *him*? Struck me he pulled round wonderfully, once you'd brought him to. He talked as cheery as a grig.'

'H'm – yes,' said the doctor; 'he has been talking like that ever since; only he hasn't been talking sense. Calls me names for keeping him in bed, and wants to get out and repair that stanchion. I told him it was mended. "Nothing on earth is the matter with me," he insisted, till I had to quiet him down with bromide. By the way, did you send off any account of the accident?'

'By wireless? No; I took rather particular pains to stop that – gets into the papers, only frightens the family and friends, who conclude things to be ten times worse than they are. Plenty of time at Southampton. Boat Express'll take him home ahead of the scare.'

'Lives in Park Lane, doesn't he? – that big corner house like a game-pie? ... Ye-es, you were thoughtful, as usual ... Only someone might have been down to the docks to meet him. Wish I knew his doctor's address. Well, never mind – I'll fix him up so that he reaches Park Lane, anyway.'

'He ought to do something for Rendal,' mused Captain Holditch.

'He will, you bet, when his head is right – that's if a millionaire's head is ever right,' added the doctor, who held radical opinions on the distribution of wealth.

The captain ignored this. He never talked politics even when ashore.

'As plucky a rescue as ever I witnessed,' he answered the doctor. 'Yes, of course I'll spare the lad. Slip a few clothes into his bag, and tell him he can get off by the first train. Oh, and by the way, you might ask him if he's all right for money; say he can draw on me if he wants any.'

The doctor took his message down to Dick Rendal. 'We're this moment passing Hurst Castle,' he announced cheerfully, 'and you may tumble out if you like. But first I'm to pack a few clothes for you; if you'll let me, I'll do it better than the steward.'

'I suppose I ought to come the handsome out of this.' Dick passed a hand over his forehead as he spoke slowly and, as it were, grudgingly. 'But somehow I – I hate – yes, *hate* – wish I knew how to clear the whole damn score – handsomely of course.' His voice trailed off.

'What you want,' said the doctor, vaguely disappointed in the lad, 'is ten grains of bromide.' He spoke sharply, and continued: 'The Old Man says you may get off as soon as we're docked, and stay home till you've recovered. I'll allow you the inside of a week before you're fit as ever,' he wound up.

'The Old Man? Yes – yes – Captain Holditch, of course,' muttered Dick from his berth.

The doctor looked at him narrowly for a moment; but, when he spoke again, kept by intention the same easy rattling tone.

'Decent of him, eh? – Yes, and by the way, he asked me to tell you that, if you shouldn't happen to be flush of money just now, that needn't hinder you five minutes. He'll be your banker, and make it right with the Board.'

Dick lay still for half a dozen seconds, as though the words took that time in reaching him. Then he let out a short laugh from somewhere high in his nose.

'Be my banker? Will he? Good Lord!'

'May be,' said the doctor, drily; laying out a suit of mufti at the foot of the bed, 'the Old Man and I belong to the same date. I've heard that youngsters save money nowadays. But when I was your age that sort of offer would have hit the mark nine times out of ten.'

He delivered this as a parting shot. Dick, lying on his back and staring up at a knot in the woodwork over his bunk, received it placidly. Probably he did not hear. His brow was corrugated in a frown, as though he were working out a sum or puzzling over some problem. The doctor closed the door softly, and some minutes later paid a visit to Mr Markham, whom he found stretched on the couch of the white-and-gold deck-cabin, attired in a grey flannel sleeping-suit, and wrapped around the legs with a travelling rug of dubious hue.

'That's a good deal better,' he said cheerfully, after an examination, in which, while seeming to be occupied with pulses and temperature, he paid particular attention to the pupils of Mr Markham's eyes. 'We are nosing up the Solent fast – did you know it? Ten minutes ought to see us in Southampton Water; and I suppose you will be wanting to catch the first train.'

'I wonder,' said Mr Markham, vaguely, 'if the Old Man will mind.'

The doctor stared for a moment. 'I think we may risk it,' he said, after a pause, 'though I confess that last night I was doubtful. Of course, if you're going to be met, it's right enough.'

'Why should I be met?'

'Well, you see – I couldn't know, could I? Anyway, you ought to see your own doctor as soon as you get home. Perhaps, if you gave me his name, I might scribble a note to him, just to say what has happened. Even big-wigs, you know, don't resent being helped with a little information.'

Mr Markham stared. 'Lord!' said he, 'you're talking as if I kept a tame doctor! Why, man, I've never been sick nor sorry since I went to school!'

'That's not hard to believe. I've ausculted you – sound as a bell, you are: constitution strong as a horse's. Still, a shock is a shock. You've a family doctor, I expect – someone you ring up when your liver goes wrong, and you want to be advised to go to Marienbad or some such place – I'd feel easier if I could shift the responsibility on to him.'

Still Mr Markham stared. 'I've heard about enough of this shock to my system,' said he at length. 'But have it your own way. If you want me to recommend a doctor, my mother swears by an old boy in Craven Street, Strand. I don't know the number, but his name's Leadbetter, and he's death on croup.'

'Craven Street? That's a trifle off Park Lane, isn't it? – Still, Leadbetter, you say? I'll get hold of the directory, look up his address, and drop him a note or two on the case by this evening's post.'

*

A couple of hours later Mr Markham and Dick Rendal almost rubbed shoulders in the crowd of passengers shaking hands with the ever polite Captain Holditch, and bidding the *Carnatic* good-bye with the usual parting compliments; but in the hurry and bustle no one noted that the pair exchanged neither word nor look of recognition. The skipper gave Dick an honest clap on the shoulder. 'Doctor's fixed you up, then?

That's right. Make the best of your holiday, and I'll see that the Board does you justice,' and with that, turned away for more handshaking. One small thing he did remark. When it came to Mr Markham's turn, that gentleman, before extending a hand lifted it to his forehead and gravely saluted. But great men – as Captain Holditch knew – have their eccentric ways.

Nor was it remarkable, when the luggage came to be sorted out and put on board the boat express, that Dick's porter under his direction collected and wheeled off Mr Markham's; while Mr Markham picked up Dick's suit-case, walked away with it unchallenged to a third-class smoking compartment and deposited it on the rack. There were three other passengers in the compartment. 'Good Lord!' ejaculated one, as the millionaire stepped out to purchase an evening paper. 'Isn't that Markham? Well! – and travelling third!' 'Saving habit – second nature,' said another. 'That's the way to get rich, my boy.'

Meanwhile Dick, having paid for four places, and thereby secured a first-class solitude, visited the telegraph office, and shrank the few pounds in his pocket by sending a number of cablegrams.

On the journey up Mr Markham took some annoyance from the glances of his fellow-passengers. They were furtive, almost reverential, and this could only be set down to his exploit of yesterday. He thanked Heaven they forbore to talk of it.

4

In the back-parlour of a bookseller's shop, between the Strand and the Embankment, three persons sat at tea; the proprietor of the shop, a grey little man with round spectacles and bushy eyebrows, his wife, and a pretty girl of twenty or twenty-one. The girl apparently was a visitor, for she wore her hat, and her jacket lay across the arm of an old horsehair sofa that stood against the wall in the lamp's half shadow; and yet the grey little bookseller and his little Dresden-china wife very evidently made no stranger of her. They talked, all three, as members of a family talk, when contented and affectionate: at haphazard, taking one another for granted, not raising their voices.

The table was laid for a fourth; and by and by they heard him coming through the shop – in a hurry too. The old lady, always sensitive to the sound of her boy's footsteps, looked up almost in alarm, but the girl half rose from her chair, her eyes eager.

'I know,' she said breathlessly. 'Jim has heard – '

'Chrissy here? That's right.' A young man broke into the room, and stood waving a newspaper. 'The *Carnatic*'s arrived – here it is under "Stop Press" – I bought the paper as I came by Somerset House – "*Carnatic* arrived Southampton 3.45 this afternoon. Her time from Sandy Hook, 5 days 6 hours, 45 minutes."'

'Then she hasn't broken the record this time, though Dick was positive she would,' put in the old lady. During the last six months she had developed a craze for Atlantic records, and knew the performances of all the great liners by heart.

'You bad little mother!' – Jim wagged a forefinger at her. 'You don't deserve to hear another word.'

'Is there any more?'

'More? Just you listen to this: "Reports heroic rescue. Yesterday afternoon Mr Markham, the famous Insurance King, accidentally fell overboard from fore-deck, and was gallantly rescued by a young officer named Kendal" – you bet that's a misprint for Rendal – error in the wire, perhaps – we'll get a later edition after tea – "who leapt into the sea and swam to the sinking millionaire, supporting him until assistance arrived. Mr Markham had by this afternoon recovered sufficiently to travel home by the Boat Express." There, see for yourselves!'

Jim spread the newspaper on the table.

'But don't they say anything about Dick?' quavered the mother, fumbling with her glasses, while Miss Chrissy stared at the print with shining eyes.

'Dick's not a millionaire, mother – though it seems he had been supporting one – for a few minutes anyway. Well, Chrissy! how does that make you feel?'

'You see, my dear,' said the little bookseller softly, addressing his wife, 'if any harm had come to the boy, they would have reported it for certain.'

They talked over the news while Jim ate his tea, and now and again interrupted with his mouth full; talked over it and speculated upon it in low, excited tones, which grew calmer by degrees. But still a warm flush showed on the cheeks of both the women, and the little bookseller found it necessary to take out his handkerchief at intervals and wipe his round spectacles.

He was wiping them perhaps for the twentieth time, and announcing that he must go and relieve his assistant in the shop, when the assistant's voice was heard uplifted close outside – as it seemed, in remonstrance with a customer.

'Hallo!' said the little bookseller, and was rising from his chair, when the door opened. A middle-aged, Jewish-looking man, wrapped to the chin in a shabby ulster and carrying a suit-case, stood on the threshold, and regarded the little party.

'Mother!' cried Mr Markham. 'Chrissy!'

He set down the suit-case, and took two eager strides. Old Mrs Rendal, the one immediately menaced, shrank back into Jim's arms as he started up with his throat working to bolt a mouthful of cake. Chrissy caught her breath.

'Who in thunder are you, sir?' demanded Jim. 'Get out of this, unless you want to be thrown out!'

'Chrissy!' again appealed Mr Markham, but in a fainter voice. He had come to a standstill, and his hand went slowly up to his forehead.

Chrissy pointed to the suit-case. 'It's – it's Dick's!' she gasped. Jim did not hear.

'Mr Wenham,' he said to the white-faced assistant in the doorway, 'will you step out, please, and fetch a policeman?'

'Excuse me.' Mr Markham took his hand slowly from his face, and spread it behind him, groping as he stepped backwards to the door. 'I – I am not well, I think' – he spoke precisely, as though each word as it came had to be held and gripped. 'The address' – here he turned on Chrissy with a vague apologetic smile – 'faces – clear in my head. Mistake – I really beg your pardon.'

'Get him some brandy, Jim,' said the little bookseller. 'The gentleman is ill, whoever he is.'

But Mr Markham turned without another word, and lurched past the assistant, who flattened himself against a bookshelf to give him room. Jim followed him through the shop; saw him cross the doorstep and turn away down the pavement to the left; stared in his wake until the darkness and the traffic swallowed him; and returned, softly whistling, to the little parlour.

'Drunk's the simplest explanation,' he announced.

'But how did he know my name?' demanded Chrissy. 'And the suit-case!'

'Eh? He's left it – well, if this doesn't beat the band! Here, Wenham – nip after the man and tell him he left his luggage behind!' Jim stooped to lift the case by the handle.

'But it's Dick's!'

'Dick's?'

'It's the suit-case I gave him – my birthday present last April. See, there are his initials!'

5

Dick Rendal, alighting at Waterloo, collected his luggage – or rather, Mr Markham's – methodically; saw it hoisted on a four-wheeler; and, handing the cabby two shillings, told him to deliver it at an address in Park Lane, where the butler would pay him his exact fare. This done, he sought the telegraph office and sent three more cablegrams, the concise wording of which he had carefully evolved on the way up from Southampton. These do not come into the story – which may digress, however, so far as to tell that on receipt of one of them, the Vice-President of the Hands Across Central New York Office remarked to his secretary 'that the old warrior was losing no time. Leisure and ozone would appear to have bucked him up.' To which the secretary answered that it was lucky for civilization if Mr Markham missed suspecting, or he'd infallibly make a corner in both.

Having dispatched his orders, Dick Rendal felt in his

pockets for a cigar-case; was annoyed and amused (in a sub-conscious sort of way) to find only a briar pipe and a pocketful of coarse-cut tobacco; filled and lit his pipe, and started to walk.

His way led him across Westminster Bridge, up through Whitehall, and brought him to the steps of that building which, among all the great London clubs, most exorbitantly resembles a palace. He mounted its perron with the springy confident step of youth; and that same spring and confidence of gait carried him past the usually vigilant porter. A marble staircase led him to the lordliest smoking-room in London. He frowned, perceiving that his favourite arm-chair was occupied by a somnolent Judge of the High Court, and catching up the *Revue des Deux Mondes* settled himself in a window-bay com-manding the great twilit square of the Horse Guards and the lamp-lit Mall.

He had entered the smoking-room lightly, almost jauntily; but – not a doubt of it – he was tired – so tired that he shuffled his body twice and thrice in the arm-chair before discovering the precise angle that gave superlative comfort . . .

'I beg your pardon, sir.'

Dick opened his eyes. A liveried footman stood over his chair, and was addressing him.

'Eh? Did I ring? Yes, you may bring me a glass of liqueur brandy. As quickly as possible, if you please; to tell the truth, George, I'm not feeling very well.'

The man started at hearing his name, but made no motion to obey the order.

'I beg your pardon, sir, but the secretary wishes to see you in his room.'

'The secretary? Mr Hood? Yes, certainly.' Dick rose. 'I – I am afraid you must give me your arm, please. A giddiness – the ship's motion, I suppose.'

The secretary was standing at his door in the great vestibule as Dick came down the staircase on the man's arm.

'I beg your pardon,' he said, 'but may I have your name? The porter does not recognize you, and I fear that I am equally at fault.'

'My name?' – with the same gesture that Mr Markham had used in the little back parlour, Dick passed a hand over his eyes. He laughed, and even to his own ears the laugh sounded vacant, foolish.

'Are you a member of the club, sir?'

'I – I thought I was.' The marble pillars of the atrium were swaying about him like painted cloths, the tessellated pavement heaving and rocking at his feet. 'Abominably stupid of me,' he muttered, 'unpardonable, you must think.'

The secretary looked at him narrowly, and decided that he was really ill; that there was nothing in his face to suggest the impostor.

'Come into my room for a moment,' he said, and sent the footman upstairs to make sure that no small property of the Club was missing. 'Here, drink down the brandy ... Feeling better? You are aware, no doubt, that I might call in the police and have you arrested?'

For a moment Dick did not answer, but stood staring with rigid eyes. At length:

'They – won't – find – what – I – want,' he said slowly, dropping out the words one by one. The secretary now felt certain that here was a genuine case of mental derangement. With such he had no desire to be troubled; and so, the footman bringing word that nothing had been stolen, he dismissed Dick to the street.

6

The brandy steadying him, Dick went down the steps with a fairly firm tread. But he went down into a world that for him was all darkness – darkness of chaos – carrying an entity that was not his, but belonged Heaven knew to whom.

The streets, the traffic, meant nothing to him. Their roar was within his head; and on his ears, nostrils, chest, lay a pressure as of mighty waters. Rapidly as he walked, he felt himself all the while to be lying fathoms deep in those waters, face downwards, with drooped head, held motionless there while something within him struggled impotently to rise to the surface. The weight that held him down, almost to bursting, was as the weight of tons.

The houses, the shop-fronts, the street-lamps, the throng of dark figures, passed him in unmeaning procession. Yet all the time his feet, by some instinct, were leading him towards the water; and by and by he found himself staring – still face-downwards – into a black inverted heaven wherein the lights had become stars and swayed only a little.

He had, in fact, halted, and was leaning over the parapet of the Embankment, a few yards from Cleopatra's Needle; and as he passed the plinth some impression of it must have bitten itself on the retina; for coiled among the stars lay two motionless sphinxes, green-eyed, with sheathed claws, watching lazily while the pressure bore him down to them, and down – and still down ...

Upon this dome of night there broke the echo of a footfall. A thousand footsteps had passed him, and he had heard none of them. But this one, springing out of nowhere, sang and repeated itself and re-echoed across the dome, and from edge to edge. Dick's fingers drew themselves up like the claws of the sphinx. The footsteps drew nearer while he crouched: they were close to him. Dick leapt at them, with murder in his spring.

Where the two men grappled, the parapet of the Embankment opens on a flight of river-stairs. Mr Markham had uttered no cry; nor did a sound escape either man, as locked in that wrestle, they swayed over the brink.

*

They were hauled up, unconscious, still locked in each other's arms.

'Queer business,' said one of the rescuers as he helped to loosen their clasp, and lift the bodies on board the Royal Humane Society's float. 'Looks like murderous assault. But which of 'em done it, by the looks, now?'

*

Five minutes later Dick's eyelids fluttered. For a moment he stared up at the dingy lamp swinging overhead; then his lips parted in a cry, faint, yet sharp:

'Take care, sir! That stanchion – '

But Mr Markham's first words were: 'Plucky! Devilish plucky! – Owe you my life, my lad.'

STEP O' ONE SIDE

The Story is told by James Pascoe of Menadarva, in the Clay District of Cornwall

I

I WAS a small boy when Joseph Pooke laid a sort of spell on our parish; and as the beginning of it happened in the bar-kitchen of 'Step o' One Side' (which is our local name for the Wesley Arms, by reason of its standing, respectable yet in some ways convenient, a short step off the main street), I can only report of them by hearsay; my chief witness being Sam Trudgian, a clay-worker and a moderately sober man all his days.

This Joseph Pooke, then, came on a Friday night in December and out of a tearing sou'westerly gale, to the astonishment of the company seated around on bench and settle and all the cosier for the squalls of rain bursting against the windows. For you must know that the little off-parlour beyond the bar-kitchen served, in those days on Fridays nights, for a sort of counting-house, where the three Clay-lords (as we called them), who owned the great One-and-All Pit, paid out the men's wages; which done, they would light their long pipes and linger for a couple of hours over two goes apiece of brandy-hot and discuss the news of the day.

Old Zebedee and Cornelius Bunt, brothers and twins at that, were the two seniors, both equally rich by repute; with William Pendrea, their sister's son – they being unmarried – for junior partner and manager. Lawyer Simmons of St Austell regularly made up the fourth; and there they would sit content with the world, a door and a curtain only dividing them off from the big kitchen bar where the men handselled their pay – thirty it might be and more, thinning down to a dozen as the staider ones sloped away home to their wives.

Well, there the place was full – Renatus Lowry, the landlord,

stirring the great fire and taking orders; his wife behind
the bar mixing 'Schenacrum' (which is ale and rum with
ingredients); and their daughter Annie, a slip of a girl all but
husband-high, slicing lemons or running to and from the
back kitchen with the kettle. And in the midst of this busy-all
the front door banged to, and close on the sound of it the
foreigner walked in. I should explain perhaps that any with a
face unknown or a stranger in any way from outside the
parish is a 'foreigner' to us in Menadarva. But this man had
the look of a far-travelled man as he stood a moment framed
in the kitchen doorway, the lamplight glistening on the wet
that poured off the rim of his sou'wester and down his yellow
oilskin. Also when he pulled off his headpiece and the company caught sight that a pair of ear-rings glinted behind the
draggle of his side locks, it took them aback to hear him speak
good Cornish.

'Evenin', neighbours all!' says he, taking in the room with
a smile and a bit of a laugh. 'A red light at times may be a
warnin', but ashore and through red curtains it spells good
entertainment – or should, eh, missus?' He turned to Mrs
Lowry.

'For them as can pay and behave themselves,' answered that
cautious woman. Her husband just at that moment came from
the inner room, a tray of empty glasses in hand. Belike the
bang of the door had fetched him forth of a sudden.

'Hullo!' says he with a stare, handing the tray to the
woman; and then: 'What's this? – a wreck ashore?'

'Timbers sound, I hope,' says the stranger, tapping a longish bundle wrapped in tarpaulin that he carried under his left
arm. With no more ado he stepped across to the fire-place,
unslung a haversack from his shoulder, set down the bundle,
and slowly stripped himself of his oilskins – a well-set fellow,
broad of shoulder, and cased in good sea-cloth. His boots,
too, though mired, were stout and serviceable.

'You're kindly welcome anyways, my son,' said Renatus,
perhaps noting this. 'A seaman, I reckon?'

'Miner. And my name's Pooke – Joseph Pooke – St Joseph
was in the tin trade once, as maybe you've heard tell. But

you've made no bad cast at it, either: seein' that I've come here by way of The Horn.'

This made all stare, respectfully.

'Plymouth bound?'

'Not to-night, anyway. And I've not broke ship, if that's what you're hintin'.'

'For shame, Renatus!' put in the wife across the counter. 'Cattychisin' like this, and him just in from the weather.' The sight of the man's good clothes had reassured her, no doubt.

He stepped to the bar. 'Thank 'ee, ma'am. And as for your husband's name I can read it from the notice above the dresser: RENATUS LOWRY, LICENSED TO SELL BEER, SPIRITUOUS LIQUORS AND TOBACCO. Well, that's a suggestion. What about drinks all round, if the company will name their fancy?' He pulled out a fistful of silver and slid a couple of half-crowns across. 'That's a pretty piece, too, you keep here.'

'I'll trouble you to speak respectful of my daughter,' Mrs Lowry fired up.

'Certainly, ma'am. But I was speakin' of your counter. A prettier piece of copper, nor a brighter kept as proud to image two handsome faces, hasn' delighted the eye this long while. I'm a miner, ma'am, as I said just now; and by haveage – my father and mother having broken up home under Carn Brea and gone out to the States with a cousin or two in the forty-nine when the mines closed, down-along. In Nevada I was born and reared. Underground mostly ... Drinks around, landlord, if you please! ... And what might be *your* name, my dear?' he asks the girl. 'N or M? as the book says.'

'Annie, sir,' answers she, bending low, and her hand shaking a bit as she pushed his drink towards him so that it spilt a drop.

'Careless, Annie!' says the mother.

'Annie? – Annie Lowry? Eh now – "Maxwellton braes are bonny" ... No, ma'am, I'm not teasin' your daughter. 'Tis the name of an old song, and the world-widest on earth I reckon.'

'Is it out of Wesley?' she asked.

' 'Tis a tune two innocents have sung together often enough, each holding a corner of Wesley's hymn-book. And you shall hear it, with the company's leave.'

He went over to the corner, unwrapped a long box from the tarpaulin, drew from it fiddle and bow. Now I should tell you we have a great ear for music in Menadarva. So all waited agog while he resined and tuned, and it didn't need a scrape of his foot when ready, nor the flourish he gave to his bow, to call for silence.

First he played the air of the old song in single notes, very quiet and true: next he repeated it, holding the fiddle to his ear and plucking the strings: then it went under his chin again and fetched out the thing in great chords 'so as (I am quoting Sam) you didn't scarcely know the fiddle's inside from your own'. And with that he started off on variations faster and faster till the tune mazed itself in a kind of devil's jig. In the whirl of it (says Sam) you couldn't tell man from music, nor the music from the play of his wrists and the glint of his ear-rings; till sudden with a stamp of his foot he broke off, waited whilst you might count five and then, soft as before, plucked out the tune, note by note.

With that it was over. In the middle of the clapping Sam turned – he didn't know why – towards the girl Annie, and her face was white as a peeled hazel. Belike, though, he was the only one to mark this, the others slewing about at the moment towards the inner doorway, where stood the Clay-lords themselves, fetched forth by the music.

'Brayvo! Brayvo!' cackled the twins together. 'But who the devil is it?' asked Lawyer Simmons.

Pendrea, as manager, took charge. 'That's a rare gift of yours, my man,' says he. 'Travellin' in music, eh?'

'Travellin' *to* music,' the stranger corrected him. 'Joseph Pooke's my name, at your service; mining's my occupation – metalliferous; and the jig I played just now is the tune I travel to, mostly. You may call it "Over the Hills and Far Away".'

Pendrea stood and eyed him a bit, finger on chin. He was a leading Methodist and took a great interest in his choir, so that all guessed what worked in his mind.

'Know anything about clay?'

'Adam was made of it, I've heard tell.'

'China-clay, I mean.'

' – and the sons of Adam hereabouts dig it for the making of things to be broken, like their father and other vessels of promise.'

'Well, if you're minded for a job' – Pendrea flushed a trifle as he said it, being a masterful man and not caring to be answered thus before company – 'come to my office to-morrow, at ten sharp.'

'Likely I may, when I've slept upon it' – with a side glance at the landlady.

'Annie, girl, fit and heat the warming-pan,' commanded she.

2

In this way Joseph Pooke came to us, to take charge, as you might say, of the parish. Next morning he signed on at the Great Goonburrow Pit, under the 'One and All', and moved in his traps to Aunt Sandercock's, over her general store; and – it being Saturday – took a longish walk over the moors. Sunday morning he attended church, and the Methodists reckoned they had lost him. But evening found him seated in chapel, just as attentive as to the parson's sermon; and singing, when the hymn came, in a clear light tenor.

Pendrea got hold of him afterwards. 'Glad to see you're one of the Connexion.'

'It's news to me,' answered Pooke. 'But there's a wheeze in that harmonium of yours that I could cure, if you gave me leave to try.'

Within a week, having fitted up a bench and conjured some tools out of goodness knows where, he had the instrument to pieces and refitted, bit by bit.

'You've made it speak like an angel,' said Miss Lasky, the choir leader, with a blush for her forwardness.

'Well,' said he, 'God Almighty *might* make an angel speak like a harmonium; but He's merciful. A harmonium's the devil at the best, if you'll excuse me. Your choir, now; a better set of natural voices you couldn't get together, not if you combed the Pacific slope; and yet all singing *tremolo* and because of *this*.' He banged his palm on the lid.

'But, but, Mr Pooke – I *like* to hear them sing *tremolo*! It shows that their feelings are moved.'

She remembered his answer to this and told it to me years after. 'Music don't wobble, miss, any more than the stars singing their Maker's name.'

'Oh!' said Miss Lasky, puzzled. 'I didn't know you were religious – in that sense,' she went on, recovering herself and being (as I can guess now) not more averse than most spinsters of her age from discussing religion with a man.

He made no answer then; but later, being called in to train the choir, with no help but his fiddle he taught them how to hit their notes clean every time, till they chorused away like larks, unaccompanied, and the fame of it drew folks of a Sunday from miles around to hear.

Before this, though, he had a wood shed built at the back of Aunt Sandercock's, with a whole gamut of tools and gadgets. And by degrees it came about that if you wanted watch or clock put to rights, or your pump wouldn't work, or your chimney smoked, or you had a tooth to be pulled, or a child with the croup, or a swarm of bees to be hived, Pooke was your man.

With all this he never again played the fiddle in public, save to give the note at choir practices. 'This clay-heaving deadens the touch,' he explained one night to the company in 'Step o' One Side'. 'Metal and clay be two different things. Fire made 'em both; but in metal – gold, silver, tin, copper, call it what you will – fire's in the veins working, and you follow it like a lover – eh, Miss Annie? While, with clay, what is it but ashes, burnt out and dead.'

None the less he did his job at the works well enough, and specially in packing a truck. Only one day, happening to cross the pit with Pendrea, says he with a jerk of his thumb back towards where a two-three men were shovelling. 'There's a cornice of over-hang yonder. None too safe as I reckon.'

Now it may be that Pendrea had started to envy the man's popularity. At any rate he answered stiff and in the hearing of several: 'Your job's over there with the loading, I believe.'

'Sorry,' said Pooke polite. 'But my father was killed by a fall of rock; and the shock so told on my mother that my brother Noah was born a week later, before his time. Whereby, being his older by nine years, I had to look after him as he grew up. She being weak of health, her terror day and night was of earth or rock giving way and smothering him. Woman's foolishness, no doubt; but that's how I grew up nervous about overhang.'

Two days later, as fate would have it, nine or ten tons of that very cornice came down and crushed a couple of workers. Reuben Oates and Jim Narcarrow by name. Pooke, as one of the foremost on the spot, to dig out the bodies, had to give evidence at the inquest, but not a word did he speak to cast any blame on Pendrea, and the other witnesses took their cue from him. So the verdict was 'accidental death' and no more, though whisperings went around.

He never took advantage of the manager over this, unless you count a day when he walked into the office and asked for a week off.

'It's like this,' he answered Pendrea – 'I was in that church of yours, on hands and knees, after hours, rubbing at a couple of brasses, when old Parson Vine came stumbling in, blind as a bat, and fairly pitched over me. Like leap-frog it was. And so, one thing leading to another, I told him that two of his organ-pipes were rotten as touch and proved it by poking a hole in 'em with my finger. And I want the hire of a lorry, too, if you'll oblige.'

'You're not joining our friends the Anglicans, I hope?'

'Nothing worse than helping brotherly love,' said Pooke. So off he drove next day, and came back inside a week with four brand-new organ pipes, and in ten days had all the rest gilded to correspond.

But his last feat was with the Parish Band, which included church and chapel alike, but had been going to pieces ever since the death of old 'Waxy' Cann, their bandmaster. He spent three weeks going around collecting the old instruments and refitting them; and then turned to the piles of old music scores. 'B flat, B flat – the whole damn lot!'

''Tis the easiest key to play,' explained Archie Govett, leader and first cornet.

'Yes, and like kissing your sister.'

With that he set to work again, transposing the better pieces back into their proper keys. Hours it must have cost him and reams of music sheets; but by August he had Menadarva Band fit to enter for the County Competition at Redruth, and that albeit he never put lip to the brass or the reeds himself. 'I was brought up on strings,' he'd say. 'If you want to know what brass can do, or a silver cornet, you should hear my brother Noah.'

It was during these practices that he started – and, once started, kept on going – with talk about this wonderful brother of his. 'He's a masterpiece, is Noah! Built for the brass, as you might say: six foot two, forty-eight round the chest at nineteen, and yet will fetch forth a note like a maid's whisper and not a slur in it.' Seemingly, too, this nonesuch had other accomplishments – 'could sing a high tenor, most pleasing, and shift a ton of broken rock against any two men of his near size,' and so on, and so on.

Well, the explanation came before we wanted; and with it the blow fell.

In mid-August the band, with Pooke as conductor, fared down to Redruth in a four-horse brake. They didn't carry off the cup; but they brought home second prize, with a special for the 'Self-Chosen Item', which was no less a teaser than the overture to *Semiramide;* which again made excuse for a grand supper in 'Step o' One Side'. Having, of course, to speak to the toast of his health: 'You'll do better next time,' he said, 'and why? Because I'm leaving you, and by the five-forty tomorrow . . . Passage booked back to the States on the *Dalmatic*, sailing Southampton, Tuesday. But 'tis no losers you'll be. You've heard me tell, often enough, of my brother Noah? Well, among his other merits he always does as I tell him. We've arranged to exchange jobs, and he'll be arriving, as we've planned, towards the end of March next. And so I thank you, friends all!' He lifted his glass and sat down of a sudden, the company left to stare as though they'd seen a ghost through the tobacco-smoke.

Next morning there was some talk of a testimonial, but no time for it. The band assembled in the afternoon and played him down to the station: and the last we saw of him was a hand waving from the carriage window at the bend of the curve.

3

It is here that, in a small way, I happen into the story, and with a confession. The train gone, and the crowd trooping back to the village to drink to the hero's health, it came into my unregenerate head (such temptations do assail a boy rising ten) that the coast lay clear for a raid on Mr Rosveare's summer orchard of quarendens and ribstones on the hither side of the railway line.

It was latish, and the young moon already clear between the apple-branches, when I started to fetch a circuit for home, first across a network of sidings, and then in cover of a line of clay-trucks anchored and waiting delivery at Tray jetties. Here, to the right of my path, ran a stream that came down past the end of our garden, where was a plank for crossing.

But before I came to this a sound fetched me up short. Queer it was, and human, sobbing between the noises of the running water; and for the instant – there being no other cottage nigh – I could think of nothing but that it must be mother out in the garden and in some terrible distress. Heart in mouth I ran towards the plank, but was fetched up again in my stride.

Years ago, in the days before the railway reclaimed the marsh, and when barges plied high up our stream until the clay-washings choked it, someone had planted an old iron cannon for a bollard. Time had sunk it to half its height and plugged up the mouth with driftings of sand and clay-dust . . . And there on it a girl was seated, rocking herself and sobbing. 'Twas the maid Annie Lowry. But what with the slip of the moon slanting down an angle of light through a break in the double line of trucks on the clay-dust spread everywhere white as snow, and her in a black shawl half covering her white frock, like a ghost she frightened me, and as like a ghost I must have come upon her, the clay muffling my tread.

'What are you doing here, boy?' she gasped out, jumping to her feet. 'Go away!'

Well, as for the question I reckoned it belonged to me, and I put it back on her. 'But if you're in trouble, Miss Annie,' I said, 'there's my mother handy, and you know her.'

She cut me short. 'I don't want your mother, Jim Pascoe' – she wiped her eyes bravely – 'and I want nothing of you but to go away. There's nothing the matter with me, either.'

'If that's so,' I stammered, taken aback by the flat lie, 'won't you have an apple?'

Upon this she broke into a high laugh. But it ended quick, overtaken by a sort of guggle in her throat.

'You funny boy! . . . Yes, I'll take your apple . . . And I'll give you something in change for it – and a promise.'

'What's that?' I asked.

She put down her head close and whispered. 'I'll give you a kiss, Jim, if you promise never – never on your oath – to tell any soul that you saw me here.'

Well, it happened to me so, at that age: and I vow that as she bent and kissed my cheek a glory of heaven broke all about me, and her breath was all flowers and fire. It was over in a moment, and she held out a hand for my apple.

'Word of honour you won't tell?'

'Not for wild horses, Miss Annie!'

Upon that she told me to run, and I ran.

4

'*Balearic timed Plymouth Saturday next Brother to wire arrival.*' – So Joseph Pooke was as good as his promise. The cablegram reached the Clay Company's office on the Wednesday before Easter, and the telegram from Plymouth on the Saturday morning (our post office receiving none on Good Friday). So again there was no time for organizing preparations to welcome the paragon. But Pendrea hurried around to engage the old lodgings at Aunt Sandercock's, enlisted some women to rig up a public tea in the Wesleyan School Room – it being a holiday, of course – and got together a small reception committee, including the vicar, to meet the 4.45 train. The station-master, too, was good enough to lay a score of fog-detonators up the line by way of welcome.

The banging of these may have shaken our man a bit. Anyhow, as the train drew in he had his head thrust out as if to inquire about the accident, and heaved forth upon the platform before Pendrea, hurrying up, had time to reach the compartment door.

So there Noah Pooke landed among us, with a kind of wondering smile on him: a monstrous fine fellow for all to see, strapping in height, with shoulders to match, in noways resembling his light-limbed brother, and least of all in his face, which was fair-complexioned and pinkish, the lower part straggled over by a thin growth of beard, hay-coloured and curly. In his left fist he clenched the brass-handled case, which we guessed to contain the famous cornet; in his right a carpet-bag (or 'grip', as he called it), which he had to set down for the hand-shaking. But to the case he stuck until, the schoolroom reached, he looked around and stowed the thing carefully under his chair. Then with a vague sort of smile he cast a second look over the feast, and the first word he said was 'Fattening.'

One of the helpers pushed a plate of jam and cream splits under his nose. 'Come now, Mr Noah, make a beginning!' – this with a blush for using his Christian name so forwardly.

'Thank 'ee, miss – a cup of tea and one slice of bread and butter. No sugar, if you please. Doctor's orders.'

He retrieved himself, however, at Easter Service in chapel next morning, with a cornet solo, O for the Wings of a Dove! clear as an angel speaking and persuading. There was no question but he must take over his brother's charge of the choir – and of the band, too, next session.

Also when, on Tuesday, he started work at the pits he soon showed that, though no match with his brother at packing, he could heave clay with the best or a trifle better.

But – no one could tell just why or how or when it began –

for some reason or other the practices of band and choir fell way by degrees from the standard to which his brother had worked them – that is, unless you accept Sam Trudgian's explanation: 'When the billies slurred up so much as a note, Joseph would hammer the desk and cry "Dammit", no matter how holy the edifice; whereas with this chap 'tis "No, no," or "Shall we try again?" at the strongest.'

Aunt Sandercock, too, had an early word about him. You couldn't say she whispered it, either, that being foreign to the pitch of her voice. She kept Wyandottes, and the freshness of their eggs was dear to her as her Bible. 'But every morning, sure as I lays – or sets, if you'll excuse me – his egg afore him, he looks at it, then up at me with "Are you sartin 'tis quite fresh, Mrs Sandercock?" There's limits to innocence, if you ask me!'

Now I should tell you that from first sight of him I had worshipped the man for his strength and stature; and he clinched it on the day when he promoted me to tap the triangle in the band. Fine and proud my mother was when she buttoned the frogs of my uniform jacket, though she didn't know I'd had to fight two boys for it. The worse shock, therefore, it gave me when she fell to discussing him with Father over our Sunday dinner. At the mention of Noah Pooke I had pricked up my young ears.

Mother was saying ' – and one of these days there'll be a scandal. Twice during sermon the minister faced around, lookin' where the noise came from.'

'Asleep,' suggested Father, 'or wind, maybe. He suffers from it, as the parish knows.'

'He's soft as' – Mother shifted knife to fork hand and pushed finger half-way towards the figgy-duff she was carving – 'as *that*. Put in with the bread and took out with the cakes.'

I flared up at this, though it misbecame my years. 'Mr Pooke is the finest man in Menadarva,' I blurted out; 'and the handsomest, and the kindest.'

'When you've finished your plate,' said Father after a slow stare, 'you just run along to garden and listen if the bees be threat'nin' a second swarm.'

Then, within a month, all of a sudden my hero's stock went up; it being gossiped about that he was courting the Lowry maid. They had been met in the dusk, walking out together. 'A promising match, too,' the parish agreed, while yet some added, 'Likely enough 'twill be the making of him,' Annie being reckoned a girl with a head on her shoulders.

But at the end of five weeks or so another rumour went round that the courtship had been broken off. And one evening in the bar-kitchen – Annie being away at the back somewhere, washing up – Bert Leggo, an impudent chap, tackled her mother for news of it. 'You'd better ask her,' answered Mrs Lowry short and sharp. 'Some time when you've stopped winkin' and don't mind having an ear boxed.'

Anyway, it told upon Noah, who took to walking by nights, all alone, and going by day (as the word goes), looking a man that had lost sixpence and found a farthing. And the band went down to Redruth and came back without a prize.

But it was not until close on Christmas that the crash came.

5

The vicar had a niece, or grandniece, down for a visit; an upstanding lady, with a full, deep contralto voice and reputed to be making a fortune at the concerts in London. These artists, I'm told, can never rest on a holiday: and what must she do but get up a concert? – proceeds to be given to an ambulance class that had been formed after the accident at the pit and was already short of funds. This was an object for which the church and chapel could work together, and they made a fine success of it up to a point. The band made up in noise what they'd unlearnt of Joseph Pooke's teaching. The vicar read out to us how the waters came down in all sorts of ways at Lodore, and later quavered out 'O that we two were maying!' with the postmistress – of all the unlikeliest capers! After that came an item or two, and then, of course, our visitor bore away the bell with some Italian thing, all runs and shakes. All encored this, as in duty bound, and she gave us *Caller Herrin'*, with wonderful effect from her lower throat, as you might say. Next came Noah's turn; and, pulling himself together, as it were, he rendered *The Lost Chord* and *I Dreamt that I Dwelt* in his best style; so outstanding that when he ended the lady came up in her imperative way, shook him by the hand and almost kissed him. 'Wonderful!' she cried out, turning on the audience. 'This gentleman must really, yes really, try an *obbligato* to me with Miss – I forget your name for the moment – I'm so excited – oh, yes! – with Miss Hender at the piano, of course.' So Noah had to blush and bow.

Well, when the lady's next turn came and she sang *Bid me discourse*, he managed it to admiration, bending over Miss Hender's shoulder and fitting in, soft, on the right notes. And in the storm of applause Miss Hender found herself gently pushed off the music-stool and the lady seated in her place.

'You'll not need any score for this,' says the lady. 'It's the dear old *Annie Laurie*, key of G,' and she struck a couple of chords. Noah's cornet went up to his lips. He kept his smile but both his hands shook.

'*Maxwellton braes are bonny.*'

– And just then a voice – Bert Leggo's – spoke up from somewhere at the back: 'Damme! the man's blubbing.'

It was true, too! Big tears were running down his cheeks as he puffed them for the next stave. There's no saying whether he heard Leggo or not. Anyway he lowered his cornet, looking about him as one dazed, tucked the thing – quick – under his arm, and fled off at the back of the platform.

6

That broke him. From that day he went about, eyes down, shunning his fellows, pitiful to see; the worst being that he kept his silly smile, full of pain as his eyes would be when he lifted them. Soon Aunt Sandercock let out that she dusted his tool-bench every morning and 'though he'll sit there half the night, wasting good oil at eleven three-farthings a gallon, there's every tool in its place untouched, same as I left it – and him the untidiest by habit that ever I lodged.' Soon, too, he took to lying a-bed and turning up late at the pit; until there came a Friday when Pendrea very reasonably lost his temper and sacked him on the spot.

Next morning I overtook and ran past him to catch up with a parcel of boys on the road to the moors – a waste of land that stretched for three miles and more at the back of the pits. It was unreclaimed for clay as yet; all peat, heather, and bog-plants, criss-crossed by small brown trickles of streams in which our game was to hunt for minnows, efts, dragon-flies, anything we could fetch home in pickle-jars.

He was carrying a fishing-rod, jointed up in a bag, and his cornet-case in his right hand. After passing him, something moved me to halt; and as he came up he must have read in my face what I couldn't put into words. For he bade me run after the rest, and then, still with that smile of his, ' Joseph is a fruit-ful bough,' said he; 'but Issachar a strong ass couching down between two burdens' – words that puzzled me at the time and puzzled me later when I found them in the Scriptures.

There were trout, small but plenty, lower down where the main stream made a long bend by the west; and when we parted he would be after these. But I never heard of his taking any, that day or after. What happened was that he wandered far off, away from sight, and there played tunes to himself on his key-bugle by the water. Times again, while hunting for minnows, we boys would hear the lonesome notes of it float-ing up, wailing across the moor. Sometimes it might be *Trafalgar's Bay* or *Come, cheer up, my Lads*; but always, and whatever the tune, it put you in mind of a creature lost and in pain.

And there the man died.

They found him stretched out by a small stream, his rod (unspliced) and his key-bugle on the bank beside him. Staring up and smiling he lay: death must have come upon him merci-fully. The vicar pursed out the money to pay all expenses with a balance for the headstone: it appeared that of late he had been getting remittances from the States and paying them out quietly to the poor fellow.

But that doesn't quite end the story. One evening, towards

Christmas, Joseph Pooke returned to Menadarva – it turned out, to visit the grave and settle up with the vicar. One or two put it about they had passed his ghost in the dusk. But it wasn't his ghost, nor his business alone with the vicar.

For that night the girl Annie ran off with him, to be married in London ... Yes, by licence and all in form: for two days later the proper certificate came to 'Step o' One Side', with word she was off to the States with the best man in the world: and later Mr Lowry showed around the photographs of two healthy children, twins.

'And a very ordinary pair,' was Sam Trudgian's comment. 'Heavy, like that unfortunate uncle of theirs, if you ask me. But 'tis curious how gifts will skip about in families.'

BARCHESTER TOWERS

Anthony Trollope

1180

This second novel of the Barsetshire series resumes the story of
the characters and the local church politics of Barchester and its
Cathedral close to which Trollope first introduced us in *The
Warden*. The author develops the characters of the two enemies,
Mrs Proudie – whose husband here becomes the new Bishop of
Barchester – and Dr Grantly, into the shape they will retain in
the later Barsetshire novels.

Here, more than in any other novel of the series, Trollope
displays – especially in that great creation Mrs Proudie – the
sense of pure comedy for which too little credit was given him
until the recent revival of interest in his work. His breadth of
judgement and his tolerance are at their most endearing, and his
deftness of touch in depicting and developing character has full
scope amid a group of men and women of a variety unexpected
in a mid-Victorian cathedral city.

SEVEN MEN

Max Beerbohm

1010

This famous book of short stories (to which have been added
memories of two other men) is a wonderful parody of the literary
world of the eighteen-nineties and the social behaviour of the
people who belonged to it. Readers of *Zuleika Dobson* will not be
amazed by the element of fantasy which unobtrusively changes
the nature of some of these stories – for instance the diabolism of
poor Soames (a writer who only felt the breath of Fame when
Will Rothenstein painted his portrait out of pity) and the
mysterious conduct of Stephen Braxton, who ruins more than a
house-party for the author of 'Ariel in Mayfair'. The collection
includes a penetrating study of a man who was not only born
but died a gambler, the story of pseudo-palmist, the unfinished
dramatic work of an inveterate second-nighter, and a touching
account of a writer whose reputation entirely depended on the
references to him in the published correspondence of his late
colleagues.

NOT FOR SALE IN THE U.S.A.